"The Unseen Killer"
and
"The Golden Masks"

TWO CLASSIC ADVENTURES OF

by Walter B. Gibson
writing as Maxwell Grant

with a new historical essay
by Will Murray

Published by Sanctum Productions for
NOSTALGIA VENTURES, INC.
P.O. Box 231183; Encinitas, CA 92023-1183

This Nostalgia Ventures edition is an unabridged republication of the text and illustrations of two stories from The Shadow Magazine, as originally published by Street & Smith Publications, Inc., N.Y.: The Unseen Killer from the December 1, 1934 issue, and The Golden Masks from the September 1, 1936 issue. Typographical errors have been tacitly corrected in this edition. These stories are works of their time. Consequently, the text is reprinted intact in its original historical form, including occasional out-of-date ethnic and cultural stereotyping. Typographical errors have been tacitly corrected in this edition.

International Standard Book Numbers:
ISBN 1-932806-97-0   13 digit 978-1-932806-97-7

First printing: May 2008

Series editor/publisher: Anthony Tollin
P.O. Box 761474
San Antonio, TX 78245-1474
sanctumotr@earthlink.net

Consulting editor: Will Murray

Copy editor: Joseph Wrzos

Cover and photo restoration: Michael Piper

The editor acknowledges the assistance of Dwight Fuhro in the preparation of this volume.

Nostalgia Ventures, Inc.
P.O. Box 231183; Encinitas, CA 92023-1183

Visit The Shadow at www.shadowsanctum.com & www.nostalgiatown.com.

Volume 18

CONTENTS

Two Complete Novels From The Shadow's Private Annals As told to Maxwell Grant

Thrilling Tales and Features

THE UNSEEN KILLER by Walter B. Gibson (writing as "Maxwell Grant") 4

INTERLUDE by Will Murray 66

THE GOLDEN MASKS by Walter B. Gibson (writing as "Maxwell Grant") 68

**Cover art by George Rozen
Interior illustrations by Tom Lovell**

Spawned amid the test-tubes of science

The Unseen Killer

escapes, to involve The Shadow in an amazing struggle for Justice!

A Complete Book-length Novel from the Private Annals of The Shadow, as told to

Maxwell Grant

CHAPTER I
PLANS COMPLETED

"THAT'S Trip Burgan—"

"The gambler, eh? He looks like a big shot, all right."

"Looks like one? He *is* one. Riding easy on the dough he's taken in—"

The comments were audible to "Trip" Burgan as he strolled through the lobby of the Hotel Revano. A cold smile appeared upon the gambler's lips. The expression changed, however, as Trip entered the elevator and turned toward the door. Those who could still see him from the lobby observed an emotionless countenance.

The term "poker-faced" applied to Trip Burgan. His sallow visage was one that maintained a fixed appearance. Only his eyes were shifty; but Trip had gained the habit of changing his gaze in a natural fashion that proved deceptive to those who observed it.

The cold smile reappeared when Trip stepped from the elevator at the sixth floor. This showed that the gambler had not forgotten the comments from the lobby loungers. Those statements were to Trip's liking, particularly the reference to the fact that he was "riding easy." For Trip, retired from active practice at the gaming table, had been seeking to establish that very impression.

Arriving at a doorway near the end of a corridor, Trip inserted a key and turned the lock. He stepped into a thickly furnished living room, just as a thick-set man bounded up from a chair to see who was entering. A sheepish grin showed on the fellow's thick-lipped face.

"Ought to have known it was you, Trip," remarked the man, apologetically. "Guess I was kind of half asleep here in the chair. You clicking the key woke me up."

"All right, Chuck," returned Trip, in a brusque tone. "Well, what's doing? Is he here yet?"

"Crofton?"

Trip Burgan's eyes narrowed. His face formed a scowl that made Chuck shift uneasily. The hard-faced fellow began to stammer apologies for his blunder. Trip cut him short.

"Listen, you mug," spat the gambler. "Forget that name. Understand? You've never heard of Miles Crofton. He's never been here. Get it?"

"Sure, Trip—but when I'm talking to you—"

"Let me mention the name if anybody does." Trip paused abruptly to fling aside hat, coat and scarf. Then, reverting to his original question, he snapped: "Well, is he here?"

"Sure," returned Chuck. "In the next room. I showed him in there about fifteen minutes ago."

"All right. I'm going in to see him. If anybody asks for me, I'm busy."

WITH that admonition, Trip Burgan opened the door to the next room and entered. He closed the barrier behind him.

Across the room, which was one of the bedrooms of Trip's apartment, a man was standing at the window, looking toward Broadway, half a block distant. The visitor turned when he heard Trip close the door.

Miles Crofton formed an odd contrast to Trip Burgan. Both men had expressionless faces; but there the likeness ended. Where Trip looked the part of a crafty schemer, Crofton had the appearance of a deliberate thinker.

Though Crofton's countenance betrayed no emotion, his whole bearing was one that would inspire the confidence of associates. It was not until Trip delivered a slight grin that Crofton relaxed. Even then, his facial expression did not lose its seriousness.

"Had to give Chuck a call-down," remarked Trip, as he waved his visitor to a chair. "I told him never to mention your name, not even to me; but he forgot it when I came in. He won't do it again, though."

Crofton nodded.

"Well," queried Trip, "what's doing up at the professor's? Everything set?"

"For tonight."

"Yeah?" exclaimed Trip, when he heard Crofton's matter-of-fact statement. "Say! That's the ticket! I didn't think he was going to pull the stunt until next week. What made him set it ahead?"

"Findlay Warlock came in to see him."

"Still singing his hard-luck song?" questioned Trip. "How he's counting on the prof to come through with the new invention?"

"Yes," replied Crofton. "Warlock talked while I was working in the lab. Professor Lessep told him that the new apparatus was ready. Warlock persuaded him immediately to make the test tonight."

As Crofton paused, his stolidness impressed Trip with the idea that something might be wrong. Poker-faced, the gambler studied his visitor; then questioned:

"Don't you like the idea? Aren't you set for it?"

"I'm ready," replied Crofton seriously. "It was something Warlock said that bothers me. Just before he left, he told Professor Lessep that he's invited the police commissioner."

"Great!" exclaimed Trip. "Say—that's going to spread the thing wide! Plenty of publicity—"

"Perhaps too much," interposed Crofton.

"How come?" questioned Trip.

"To begin with," replied Crofton, "the commissioner may be suspicious of the whole experiment. After it goes through—supposing there's no hitch—he may start an investigation of my past."

"What if he does? What'll he find out? War hero—soldier of fortune—stunt flier—"

"That part's all right. But he may learn that I was a pal of Rouser Tukin."

"How? You kept in the clear when Rouser pulled that bank job. A couple of cops got killed, but Rouser was bumped in the fight. He's not around to talk."

"They're still looking for some of the mob."

"But they haven't found them. Anyway, who's going to blab your name? Nobody's got anything on you."

"You never can tell what some stool pigeon has heard. Listen, Trip: I don't want this thing to stir up too much hullabaloo right at the start."

"It won't." Trip seemed positive. "But you're wise to look at it that way, Crofton. You'll have to lay low in a hurry. But that's all set. The hideout's ready. Steer there as soon as you leave the prof's."

"The hideout," repeated Crofton. He indulged in a slight chuckle. "It seems funny, calling it a hideout. It's necessary, though. All right"—he shrugged his shoulders—"we can take a chance on the commissioner. Maybe he won't make any trouble up at Lessep's."

"He's a dumb egg," assured Trip. "The old commissioner, Ralph Weston, might mean something. But this guy Wainwright Barth—well, maybe he's as cuckoo as Professor Lessep. He won't get wind of anything."

"He might trace you, Trip—"

"How?"

"Through Professor Lessep."

TRIP BURGAN arose and stalked over by the window. The fading afternoon light revealed an ugly twist to his lips as the gambler faced Miles Crofton.

"The old prof won't blab," asserted Trip. "It would queer him if he did. I slipped him dough when he needed it. If it wasn't for that, this new invention would be listed as a flop along with the others.

"What's more, I've been playing a steady game. I picked this hotel because it wasn't too cheap nor too ritzy. Just the place where a guy like myself would stop if he had retired. Nobody's got anything on me.

"I fixed it so you got in with the prof as his assistant. But what if he says so? I'll deny it; he'll have no proof to back it up. He'd only put himself in trouble.

"But that's not all. After you fade out, I'm going to keep away from where you are. Chuck Galla fixed the hideout. He'll have his own men planted there after you move into the joint tonight. If the bulls begin to quiz me, Chuck will keep away from here and I'll play dumb.

"If the prof begins to weaken, we'll find out about it soon enough. There'll be a way to handle him. You're not seeing me anymore; and I'm not seeing you"—Trip paused to deliver a slight grin—"in fact, nobody's seeing you. It looks to me like we're all set."

"We are." Crofton rose as he spoke. "I just wanted to sound you out, Trip. I've been studying Professor Lessep at close range. I feel sure that he won't crimp the game. As you say, it would queer him worse than anyone else.

"But I wanted to make sure that you weren't overconfident. It may sound funny for me to say that, after the risks I've taken to grab off coin. But I've always studied consequences and given them their full value, even when everything looks like a setup. That's why I'm still alive.

"The weak link lies between you and Professor Lessep. There's always a weak link. My policy is to look for it. I wanted to be sure you saw it. You've seen it and you'll be ready for it. That settles the matter. The commissioner won't worry me."

Crofton strolled toward the door that led to the living room. Trip followed. He stopped his visitor with a low-voiced question. This time it was Trip who expressed concern.

"You're sure the apparatus will work?" he questioned. "The old prof won't get excited and bungle it?"

"Not a chance," returned Crofton. "We tested it after Warlock left today. Lessep has it timed to the exact second. I've taken your word for it that the prof will keep mum. You can take mine that he won't slip when he works his experiment."

"There'll be no worry after tonight," assured Trip. "Listen, Crofton. In a pinch, you can blow in on the old prof. End the whole game before he makes up his mind to blab. Let him know that he's got plenty to lose—"

Crofton was nodding as he opened the door. Trip broke off so that Chuck would not hear the finish of the sentence. Solemnly, the ex-gambler shook hands with his visitor. Then Trip opened the door, peered into the hall and gave Crofton the signal to stroll forth.

AS soon as he had closed the door Trip Burgan turned to Chuck Galla. Trip made no effort to suppress the enthusiasm that he felt. His hard lips widened; he showed an elation that amazed his underling.

"Give the gang the tip, Chuck," ordered Trip. "We're going to cover the hideout, beginning with tonight."

"You mean Croft—"

Trip laughed as Chuck caught himself before completing Crofton's name.

"Crofton's the guy," informed Trip. "He's going in there. But nobody's going to see him go in; and nobody's going to see him when he comes out. That's why I told you to fix the hideout the way I described it.

"We're in the big dough, Chuck. You'll get plenty by the time we're through. The best of it is that we can sit back while Crofton's doing the work. All we've got to do is cover up. Make it easy for him."

Chuck looked puzzled.

"Can't figure it, eh?" chuckled Trip. "Well, you haven't heard anything yet. We're playing the old professor for a sap, to begin with. If the thing works—well, after tonight, it will be a cinch. Crofton bringing in the gravy—"

"But the bulls—"

"They'll never find him." Again a chuckle from Trip as he spoke. "They can't find him. Nobody can find him after tonight."

"Give me the low-down, Trip."

"All right. Listen."

Chuck sat down, still puzzled. Trip began to speak in a steady, convincing tone. As Chuck listened, his eyes began to blink. He looked at Trip, wondering if the gambler had gone insane.

But Trip's persuasive voice belied all madness. In spite of himself, Chuck began to be convinced. Doubt became bewilderment. In turn, bewilderment changed to amazement. But with amazement came belief.

Nodding mechanically, Chuck was sitting upright in his chair when Trip completed his statements and his orders. The gambler's hand clamped upon the underling's shoulder. Chuck arose; Trip moved him toward the door.

"You've got it now," declared Trip, steadily. "So keep it in your noodle, where it belongs. You're in on something big, Chuck. Get going. Fix things at the hideout."

With an effort, Chuck snapped out of his trance. He left and took an elevator to the lobby. Dusk had settled when Chuck Galla came out into the street. The lieutenant started away at a steady pace.

But as he walked along, Chuck mumbled to himself. He was repeating words that he had heard from Trip. Chuck was strengthening his conviction that the impossible could be true.

For from Trip Burgan, Chuck Galla had learned the details of new plans for crime. He had heard a plot that had seemed incredible; a scheme that all the power of the law could not combat.

CHAPTER II
FROM THE CONFERENCE

A GROUP of men was gathered about a long conference table. Situated in an office high in a Manhattan skyscraper, they commanded a complete view of the Times Square district. Dusk had settled over the metropolis. Blinking signs flashed their intermittent glow into the ruddy sky above the city. But the sight meant nothing to these men. They were concerned with the misfortunes of the Centralized Power Corporation.

At one end of the long table was a solemn-faced, gray-haired man. Benign of countenance, he held an attitude of friendship. Glumness, however, was imprinted upon his features. He could not shake off the pall of gloom that had captured him. This was Findlay Warlock, president of the corporation.

Stockholders—represented by men seated on both sides of the table—had once looked to

Warlock as master of their fortunes. But that had been before the advent of disaster. Warlock, no longer a leader, had been supplanted by the man who now sat at the other end of the conference table. This was Marryat Darring, recently appointed as executive secretary.

In contrast to Warlock, Darring was a man of rugged vigor. Black-haired, keen-eyed, dynamic in every action, the executive secretary was tracing the events that had led to the crash of Centralized Power. Stockholders listened while he spoke; their nods showed their unanimous approval of Darring's findings.

"Centralized Power," the black-haired man was saying, "was an ill-advised project. Its very inception predicted its ultimate failure. The company planned the building of a huge dam in a district where there was no concentration of population.

"Mr. Warlock, as president, advised the step in the belief that the region would expand once the power project had been completed. We all agree that Mr. Warlock is a man of vision. In this instance, however, he was a man of too much vision.

"He looked ahead to the establishment of industries; to the growth of cities—all produced by the magic of power development. Instead of following the old rule of producing a supply to fill a demand, he adopted the policy of believing that a demand would arise as a result of the supply."

Darring paused; he looked about at the approving nods which continued. Even Warlock had joined in the approbation. The president was admitting the truth of the statements which the executive secretary had made.

"Despite those mistakes," resumed Darring, in a modulated tone, "Centralized Power might have achieved its organizer's hopes. It is not my province, gentlemen, to make too severe a criticism. I say that the project was ill-advised. I do not state, however, that it was impossible of attainment, so far as the basic idea was concerned.

"The real mistake came when Mr. Warlock, convinced that his dreams would become realities, advised the purchase of land that was offered at outrageous prices. He also bought out the options and rights of smaller concerns that had gained claims upon that territory.

"Then, as the colossal blunder, he permitted the awarding of contracts that were set at wartime figures. In brief, he allowed the expenditure of several million dollars that could very well have been saved. Am I correct, Mr. Warlock?"

"You are," responded the gray-haired president, in a wheezy voice. "I must state, however, that the estimates proved that these extravagances would be repaid eventually—"

BURSTS of indignation came from stockholders. Warlock slumped pitifully in his chair. Accusing voices sounded in his ears. It was Darring who silenced them with a powerful rap upon the end of the table.

"One moment, gentlemen!" roared Darring. "This is no time for spitefulness. Accept Mr. Warlock's statement at its true value. He admits extravagances, but"—Darring's tone eased as his eyes moved about the silenced group—"he also states a fact when he declares that the heavy expenditures would have been absorbed by the completion of the project.

"In a nutshell, gentlemen, Mr. Warlock is free from condemnation. His were errors of omission, not of commission. He believed—he still believes—that his expenditures would have been justified. We can not take issue on that point."

Warlock smiled gratefully as he heard these statements. Antagonism faded as the stockholders were swung by Darring's persuasion. Though their faces remained glum, they gradually began to coincide with Darring's assertions.

"The real failure of Centralized Power," resumed the executive secretary, "lies in the matter of riparian rights. As I said a moment ago, Mr. Warlock's error was one of omission. He neglected to obtain full information on a subject that was vital to the success of Centralized Power.

"A few months ago, certain directors of this company became alarmed by the high expenditures that Mr. Warlock had instituted. They urged my appointment to the position of executive secretary. I went into all matters in detail. I must say, gentlemen, that Mr. Warlock spared no effort to aid me in my investigation, even though it was a reflection upon his handling of the company management."

Warlock nodded approvingly. Stockholders, toned down by Darring, looked sympathetically toward the president. They recalled that Warlock, himself, was a heavy stockholder in the company. He, too, was losing a fortune.

"Thanks to Mr. Warlock's cooperation," declared Darring, "I was able to make a thorough study of matters as they stood. Aided by my experience as receiver for certain defunct power companies, I went deeply into the entire affair. In fact, I started from the beginning. I wanted to learn about the water supply that the great Centralized dam was to hold.

"Everyone else—Mr. Warlock included—had taken the riparian rights for granted. I took nothing for granted. Almost at the start of my survey, I uncovered the astounding fact that all the streams from which Centralized Power expected to store up water were controlled by other interests.

"There we had it. A huge dam, half built.

Contracts calling for equipment. New property options to be exercised. All for a project that was doomed to failure because the one needed element, water, was not obtainable. There was but one course to take. Empowered as executive secretary, I suspended further construction of the dam.

"Since then, I have been actively engaged in my investigation. I find that we are confronted by an absolute dilemma. We must either abandon our entire enterprise, calling it a complete loss, or we must buy out all the companies that hold riparian rights. That would mean a cost that could never be absorbed."

THE truth of Darring's statements seemed obvious. Haggard-faced, the stockholders looked from one to another and shook their heads.

There was only one who seemed unperturbed by the situation. This was a tall, silent personage who was seated midway at the table. Turning toward Darring, he spoke.

"Let me introduce myself," he said, in a quiet tone. "My name is Lamont Cranston. I have but recently returned from abroad, to find that my broker had purchased shares of Centralized Power securities. Though my holdings are not proportionately large, I am as interested as anyone present regarding the ultimate fate of this corporation. What do you propose, Mr. Darring, as the best solution?"

Darring faced the speaker. He observed a keen, chiseled countenance that was almost masklike in appearance. An aquiline nose, steady, burning eyes—these were the predominating features of Lamont Cranston's visage. Marryat Darring recognized that he was dealing with a person of importance. He spoke frankly.

"There is no exact solution," admitted the executive secretary. "But of the two courses that I have mentioned, I should suggest the first. A petition for bankruptcy would be our method to abandon the enterprise."

"No! No!" exclaimed Warlock, coming to his feet. "We must raise more money, gentlemen! Enough to buy out the other interests—"

"And to burden ourselves," put in Darring, "with expenditures that would certainly result in even greater loss."

Warlock subsided. Cranston again took up the matter with Darring.

"The newspaper reports," stated Cranston, "mention the names of three promoters who profited heavily through the formation of the Centralized Power Corporation. Suppose, Mr. Darring, you give us a statement of their present status."

"I shall," responded Darring. "The three men in question are Nathaniel Hildon, Peters Amboy

FINDLAY WARLOCK

and Wallace Norgan. They are the ones who sold property to Mr. Warlock. They also turned over the stock of the subsidiary companies that Centralized Power absorbed. They had options on many contracts.

"Unquestionably, those three have profited heavily through Centralized Power. By suspending operations, I have stopped their gain. If we go into bankruptcy, our remaining funds will be required to make them further payments.

"If we continue, we will require more money to meet the debts that Hildon, Amboy and Norgan have saddled on us. Such payments will have to be made before we can begin to buy out the companies that hold riparian rights. All that means further loss."

As Darring paused, Warlock arose. The gray-haired president was trembling with suppressed anger. His wrath, however, was not directed toward Darring. Warlock's fury had been fanned by the mention of the three promoters.

"They were swindlers!" cried Warlock. "The three of them. Hildon, Amboy and Norgan! Those parasites have fattened themselves with the funds that we have invested in Centralized Power!"

"But you met their demands," reminded Darring.

"I met them in good faith," declared Warlock. "Despite their exorbitant terms, I believed that we could make our project pay. It is this question of riparian rights that has ruined us; and I am convinced that those scoundrels are in back of it. Another scheme to bleed us!"

"Yet you advise our continuance?" questioned Darring.

"Only if we can first bring those rogues to justice," returned Warlock. "Make them disgorge their ill-gotten millions. Regain the funds that are rightfully our own—"

"ONE moment," interposed Darring, with a wave that curbed Warlock. Then, to the stockholders: "Gentlemen, if we could prove these accusations against Hildon, Amboy and Norgan, our case might be different. But it is impossible to show actual conspiracy on their part.

"I have visited them, with Mr. Warlock. All have denied any knowledge in this matter of riparian rights. All of their sales and contracts were legal. None of them involved the matter of water supply. Moreover, they take the stand that if the president of Centralized Power knew nothing about the situation that existed, why should they be expected to have such knowledge?

"I argued with them from another angle. That of exorbitant charges on property, options and contracts. There, again, I was balked by the previous actions of our president. Hildon—Amboy—Norgan—all three pointed out that Mr. Warlock had invested in turbine motors that had proven worthless. Hence his payments to them—for actual property and materials delivered—were not out of keeping with his system of management.

"No, gentlemen, the most that I can hope to do is to induce Hildon, Amboy and Norgan to waive certain claims which they still hold upon our company. That, at least, would benefit the stockholders. But I can not accomplish such a result while Mr. Warlock insists upon denouncing them as scoundrels."

A momentary silence. Then a stockholder made a motion that Marryat Darring be empowered to treat with the three promoters on the matter of waiving the existing claims. The motion was seconded and carried. Then came a motion for adjournment. It passed; the meeting ended. Warlock approached Darring.

"You were right," said Warlock to the secretary. "I have been tactless in my dealing with those three. You know as well as I that they are thieves; but you have sense enough not to mention it."

"Exactly!" replied Darring, with a smile.

"But their reference to Lessep was uncalled for,"

resumed Warlock. "I made an appropriation for his turbines, I admit. But the money was for experimental purposes. Had the turbines proven practical—"

"Unfortunately," interrupted Darring, "Professor Lessep has a bad record so far as his inventions are concerned. He, more than the promoters, can be said to have swindled you. I saw those turbines, Warlock. They were hopeless. You have made a great mistake, Warlock, in giving credit to the ideas of an eccentric inventor like Melrose Lessep."

"You are wrong, Darring. Gentlemen"— Warlock turned to the departing stockholders—"I call you to witness! Would it restore some of your faith in me if I proved that Professor Lessep is a capable inventor?"

"Yes," came a reluctant response.

"Very well," announced Warlock. "Tonight, at his laboratory, Professor Lessep intends to perform an experiment in the devisualization of solids. I intend to witness it. I feel that Mr. Darring and others should be present."

"It does not concern the corporation," objected Darring. "I told you that long ago, Warlock, when you first mentioned this new invention of Lessep's. Devisualization of solids has nothing to do with turbines."

"But Lessep's success tonight can justify my belief in his inventive genius. It will prove that I was not unreasonable in spending money on his turbines."

"What do you think, gentlemen?"

Darring's question brought nods from the stockholders. They seemed to agree that Warlock needed vindication. Darring turned to the president.

"In response to your request," he said, "I shall attend tonight's experiment. I would suggest, also, that two of the stockholders be present in addition to myself. Two—or more—"

One man volunteered. The others, however, pleaded previous engagements. It was then that Lamont Cranston stepped forward, just as Findlay Warlock was making another remark.

"The police commissioner will be there," Warlock was saying. "I have invited him in the belief that Lessep's experiment may be of use in crime solution. If anyone else—"

"I shall be present," came Cranston's quiet interruption.

The impromptu meeting adjourned. Stockholders went their separate ways. Warlock and Darring departed together, intending to have dinner; then to go to Lessep's. They invited Cranston; but he declined, stating that he would meet them at the laboratory.

ON the street, Lamont Cranston hailed a taxi. He ordered the driver to take him to the exclusive Cobalt Club. As the cab rolled along, Cranston leaned back in the cushions of the rear seat and laughed softly through immobile lips.

A strange whisper, that repressed mirth! Yet it told a story of its own. It revealed the true identity of this personage who wore the masklike countenance of Lamont Cranston; it marked a secret purpose—a design of The Shadow!

For this was not the real Lamont Cranston. The actual man who held stock in Centralized Power was still abroad. Guised as Cranston, The Shadow had attended the stockholder's meeting to gain first-hand information of the swindle that he knew must lie behind the corporation's failure.

As Cranston, he had heard something that interested him as The Shadow. Professor Lessep's experiment—one that involved crime solution— was a project that might concern The Shadow in the future.

Police Commissioner Wainwright Barth dined nightly at the Cobalt Club. Barth was a friend of Cranston's. He would be pleased to learn that Cranston had returned from abroad; glad to know that his friend was also invited to the affair at Lessep's. They would go there together, once they had met at the Cobalt Club.

Wainwright Barth considered The Shadow to be a myth. That was the occasion for The Shadow's laugh. For tonight, the police commissioner would have the honor of accompanying The Shadow— in person—to an event that promised unusual developments.

Yet even The Shadow, at this moment, did not

MARRYAT DARRING

suspect the strange doings that lay in store. Chance was leading him to a happening that was destined to have amazing consequences. The Shadow was approaching the beginning of a trail that would bring astounding crime!

CHAPTER III
THE EXPERIMENT

"HERE we are, Cranston."

The commissioner's car had pulled up in front of an old, moldy-looking house on the upper East Side. Brick-fronted, with white steps cracked above a grimy sidewalk, the place did not seem fitting as the abode of a prominent scientist.

Wainwright Barth stared askance as he viewed the grimy windows, where dull light trickled through crimped shades. The commissioner was a man who considered wealth important; and this first sight of Professor Lessep's house made him lose stock in his preconceived impressions of the inventor.

Standing on the curb, Barth turned a ruddy, beakish face toward Cranston. Staring through pince-nez spectacles, the commissioner voiced a disapproval that sounded much like an apology.

"I've never seen this chap," said Barth. "Heard of him, only. Professor Melrose Lessep. Come to think of it, his reputation is a bit unsavory. However, he may be a genius, and I have promised to attend his experiment. Let us enter."

Barth rang the doorbell. The barrier was opened by the professor himself. A tall, wild-eyed man, with a huge shock of unkempt white hair, Melrose Lessep appeared deserving of the title "eccentric." Yet he was keen in recognizing the visitor who stood on his doorstep.

"The commissioner!" exclaimed Lessep, in a crackly voice. "I am right? Yes? And a friend with you. Come in, gentlemen. This way. To my parlor, where the others await."

Lessep led the way through a dingy hall, then into a musty parlor that had evidently been opened for tonight's event. One dozen men were gathered in the little room; among them, Findlay Warlock and Marryat Darring. It was Warlock who sprang forward to greet Barth. The professor made a bow and retired into the hall.

"The laboratory is in there," explained Warlock wheezily, pointing to a door at the rear of the room. "The professor's assistant is busy arranging the apparatus. They will call us when they are ready."

Barth nodded. The presence of men of prominence offset the drab surroundings. Warlock introduced Darring. Barth shook hands with enthusiasm. He had heard of Darring, for the man had accomplished remarkable results in handling the affairs of bankrupt corporations. He knew of Darring's connection with the Centralized Power Corporation.

"Warlock has told me of his misfortunes," remarked the commissioner. "From his description of the circumstances, it looks like a swindle on the part of the promoters. What is your opinion, Mr. Darring? Have you—"

"Matters are still undecided," interposed Darring, in a cautious tone. Then, with a glance about him, he made a nudge toward the corner. "I think we have some reporters here tonight. It would be best to keep them off the subject of Centralized Power."

Barth followed Darring's gaze. He recognized two men as reporters. He smiled, for he knew them to be newshawks of little consequence. Evidently the morning newspapers had not counted on Lessep's experiment as good meat for a story.

"Warlock has faith in Lessep's inventive genius," explained Darring, in an undertone. "Personally, I think the professor is a faker. He sold impractical turbines to Centralized Power. That is why I am here tonight.

"I hope that Lessep succeeds in this experiment, whatever it is. Warlock calls it 'solid devisualization' or something of the sort. The term is new to me. My sympathies are with Warlock, for the failure of Centralized Power has been a blow to him. If he can prove that Lessep is a capable inventor, it will strengthen his position with the stockholders.

"As for the other matter, Warlock has probably told you all the details of the case. Unfortunately, it offers no opportunity for prosecution. Unless"—he broke off, while still keeping his wary eye upon the corner—"ah, here come the reporters. Probably to interview you, Commissioner."

Darring was right. The two reporters had sauntered from the corner. In the accepted journalistic fashion they introduced themselves to the commissioner and began to press him for statements regarding Professor Lessep. Barth pleaded ignorance and replied that he would talk after the experiment.

At that moment, the rear door opened; Professor Lessep stood framed in the brilliant light of the laboratory. Wearing a white gown and beckoning with a scrawny finger, he invited his guests to enter the room beyond.

The reporters headed in that direction. Barth looked for Cranston. Finding his friend close by, the commissioner joined him and they entered the lab.

KEEN eyes gazed from the immobile countenance of Lamont Cranston. The Shadow was prompt to note the arrangement of this room which they had entered. Whatever his reputation, whether genius or madman, Professor Melrose Lessep had certainly fitted up a most remarkable laboratory.

The room was some thirty feet in length. At the near end, where the group had entered, were a dozen folding chairs, arranged against the wall. Beyond were numerous contrivances. Some looked like electric motors of odd design. Others were light projectors of curious shape. One machine appeared to be a squatty camera.

The windows—on the right side of the room—were shuttered. Illumination came from bluish bulbs in the ceiling. At the far end of the room were two doors, both opened. One showed an extension from the rear hallway; the other revealed a little office at the right.

Between the doors, and just beyond the center of the room, was the most striking object in the laboratory. This was an upright cabinet, more than six feet high and three feet square, mounted upon a square base that measured five feet in each direction.

Most curious was the fact that cabinet and base were both constructed almost entirely of glass. The framework alone was of chromium-plated metal. It formed a skeleton in which the sheets of plate glass were set.

The square base, metal rimmed, was mounted upon four slender legs of shining metal. This raised the bottom of the cabinet two feet above the floor. The professor, beckoning, invited all comers to inspect the apparatus. The two reporters led the march.

"Be careful," warned Lessep, in his crackly tone. He opened the glass door that formed the front of the cabinet. "You may step inside if you please; but remember that the substance is breakable. Be careful."

While the examination was going on, a young man came from the little office and took his stand beside Professor Lessep. Steadily, with almost indifferent gaze, he looked about at the persons present. This was Miles Crofton. Like the professor, he was wearing a white gown.

"My assistant, Mr. Crofton," introduced Lessep. "He is to play an important part in tonight's experiment. Seat yourselves, gentlemen. Please. We are delayed a trifle already. Please be seated."

When the group had obeyed the injunction, the professor stood for a moment with quick-blinking eyes. Then, leaving Crofton by the cabinet, he went to the door that led into the hall. He closed it with a clang that revealed its metal surface. Then, solemnly, Lessep drew a big bolt that locked the door.

He walked to the door of the little office, closed it, and shot a similar bolt. Then he stalked to the door through which the throng had come from the parlor. He closed this barrier, showing a metal inner surface, and pressed home another bolt.

"We must not be disturbed," chuckled the professor, with a peculiar smile. "That is why I have made the doors fast bolted. When I work herein, with my capable assistant, we keep the doors fast bolted that none may enter."

The professor walked back to the cabinet, where Crofton was awaiting him. At that moment, a telephone bell began to ring. The sound, coming from beyond the door that led to the little office, was barely audible.

"Shall I answer it, Professor?" questioned Crofton.

"No!" returned Lessep, testily. "I do not wish disturbance. Let it continue to ring. It will stop soon. We must make ready with my experiment."

CROFTON nodded. He and the professor moved two different machines up beside the cabinet. Looking toward the walls, the witnesses saw a dozen different floor plugs from which current could be supplied. Crofton produced several lengths of wire, each with plugs on both ends. The professor began making attachments. He needed more wires. Crofton brought them.

The telephone ceased ringing before Lessep had completed his arrangements. Wires ran from floor plugs to machines. Others stretched from one machine to corners of the cabinet. The rest were left dangling from the second machine, for later use.

Nodding busily, Lessep decided that everything was ready. He spoke to Crofton. The young man removed his white robe. Underneath, he was wearing an outfit that looked like an aviator's garb, except for its color, which was black. As Crofton stepped into the cabinet, it was apparent that his shoes were fitted with heavy rubber soles.

The professor produced a helmet. Crofton donned it. Then he put on dark brown gloves, made of thick rubber. Cautiously, he stepped into the exact center of the cabinet. The professor closed the glass door. The observers could see the man inside.

Lessep pressed a switch on the hooked-up machine. Crackly sounds came from the glass walls of the cabinet. Flickers of light flashed from the connections. The sides of the cabinet and the glass base began to turn misty.

There was something insidious in Professor Lessep's manner as the old man turned toward his audience. A profound hush had been created; now it was broken only by the buzz of the motor and the dying crackles from the glass. In a high-pitched, fanatical tone, the professor began to speak.

"I have found it!" he exclaimed. "The secret of devisualization! Through this experiment I shall make a solid appear as a vapor. A solid—a living solid!

"Look to that cabinet. What have you seen there? First you have seen glass. Then, inside, a man. What do you see now? A vapor—like steam—a vapor from the air."

The walls of the cabinet were frosting. Crofton's form was almost obscured from view. Chuckling, the professor waited until the misted glass had totally hidden his assistant. Then he consulted a clock dial upon the machine.

"You see vapor," clucked Lessep, turning to the silent group at the end of the room. "That vapor is air, which I have made to show itself by the application of heat. You understand? You see air—which you could not see before—and later you will see that air no longer.

"But a little while ago you saw a man inside the cabinet. You cannot see him now. Why? On account of air. Air, which is vapor, surrounding him. I have made a man unseen, by surrounding him with air of a certain sort.

"Now comes my secret"—the professor paused and wisely tapped his forehead—"which I have formulated here in my brain. If air, when like a mist, can hide a solid form, why cannot air, when it is no longer mist, still hide that form?

"It is impossible? That is what you would say. But I shall show you different. Far different. The vapor that you see is on the walls of the cabinet only. But the air inside that cabinet is possessed of the same power.

"That air alone will hide the solid form. That air which you cannot see! You cannot see it—nor can you see what is within it. The vapor has done its part. It is no longer needed. But it will take a while to go. I shall not try your patience by forcing you to wait."

WITH hurried, almost frenzied speed, the professor bobbed about the cabinet, detaching wires. He turned off the buzzing machine. He attached the connections from the second motor. All the while, the silent watchers were staring at the whitened walls of glass, for the sides of the cabinet had become completely frosted.

Ready, with one hand upon the new motor, Professor Lessep raised his other hand and lifted an impressive forefinger. Leaning forward, prophetic with his garb and hair of white, the old man spoke in his odd, crackling tone.

"He is within that cabinet," announced the professor. "This man who has been willing to take the risk of my experiment. Science owes much to him—to Miles Crofton. He is a man who has taken great risks; but none to equal this.

"He can come out only by that door which you see in the front. I shall have him open that door; but he must stay within the cabinet. For at this moment, my friends, no living eye could see Miles Crofton. He is devisualized! Within air that hides him and all that he may carry within that space. Not until I use the second process will he come back to view."

The professor paused. Still holding his fixed position, he turned his eyes toward the cabinet and waited amid complete silence. Then he spoke:

"Open the door of the cabinet."

A pause. The door trembled. Then, impelled by some force, the white, frosted barrier swung outward.

Staring spectators blinked; the only eyes that were steady were those of The Shadow—the optics that peered from the countenance of Lamont Cranston.

Where the dark-garbed form of a man had been, whiteness alone came to view. The sides, the top, the base of the cabinet—these showed with their coating of thick frost, a solid-walled interior.

The cabinet, itself, was empty! Professor Lessep's fantastic experiment had fulfilled his strange prediction. Miles Crofton had vanished from human sight!

CHAPTER IV
CARDONA SPEAKS

TRIUMPH showed on Lessep's face as the old professor stepped forward from the motor. A peculiar awe lay over the little audience that had witnessed the evanishment of Miles Crofton.

The telephone began to ring again from beyond the door of the adjoining office. Professor Lessep gave it no heed; nor did the persistent ringing break the spell that had come over the assembled group.

With sharp, steady gaze, the white-haired inventor surveyed the spectators. He was ready for a challenge; for quizzical expressions; but none came. It was not until his gaze reached a certain point that the professor became perturbed.

There, Lessep's stare encountered the burning glare of eyes far sharper than his own. Those were the orbs that peered from the visage of Lamont Cranston. All others seemed bewildered; they were looking toward the frosted cabinet. But this one member of the audience had chosen the professor as his visual target.

Lessep alone saw the focused brilliance of those eyes. They were the eyes of The Shadow. They troubled the old man in his triumph. They carried a challenge that brought a quiver of fear to the professor's wasted frame.

As suddenly as if he had received a shock from one of his own machines, Lessep sprang sidewise toward the cabinet. Shaking a scrawny hand toward the opened door, he issued a new statement that came amid the muffled ringing from the telephone bell in the office.

"He is standing there!" exclaimed the professor. "Within the glass walls of the cabinet! Yet you cannot see him. Sharp though your eyes may be"—

wildly, Lessep paused to catch the gaze of The Shadow's burning optics—"you can see—nothing!

"Yet he is there! Miles Crofton, in the flesh, stands in the center of the cabinet. Held within walls of glass. Encased where he cannot escape. Still solid, yet surrounded by an aura that renders him unseen. An invisible mist, about a living form. I shall prove it!"

With that, Lessep thrust his right hand into the cabinet. He moved it about, as though touching an invisible form. The action was impressive.

Commissioner Barth, straining forward, sought to make out a living shape, but failed.

"You may step forward—"

Professor Lessep stopped short in his statement; then betrayed a look of alarm. He had half withdrawn his hand from the cabinet; now he was thrusting it in again. Wildly, the professor grappled into the opened space, this time encountering nothingness.

"He is gone!" shrieked the old man. "Out of the cabinet. Stay where you are, until I find him. Crofton! Crofton! Where are you?"

THERE was no response. The professor leaped back to his new motor. He pressed a switch. Lightninglike flashes crackled through the cabinet. The odor of ozone charged the air. The ringing of the telephone bell had ended. This new sound alone pervaded the room.

"He has left the cabinet!" shrilled Lessep, above the crackle of electricity. "He had no right to do so. Stop him—wherever he may be! Look to the doors— stop him—there, by the door to the parlor—"

Men were coming to their feet. In response to the professor's plea, they swung as one toward the door that Lessep had indicated. It offered the logical avenue of departure, that door through the front of the house.

"The bolt!" cried Lessep. "The light switch! Watch them"—the professor was swaying as he leaned heavily upon his buzzing motor—"watch them before—before—"

The admonition came too late. While those nearest the door were staring, the bolt of the door was drawn back, as though plucked by an invisible hand. The knob turned. The door swung open. Then, as the barrier wavered, the light switch was pressed upward. It clicked. The room was plunged in blackness. An instant later, the door closed with a sudden slam.

Men were groping blindly for the wall. The light switch was beyond the corner of the room, a hard spot to locate in the darkness. The crackle of the motor continued, with the professor's voice shrilling above it. Then, after moments that seemed interminable, the switch was found. It clicked. Startled men blinked in the light.

Most of the persons present were clustered along the wall or by the door. There was one exception. The tall form of Lamont Cranston had moved in a different direction. Staring toward the cabinet, Professor Lessep saw this one visitor almost beside the frosted apparatus.

Lessep had turned on more power. He motioned wildly with his hands, his gestures signifying for Cranston to stay away from the cabinet. Calmly, the tall witness watched; then others turned in the same direction.

Electric sparks were crackling against glass panes. They were knifing their way through frosted white- ness. Icy mist was fading. The walls of the cabinet were becoming clear. As silent men stared, they saw the glass sides regain their original clearness. The cabinet and its base stood as transparent as they had been at the beginning of the experiment.

Lessep turned off the motor. Sagging above the machine, he pointed toward the unbolted door, where Commissioner Barth stood facing him. The commissioner, bald-headed, yet austere, had backed against the closed barrier, determined that no one else should leave.

"Bolt the door!" suggested Lessep, gasping.

Barth complied. The professor then glanced all about the room. Others followed his gaze as it wandered from door to door. The exit to the hallway was bolted, as before. So was the entrance to Lessep's little office. With a broad sweep of his hand, the professor invited a complete search. He began to detach the wires from his motors.

HALF quivering, men began to look about. Wainwright Barth boldly approached the glass cabinet. He was followed by the two reporters, who tapped the transparent panels and looked at each other in puzzled fashion.

Findlay Warlock, in a high state of excitement, began to join in the inspection. The others were a bit slower; yet they gained encouragement as they proceeded.

Lessep, suddenly subdued, kept on coiling wires. At times he looked up. He encountered the steady gaze from Cranston's eyes. He blinked and looked away.

By the door, Lessep saw the rugged form of Marryat Darring. Where Cranston's eyes had been challenging, Darring's were skeptical. Lessep faced their gaze; he saw an unbelieving smile appear upon Darring's lips. The old man responded with a glare. Then Commissioner Barth's arrival proved an intervention.

Barth had satisfied himself that the room was empty. He was also sure that no one could have made exit from it, except by the door that he had seen open and close. Faced by the incredible, the bespectacled commissioner demanded a statement from Professor Lessep.

"Tell me, Professor," ordered Barth. "Did this man Crofton actually attain a state of invisibility?"

"Yes," assured Lessep. "In the exact manner that I explained. The experiment worked perfectly, Commissioner. It is a case of total devisualization. Indeed, it amazed me."

"How so?"

"Because I had never before attempted the devisualization of a living object. The atmospheric state that I created has adhered to Crofton's form. You saw him go out the door. You saw him press the light switch. Did you catch one glimpse of his actual form?"

"Not one."

"Ah! It is too bad."

Barth looked perplexed. Warlock, enthused by the success of the experiment, could not understand the professor's sudden turn. Both wanted an explanation. Lessep gave it.

"It is too bad," he cackled, gloomily, "that I should have spoken so much to Crofton. I told him that the experiment would be complete. More than that, I said that his risk would be great because he could lose his devisualized state only through the application of the rays from the second motor.

"I meant it as a warning, Commissioner, a warning that Crofton should have heeded. But now I fear that he took it in a different sense. Could it be that he had some reason? So it seems. But he gave me no reason to think that he would wish to remain unseen."

"You mean," questioned Barth, anxiously, "that this man Crofton will not be visible again until you have subjected him to the second treatment?"

"Exactly so!" assured Lessep, glumly.

"It seems incredible!" declared the commissioner. "Beyond all belief—"

"It is a hoax!" The interruption came from Darring. The black-haired man had approached the cabinet. "Don't let it worry you, Commissioner. A man can't vanish into thin air."

"But we have seen it," stated Barth. "The man could not have walked from the cabinet without observation."

"Except in the darkness."

"I was at the door. I gained that post immediately after the lights went out."

"The other doors?"

"They are still bolted."

HANDS in pockets, Darring strode over to examine the doors that the others had already inspected. He found them tightly bolted. A bit puzzled, yet still skeptical, Darring came back. He looked toward Lamont Cranston, as though seeking assurance from the one other person who did not stand convinced.

"What do you think of it?" he inquired. "Do you share my view, Mr. Cranston? A hoax?"

"It is no hoax," put in Warlock, suddenly. "You are unfair, Darring. I call upon the commissioner to support me when I say that this experiment was fairly conducted and proves Professor Lessep's claim."

"Incredible though it appears," decided Barth, "we are faced by the definite fact that a man has vanished. I am forced to agree with Mr. Warlock. This is no hoax."

The reporters were quick with their pencils. They wanted a further statement. Barth, a little flustered, began to polish his pince-nez spectacles, after carefully removing them from the bridge of his nose.

"A statement?" queried the commissioner. "Hm-m-m. It might be best to hear others first. By the way, Cranston, what is your opinion of this experiment?"

"I am interested in the subject," came the quiet response. "I should like to know—from Professor Lessep—why Miles Crofton was chosen for this experiment in devisualization."

"For two reasons," returned Lessep, promptly. "First, because he had proven to be a competent assistant. Second, because he was a man who had undergone many hazards. He had been an aviator, a soldier of fortune—"

"How did he happen to come into your employ?"

"I advertised for an assistant who understood electrical appliances. I specified that I would need a man who would take unusual risks—"

"And Miles Crofton responded?"

"Yes."

Before another question could be asked, a sudden pounding broke out from the door that led into Lessep's parlor. For a moment, Commissioner Barth was startled. Then, adjusting his pince-nez, the official smiled wisely.

"Perhaps Miles Crofton has returned," he decided. "Remain as you are everyone. I shall answer this knock."

Barth strode to the door and unbolted it. The barrier opened. In stepped a stocky, swarthy-faced man, with two others close behind him. Barth stood astonished. This was Detective Joe Cardona, the ace from headquarters.

Cardona looked about the room; then turned to nod to Barth.

"Called you from headquarters, Commissioner," said Joe. His right hand was half out of his pocket; it was plain that his fingers clutched a gun. "No answer, so I came up here. Told Markham to call you later."

"We heard the bell ring," returned Barth. "But neither call was answered by anyone—"

"I see." Joe was looking about the group as he made the interruption. "Which one of these men is Miles Crofton?"

"Miles Crofton?" exclaimed Barth. "Why—why—Crofton is gone. Did you want him?"

"Yes," responded Cardona, grimly. "For murder!"

CHAPTER V
THE QUEST BEGINS

IT was midnight. The lights were on in Commissioner Barth's office. The high official was holding council. Present was a select group that had accompanied him from Professor Melrose Lessep's laboratory.

Barth had chosen this spot for a consultation with Joe Cardona. He had insisted that his friend Lamont Cranston come along. Findlay Warlock, as the patron of Professor Lessep, had also been invited. Warlock, in turn, had requested the presence of Marryat Darring.

"The facts of the case," summarized Barth, as he sat importantly behind his mahogany desk, "are these. A man—one Miles Crofton—is at large. He has disappeared completely from human sight. Professor Melrose Lessep, the person responsible for this disappearance, attributes it to a process that he has termed 'devisualization.'

"Our repeated search has given more and more substantiation to the professor's claim. His cabinet, his laboratory, his office and his bolted doors have added mute testimony to his assertion. Four of us were witnesses to Crofton's disappearance. Two of us—myself and Warlock—have admitted that devisualization must be the answer to Crofton's departure.

"You, Cranston, have simply reserved opinion. For the present, we may regard your view as neutral. As for you, Darring, you hold to the belief that the whole affair was a hoax. Yet you have not produced any evidence to support your claim."

"None," interposed Darring, testily, "except that of common sense. You can't make a man vanish, unless there's a trick to it. I've got to see something more tangible."

"We are dealing with a scientific matter," asserted Barth, reprovingly. "The professor's theory of devisualization has merit. Many facts, scientific ones, have been discovered that are quite as incredible as this one.

"However, we can resume this portion of the discussion later. What concerns us as much as Crofton's disappearance is the matter of Crofton himself. Cardona, let us hear your exact statement once again, in reference to Miles Crofton."

"Well," declared Cardona, gruffly, "I'm only following a tip, as I said before. We've been looking for the crew that worked with Rouser Tukin. Hadn't been able to trace any until tonight.

"Down at headquarters I got a phone call from a

PROFESSOR MELROSE LESSEP

stool pigeon. Fellow that's been A-1 reliable, the little I've used him. Just had a couple of minutes to put me wise to something, he said. So I listened.

"His story was that Miles Crofton was in with Rouser. What's more, he swore that Crofton was the fellow who killed one of the policemen. Didn't say where he got the dope, this stoolie didn't, but he promised more next time he got in touch with me. But he told me where Crofton was. Said the guy was working for an inventor named Melrose Lessep. What's more, the stoolie said the commissioner was going to be up at Lessep's tonight."

"Your man was remarkably well informed," observed Barth, dryly. "You yourself did not know where to reach me, at first."

"That only proves the stoolie knew his stuff," returned Cardona. "I called the Cobalt Club; they told me where you were. So I called you, Commissioner. Getting no reply, I started up, leaving Markham to keep calling you."

"We know the rest," declared Barth. "Therefore, we are safe in saying that a killer, an unseen killer, is at large. We cannot hold Professor Lessep culpable. There is no way in which he could have known of his assistant's past.

"But we must begin at once!" Barth thumped his

fist upon the desk. "We must spare no effort in tracing this dangerous man. That is why I gave a full statement to the newspapers. The Unseen Killer is at large. It is up to you, Cardona, to find him."

"You can't track a man you can't see," objected Joe. "It's easy enough to get pictures of Crofton, but what good will they be? If this wild stuff is on the level—if the guy's lost to sight—how are you going to grab him?"

"That must be determined," replied Barth, sagely.

Cardona waited for a further statement. None was forthcoming. The commissioner had propounded an unanswerable riddle.

A THIN smile showed upon the lips of Lamont Cranston. It was unobserved by the others.

"Where are you going to start?" quizzed Cardona. Then, answering his own question: "The professor looks like the best bet to me. If it wasn't for him, we'd have Crofton right now. The way I figure it, Commissioner, the professor is responsible."

"Professor Lessep has committed no crime," objected Barth. "His experiment was scientifically conducted."

"If one can regard a hoax as a scientific experiment," put in Darring. "I should think that the law could deal with the perpetrator of a hoax."

"The professor has proven his sincerity," declared Warlock, hotly. "This attempt to damage his reputation is unfair. It is not his fault that Crofton took criminal advantage of his invention."

"We are back to the same point," decided Barth, in an irritable tone. "Unless we can come to a definite agreement on this matter, we will arrive nowhere. I am willing to bring pressure upon Professor Lessep, provided that it can be done in a reasonable manner."

"No pressure is necessary," insisted Warlock. "Professor Lessep was quite willing for people to witness his experiment. He even set it in advance of the date originally scheduled. He offered no objection to making his demonstration under rigid conditions."

"I have it!" exclaimed Darring, suddenly. "We can settle this matter very easily. Why not have the professor repeat the experiment?"

Cranston's smile remained immobile. The suggestion had come at last. Darring had struck upon the obvious solution, the logical way to learn whether or not the devisualization system would stand a thorough test.

"Excellent!" said the commissioner. "That, at least, would establish one point, namely: whether or not your cry of 'hoax' is a fair one, Darring. But it offers a danger, besides."

"What is that?"

"The possibility of putting a second person into the realm of the invisible. One is bad enough."

Joe Cardona nodded at the commissioner's statement. The detective added an opinion of his own.

"I'm supposed to track one fellow that I can't see," he declared. "Why double the odds against me?"

"My suggestion," remarked Darring, "could produce the opposite effect. If devisualization is a genuine process, it can be used to advantage."

"How so?" inquired Barth.

"By choosing the proper person," replied Darring. "Detective Cardona, for instance. Why not dispatch him into the invisible?"

"Jove!" exclaimed Barth. "You've struck it, Darring. The effect would be tremendous!"

"It wouldn't help me trace Crofton," objected Cardona, in an uneasy tone.

"But it would give you a marvelous advantage," argued Barth, with enthusiasm. "Furthermore, it would settle all this controversy. Of course, Cardona, I shall not insist that you take on this task—"

"I'M game," interrupted Joe, "but it sort of gives me the creeps. It don't sound real. I'll take a chance on it, though, if the professor will stand for the deal."

"I think I can persuade him to do so," put in Warlock, a bit troubled. "He might object; but I think that he would listen to my arguments. I have sponsored this invention, in a sense. Let me communicate with Professor Lessep in the morning."

"Very well," agreed Barth. "A request from you, Warlock, would be better than an order from me. For a beginning, at least. Arrange for an experiment tomorrow night, with Cardona as the subject. If you fail, I shall handle the matter."

"This experiment business works both ways, don't it?" queried Cardona. "I mean the professor can bring a man back to sight, just like he can put him away?"

"So he claims," stated Barth. "That was precisely what he intended to do with Miles Crofton; but the fellow made an escape in the midst of the experiment."

"Have no qualms," assured Warlock. "The professor is thoroughly reliable. I feel sure that you will encounter no danger when you visit his laboratory tomorrow night."

"Agreed," added Darring, mildly sarcastic. "You won't have much to worry about, Cardona."

"Why not?" questioned the detective, seeing significance in Darring's tone.

"Because," predicted Darring, "the professor will have some excuse for postponing the experiment. The thing is a hoax, I tell you. He will not dare to repeat it except with some person of his own choosing."

Warlock began to protest. The commissioner interrupted him. He wanted no further controversy. Blinking in owlish fashion, Barth delivered his decision in the matter.

"All will be settled tomorrow night," he declared. "We shall rely upon Mr. Warlock to persuade Professor Lessep to undertake the new experiment, using Cardona in the test. If Warlock fails, I shall threaten Lessep with arrest unless he proceeds.

"We shall all be present to witness the result. Then we can fairly judge the circumstances. We can decide whether Mr. Warlock's faith in the professor is justified; or whether Mr. Darring's skepticism is correctly founded.

"Personally, I incline toward Warlock's belief. You, Cranston"—Barth turned to his silent friend—"appear to be somewhat in accord with Darring. That balances the committee. With Cardona as the chosen subject for the new experiment, we have every advantage. Let us adjourn until tomorrow."

ONE hour after the meeting had ended in the commissioner's office, a sharp click sounded in a blackened room. A bluish light threw shaded rays upon a table in the corner. Long, white hands appeared upon a polished surface. The Shadow was in his sanctum.

A soft laugh from hidden lips. Producing pen and paper, the hands began to work. While the left steadied the sheet beneath the light, the right began to draw a floor plan of Professor Lessep's laboratory.

Blue-inked lines faded. Such was the way with The Shadow's writing. Then came carefully written words; and all the while, traces of the soft, mocking laugh. The Shadow was reviewing the bizarre events that had taken place in the professor's lab.

The Shadow could see the real reason behind the episode at the professor's, so far as Lessep himself was concerned. The old inventor's reputation had been none too high. He had needed an astounding success to restore faith in his genius. He had scored the result that he required.

A living being banished out into the unknown! What a triumph for Lessep! Hoax or reality—either had achieved the same result. Lessep had paved the way to tremendous publicity. That, as The Shadow saw it, was the professor's game.

"Miles Crofton."

The Shadow's hand inscribed the name of Lessep's assistant. Here was another factor. At the outset of the experiment, Crofton had figured purely as the subject whom Lessep had chosen. The Shadow, present in the guise of Lamont Cranston, had seen no reason to interfere with the professor's game.

Joe Cardona's arrival had been the startling factor. The detective's accusation of Miles Crofton had changed bewilderment into consideration. Yet this fact fitted into the scheme of things. Miles Crofton—wanted for murder—there was a tie-up that would bring Professor Lessep's experiment into front-page headlines.

It transformed Miles Crofton from a prank-player into a menace. Instead of being a missing assistant, the man had become an unseen killer. The bigger the news, the better from the professor's standpoint.

Viewed from that aspect, Cardona's tip from the unnamed stool pigeon looked like more than a coincidence. But The Shadow had passed from his consideration of Professor Lessep's peculiar interests. He was studying the part played by Miles Crofton.

It was quite conceivable that the assistant would have agreed to work with the professor. Crofton's startling disappearance had added a touch of real drama to the events in the lab. But would Crofton have agreed to go forth branded as a murderer?

The Shadow's laugh was a negative answer. No matter what Crofton's present situation might be, the charges against him were dangerous. The cry of "murderer" had made him a hunted man. Cardona's timely gained tip might prove a boomerang to the missing assistant.

Coincidence? A double cross by the professor? The action of some new player in the game? These were questions that concerned The Shadow. They brought a new laugh from his lips; a burst of sardonic mirth that was creepy in its tone. They told of a definite purpose.

HANDS stretched across the table. Earphones clattered from the wall. A tiny bulb glittered from the blackness, telling of telephonic connection. Then came a quiet voice:

"Burbank speaking."

"Instructions to all agents," whispered The Shadow.

The weird voice continued through the sanctum, hissing its sibilant tones, while Burbank, The Shadow's contact man, listened at the other end of the wire. The Shadow's tones ended. From the receivers came Burbank's final response:

"Instructions received."

Earphones slid back. The bulb went out. A click; the bluish light was extinguished. Amid the darkness of the sanctum came an eerie laugh that died with lingering echoes. The Shadow had departed. But while the law was lingering, he had taken up a quest.

Miles Crofton was the man The Shadow wanted. Agents of The Shadow would locate him. Visible or invisible, Lessep's assistant would be found; for The Shadow had seen possibilities that had escaped the law.

Whatever Miles Crofton's present state of being,

the man would need a hideout. A visible man, hunted by the police, would have to stay out of sight. An unseen crook would have to maintain a secret headquarters.

"You can't track a man you can't see—"

Such had been Cardona's verdict. All had accepted it, with the exception of The Shadow. He knew that Cardona had made a misstatement. Laughing softly in the seclusion of his sanctum, The Shadow had pictured the difficulties of an unseen killer. Troubles quite as great as those that would surround a visible criminal.

Food, shelter, security—Miles Crofton needed them. Whatever his game, he had probably pre-arranged those necessities. There must be other men who would aid him. Through them, Crofton could be traced. Agents of The Shadow would filter forth through the reaches of the underworld, seeking trace of a hideout.

Keen had been The Shadow's finding. Yet his parting laugh, satirical in its mirth, had revealed a trace of levity. Although he had instituted a search for Miles Crofton, The Shadow had seen no need for haste. As yet, he considered menace lacking.

Seldom did The Shadow err in judgment. Even now, his calculation was wrong only so far as time was concerned. In starting the manhunt, The Shadow had sensed possibilities of crime at some future time. Crofton, goaded by the fact that he was wanted as a murderer; might eventually prove dangerous.

Yet the menace was immediate. Already crime was planned. It would strike with a suddenness that would prove startling even to The Shadow. For the threat of an unseen killer was backed by the machinations of an evil brain.

CHAPTER VI
THE PROFESSOR BALKS

AT eight o'clock the next evening, Commissioner Barth's car pulled up in front of the residence of Professor Melrose Lessep. Three men alighted from the machine: Wainwright Barth, Joe Cardona and Marryat Darring.

They ascended the cracked stone steps. The commissioner rang the bell. After a short interval, the door opened.

Professor Lessep, shock-haired and wild-eyed, stood viewing his visitors. A broad smile appeared upon the inventor's lips.

"Ah! Good evening!" exclaimed Lessep. "Come in, my friends. At once. Mr. Warlock has been here this half hour, expecting your arrival. Come. Into the laboratory."

The visitors divested themselves of hats and coats, which they hung on a rack in the hall. Lessep led them through the parlor to the laboratory door.

There he paused to rap. There was no response until Lessep knocked louder than before. Then came muffled footsteps. A bolt was drawn; Findlay Warlock admitted them.

"I was looking about," said Warlock, in a wheezy, apologetic tone. "I wasn't sure that I heard you knock."

"Quite all right," assured the professor. "You see, gentlemen"—his tone was uneasy—"I was not certain who might be at the door. I did not like to leave the laboratory. So Mr. Warlock said that he would bolt the door while I was making sure that the proper visitors had arrived."

"What did you do when Warlock arrived?" questioned Barth, a bit suspiciously. "You had to leave the laboratory open then, didn't you?"

"No," replied the professor. "I had not opened the laboratory before his arrival. You see"—he waved his hand toward the door that led into the rear hall—"there is a lock also on that door, as well as a bolt. I have the key to open it. It is only when we are inside that I keep all the bolts closed."

Barth nodded. He could see the closed bolt on the far door. The door to the office was also bolted. Lessep had shot the bolt of the door through which they had entered.

"This is the key," remarked Lessep, producing the object. "But it will be necessary, I now fear, to have a new lock placed on that one door."

"Why?" asked Barth.

"Because," replied the professor, "there is another key which I do not have."

"Who has it?"

"Miles Crofton."

BARTH'S eyes blinked through the pince-nez. The commissioner was about to make a comment, when Lessep saved him the trouble.

"Ah, yes," affirmed the professor, in a troubled tone. "I have thought of what you wish to say. Crofton—that ungrateful assistant—still has access here. I was thinking about it, all this very afternoon. How he might even be here, watching me!"

As he spoke, the professor looked warily about. His eyes strained as though seeking view of an invisible object. Findlay Warlock nodded seriously.

"I had the same impression," he declared. "Alone here, during the past few minutes. That of unseen eyes—"

"It's ridiculous," Marryat Darring snorted the interruption. "Come, come! This is carrying a hoax too far. What about tonight's experiment? Are we going through with it, Professor?"

"Certainly," replied Lessep, in a crackly tone. "If you so wish. It was at one o'clock this afternoon that I came into this laboratory, to work until five. Hardly had I been here before the telephone rang in my office. It was my good friend here, Mr. Warlock.

Leaning close to the motor, Lessep uttered a sudden exclamation. He blinked nervously as he looked at the others.... "It is gone!" cried Lessep. "The connecting lever! The integral part of this machine!"

"I told him that I would do the experiment as wished. I worked on then until five o'clock. Then I went out and locked the laboratory behind me. After having dinner at the restaurant, I came back. But I did not again open the laboratory until Mr. Warlock arrived."

"The experiment is what interests us," declared Darring, impatiently. "The commissioner wants you to perform it with Detective Cardona as the subject."

"So I understand"—Lessep paused warily, to look at Cardona—"but it is very dangerous. I must tell you that beforehand. It is a risk—"

"I'm ready for it," interrupted Cardona.

"And we're ready to watch it," added Darring.

"We must wait for Cranston," remarked Barth. "He should be here shortly."

"But that's no reason why the professor can't get started," interposed Darring. "How about hooking up those motors, getting the machinery ready?"

"Proceed, Professor," ordered Barth, with a pompous nod.

Professor Lessep bowed. Methodically donning a white robe, he drew the glass cabinet from the far wall. Then he rolled up one electric motor and began to make attachments. It was while he was plugging in a cord that his face became troubled.

Leaning close to the motor, Lessep uttered a sudden exclamation. He blinked nervously as he looked up at the others; then made a sweeping motion with his hand, to indicate the screw-end of a bolt that projected from the machine.

"It is gone!" cried Lessep. "The connecting lever! The integral part of this machine. Someone has removed it without my knowledge!"

"HOW long ago?" quizzed Barth, sharply.

"Since after five o'clock," replied Lessep, seriously. "I remember; I made one examination of this motor before I left for my dinner. He has been here!" Lessep's voice rose shrilly. "Crofton has been here!"

"When?" demanded Barth.

"How could I know?" asked Lessep. "But I think—maybe—that I could guess. It must have been before one o'clock that he entered, with that key which he has."

"Why before one?"

"So that he could have listened while I heard word from Mr. Warlock. Then, after I had gone, at five o'clock—"

"He wanted to block the experiment," interposed Barth. "How much did you say over the telephone, Professor, when you talked with Warlock?"

"A great deal. Too much, I fear."

"A fine stall!" The sarcastic comment came from Darring. "I predicted this, Commissioner. I told you, last night, that the professor would find some excuse. He has hidden the lever himself, I believe."

"Look for it if you wish!" exclaimed Lessep. "Here; in the little office. Anywhere about."

"All right," agreed Darring. "What does the lever look like?"

"I shall show you." Lessep turned and led the way into the adjoining office.

It was a little room, plainly furnished. A filing cabinet in one corner; a desk in another. A single window, metal-shuttered, like those in the laboratory. These arrangements were revealed when Lessep pressed a light switch just inside the door.

The room was illuminated by the action, from a single light in the ceiling. Lessep went to the filing cabinet. There he turned on a hanging light. Under the increased glare, the professor opened a drawer; he found a photograph of the motor that was in the laboratory. He pointed out the lever in question.

Darring examined the picture.

"You have a better photograph," remarked Warlock. "Where is it, Professor?"

"I must have left it in the desk," replied Lessep. "Let me see." He went to the desk and turned on another light. "Ah, yes. Here it is."

He brought the photograph to Darring, who had handed the first picture to Barth. Cardona was also looking on, when an exclamation came from Warlock, who had gone over to the desk.

"Here's a note for you, Professor," announced Warlock. "Addressed in your name, with the word 'important' added. It hasn't been opened."

He handed the envelope to Lessep. Photographs were temporarily forgotten while the professor fumbled excitedly in opening the message. Lessep unfolded a sheet of paper. His lips began to quiver. The note nearly fell from his shaking hands.

Commissioner Barth seized the paper. He read aloud:

"To Professor Melrose Lessep:

"The missing lever is proof of my ability to thwart your actions. This letter is my warning. If you attempt to repeat your experiment in devisualization, you shall die.—THE UNSEEN KILLER.

"It's typewritten," remarked Barth. "With the signature in red. This is a result of that newspaper story, Cardona. Those reporters termed Miles Crofton the 'Unseen Killer' and he has adopted the title. This constitutes a threat."

"All the more reason," put in Darring, "why you should proceed with the experiment, Commissioner."

"I agree," declared Barth. "Come, Professor. Let us search for that lever. Where would Crofton have hidden it? Here or in the laboratory?"

"He might have taken it with him," replied Lessep, in a quavering voice. "You may search if you wish, but I feel—"

"Crofton may still be here," suggested Warlock,

in a troubled tone, as further words failed Lessep. "Remember, the man is unseen. A search might bring serious consequences."

"Still a hoax," scoffed Darring. "What about a search, Commissioner?"

BARTH nodded in agreement. The search began. The office was a simple task. Desk drawers revealed no traces of the lever, nor did the filing cabinet. Cardona lifted a covered typewriter from a small table, but did not find the lever beneath it.

Lessep was replacing his photographs in the filing cabinet when the others started out to search the laboratory. Only Darring remained, making a second search of the desk when the clang of a house-bell announced someone at the front door.

Wainwright Barth stood momentarily startled. He was in the center of the laboratory when he heard the sound. Then he saw Professor Lessep come trembling from the office. The old man's face was pitiful.

"It's Cranston," reassured Barth. "Answer the door, Professor. Warlock will go with you"—then, as Warlock hesitated—"and Cardona also. Come." The bell tingled again. "Do not keep Cranston waiting."

Barth led the way to the door and unbolted it. The professor went into the parlor. Cardona followed him promptly. Warlock hesitated; then remained. While he was standing beside Barth, Darring strolled up and joined them.

"It's Cranston," assured Barth.

Darring nodded. He stood beside the commissioner and waited, while Warlock nervously edged away. A full minute elapsed. It was one of increasing tension. Then Barth, whose ruddy face had begun to show a strain, smiled weakly in relief.

The professor and Joe Cardona were returning. With them was Lamont Cranston. Sight of his friend's calm face had eased the commissioner's worry. For Wainwright Barth, unconsciously, had begun to feel the presence of an unseen killer.

His forced belief in an invisible menace had brought Barth to a state almost as fearful as that evidenced by Melrose Lessep and Findlay Warlock. The arrival of Lamont Cranston, through some singular reason, brought Barth a renewal of confidence.

CHAPTER VII
THE KILLER STRIKES

COMMISSIONER WAINWRIGHT BARTH became dramatic as soon as the three men had entered the laboratory. He closed the door and bolted it. Turning to Cranston, he beckoned. Then he led the way to the motor which Professor Lessep had attached to the glass cabinet.

"Strange things have occurred here, Cranston,"

explained Barth. "An important connecting lever has been stolen from this motor. Apparently the theft took place after five o'clock this afternoon."

The commissioner paused as he saw Cranston nod. The new arrival was examining the bolt from which the lever had been removed.

"Professor Lessep had a photograph of the complete motor," resumed Barth. "If you wish to see it—"

"That is not necessary," came Cranston's quiet interruption. "I noted this motor very carefully last night. I recall the appearance of the part that is missing."

Professor Lessep blinked as he heard this statement.

Silently, Cranston turned away and looked at the second motor. One by one, he picked up loose cords that were plugged to it.

"Some of these have been changed also," he remarked. "See, Professor? The ones with the special plugs are no longer here."

"The special plugs?" inquired Lessep. "You must be mistaken, Mr. Cranston. There were no special plugs. Those are merely for making electrical connection. They have no other purpose."

"Two of them were different from the others," returned Cranston. "One which connected to the cabinet; the other to the floor socket."

"I never knew it," declared the professor. "All were standard cords and plugs. Of course, such items of electrical equipment differ in certain details."

"These had unusually long contact points." Cranston's tone was methodical. "I noticed them, particularly, after they were detached last night."

"But they are unimportant—"

"The professor is right," put in Barth. "Perhaps some of these cords were moved about; but no important parts are missing, Cranston. What we must find is that lever. Aid the professor, gentlemen, while he resumes the search. I want Mr. Cranston to see the note that was left in the office."

Lamont Cranston's keen eyes watched the professor's nod. Lessep started about the laboratory, with Cardona following him. Darring shrugged his shoulders; then joined in the search. Warlock appeared from the door of the little office. Seeing what the others were about, he entered into the hunt.

"Come into the office, Cranston," suggested Barth. "I want you to see exactly where the note was found. Here—read it for yourself."

They entered the office. Only the ceiling light was on. Barth approached the desk, clicked on the hanging lamp and pointed to the spot where the note had been.

Cranston nodded. He finished his examination of the note; then began to open the desk drawers.

"Nothing of importance in there," said Barth. "Just carbon copies of letters—a box of electric lightbulbs—"

He stopped as he saw Cranston pick out a yellow sheet of paper. It was a carbon copy of some letter sent by the professor. Barth watched Cranston compare the yellow sheet with the note that had come from the Unseen Killer.

"Agate type," was Cranston's comment. "Not well lined. An old-style machine, evidently purchased secondhand at a bargain price. Odd, Commissioner, how some of these letters correspond—"

Pausing abruptly, Cranston turned to the little table that bore the covered typewriter. He whisked away the cloth covering and smiled slightly, as he stooped forward. Then he motioned Barth toward the machine.

"Notice anything, Commissioner?"

"Nothing in particular—"

"The ribbon?"

Barth adjusted his pince-nez.

"Ah, yes," he said. "Two-colored—half red and half blue. Not uncommon for—"

He looked up to see Cranston's smile; then noted the Killer's message, that Cranston was holding toward him. The red signature, in its capital letters, was directly before the commissioner's eyes. Barth uttered an exclamation.

"Examine the ribbon more closely," came Cranston's suggestion. "Particularly the red portion."

Another exclamation from the commissioner. Barth, close to the typewriter, noted blue letter-marks—capitals—imprinted on the red half of the ribbon.

"What do those letters spell?" queried Cranston, still holding his thin smile.

"The Unseen Killer!" cried the commissioner.

"WHEN the red portion of the ribbon is seldom used," reminded Cranston, "the keys invariably leave blue marks when they first strike it."

The others had arrived. Barth's shout had been heard in the lab. As they crowded up, four together, the commissioner turned and pointed to the typewriter.

"Mr. Cranston has made a discovery," declared Barth. "The threatening letter was typed on your machine, Professor. Here, in this office!"

Lessep shook. He bent forward as the commissioner pointed out the marks on the ribbon. For a moment, the professor seemed worried and speechless. Then, gathering himself together, he spoke.

"This proves that Crofton has been here," declared the old man, solemnly. "Here, with his own unseen hands, he typed his warning. Even while we were first gathered in my laboratory, he could have prepared his terrible message."

"Hardly," came Cranston's quiet objection.

"Why not?" queried Barth.

"The note," explained Cranston, "was typed by someone who was alone in this office. Had any other person been present, the clicking of the keys would have been heard."

"Correct," agreed Barth. He made a calculation. "Then the message must have been typed between five o'clock and seven thirty, while the professor was out to dinner."

"Only if the Unseen Killer typed it," put in Darring.

"What do you mean?" inquired Barth.

"He means," came Cranston's steady response, "that you are accepting the note on the value of its typewritten signature. Mr. Darring, apparently, still holds to his opinion that Crofton's disappearance was a hoax."

"I do," declared Darring abruptly. "We came here for a second experiment. Professor Lessep has avoided it. In my opinion, this devisualization stuff is still hypothetical. Anybody could have typed that note. Whoever did type it could have been seen, as well as heard."

"I was here from one until five," declared Lessep solemnly. "I saw no one in the laboratory during those hours."

"And you returned at seven thirty."

"Yes. With Mr. Warlock."

"And after that?" queried Barth, swinging to Warlock's way of reasoning.

"The two of us were here," affirmed Lessep, "until eight o'clock. Then I went out to admit you, Commissioner. I left Mr. Warlock here alone."

"For about five minutes," interjected Warlock. "I was in the laboratory all that while. I heard no sounds of typing."

"This business is serious," announced Barth, glaring about the group. "Here is new evidence that cannot be minimized. If this should be a hoax"—he paused to nod approvingly toward Darring—"I intend to treat it as an actual crime.

"Let us forget Miles Crofton for the moment. You were here, Professor, four hours this afternoon. You could have typed that note. You could also have removed the parts from the machine."

Lessep began a protest. Barth silenced him with a fierce gesture. The commissioner then turned to Warlock.

"You were here also!" thundered Barth. "Alone, for five minutes. A short time yet sufficient to have done the work. Jove! This talk of an unseen man is maddening me. I intend to deal with those who are visible. Who else was in here alone?"

"I was," replied Darring, calmly. "While we were searching for the lost lever—"

"That was after the message was found,"

interrupted Barth. "After the lever was stolen. I mean before we discovered this note. "Who else was here beside you two?" He glared at Lessep; then at Warlock. "Who else could have been in here?"

"Miles Crofton," replied Darring.

"MILES CROFTON?" spluttered Barth, in total surprise. "But—but you, Darring, you were the one who termed it all a hoax. You claim that Crofton could not have become unseen—"

"I still hold my claim," responded Darring. "But do not forget, Commissioner, that there was an interval between five o'clock and seven thirty, while neither the professor nor Warlock happened to be here.

"Neither you nor I could have been here during that period, for you met me at my office at five and we dined together. But Crofton could have come here. Not unseen, but visibly. Or he could have sent someone. Anyone who had a duplicate key."

"That's right," admitted Barth. He mopped his forehead with a silk handkerchief. "This whole case is maddening. It brings us in circles, back to where we started. I don't know where it will end, unless—"

"Unless," completed Darring, in his skeptical tone, "the professor gives us proof that his devisualization is fact, not fancy. Just how long, Professor"—he wheeled to Lessep—"would it require for you to replace that missing lever?"

"Some time," responded Lessep, in a troubled tone. "It is a vital portion of the mechanism."

"How vital? Just what is the mechanical principle involved?"

"That is my secret," pleaded Lessep.

Darring looked hopelessly at Barth. The commissioner towered in indignation. He waved his hand toward the laboratory.

"Come, Lessep!" he ordered the professor. "This is no time for secrets. I shall guarantee protection to your invention. But unless you are willing to cooperate, I shall order your arrest."

THEY entered the laboratory, and formed a group about the first motor. Lessep reluctantly began to point out mechanical features of the device. His words became incoherent. Barth became brusque. Lessep pleaded.

"I am afraid," he declared. "Crofton is a menace."

"Proceed with your explanation," insisted Barth.

"It is useless," crackled Lessep. "So much depends upon the missing part. You would have to see it."

"We have seen the photographs," remarked Darring.

"Yes, Professor," urged Warlock, suddenly. "Bring the photographs. Let us see them. They will do to illustrate the use of the connecting lever."

Lessep rubbed his chin. At last he nodded.

Turning from the group he entered the little office. Ceiling light and desk lamp had been extinguished. The professor turned on the ceiling light; then closed the door behind him.

Lamont Cranston was examining the tall glass cabinet. He had noted that its sides were attached by clamps midway on each edge. As he unfastened clamps at the sides, the rear wall pivoted on its upper and lower fastenings; then swung back into place at Cranston's touch.

"I really believe," Barth was saying solemnly, "that the professor's fears are justified. Accept my apologies, Warlock, for accusing you the way I did. Actually I was not accusing; I was merely speculating. I wanted to find some solution other than the obvious."

"The obvious?" inquired Darring.

"Yes, the obvious," stated Barth. "For here the incredible happens to be the obvious. It sounds impossible to think that a man could be surrounded by an atmospheric condition that renders him invisible. Yet analysis tells me that Miles Crofton is actually devisualized.

"Professor Lessep knows it. That is why he fears. He realizes that Crofton—an unseen killer—could strike him down with some invisible weapon."

"You are right, Commissioner," spoke Warlock. "I knew that you would return to your first impression. It is the only sound explanation."

"Tommyrot!" ejaculated Darring. "Where is the proof? Lessep could furnish it by repeating his experiment. He has failed to do so. He removed that lever. He wrote that note.

"If Crofton is in the picture—as an unseen killer—why doesn't he strike? Why should a man in his position fail to follow up a threat? If Crofton—"

Darring never ended the sentence. From beyond the door of Lessep's study came the sudden muffled boom of an explosion. The laboratory caught the jar. The glass cabinet rattled. Those in the large room almost lost their footing.

WAINWRIGHT BARTH leaped to the door of the office and wrenched it open. With others close behind him, the commissioner was confronted by an outpouring of smoke that came from the corner by the filing cabinet.

Barth staggered back. Then, as the fumes were clearing, he led the way into the office. Lessening smoke enabled the commissioner to see Lessep's body, prone upon the floor. The filing cabinet was wrecked; the hanging lamp above it was shattered.

Lamont Cranston reached the professor's body ahead of the commissioner. His keen eyes saw that Melrose Lessep was dead. Barth, also realizing the professor's fate, turned to stare about the room.

Darring had entered behind Cranston. Now Cardona and Warlock were coming in from the laboratory.

"The Unseen Killer!" cried Barth. "He has caused this. He was here—in this room—"

He looked toward the door, diagonally opposite the demolished filing cabinet. It offered the logical spot from which a person could have projected a bomb or a grenade without danger to himself. Wildly, Barth sprang to that spot, to find nothingness. He headed into the laboratory. Warlock, Darring and Cardona were close behind him.

Staring, the commissioner saw the door that led to the rear hall. It was unbolted and open. Barth pointed, excitedly. Cardona spoke.

"I opened the door, Commissioner," said Joe. "In case there would be fumes from the office."

"You paved the way for Crofton's escape!" exclaimed Barth. "Had you kept the door bolted—"

"All our lives might have been jeopardized," put in Warlock. "He could have slain us as he killed the professor."

Back in the office, the tall form of Lamont Cranston stood above the body of Professor Lessep. There was no smile upon the firm, straight lips. Keen eyes stared—the eyes of The Shadow.

The shattered front of the filing cabinet had resulted in chunks of wood upon the floor. Beside these were slivers of glass from the wrecked lamp. The Shadow looked upward.

Turning, he moved quickly to the desk in the other corner. The lamp was illuminated there, still swaying slightly from the concussion that had caused the professor's death. Rapidly, The Shadow opened a drawer. He saw the box of lightbulbs; four in all.

One appeared to be burnt out. The Shadow removed it and closed the drawer. Resuming the slow motion of Lamont Cranston, he strolled into the laboratory to join the commissioner and the others.

"Close the door to the office," ordered Barth, turning to Cardona. "No one is to enter there from now on. I shall take charge of the investigation. With Cardona's aid. The rest of you are witnesses."

HOURS later, The Shadow entered his sanctum. A click; the blue light glimmered. A hand arose and turned the bulb in its socket. The light went out. Motion followed in the darkness. Then, suddenly, light reappeared.

It was not from the bluish incandescent. The Shadow had screwed in the frosted bulb that he had brought from Professor Lessep's office. That bulb was not burned out. Though it had been in long use, it was still serviceable.

The Shadow's hand remained motionless beneath the bulb. Then fingers unscrewed the frosted object. Again the blue incandescent came back in place. The white bulb lay in view upon the table.

Keen eyes studied this souvenir that The Shadow had brought from the scene of crime. The left hand raised the bulb and held it. Then the right hand rose upward toward the lamp. Slowly, the fingers turned the bluish incandescent; then paused.

A final twist. The blue light went out. It came on again, as the fingers reversed their twist. Off—on—off—on. The light glowed for a dozen seconds. Then a pressure of the switch extinguished it.

A soft laugh in the darkness. Then a swish. Weird, solemn echoes to hover in the gloom. For there was strange understanding in The Shadow's tone. The Shadow had gained a clue to crime.

Yet facts remained unexplained. The Shadow could see reasons for the death of Professor Lessep. He needed new links to complete the chain that would lead to a discovery of the motive. Reports from agents—received tonight from Burbank—had brought no word concerning the whereabouts of Miles Crofton.

The Shadow had gained theories; yet they conflicted. Those suppositions concerned the purposes of an unseen killer. Death had struck, almost in The Shadow's presence; nevertheless, it had left much to be explained.

Faced by one of the strangest situations that he had ever encountered, The Shadow was forced to wait. But in waiting, he would be preparing—ready to balk the next stroke of doom.

CHAPTER VIII
AT WARLOCK'S

LATE the next afternoon, a large limousine swung westward on a street well north of Times Square. It came to a stop in front of a brownstone house that was old yet imposing in appearance. A chauffeur alighted and opened the door. Lamont Cranston emerged; then Police Commissioner Barth.

"Wait here, Stanley," said Cranston, to the chauffeur. "We shall not be long."

The chauffeur saluted. Cranston and Barth ascended the steps and rang the bell. While they waited, the commissioner made comment.

"Glad you happened in, Cranston," he said. "I didn't care to make this visit appear too much in the nature of my official capacity. Since you came with me, I can express my arrival in the light of a friendly call.

"I think it best to be diplomatic with Findlay Warlock. He is actually apart from these strange events that ended in Melrose Lessep's death. Yet it so happens that he is the one man who actually knew the professor—"

Barth cut his sentence short as the door opened. A tall, withered-faced flunky gazed inquiringly at

the visitors. Barth glanced at Cranston. The latter spoke.

"We have come to see Mr. Warlock," he said quietly. "Mr. Cranston and Commissioner Barth."

The flunky nodded. He ushered the visitors into a gloomy living room, where fading embers were glowing in a stone fireplace.

Barth looked about at dull oak-paneled walls. He shrugged his shoulders after the servant had left.

"Moldy old place, isn't it?" questioned the commissioner. "I wonder how Warlock happened to choose this house as a residence. I should think he would prefer to live at a hotel."

A nod from Cranston; but no reply. Footsteps were already coming from the stairs. Findlay Warlock appeared. He bowed in welcome to his guests; then invited them toward the hall.

"It's more cheerful in my study," he observed. "On the second floor. Shall we go up? Good. An odd old house"—Warlock talked steadily as he led the way—"and I suppose you asked yourselves the usual question: Why I chose it. The answer is simple." Warlock chuckled. "It was thrust upon me."

He paused in the upper hallway to open the door of the study. They stepped into a well-furnished apartment that was directly above the living room. Here was contrast. Paneled walls, but lighter in color. A cheery fire in the hearth. Everything spoke of comfort.

"Better than the living room, isn't it?" questioned Warlock, with a benign smile. "This study explains why I live here. A most comfortable sort of a room. This house, I understand, had been vacant for several years. A new purchaser took it over a few months ago and had it refinished; then decided to get rid of it.

"A real estate agent offered it to me at a surprisingly low price. So low that it would have been folly not to take it. I moved in here with Cluett, the servant who admitted you. I have found the house very satisfactory. It has a third floor, also. All refinished—"

"Quite interesting, Mr. Warlock," observed Barth, finding opportunity for an interruption. "But now that you have told us about the house, let us turn to the matter of Professor Melrose Lessep. My investigation of his death has brought no tangible results. I am particularly disappointed because his files show no record whatever of his devisualization apparatus.

"I have come here in hope to learn more regarding his invention. You were financially interested in the device. Surely you must have some papers

Wainwright Barth leaped to the door of the office and wrenched it open. With the others behind him, the commissioner was confronted by an outpouring of smoke that came from the corner by the filing cabinet.

pertaining to it. I do not suppose that you would have ventured money in the enterprise without first learning something about it."

"I have some of the professor's data," replied Warlock. "But—unfortunately—I do not think that it will shed much light on the matter. The most I can show you is the prospectus which Lessep originally gave me. It is here, in the wall safe, along with the file that concerns his turbines."

WARLOCK turned and went to the wall at the rear of the room. There, he opened a small safe that was set in the paneling. He drew out a portfolio, laid it aside; then rummaged about among loose papers.

"Very convenient, this wall safe," remarked Warlock. "It was installed by the previous owner. It makes an excellent strongbox. I changed the combination to suit myself and it saved me the trouble of having one of the small safes shipped up from the office."

"Could I see the papers?" inquired Barth.

"Certainly," replied Warlock. He brought over the portfolio and opened it. "Most of these deal with the turbines. Here are a few papers, though, that relate to the devisualization apparatus."

The commissioner examined the documents. He shrugged his shoulders and passed the papers to Cranston. Barth was obviously disappointed.

"Nothing but sketchy claims," he declared. "Not even worthy to be called a prospectus. I am amazed, Warlock, that a man of your judgment should have advanced money on so doubtful a proposition."

"I had faith in Lessep," explained Warlock. "I felt that the failure of his turbines had been a misfortune. He wanted to preserve secrecy about his new invention. That was why he gave me so little information concerning it. But he came here, several times, to tell me how his devisualization experiments were progressing."

"He came here?"

"Yes. With Miles Crofton."

"Ah! This is interesting. Why did he bring Crofton?"

"Because he had the greatest confidence in his assistant."

"Tell me," urged Barth. "Just what did you learn from either Lessep or Crofton?"

"Only that the experiment was succeeding," replied Warlock. "The professor said that he had partially devisualized small objects. He said that greater success was sure. Naturally, I discounted his statements. I felt that he might be overenthusiastic, as he was with the turbines.

"But Crofton supported the professor's claims. Moreover, Crofton impressed me as a man of sound judgment. I told Lessep, of course, that I could

advance no more money. That was because of the financial difficulties that I had experienced with Centralized Power."

"What was the reaction?"

"Lessep wanted no money. He said that other investors would respond as soon as his invention demonstrated its worth. That the cash that I had advanced would be increased a hundredfold."

"And Crofton?"

"He agreed with the professor. They were both convinced of success. That was why I was not surprised when the devisualization experiment succeeded the other night."

Barth nodded thoughtfully. Then he stared, eagle-like, through his pince-nez. He spoke seriously.

"WE found no plans of Lessep's apparatus," declared the commissioner. "The photographs seem insufficient. We cannot replace that missing lever. Experts have examined Lessep's machine. They cannot fathom its working.

"That is why I want to learn more about Lessep as an individual. I want to know all I can concerning his associates. But I have failed to uncover anything of importance. The same applies to Crofton.

"He—Crofton—seems to glory in his role of unseen killer. His past shows him to be an adventurer. The only stigma of crime lies in his association with Rouser Tukin. Yet even there, Detective Cardona has learned no more than he first gained.

"Underworld talk has it that Crofton knew Rouser. The two had been seen together. We have reason to suppose that Crofton aided Rouser in crime. But that is all. Until Cardona locates the stool pigeon who gave the original tip-off, we can hope for no more definite information."

"The stool pigeon is missing?" inquired Warlock, in apparent surprise. "I thought he intended to report to Cardona again."

"He has not done so," replied the commissioner.

"Who is he?" asked Warlock.

"Cardona wanted to keep his name a secret," observed Barth. "But I see no reason why I should not mention it here. The stool pigeon is an occasional informant named Lagran. 'Crazy' Lagran, they call him. One of the sordid characters who prowls the underworld.

"Crazy Lagran works from undercover. That is why Cardona did not press him. But since his tip-off, Lagran has kept completely out of sight, not even communicating with Cardona. This, I believe, may be attributed to the fact that the newspapers have dubbed Miles Crofton the 'Unseen Killer.' Cardona thinks that Lagran is afraid of Crofton."

"A logical supposition," decided Warlock.

A momentary gleam had appeared in the eyes of Lamont Cranston. The matter of the missing stoolie had not previously been mentioned by Commissioner Barth.

There was a rap at the door. It proved to be Cluett, the servant. The flunky announced that Mr. Darring had arrived and was waiting in the living room below.

"Tell him to come up at once," ordered Warlock. Then, to Barth and Cranston, he added: "I hope that Darring is bringing good news regarding Centralized Power. A receivership seems imminent. Our one hope is to salvage what we can from the wreck.

"I wanted to proceed with further operations; but I realize now that I was wrong. We are threatened by a lawsuit. Hildon, Amboy and Norgan—leeches, the three of them—intend to sue for unpaid claims. Their lawyer made a statement to the newspapers."

"I did not see it," remarked Barth.

"Here it is." Warlock scowled as he picked up an evening newspaper. "Pushed to the second page, probably because the Lessep case took up so much front-page space. Read it, Commissioner."

As Barth took the newspaper, the door opened and Darring entered. The black-haired man was surprised to see Barth and Cranston. He shook hands; then noted the newspaper that Barth had opened.

"The newshawks made a great furor over Lessep's death," remarked Darring. "Have you given them new statements, Commissioner, regarding the Unseen Killer?"

"No," replied Barth. "I was just about to read the story that concerns Centralized Power. Mr. Warlock called my attention to it."

"You can tell us more, Darring," put in Warlock. "Have you seen the attorneys whom these three rogues have hired to sue us?"

"Yes," replied Darring. "I have come from their offices."

"Any luck?" questioned Warlock.

"On the matter of contracts, yes," returned Darring. "I convinced them that we would not have to go through with further construction work. By stopping that labor when I first took charge, I have saved Centralized Power Corporation a few hundred thousand dollars."

"Excellent!" cried Warlock. "But the options?"

"They cannot be canceled," answered Darring. "It looks as though the corporation will have to sacrifice at least a half million."

The effect of this statement was surprising. Warlock's pleasantness turned to anger. Clenching his fists, the gray-haired corporation president paced across the room. Turning, he delivered imprecations.

"They are thieves!" he cried, furiously. "The three of them! Rascals who masquerade as honest men. All of a kind; Hildon—Amboy—Norgan. I denounce them! They have bled us for millions!"

"Which they deny," reminded Darring.

"They lie!" stormed Warlock. "They are rogues without scruples—"

"Which cannot be proven."

Warlock stopped short. His fists unclenched; but his expression remained fierce. Finally, he relaxed entirely.

"You are right, Darring," he admitted. "They have us beaten. We are helpless, because we are honest. But mark my words: the fruits of evil can seldom be retained.

"They have been bold, those three. They have brazenly flaunted their crookedness into the eyes of the world. They glory in the fact that they have gained wealth which the law cannot take away. Of course they deny that they have profited; but their denial is a mere gesture.

"They mock honest men, those three. They have made their gain. But there are others in this world—others as grasping as those knaves. Others who may defy the law as well as circumvent it. Sometime, someone may step forth to deprive them of their ill-gotten wealth."

Warlock became calm. His moment of rage had ended.

Darring produced a stack of papers; documents that he had brought from the lawyers. He remarked that they would have to be examined and approved by Warlock. Commissioner Barth spoke.

"We must be leaving, Cranston," he remarked to his friend. "Good afternoon, gentlemen"—Barth had turned to Warlock and Darring. "I hope that you will find some solution to the affairs of Centralized Power Corporation."

"Suppose I go along with you," suggested Darring. "I am due at my hotel. Mr. Warlock can study the reports without my assistance."

TWENTY minutes later, Marryat Darring alighted from Lamont Cranston's limousine at the entrance of a hotel near Times Square. The car continued on to the Cobalt Club. There, Commissioner Barth stepped forth. The limousine pulled away. Lamont Cranston, presumably, was going to his New Jersey home.

An order through the speaking tube changed that plan. Stanley veered left. He traveled east; then north. He parked on a secluded street not far from the deserted home of Professor Melrose Lessep. The rear door of the car opened. A blackened shape glided into darkness.

Garbed in hat and cloak, produced from a bag in the limousine, Lamont Cranston had become The Shadow. His course was untraceable. The next manifestation of The Shadow's presence came when the rear door of Lessep's laboratory opened under the action of a probing, picklike instrument.

A tiny flashlight glimmered. The motor with the missing part was absent. Also the glass cabinet. These had been removed for tests. But the second motor—the one that had played no part in the devisualization of Miles Crofton—was still standing by the wall. The experts had left it here.

The flashlight glimmered on a cord with special, long-pronged plugs that The Shadow produced from beneath his cloak. Then the light went out. With a soft laugh, The Shadow approached the motor. The light glimmered while he made a wall connection. Then the flashlight went out to stay.

LATER, Stanley, drowsing behind the wheel of the limousine, heard the voice of Lamont Cranston through the speaking tube. His master had returned to the car. The limousine pulled out and rolled to a new destination. Again, The Shadow emerged.

Soon afterward, a light glimmered in The Shadow's sanctum. Gloved hands reached for the earphones. New orders went across the wire to Burbank. After that, blackness; then the departing laugh of The Shadow.

The quest for Miles Crofton was still on. To it The Shadow had added another task for his searching agents. There was another to be sought within the underworld. "Crazy" Lagran, the missing stool pigeon.

CHAPTER IX
DEATH DELIVERED

CULBERLY COURT was considered an exclusive residential district of Manhattan. There, a row of old-fashioned houses fronted on a quiet street. Quaint structures, like homes in a small town, they looked out of place, even in this low-built portion of the metropolis. That was why these houses commanded high prices. They were different.

At a distance, the Culberly Court houses looked alike. Close at hand, they differed. Each house had an areaway on both sides. Bay-windows, odd-shaped gables, little roofs above side porches; these were the individualities that gave distinction.

It was easy to pick out one particular house after having seen it before. Nevertheless, at night, that process required a careful inspection as one went by the row of residences. Hence people who came here by automobile often moved along very slowly, house to house.

On the night following The Shadow's secret trip to Lessep's abandoned laboratory, a car appeared at the near corner of Culberly Court and began to perform the slow-motion routine. The chauffeur was trying to pick out a certain house. He knew that he could find it, because the house just beyond it was closed and boarded up.

Furthermore, the house that the chauffeur wanted had a green-glass transom just above the doorway. If the hall light happened to be on, the driver knew that he could spot the house very easily. The house that the chauffeur wanted was the home of Nathaniel Hildon.

While the car—a limousine—moved at its snail's pace, two impatient men were talking in the back seat. The glare of a street lamp showed their faces. Neither man was more than forty years old; both were keen-faced.

One, sallow and with bristling mustache, was Peters Amboy. The other, square-jawed and with bulldog countenance, was Wallace Norgan. They were talking in low voices and their tones were troubled. They did not want the chauffeur to hear their words. The partly closed glass partition aided their purpose.

"You called Hildon at eight?" Amboy was asking. "Are you sure, Norgan, that it was not later?"

"Exactly eight o'clock," replied Norgan. "Then again at nine. There was no answer."

"Yet he said that he intended to stay at home. He said that when we lunched with him."

"Yes. That is why I decided to come in from Long Island. After I reached town, I called your apartment, Amboy. I was glad to hear your voice."

"I don't blame you, Norgan. By the way, you brought your note?"

"Yes. That's why I asked you to have yours with you. We cannot tell when the—"

The car had stopped. The chauffeur had alighted. As the man opened the door, a clock began to strike the hour of eleven. Norgan looked anxiously at Amboy. His friend whispered something. Norgan nodded.

"You had better come in with us, Jedrey," said Norgan, to the chauffeur. "I do not know how long we will be here."

"Very well, sir."

The chauffeur opened an iron gate and ascended steps to ring the bell. Light was shining through the green transom. Jedrey wondered, however, why this visit was so late. He had brought Mr. Norgan here often; but never so late as eleven o'clock.

Amboy and Norgan had joined the chauffeur and Jedrey had repeated his ring at the doorbell before there was any sign of an answer. Then locks turned; a woman's face peered past the edge of the door. Suspicious eyes recognized the visitors; the door opened to show a fat woman who looked like a servant.

Both Amboy and Norgan recognized Katy, the cook of the Hildon household. The woman was prompt with an apology for her delay in answering the door.

"SURE, it's you, Mr. Amboy," she declared. "And Mr. Norgan. I couldn't think who might be here at this late hour. With the butler away for the night, and me not thinking who might want to see Mr. Hildon."

"Mr. Hildon is at home?" quizzed Norgan, promptly.

"Indeed, yes," returned Katy. "Ever since he ate the big dinner that I cooked for him, he has been upstairs reading in his own room. It's a wonder he didn't hear the doorbell before I did, sir. The light was shining under his door."

"He is awake then?" queried Amboy.

"I'm thinking he is asleep, sir," answered Katy. "But I'll go up to rap and find if he will wake up."

The woman waddled toward the stairs. Amboy and Norgan exchanged anxious looks. They drew in closer to the stairway, where Amboy made a remark:

"The telephone is located in Hildon's room—"

"Yes"—Norgan's tone was anxious—"but even if it didn't wake him, the woman should have heard the call from the third floor."

"Maybe her door was closed—"

"Wait here, Jedrey." Norgan turned nervously toward the chauffeur. "After we see Mr. Hildon, we will tell you how soon we intend to leave."

"Yes, sir."

"Mr. Norgan!" The call came from the top of the stairs. It was Katy, the cook. "Mr. Amboy!"

"Yes?" responded Amboy.

"The light is on, sir," called Katy, "under Mr. Hildon's door. But answer he does not. I've been pounding—"

Amboy started toward the stairs. Halfway up, he looked back. Norgan followed; then motioned to Jedrey to come along. The three men reached a door at the side of the house. They could see the light beneath. Amboy pounded. There was no response.

"You're sure he is in?" questioned Norgan, of Katy.

"Sure of it, sir," blurted the woman. "It was upstairs I was, but I would have heard had he gone out."

"Did you hear the telephone bell ring?"

"No, sir. Not this evening."

"He doesn't answer," said Amboy. He tried the doorknob. "It's locked—seems to be bolted."

"We'll call the police," returned Norgan, grimly.

"The telephone is in Hildon's room," reminded Amboy.

"Who lives next door?" questioned Norgan, turning to Katy.

"Mr. Willings, sir," replied the cook. "He would let you use the telephone."

"Let us go there," decided Norgan. "Jedrey, you stay here with Mr. Amboy."

WHEN the police car reached Hildon's, it was only a few seconds ahead of another automobile that had come from headquarters. Two officers of the radio patrol had been ordered to Number 58, Culberly Court; and Joe Cardona had started at the time the order was given.

The ace detective, at present an acting inspector, joined the uniformed men on the steps. Trouble at a spot like Culberly Court was sufficient to bring Joe on the job. Cardona was the first to enter the open door.

He found Peters Amboy and Wallace Norgan awaiting him. Norgan explained about the telephone calls while they were ascending the stairs. Joe nodded. At the top, he eyed Jedrey; then learned that the man was Norgan's chauffeur. Katy was also present; the detective nodded when told that she was the Hildon cook.

Cardona eyed the door. He knocked. He tried the knob. He noted the light that shone from beneath. Then he beckoned to the two officers from the radio car. They launched themselves against the door. The barrier cracked.

Joe motioned the officers back. He rammed his shoulder against the door for the final urge. The hinges had broken; Joe entered as the door swung loose at that side. The others peered through the opening. What Cardona saw, they saw.

In the center of a large bedroom lay Nathaniel Hildon. He looked tall and frail, sprawled like a toppled scarecrow. His face showed him to be a man of less than forty—slightly younger than either Amboy or Norgan—yet less robust than either of his associates.

Hildon's gaping face was staring upward. His eyes were bulged in death. There was no question as to the manner in which he had died. Purplish marks about his throat showed that the victim had been strangled by some powerful killer.

Yanking a revolver from his pocket, Joe looked warily about the room. The patrolmen, shoulders at the door, had guns in readiness. Dropping to one knee, Cardona peered beneath the bed. The space there was vacant.

There was a closet in the corner. The door stood ajar. Cardona moved in that direction and peered in to find nothing but hanging clothes. He shook the garments. Satisfied that the closet was empty, he swung back toward the door through which he had entered.

The reason why the door had given at the hinges was because of the powerful bolt that barred it. The bolt was still shot. It proved that no one could have used the door as an exit. That meant a window. There were two of these; one at the side of the room, the other at the rear.

Cardona went to the side window. There the

detective found something that perplexed him. The window was of the type that swung open on hinges. Those hinges were on the inside. Furthermore, the fastening consisted of a heavy bar that fitted over a bolt, with a wing nut to hold it there.

The bar was in place. The bolt was topped by the nut, screwed tightly in place. A fastening at the side of the window was also firm. The windowpanes were large but unbroken. This window could not have been the exit. That left the one at the rear.

JOE could see a light from a rear alleyway, shining through the solid panes of the rear window. That was why he had picked the side window first; because he could not picture a killer foolish enough to choose the window where the light shone. But as he moved to the rear window, Joe was positive that it must have formed the avenue of escape. He stopped, more astonished than before.

The rear window was fastened like the side one. Catch at the side; bar on the sill; nut tight on bolt. As with the first window, no one could possibly have closed and fastened this one on the inside.

The cops at the door could see the blank look on Cardona's face when the sleuth turned back into the room. Rubbing his chin, Joe looked for some new hiding place. He gripped his gun more firmly. But this quest, too, was useless. There was not a single place—other than beneath the bed or in the closet— where any one could have hidden.

Then Cardona spied the telephone. He saw why calls had not been answered. Someone had wadded tissue paper about the bell, just beneath a small desk in the corner. Carefully, Cardona pulled away the wadding. He laid the paper on the desk.

Slowly, a grim look came over Cardona's features. Standing just within the door, the detective was viewed by Amboy and Norgan, who were peering past the watching cops. The dead man's friends saw Cardona pick up the telephone. Joe made a call and they listened tensely as they heard his words.

"Hello... Markham... Yes, Cardona... Up at 58, Culberly Court. Man murdered here. Nathaniel Hildon... Yes... Listen, Markham. Put in a call to the commissioner... Yes... You'll probably get him at the Cobalt Club...

"Yes... Certainly. He'll want to come down here... Tell him it's murder. And tell him it's more than that... More than murder... Another job by the guy we're after... Miles Crofton... The Unseen Killer..."

Gasps from Amboy and Morgan. The two dropped back from the door. The patrolmen tightened fists on their guns. Joe Cardona's words had produced an electrical effect.

Already, Manhattan had rung with news of the Unseen Killer. Here was murder—new crime that Joe Cardona could attribute only to the prowess of that same invisible fiend!

CHAPTER X
THE LAW AND THE SHADOW

ONE hour later. Commissioner Wainwright Barth was standing in the downstairs parlor of Nathaniel Hildon's quaint home. Present was his friend Lamont Cranston, who had come with him from the Cobalt Club. Also present were Peters Amboy and Wallace Norgan. In addition, Detective Joe Cardona.

The sleuth was glum. He had occasion to be, for Barth was reprimanding him, despite the presence of these witnesses. The commissioner had completed a survey of the dead man's bedroom. He had agreed that the Unseen Killer was again responsible for murder. That was why Barth was finding fault with Cardona.

"You should have profited by experience," chided the commissioner. "You were there, in the room. You had patrolmen at the door. Then you ordered them to conduct everyone else downstairs. You were temporarily alone; worse than that, you left the door unguarded.

"Remember, Cardona, we are dealing with a physical being. Miles Crofton may be devisualized; but he is not dematerialized. If he slew Nathaniel Hildon—as seems obvious—he must have remained within that room.

"Your one chance was to hold him. To cleverly keep the doorway bolted. Instead, you opened the path. Like you unwittingly did at Lessep's. Our quarry has eluded us. Stupidity, Cardona. Stupidity."

"I admit it," growled Joe. "When I saw the room empty, I took it for granted the guy was gone. The way he worked before—well, it was like he became air. It seemed the same here. It kind of knocked me, Commissioner, when I saw those bolted windows."

"Well, the mistake has been made," acknowledged Barth. "The evidence, every bit of it, points to the Unseen Killer. Nathaniel Hildon has lived in this house for three years. We have absolute testimony from these two gentlemen"—he indicated Amboy and Norgan—"that nothing unusual has occurred about this place. The cook says the same; also the butler, whom you called in from Brooklyn.

"Walls—floors—ceiling—those could have been the only other modes of exit. They were solid. We are back again to the doors and the windows. All bolted. Any ordinary murderer would have been forced to leave door or window open.

"You can't close a bolt through solid woodwork. You can't push an arm through a windowpane without breaking it. My verdict is the Unseen Killer. But this time he sent no warning."

The commissioner paused. He stared through his

spectacles, looking first at Cardona, who nodded; then at Cranston, whose expression remained unchanged. During the momentary lull, Amboy whispered to Norgan, who nodded nervously.

Commissioner Barth had caught the whisper. He stared inquiringly. Norgan coughed and mopped his forehead. Then, in a rather strained tone, he spoke.

"NATHANIEL HILDON did receive a warning," he declared. "We intended to speak of it, Mr. Amboy and I, but we thought it best to wait until you had completed your inspection. You see, we—"

"A warning?" snapped Barth, querulously. "A warning—to Hildon? What kind of a warning?"

"A typewritten message—"

"From whom?"

"The Unseen Killer."

Barth stood dumbfounded. Then his eyes sparkled. Triumphantly, the commissioner looked toward Lamont Cranston. Then he asked, sharply:

"What became of that message?"

"I didn't see anything of it," put in Cardona. "I searched the room. If Hildon had it, the murderer could have lifted it."

"That is what he must have done," declared Norgan.

"How do you know?" demanded Barth. "Did you see the message, Norgan?"

"Yes," nodded the square-jawed man. "I saw it at noon today, when we had lunch with Hildon. So did Amboy."

A nod from Amboy corroborated this statement.

"Explain in full," ordered Barth.

"To begin with," stated Norgan, still a bit nervous, "I must mention that Hildon was—to an extent—associated with Amboy and myself in certain business enterprises. The three of us are erroneously reported to have made a fortune at the expense of the Centralized Power Corporation."

"I have heard of that report," returned Barth. "You do not need to go into details regarding your enterprise. Proceed with the matter of the note."

"Today," resumed Norgan, "each of us received a threatening message. All the notes were exactly alike. We met at luncheon and discussed them."

"You have such a message?"

"Yes. From the Unseen Killer."

"Where is it?"

"Here." Norgan produced a folded sheet of paper. Amboy did likewise. They passed the missives to Barth. The commissioner handed one to Cardona; then opened his and read aloud, while Cardona, nodding, acknowledged the identical wording.

Each message read as follows:

A WARNING:

You possess certain funds which represent ill-gotten gains. You are not alone. Two others share your spoils. They, too, are receiving warnings.

All this wealth—not one cent excepted—must be delivered into my hands, intact. To pass me your hidden funds, you must first communicate with me.

Issue a statement to the evening newspapers announcing that you have received a threat from me. Unless some such account appears by the final editions, one of you will be dead by tomorrow morning.

THE UNSEEN KILLER

"Well?" questioned Barth, sharply. "Why did you not inform the police of these threats? You have witnessed the result. Hildon is dead—"

"We thought the notes a trick," put in Amboy. "Some game, worked by enemies who have been trying to force us into admission of profits that we have not made."

"Or a blackmailer's scheme," added Norgan. "Possibly the work of a crank—anyone who might have read the newspaper accounts of the unseen murderer who slew Professor Lessep."

"So you decided to do nothing about it?" quizzed the commissioner.

"Exactly," admitted Norgan. "The three of us met, compared the messages that we had received and agreed to make this crank show his hand. We wanted no notoriety. We felt that we were safe.

"I went to my home on Long Island; Amboy to his apartment. Hildon came here. Then, about eight o'clock in the evening, I began to worry. About Hildon. I felt that his position would be the least secure. This district is secluded."

"That is why you telephoned him?"

"Yes. At eight o'clock. No answer. I telephoned again. Still no response. I decided that servants must certainly be here, even if Hildon had gone out. So I drove in town and picked up Amboy. You know the rest, Commissioner."

BARTH paced for a few moments. Then he paused to eye the two threatened men. Amboy and Norgan looked solemn. Barth adjusted his pince-nez.

"I predict," he said, wisely, "that you will receive new messages tomorrow morning. This Unseen Killer—Miles Crofton—possesses powers that are almost unlimited. We must draw him out.

"Notify me if you receive new threats. Then we will give him the statement that he wants. In the meantime, I shall place officers on guard at your respective homes.

"It seems obvious, after reading those threats, that the Unseen Killer did not want you to learn of Hildon's death until the morning. That is why he muffled the telephone bell. His entire purpose is now explained.

"Despite the fact that you gentlemen have sought to shun publicity"—Barth paused dryly—"your names have appeared in print. Only yesterday, the newspapers carried an account of your proposed lawsuit against the Centralized Power Corporation.

"It is generally acknowledged that you gained profits through your transactions, even though the amounts may be exaggerated. By merely reading the newspapers, the Unseen Killer could have picked upon you two—with Hildon—as a trio of wealthy men."

Amboy and Norgan stood silent. Having summed the case as he saw it, Wainwright Barth made prompt arrangements. He detailed officers to accompany both men to their homes. He saw Amboy and Norgan leave. Then, accompanied by Lamont Cranston, Barth went upstairs for a final examination of the room wherein Nathaniel Hildon had died. After that, Barth departed with Cranston.

A CLOCK chimed four. It was the same clock that Norgan and Amboy had heard, hours before. Solemn strokes above the gloom that pervaded that isolated thoroughfare called Culberly Court.

Patrolmen heard it as they paced in front of the silent, almost ghostly houses that stood as relics of the past. The sound drifted to the alleyway at the rear of the old-fashioned homes. There, another patrolling officer caught the notes.

Blackness persisted from the shrouding trees of a parklike square across the way. Then came motion; inkiness detached itself from the gloom. A blot moved along the sidewalk, just within the area of a street lamp's light.

A hazy form glided across the thoroughfare. It moved past the house where the green glass glowed above the front door. The strange shape entered the obscurity of the side areaway between Hildon's home and the empty house that adjoined it.

Projecting ornamental bricks offered a hold for hands and feet. Eerily, a phantom figure scaled the wall close by a little alcove. Then the moving shape stilled. Batlike, it clung to the vertical surface.

A policeman was coming through the areaway. His flashlight flickered. Its beam reached the wall; but not quite high enough to reveal that form. The light went on. The Shadow, motionless as night itself, remained undiscovered.

The weird form resumed its brief ascent. The Shadow edged sidewise past the corner of the alcove. He gained the roof above a small inset porch at the side of the house. Prone upon the slanting surface, he reached the window.

The Shadow was looking into Hildon's second-floor room. A hall light's rays filtered past the broken door. The dull illumination showed the death chamber. Furnishings were hazily outlined before The Shadow's gaze.

The Shadow, guised as Lamont Cranston, had viewed that room before. He had walked about within its walls with Police Commissioner Wainwright Barth. Together, they had gone over the ground covered by Detective Joe Cardona.

But now The Shadow was viewing the room from a new angle. He was outside, looking in, perched comfortably in a perfect hiding place beneath. The extended house wall hid him from the street in front. The porch roof kept him concealed from eyes below.

Darkness prevented a prying view from the alleyway at the back of the house. The next building—its windows boarded—could not have been an observation post. This little roof was the strategic spot from which to enter or to look into Nathaniel Hildon's bedroom. Any prowler could have chosen it as a vantage point.

Yet what had it to do with the murder of Nathaniel Hildon? Nothing, so far as Cardona and Barth had seen. A window, panes unbroken, fastenings intact within, could not have aided a visible killer to make his escape. As for the Unseen Killer—to him the window was unnecessary.

A square window, measuring four feet in either direction. A stout vertical post from bottom to top. Gloved hands issued from the darkness; one pressed against each pane, while The Shadow's head, tilting a trifle to the right, took a position from which keen eyes could study all that lay within the room.

Hands dropped from the solid set panes. Edging backward, The Shadow produced his tiny flashlight. Blinking guardedly, the beam ran up around the window, down the center division, then to the porch itself. There, The Shadow's left hand moved idly. Fingers traced streaks in the grime of the roof. They crumpled a bit of dried, claylike substance. The light went out.

A patrolman passed by the side of the house. His footfalls clicked through the alleyway.

The Shadow's light blinked intermittently, close to the roof. Then it went out finally. The black-cloaked form edged from the roof and descended easily by the ladderlike bricks that lined the wall.

An officer on the front street failed to see the gliding form that issued from the alleyway. The Shadow crossed to the square. He merged with the blackness of the trees. His course was untraceable as he moved away from Culberly Court. It was not until he had gained a spot two blocks away that he gave another manifestation of his presence.

Then, gliding silently past the front of unpretentious houses, The Shadow laughed. A ghostly chuckle in the darkness; a touch of suppressed mirth that was grim. Turning to a sinister whisper, the laugh throbbed and faded.

Though his agents in the underworld still pursued a hopeless quest for missing men, The Shadow, himself, was making progress. He had learned facts about the Unseen Killer. He could wait until the morrow.

For Commissioner Barth was determined to bait the Unseen Killer. That course was to The Shadow's liking. Wealth was the criminal's aim. To obtain it, he would have to act.

Action by the Unseen Killer would bring him within The Shadow's range.

CHAPTER XI
THE BLACK BOX

THE next morning, both Peters Amboy and Wallace Norgan received new threats from the Unseen Killer. The letters came in the first mail. They were typewritten as before. They delivered the same ultimatum. A statement to the afternoon newspapers of death to one of the pair within twenty-four hours.

They communicated at once with Commissioner Barth. He ordered the statements to the newspapers. Already, headlines were telling of Nathaniel Hildon's death. The statements from Amboy and Norgan were boxed on front pages. They brought quick results.

At five o'clock that afternoon, Findlay Warlock, president of the fading Centralized Power Corporation, was surprised when he opened a letter that came in the late mail. It had been posted only a few hours previously shortly after the newspapers had carried their flash regarding the new threats received by Amboy and Norgan.

The note to Warlock was typewritten. It read as follows:

A REQUEST:
Two men, Peters Amboy and Wallace Norgan, are anxious to deliver funds into my possession. This can be facilitated if they put the moneys in a place of easy access.

There is a wall safe in your study. Would you cooperate by letting them put their funds in that strongbox? Before 8:30 tonight. Lock the safe, but put the combination in an envelope and seal the flap of the envelope to the front of the safe. Let the envelope remain open.

At 8:30, open the doors to your study. All must leave the room, either going downstairs or remaining in the hallways. At 9:00 close the doors of the study. Reopen them at 9:15. Do not reenter the room until 9:30. At all times, the doorways must be unblocked. Also doors to the house and ground floor windows must be left open.

Witnesses, police, interested parties all are welcome, provided only that the conditions are exactly fulfilled. I promise immunity to all who play fair. Treachery will mean DEATH.

THE UNSEEN KILLER

Cluett was present when Findlay Warlock received this note. Warlock had just come in from the office; Cluett was startled by the trembling that came over his master. He thought that Warlock had experienced a stroke.

Then Warlock recovered. He made a telephone call to the Melkin Hotel, was connected with Marryat Darring, to whom he blurted out the news. At Darring's advice, he then made a call to the police commissioner.

Barth communicated with Peters Amboy and Wallace Norgan. Prompt arrangements were made. More wires buzzed. At eight o'clock all was completed. A group of men were assembled in Findlay Warlock's study.

POLICE COMMISSIONER BARTH had summoned Peters Amboy and Wallace Norgan. The two had arrived after a visit to an uptown bank, where they had gone to the safe deposit vaults. They had been accompanied by half a dozen detectives.

Marryat Darring was present, because of Warlock's call. Lamont Cranston was also there, thanks to the police commissioner. Barth wanted reliable witnesses who had seen the actions of the Unseen Killer on that night at Lessep's.

Joe Cardona and three detectives were in the study; besides these men, there were a dozen other dicks downstairs, including the six who had acted as guards for Amboy and Norgan.

"Tonight," declared the commissioner, "we intend to deal with Miles Crofton, alias the Unseen Killer. He has imposed certain conditions that give us definite indications. They prove that our analysis of his power is correct. The man is devisualized. He cannot be seen.

"I consider it good policy to meet his conditions. Otherwise, he may resort to new murder. At the same time, I am following this course purely as matter of investigation. I have not requested Amboy and Norgan to deliver up their funds.

"That is a matter that concerns themselves. I merely asked them if they were willing to cooperate; if they were desirous of turning over wealth to the Unseen Killer because of his threat. They answered that they were."

Barth turned inquiringly as he paused. He wanted corroboration from the men themselves. Amboy and Norgan were seated by a table upon which lay a large, black metal box.

"The funds are in this box," declared Amboy, solemnly, pointing to the container. "All the funds that the Unseen Killer wants."

"Every penny," added Norgan. "We are taking this measure to rid ourselves of the menace."

"Do you wish to state the amount in the box?" inquired Barth.

Amboy looked at Norgan, who shook his head. Norgan had been staring straight at Findlay Warlock.

"We have been accused of unfair profit," asserted Norgan. "Amboy and I discussed that matter this afternoon. Let the Unseen Killer gain what he demands. But we do not care to satisfy the curiosity of others."

"Very well," agreed Barth. "Do you wish to remain here or do you want to return to your homes, under guard?"

"We will stay," responded Norgan, "but we would appreciate the guards afterward. For tonight, at least."

"We can't forget Hildon's death," put in Amboy. "We won't feel safe until the twenty-four hours are up."

"That is settled," assured Barth. "I shall provide adequate protection for both of you."

THE commissioner arose and walked toward the rear wall, where the safe stood open. The others followed him. They formed a keenly interested group. Norgan placed the black box in Barth's hands. The commissioner inserted it in the wall safe.

The strong box was a fair-sized one, with a metal-lined interior that was recessed slightly at the sides, top and bottom. The box, however, was plainly in view, even though its bottom was slightly below the level of the door.

Barth swung shut the metal front. He closed the door and turned the knob. The safe was locked. Warlock approached with an envelope. He bent back the flap and sealed it to the front of the safe. Then he produced a folded paper from his desk.

"The combination," he explained. "I typed it on this paper."

He inserted the folded sheet in the envelope. Only a corner of the paper protruded. As Warlock stepped away, Norgan moved up and started to take out the paper. Warlock shot out a hand; Norgan dropped the paper and it fluttered to the floor. Lamont Cranston picked it up and held it.

"Let me see that combination!" challenged Norgan. "That should be my privilege."

"Perhaps," retorted Warlock, "I have a right to see the contents of your black box."

"Not at all!" snarled Norgan, thrusting out his square chin. "That box is property that belongs to myself and Amboy."

"And the combination of this safe is mine," retaliated Warlock.

"Why quibble?" demanded Barth. "Let me decide this matter. Do you mind, Warlock, if Cranston or I see the combination?"

"No," returned Warlock. "But Norgan—"

"Open the paper, Cranston," interjected Barth. "We can assure Norgan that all is in order."

Cranston complied. Barth nodded when he saw the opened paper. Cranston folded it carefully and tucked it in the envelope. His long fingers pressed the envelope flat. His thumb finished the task by poking the paper out of sight.

It was nearing half past eight. Barth ordered the doors open. All left the room. While the others waited, Barth and Cardona conducted a brief tour of inspection. Warlock's study had three doors; one to a bedroom at the front, a second to a small hall at the rear. The third was the door to the main upstairs hall.

The commissioner stationed detectives—one in the bedroom, one in the side hall; a third at the rear. He then dispatched a pair of dicks to the third floor. Speaking to the men about Warlock's study, he warned them not to block the doorways.

Leaving Cardona in charge, Barth ushered the other persons to the ground floor. They assembled in Warlock's gloomy living room. Barth stationed detectives at the door. Then he delivered an order.

"I shall go up and down at times," said the commissioner. "The rest of you must remain here—with the exception of Cranston. I want him to do as he pleases. Perhaps he may be here when I am upstairs and vice versa. He and I can maintain contact with those above."

So saying, the commissioner departed.

A CLOCK on the mantel struck the half hour. From then on, minutes were monotonously slow. Findlay Warlock paced about in front of the fireplace, pausing at times to glance suspiciously at Norgan and Amboy.

Those two were seated in large chairs, saying very little. At times, they resorted to whispered conversation. That was their only form of conversation.

Marryat Darring was less serious than the others. The black-haired man was smoking a panetela. At times, he strolled about, examining pictures on the wall. At other intervals, he rested his tall frame against the wall and blew huge rings from his cigar smoke.

Barth came downstairs at quarter of nine. He found Cranston seated quietly in the corner. He suggested that his friend go up and look about. Cranston complied. The dicks were on duty just as Barth had posted them. Cranston returned shortly afterward. Barth went upstairs again.

Nine o'clock. Lamont Cranston was standing in the doorway of the living room, between the hanging curtains of the broad portal. The clock was chiming the hour. From upstairs came the sound of closing doors. Then Barth arrived to announce that the study had been closed.

Nine fifteen. Barth had gone back. He came down to say that the doors were opened. Detectives on guard. No one had been seen; nor had any unusual sound been heard. Cranston went up; then came down. Barth ascended the stairs.

Nine thirty. A call from the commissioner. Detectives stepped aside. Following Lamont Cranston, the other four ascended. Joe Cardona motioned them into the study; then followed. The group clustered about the commissioner. But as Barth advanced toward the wall safe, he paused to motion the others back.

"I remember the combination," he said. "I shall open the safe; the rest of you can watch. I think that we shall find everything intact. This begins to appear as a hoax."

"One moment, Commissioner"—the quiet words came from the steady lips of Lamont Cranston. "It might be best to remove the envelope before you open the safe. Suppose I do that."

"Very well," decided Barth. "Take a look at the paper, just to make sure that it is the same as before."

As soon as Lamont Cranston's deft fingers had removed the envelope, Barth began to work on the combination. Cranston had opened the paper; his keen eyes had studied it before the commissioner had completed the turnings of the dial.

Then that same steady gaze was fastened on the front of the safe. The combination had given its final click. Very dramatically, Wainwright Barth stepped aside and pulled back the door. There was a smile on the commissioner's face. It vanished as his eyes stared blinking through the spectacles that fronted them.

Exclamations from others. A growl from Joe Cardona. Only Lamont Cranston remained silent as he, like the others, viewed the interior of the wall safe.

The black box was gone!

The Unseen Killer had made good his boast. His claim to complete invisibility stood substantiated. The wealth delivered by Peters Amboy and Wallace Norgan had vanished as completely as the devisualized human form of Miles Crofton.

CHAPTER XII
DEATH FOLLOWS

ONE hour later. Findlay Warlock's home was deserted, save for the presence of the owner and his servant, Cluett. Flabbergasted, Commissioner Wainwright Barth had drawn off the bloodhounds of the law. He had departed, sulking because of the Unseen Killer's triumph.

Peters Amboy and Wallace Norgan had bewailed their loss. They had cried for further protection. Barth had granted it. Not only had he sent three detectives to guard each man, but he had put Joe Cardona in charge of Norgan's guards and Detective Sergeant Markham at the head of Amboy's.

Thus had Findlay Warlock's old-fashioned residence returned to its obscurity. It was no more than any other brownstone house. For Commissioner Barth was trailing the Unseen Killer; he could see no merit in keeping watch on places where the untraceable crook had been and gone.

Yet there was one who still found interest in Warlock's house. That one was The Shadow. As Lamont Cranston, he had spent very little time in taking leave of Commissioner Barth. After that, he had assumed his garb of black. Now he was returning to the scene of the Unseen Killer's triumph.

Warlock's house had high steps that showed a slight glisten in a street lamp's glare. The Shadow had avoided that betraying means of entrance. All Warlock's doors were fitted with old-fashioned locks. Anyone would do. So The Shadow chose an entrance to the basement, under the shelter of the steps themselves.

A black blob against the dull color of the door, The Shadow worked briefly with a special key. The door yielded. He entered and closed the door behind him. He found a flight of stairs that led up to the first floor.

At the top, The Shadow used his glimmering flashlight. He saw a flight of back stairs that went to the second floor. They terminated, The Shadow knew, in the little hall just behind Warlock's study.

The Shadow entered a room that led through to the living room. His light went out. Silently, through darkness, The Shadow neared the rear door of the living room. He paused. Slight sounds reached his ears.

Someone was in the darkened living room. Someone, prowling there. The intruder was trying to remain unheard. Only the keen ears of The Shadow could have detected the man's presence— until an accident occurred.

A chair scraped and slid against the wall as the man in the living room made a blunder. There was momentary silence; then some cautious footsteps moving into the hall. The Shadow moved into the living room. He could hear the steps creaking toward the back of the hall.

Here was easy prey for The Shadow. In his silent fashion he could track the man who was lost in the darkness. He did not need to see a living form. Sound—motion—those were sufficient. But as The Shadow reached the door of the living room, he was forced to stop.

Someone was coming down the front stairway. To follow the man who had moved to the back of the house, The Shadow would have to step squarely into this arrival's path. The Shadow waited. The man from upstairs arrived, fumbled for a light switch and pressed it.

Peering from behind a curtain at the living room

door, The Shadow saw Cluett. The servant's face looked anxious. Cluett must have heard the blundering sound in the living room. The Shadow saw him look along the hall. Cluett was too late. The first man had moved away.

Cluett stepped toward the living room. The Shadow faded swiftly. He whirled back into the rear room; then cut through to the back stairway to the second floor, just as Cluett turned on the living room lights.

The Shadow, however, had lost his opportunity to trail the real intruder. The man had gained a lucky break through Cluett's chance arrival. The Shadow decided to ascend the back stairs. He reached the little hall at the top. Listening at the rear door of the study, he could hear someone moving about within.

Cluett's footsteps came from the front stairs. The Shadow heard the man in the study pace across toward the side door. The Shadow moved to the turn in the hall. He saw Cluett arrive in the dim light of the second-floor hall. Then the side door of the study opened. Findlay Warlock appeared, attired in dressing gown.

"What are you doing, Cluett?" quizzed Warlock. "Were you downstairs?"

"Yes, sir."

"Why?"

"I thought I heard someone in the living room. While I was going into my own room, sir."

"Why didn't you call me?"

"I tapped at the door of the study, sir. But you did not respond."

"Humph. That must have been while I was in the front bedroom."

"I suppose so, sir. I didn't rap too hard; I feared that the sound might carry downstairs."

"You did not knock loudly enough to attract my attention, that is certain. What did you find in the living room?"

"Nothing, sir."

"I supposed that. Well, Cluett, curb your imagination after this."

WARLOCK went back into the study; Cluett to his own room.

The Shadow listened a few minutes; then moved to the rear door of the study, opened it and entered. The room was dark. Warlock had retired to the front bedroom. He had closed the door behind him.

The little flashlight blinked. Its tiny ray cleaved the darkness and settled on Warlock's wall safe. The Shadow approached. His gloved hand worked the combination. The front of the safe opened. The Shadow inspected the interior. The safe contained a few odd papers that Warlock had evidently replaced.

The light went out. The Shadow left the study and glided down the front stairs. He reached the living room. There, his light blinked intermittently as The Shadow moved along the wall. The light went out; The Shadow remained a full two minutes in the darkness. Then he moved away.

For his exit, The Shadow chose the rear door of the first floor. It opened from a kitchen. The door was locked; the key was hanging beside it. The Shadow used a skeleton key of his own. He unlocked the door, went through and locked the barrier behind him.

It was with apparent purpose that The Shadow kept to the darkness as he traveled away from Findlay Warlock's. Had he found some trail left by an outer visitor who had come to the old house? Or had some lurker waited there, to leave later by the rear door that The Shadow had taken?

Or had Findlay Warlock been the man in the living room? He could easily have reached the upstairs study before the arrival of either Cluett or The Shadow. This aftermath was odd, coming only an hour following the strange disappearance of the black box that had been placed in the upstairs safe.

A soft laugh in the darkness. It indicated that The Shadow, moving stealthily in his passage from Warlock's, had some destination known to himself alone. His course led southward after he was clear from the vicinity of the brownstone house. The Shadow was traveling in the direction of Times Square.

Mystery had fallen tonight—mystery to others, not to The Shadow. He had seen an aftermath to the delivery of the wealth in the black box. He had traced some crosscurrent in the scheming of the Unseen Killer.

EVIDENTLY, The Shadow had decided that the invisible crook's work had been performed. The acquisition of certain funds was unquestionably the Unseen Killer's aim. He had gained what he wanted. Death no longer remained as a present motive.

But there was one man in Manhattan who did not share The Shadow's opinion. Up in his apartment, Peters Amboy was talking to Detective Sergeant Markham. In his discourse, Amboy babbled his fear of death.

Amboy lived in a high-class apartment known as Surinam Hall; and Markham had felt secure as soon as they had reached the place. Amboy's apartment was on the fourteenth floor. Stepping from the elevators, they had turned left; then right; and followed clear to the end of the corridor. There they had entered the last apartment on the right.

Markham had posted two detectives in the corridor. He and Amboy were seated in the living room, the third dick with them.

"He said he was going to kill one of us," Amboy was telling the detective sergeant. "One of us to die—like Hildon died—before morning. It worries me."

"You delivered your cash," reminded Markham. "That's what this Unseen Killer wanted, wasn't it?"

"Yes. But he may still be vicious. He can go anywhere he wishes. Invisibly. Perhaps—"

"He won't come here. Just the same, I'll take a look at the place. Then you can turn in and get some sleep. That's what you need, Mr. Amboy."

Markham made an inspection. The apartment was situated at the rear of the building. All the rooms had windows in the rear wall. First was the living room. From it extended a windowless hall.

Off the hall Markham saw a bedroom. Then a bath; finally, at the very end of the hall, a door to the left. Markham stepped in there and pressed a light switch set in the far wall. The room was half study, half bedroom.

"My own quarters," explained Amboy. "This is where I intend to sleep."

"Only the one door," observed Markham.

"Yes," replied Amboy. "This is the end of the apartment."

"Why don't they have a window in this end wall then?"

"Because this is only one half of the building. There's another apartment beyond. Similar to this one."

"I see. Reached from the other side of the house, eh?"

"Yes."

Markham looked about. He asked Amboy to make sure that nothing in the room was disturbed. That established, both men left, Markham turning out the light. They went into the living room. There they sat and chatted.

Peters Amboy became less nervous during the progress of a half hour. Finally he decided to turn in.

Markham agreed to sleep in the empty bedroom, leaving the dicks in the living room. He walked along the hall with Amboy. He stopped, turned on the bedroom light and looked around.

Amboy kept on. When Markham reached the hall, the man was just stepping into the study at the end of the hall. Markham saw the door swing shut; it did not quite close. Hence the detective saw the light from the room when Amboy turned on the switch.

The detective sergeant turned to go back to the living room. Then he came to a startled stop. From beyond that partly closed door of the study came the boom of a gunshot. As Markham stood rooted, he heard a gasping choke; then the thump of a falling body.

MARKHAM sprang along the lighted hall. The dick from the living room came dashing up to join him. Together, they reached the study. Markham pushed the door open. He stared at the floor. There,

five feet away, lay the sprawled form of Peters Amboy.

Markham advanced and stopped above the body. Amboy was dead. Looking about, Markham could see no one. The detective sergeant had drawn a gun. He spoke to the dick beside him, ordering the fellow to bring in the other detectives from the hall.

The dick hurried away. Rising, Markham moved slowly toward the door; then stood with revolver in hand. Two minutes later, the three-man squad joined him. Posting his aides, Markham stalked across the room and yanked open a closet door. The closet was empty.

Space showed beneath the couchlike single bed. No spot where a man could be concealed. Markham stepped over to Amboy's body. He thought he had the solution. Suicide. Amboy had been nervous. He looked for a gun, beside or beneath the body. He found none.

Blinking, Detective Sergeant Markham arose and stared at the dumbfounded dicks. Like Markham, the members of the squad were wearing whitened faces. They formed a group that could swear to astounding murder.

Every man—even the pair in the hall—had heard the fatal shot. All had arrived through the only door whereby an exit could have been gained. Yet they had found no trace of the murderer nor any sign of the weapon he had used.

Again, the Unseen Killer had delivered amazing death!

CHAPTER XIII
NORGAN SPEAKS

MIDNIGHT. Commissioner Wainwright Barth was standing in Amboy's living room. He was surveying a group of men who had come here at his call. Findlay Warlock, Marryat Darring, Wallace Norgan; last of all, Lamont Cranston.

"I'm glad you happened to call the club, Cranston," Barth was saying. "I reached Warlock at his home; Darring in the grille room of his hotel. Norgan, of course, was at his home, with Cardona guarding him.

"But I didn't know where to reach you. That is why I left the message at the Cobalt Club. Because I wanted you to be here also. Everyone who was present at Warlock's should be here to learn the details of this new outrage by the Unseen Killer."

Barth paused as Joe Cardona entered. The detective had come from the death room at the end of the hall. Joe nodded to indicate that everything was ready. They formed a procession down to Amboy's study. They passed detectives in the narrow hall.

When they reached the death room, they saw Amboy's body lying on the floor. Markham and a police surgeon were on duty.

From beyond the partly closed door of the study came the boom of a gun-shot.... Markham pushed the door open. He stared at the floor. There … lay the sprawled form of Peters Amboy.

"I want you all to hear the reports," declared Barth. "Tell us exactly what happened, Markham."

The detective sergeant gave the details as he knew them. When he had finished, Barth mentioned another matter—the fact that Markham had failed to cover the door after Amboy's death.

"I muffed it, commissioner," admitted the detective sergeant. "I remembered what you'd told me. We've got to figure that this Unseen Killer is around even when we can't see him. I figured wrong. That's all.

"Amboy had been jittery. Hadn't been out of my sight all evening. Perked up some, just before he came in here. Then *boom!*—the shot comes all of a sudden. When I saw nobody in here, I thought that maybe it was suicide.

"It wasn't till after I looked for a gun that I knew I was wrong. By that time, the squad had come in; I'd been away from the door. The Unseen Killer could easy have made his getaway."

"Your frankness is commendable, Markham," declared Barth. "Well, gentlemen, you see before you the evidence of a crime more startling than the murder of Nathaniel Hildon. Here, the Unseen Killer committed crime almost under the eyes of watching detectives.

"Look about. I want you to fully realize the difficulty that he must have encountered. Here is this room, just as it was when Peters Amboy was slain. There is the body. Let us hear the surgeon's statement."

"Would it be all right, Commissioner, if I moved one of these floor lamps?" The question came from the police surgeon. "If I can get it closer to the body, I can show the wound more effectively."

"Move one of the lamps if you choose."

THE physician detached the cord of a lamp, pulling it from the floor plug. He carried the lamp to a spot only a few feet from the sprawled form of Peters Amboy. He carried the end of the cord to the wall switch.

There was a plug in the brass plate just beneath the switch. This plug was covered by a hinged brass disk, which the surgeon raised. He inserted the end of the lamp cord into the plug beneath. He turned on the lamp. A glow spread above Amboy's body.

"The wound was just above the heart," explained the doctor, in a methodical tone, stooping to indicate the body. "The range must have been about three feet. The man evidently staggered before he fell. It was impossible to tell exactly where he was standing when the killer fired."

"I might indicate that, Commissioner," declared Markham. "But as the doctor says, it can't be exact."

"Show us," suggested Barth.

"Well, he'd just turned on the light," said Markham. "I don't think the killer would have been mug enough to press the switch himself. So that puts Amboy here, to begin with."

Markham went over and placed his right hand against the wall switch. He did not click it; instead, he stood there, facing the wall. He held up his left hand.

"I'll give you the interval," he said. "As near as I can remember it."

He retained his position for a few moments; then lowered his left hand. Without turning, he spoke again.

"You see," he said, "I turned on this light about a half hour before Amboy did. That was shortly after he and I got into the apartment. I was looking around the place. So I can figure sort of what a man might do after turning on the light.

"He'd either look around"—Markham turned his head to the left—"or he'd turn around." He swung his body to the left. "This direction. Because he'd be coming into the room and the room is to the left.

"Now, if he'd looked around, he couldn't have got plugged while he was standing here, because the bullet's in the front of him and he was facing the wall. Something would have had to make him swing. All right. Suppose we try it. I'll look around."

Markham stood in front of the switch. He swung his head to the left and began to blink his eyes.

"Suppose I'm Amboy," he said. "I can't see anything, because I can't see the Unseen Killer. But maybe I hear something. That's why I'm staring. I shy away"—Markham swung to the left and began to withdraw, toward the right—"and that lets him bump me through the heart.

"What happens then? Well, I stagger, but I've already got a start and like as not I'll keep going back. Up against the door. But Amboy didn't wind up against the door. So he didn't turn his head, to begin with. He turned his body."

"Logical," asserted Barth. "But if he—"

"I know what you're going to say, Commissioner: If he turned his body, he'd have staggered back just the same. Well—he must have done more than turn his body. He must have turned and started away." Markham paused again. He turned and started to walk. "Like this, out here, and the shot. That finished him."

Barth nodded and looked at Cardona. Joe gave his approval of Markham's theory. It came rather unexpectedly, for Markham was not classed as an artist in deductive reasoning. Barth, however, could find no flaw.

"This comes within the time limit?" he questioned. "That is important, Markham."

"It just gets inside it," said the detective sergeant, "figuring that Amboy moved rather fast. He could have, because he was nervous. I think that clinches it, Commissioner. I'll tell you why.

"Because the only other way Amboy could have landed where he did was if he'd stayed facing the wall and gone back like this." Markham went to the switch, stood there, then staggered back, stopping just before he reached the body. "But how could he have done that? The killer couldn't have been between him and the wall."

"How promptly did you arrive here?"

"As quick as I could make it. But I'm telling you something else, Commissioner. I heard the shot. Then kind of a choke. After that, *plop!* So I know Amboy didn't do a lot of staggering. He got places quick and by the shortest route."

BARTH nodded approvingly. He motioned to the police surgeon, to indicate that the light was no longer needed.

The doctor turned off the lamp. Silent men watched him pull the cord from the wall. The little brass disk dropped shut with a click as it covered the plug in the wall plate. So hushed was the throng that the sound seemed loud.

Mechanically, eyes turned toward the body of Peters Amboy, that silent testimony to the power of the Unseen Killer. Only Lamont Cranston looked elsewhere. His gaze was toward the wall. His eyes, keen and burning, were the eyes of The Shadow.

Cardona and Markham questioned Barth; the commissioner gave them a nod. The body was to go to the morgue. That settled, Barth requested the other men to follow him. They went back to the living room.

"Peters Amboy is dead," declared the commissioner. "His murder has given us another insight into the ways of the Unseen Killer. Until now, that fiend has apparently governed himself by a code of his own.

"Tonight, however, his demand was met. He sought wealth; he received it. Yet he slew as he did before. There seems to be no explanation for his crime. Why—after that box was delivered—should he have sought the death of either Peters Amboy or Wallace Norgan?"

As he asked the question, Barth turned toward Norgan himself. Norgan's face was pallid. It showed more than fear. It registered understanding. Norgan's lips began to quiver.

A strange smile showed thinly on the features of Lamont Cranston. The eyes of The Shadow saw the answer.

Marryat Darring, too, was looking toward Wallace Norgan. Then Findlay Warlock stared at the last of the three men whom the Unseen Killer had threatened. Despite the fact that Hildon and Amboy were dead, Warlock could not forget the antagonism that he had held toward them.

In Norgan, Warlock saw the last of a trio whom he had defined as thieves. Perhaps that was why he—Warlock—was the first person to blurt out the question that his companions would soon have asked.

"Maybe you can tell us something, Norgan," exclaimed Warlock. "Something that you failed to tell before. What was in that box that you left for the Unseen Killer?"

"I—I talked with Amboy"—Norgan's sudden stammer broke—"and it was—well, both of us who decided—"

"Decided what?" quizzed Barth, suddenly.

"About the box," gasped Norgan. "What we should put in it—before we took it to Warlock's."

"You mean the box contained no funds?"

Norgan nodded weakly.

"What was in it?" demanded Barth.

"Blank papers," confessed Norgan. "The contents were worthless. We—we expected a trick—"

"So you worked one of your own—without informing me."

"I know, Commissioner. But—but we feared the Unseen Killer. He might have been listening when we talked to you—"

"Amboy is dead," interposed Barth, solemnly. "We know now why he died. That, at least, brings us back to where we were."

"My life is still in danger," choked Norgan. "Hildon is gone. So is Amboy. If I—"

"We shall protect you—to the utmost. You will be guarded at your home. Do not worry, Norgan, at least not for the present. Your two associates have died. But now that you have given us the truth, I feel confident that you will be safe until a new threat arrives. After that—"

Barth paused speculatively. Then he called Cardona. He told the detective what had happened. He placed Norgan under Joe's protection. Cardona called his squad together. Surrounding Norgan, they departed, taking Norgan to Long Island.

DETECTIVES remained in the apartment of Peters Amboy. Others were on duty in the corridor outside. They kept up a patrol between there and the center hall where the elevators stopped. Hours passed while these men of the law maintained their vigil about the place where death had struck.

They were on duty should the Unseen Killer return. They were to report any unusual event that might occur upon this floor. Hours passed; but nothing disturbed the monotony of the watch. That, however, was because one sleuth failed in his duty.

Not long after Barth and the others had gone, a figure appeared mysteriously from a stairway on the fourteenth floor of the apartment building. A detective had just paced to the elevator shafts. He had turned to go back toward Amboy's apartment.

It was then that a black-cloaked shape glided into plain view. Unseen by the detective, that phantom form moved past the elevators. The Shadow had returned, this time in his chosen guise of blackness.

It was not surprising that the dick failed to see The Shadow. For the mysterious visitant did not head toward Amboy's apartment. Instead, he moved swiftly toward the corridor at the other side of the building. He reached an apartment at the end of a long hall.

There The Shadow's key probed a lock. The spectral arrival entered an apartment that proved to be deserted. It was similar in layout to Amboy's apartment; and The Shadow followed its hallway until he reached the last room. That chamber corresponded with the one wherein Peters Amboy had died.

A solid wall separated this apartment from Amboy's. Hence The Shadow had no need to control the whispered mirth that he uttered while his flashlight blinked about the wall. Detectives in the next apartment could not hear that subdued mockery that bore a touch of grimness.

The little flashlight ended its blinks. The Shadow moved silently back along the hall. He left the apartment and made his way through the corridor. The space by the elevators was temporarily deserted. The Shadow reached the stairway and slowly descended.

Later, a laugh in the night. Traveling from the scene of crime, The Shadow found occasion for his mirth. Peters Amboy had died through his own folly. By keeping secret the fact that the black box was stuffed, he and Wallace Norgan had made their great mistake.

Through that course they had not only lost the important protection of the law. They had also failed to keep the protection of The Shadow. That weird foe of crime had not met the Unseen Killer's move purely because he had not expected a double game from Amboy and Norgan.

But The Shadow had scored tonight. As in the case of Melrose Lessep; as in the death of Nathaniel Hildon, he had once again gleaned facts that were bringing him closer to final combat with the Unseen Killer.

CHAPTER XIV
THE SQUAWKER

WHEN Commissioner Wainwright Barth had assured present safety for Wallace Norgan, he had spoken in the hope of playing a waiting game. Barth believed that the Unseen Killer would do as he had done before: deliver a new threatening message to the last of the three men whom he had cowed with statements of impending death.

The Shadow had divined the course that Barth would choose. Suiting his own action to the trend of events, he chose also to play a waiting game. Let another threat come; let Barth prepare. The Shadow would be ready.

To The Shadow, the death of Peters Amboy had merely postponed the inevitable. The Unseen Killer wanted certain funds. Wallace Norgan, alone, could deliver them. This time, Norgan would not balk.

Hence, The Shadow, too, was playing a waiting game. His stroke would come after the Unseen Killer received the wealth that he sought. Then would be the time to trap the crook with the goods in his possession.

As yet, The Shadow's agents had been unable to find traces of any hideout where Miles Crofton might be located. Nor had they tracked Crazy Lagran, the missing stoolie. Those were further reasons why The Shadow preferred to wait until the climax that he knew would come.

But the next morning brought no message to Wallace Norgan. The expected blackmail note was absent from the survivor's mail. The Unseen Killer, too, had decided to try a waiting game. He wanted to create an effect of suspense. That was a bit of subtlety that escaped Detective Joe Cardona.

Joe was out guarding Norgan's home. He was the first to see the mail when it arrived. He put in a prompt call to Commissioner Barth, to tell him that no death note had been delivered. Barth fumed across the wire. Joe made a suggestion. It went through.

Commissioner Barth, at Cardona's urge, ordered the dragnet into operation. The badlands were to be scoured for all traces of Miles Crofton, branded as the Unseen Killer. The dragnet was seldom advocated by Joe Cardona. But this was one time that the ace sleuth felt it might bring results.

Joe felt that he was after an untraceable person, so far as the man himself was concerned. But it had struck him strongly that someone might know facts concerning Crofton. Why not quiz every crook that the net brought in?

Moreover, Cardona knew of one specific person whom he wanted to locate. That was Crazy Lagran. The stoolie had handed him a prompt tip once. If Crazy could be located, there might be more coming. So the dragnet started while the Unseen Killer waited.

EVENING. Commotion in the badlands. Rats of the underworld were keeping out of sight. They were dodging cops and dicks, keeping away from the joints. Some, scared from their hideouts, had headed for parts of the city where they might elude the clutch of the law.

Those who remained within the scoured areas were furtive and skulking. They kept to alleyways. They dived for shelter on the slightest provocation. Even though they might be subjected to no more than a brief examination, they had no yearning for contact with the police. Quizzes were not to mob-land's liking.

Yet, amid the patrol of the underworld, a select crew of tireless workers still kept up a steady task. These were the agents of The Shadow. Night after night they had been looking for Miles Crofton or Crazy Lagran. Even though the dragnet was at work, the aides of The Shadow kept at their job.

Clyde Burke, a newspaper reporter; Harry Vincent, whom no cop would pick as a crook; Cliff Marsland, whose knowledge of the underworld made it simple for him to evade the law. These were three of the men who were working for The Shadow. They kept on, confident that the police would pass them by.

But among The Shadow's reserve agents was a worker of another sort. This was "Hawkeye," a cunning-faced, crafty little fellow who had once yielded to ways of crime. Those days were past. Hawkeye was taking orders that came indirectly from The Shadow.

Hawkeye was the type of prowler whom the dragnet would pick up. He ran a risk, covering the districts where the police were hauling in the riffraff. But Hawkeye was smart enough to elude the ever closing mesh. His nickname was no misnomer. He could spot a bluecoat a mile away and a dick at half that distance.

Hawkeye was working on the outskirts of the badlands. There was method in his process. Not only had he finished searching the depths of the underworld; he also knew that here he could rove more effectively while the dragnet was in operation. Hunch-shouldered, shifty of gait, Hawkeye had a way of slipping into alleys that made him as elusive as a prowling cat.

There were others of Hawkeye's ilk; but he was far more clever than the average. On this night, Hawkeye spied several who were using his own shifty plan of fringing the Tenderloin. Stationed at the entrance of an alleyway, he watched various figures shamble past. Suddenly, Hawkeye became alert.

He had spotted a pasty-faced passer. The fellow looked like a dope; but he wasn't. He was known in the badlands as "Fox" Cullis. His nickname meant that he knew much and kept it to himself. Fox, apparently, was edging away from the dragnet's range.

Hawkeye had spotted Fox twice within the past four days. On both occasions, he had tried to get hold of the fellow; but Fox had slipped from view. Hawkeye had a reason for wanting to talk to Fox. If anyone knew where Crazy Lagran might be, Fox would be the person.

Hawkeye edged from his alley. He sneaked after Fox and saw his quarry duck into a narrow street.

Then, up ahead, he spotted Fox turn between two buildings. An artful dodge; but one that did not escape Hawkeye's quick vision. Hawkeye followed Fox's path.

He was closing in on the pasty-faced shambler. Calculating, Hawkeye wondered what method would be best to use when he overtook the man he wanted. Fox's reputation for knowledge was equaled by his known capability for keeping matters to himself. Would Fox talk without persuasion?

Hawkeye grinned to himself. If persuasion proved necessary, he would use it. The job was to grab Fox before the fellow reached the next street. Hawkeye stole forward more rapidly. Then he stopped short.

The unblinking glare of a bull's flashlight had opened up from the other end of the passage between the buildings.

DESPITE his native cunningness, Hawkeye was caught squarely in the searching beam. He dived into a protecting angle of the wall just as a shout came from up ahead.

Another call responded. It came from the street that Hawkeye had left. A second glare issued from that direction. Footsteps came from both ends of the passage. Hawkeye growled to himself. It was the dragnet.

With all his artfulness, the crafty agent had been trapped in a spot that the cops had decided to search. They had caught a glimpse of his figure. They were on their way to drag him from the hole where he had found momentary shelter. It was a tight spot. One that Hawkeye did not like.

He did not fear a quiz. A few nights in a cell would be followed by discharge. But his usefulness to The Shadow would be ended during the time when it was most needed.

Footsteps were coming closer. Hawkeye edged further into the niche, found a little blind space beyond and crouched to avoid the approaching lights.

Then a thought struck him. He remembered Fox Cullis. Fox had not gotten clear of this trap. Where was Fox? Hawkeye guessed the answer. Fox must have heard sounds from the street ahead. He had dived for cover before the lights appeared.

Fox was here, in this cul-de-sac, crouching somewhere close at hand. Hawkeye had an idea. He edged along the wall of the building behind him. Finding a flight of old steps, he crept across them and huddled in a space between the steps and the wall.

Then came light. The glare of a cop's flash flooded the blind passage. It showed the steps behind which Hawkeye was hiding. It also picked out two old ash cans, near the other wall. A second cop joined the first. They made for the ash cans. They yanked the objects away.

The glare showed Fox, cringing helplessly. An officer chuckled as he recognized the pale face. Fox Cullis was small fry but it was smart business to trap as good a dodger as he was known to be. The policeman pulled his captive up into the light.

"You're coming along," he growled. Fox nodded.

"Any of your pals here?" quizzed the second cop.

"I ain't got no pals," whined Fox. "I was just comin' through here for a shortcut—"

"Never mind. Stay where you are while I look around."

Hawkeye huddled closer to the steps. He had hoped that the search would end with Fox. The cops had only seen one guy in the alley. Just like a dumb flatfoot to want to make sure.

It looked like Hawkeye's strategy was done, when voices sounded from the outer end of the space. The searching cop turned.

A stocky man had come into the light. It was Detective Joe Cardona. Acting inspector for the present, known to be the man behind the dragnet, Joe was the big boy as far as the cops were concerned.

THE policeman who had grabbed Fox Cullis was not going to miss out on his credit.

Forgetting further search, the bluecoat turned and gripped Fox's arm. He pulled the pasty-faced prowler into the light, dragging him up for Joe's inspection. Cardona nodded and grinned.

"So they got the Fox, eh?" he questioned.

"I ain't done nothin', Joe," whined Fox. "You ain't goin' to pull me in—"

"We're looking for others like him," put in the cop.

"How about it, Fox?" asked Joe, dropping his gruffness. "Anybody with you?"

"Honest, Joe. There ain't."

"All right."

Hawkeye grinned again. Fox had not heard him come in here. For Fox would not have made a negative answer had he known a brief search would prove him wrong. This was a break. It became a better one when Cardona ordered the cops to douse the glims and move out from the cul-de-sac.

The officers obeyed, puzzled. When they were gone, Hawkeye listened intently.

"Fox," said Joe Cardona, in the darkness, "I'm going to give you a chance to go your way."

"T'anks, Joe—"

"Wait a minute. They're going to take you up to the precinct; but you'll be out inside an hour if you talk straight right now."

"I don't know nothin'—"

"Can that. Listen. You know Crazy Lagran."

"Sure I know Crazy; but I ain't—"

"Wait up. You're one bird that knows enough to keep his mouth shut. That's why I'm talking to you. Do you know what Crazy is?"

"I t'ought he was a good guy—"

"He's one of my stools. You knew that, didn't you?"

There was a pause in the darkness. Then came Fox's half-reluctant reply:

"Yeah. I knowed it."

"All right." Cardona spoke quietly. "Then you know that Crazy's not going to mind seeing me. He's hiding out somewhere; but not because I'm looking for him. That wouldn't be reasonable. I want to know where Crazy is. So I can talk with him, confidentially."

"Uh-huh."

"All right. Where is he?"

Fox considered. Then came his reply, lowered to a tone that Hawkeye could barely hear.

"He's up over Mosey's hockshop," whispered Fox. "I knowed he was a stoolie, Joe. So I ain't squealin'. But don't tell him I told you where he was. Then he'd know that I knowed he was a stoolie. See?"

"I get it. Don't worry."

"I ain't doin' nothin', Joe. You said that—"

"I said you'd be loose in an hour. You will. After I've taken a look over at Mosey's. Why's Crazy hiding out?"

"I don't know. Some mugs must have wised up to him bein' a stoolie. Honest. I don't know nothin' more."

"All right. Come along."

Lights blinked as Joe took Fox out to the cops. The acting inspector gave brief orders. The bluecoats started away with Fox Cullis. Joe Cardona followed.

Hawkeye came out of his hiding place.

When he reached the next street, Hawkeye had luck. The police were nearly out of sight. Close at hand was a dumpy cigar store. Hawkeye ducked in and found a telephone in an obscure corner. He put in a call—one that would reach The Shadow. Then Hawkeye slid out into the street and moved back through the very space where he had made his lucky escape.

MEANWHILE, Joe Cardona had moved swiftly. Taking the direction opposite that chosen by Fox's captors, the ace had headed toward Mosey's hockshop. Joe had never thought of it as a hideout. The old hockshop had gone out of business. It was a black, deserted building near a corner and to all appearances it was boarded up. A fine spot for a hideout.

Ordinarily, Joe Cardona might have moved slowly on a special trip through this district. But tonight the dragnet was his cover. If skulking crooks spied him, they would think that he was merely checking up on the routine instituted by the law.

Nevertheless, the detective slowed his pace as he neared the vicinity of Mosey's old pawnshop. He strolled down the street where the place was located. He stopped a moment and noted the doorway that led upstairs. Walking further, Joe crossed the street and returned.

When he reached the doorway, he edged up against it. He tried the knob and found that the door was locked. Not only that; it was well locked. Joe paused; then looked down the street. He remembered something: Mosey's brother lived near here. Joe left the doorway.

He found the house he wanted. He rang the bell and was admitted. A blinking, bald-headed man recognized the visitor. Joe explained what he wanted. Mosey's brother produced a key. He shook his head as he handed it to Joe.

"You won't find anybody up there," he said. "I ain't been in the place because there ain't been any need to go. Maybe somebody else has got a key. But I ain't seen no lights in the house."

Cardona decided to look anyway. He went back to the door beside the hockshop. He unlocked the barrier and ascended a flight of dusty steps, using a flashlight cautiously. On the second floor, Joe saw doors on both sides of the steps. He noted a light under one. He scraped his shoe softly and waited.

It made a slight sound—just the type that a person would want to investigate but might not fear. A bolt was drawn. More light arrived as a peaked face peered out into the hall.

Joe Cardona stepped forward. The man ducked; but Joe caught the door with his foot and shouldered his way into the room.

The only window was covered with a drawn shade. The dull illumination came from an oil lamp. But the light was enough to show Joe the face of the man whom he had trapped. It gave the other fellow a look at Cardona, also.

The peaked man's hands had gone up. Now they lowered. The fellow grinned weakly. Joe Cardona's response was a pleased grunt. He had found the man he wanted, Here, in this hideout, he was facing Crazy Lagran, the missing stool pigeon.

CHAPTER XV
TWISTED TRAILS

CRAZY LAGRAN'S hideout bore all the signs of an improvised headquarters. The oil lantern was standing upon a broken soapbox. A battered army cot, covered with ragged blankets, was in a corner of the room. A rickety folding chair was the final article of furniture.

His first surprise over, Crazy grinned sheepishly. He slouched across the room and parked himself on the edge of the cot. He made a gesture toward the folding chair, an invitation for his visitor to be seated.

Joe accepted. He took the chair and watched Crazy roll a lopsided cigarette.

"Well?" quizzed Cardona, eyeing the stool pigeon steadily. "What's the idea?"

"Dis hideout?" parried Crazy.

"Yes," nodded Joe.

"I had to duck," declared Crazy, earnestly. "Honest, Joe. I was scart. After I seen de poipers—"

"When was that?"

"De day after I give you de tip-off. I was readin' about Crofton. I knowed I'd better lay low."

"Why didn't you give me another call?"

"I was scart."

Cardona watched the stoolie puff at his cigarette. Crazy, in turn, eyed the ace detective. The stoolie became uneasy. He shifted a bit; then began an explanation.

"It was dis way, Joe," he affirmed. "You know de way I work. I ain't no ordinary stoolie. I look for de real dope, don't I? You know what I told you onct. Just leave me go my way an' slip you news when it's hot—"

"I know," broke in Cardona. "Get back to Crofton. Where'd you get the tip about him?"

"I knowed de guy onct. Dat was all. Den I hears he was wid Rouser. I meets him on de street—Crofton—an' he figures me a pal. Tells me he's workin' for dat professor guy."

"When was that?"

"De day I called you. Well, after dat, I ducks out. Figurin' on findin' somebody knowin' more about Rouser. See? Den de poipers blows de woiks. I ducks in here."

"On account of Crofton?"

"Sure. Dey call him de Unseen Killer, don't dey? Ain't he liable to be figurin' dat I did de squealin'? Him bumpin' off dem big guys—say, Joe—I don't want him to know where I am."

"How did you get in here?"

"Had a key. From a mug dat used to work for old Mosey. Mosey forgot about it. Dis fellow made some extra keys."

"Who is he?"

"Aw, lay off, Joe. I can't squeal on no guy dat's helped me out. Dis guy drops in an' gives me de newspoipers. I see what's been goin' on—"

"But you couldn't get out long enough to tell me where you were."

"I was scart, Joe."

"Well, you look it. But what about tonight? Why didn't you let yourself get grabbed by the dragnet?"

"Wid dat guy Crofton runnin' around? He could plug me in de middle of a police court. I ain't tellin' nobody nothin', Joe. Nobody."

"Except the guy that slipped you the key to this place. What about him?"

"He's a regular, Joe. But I can't tell you who he is. Say—ain't I in enough of a mess? Tellin' you about a guy like Crofton? Well, dis friend of mine ain't done nothin'. So why should I—"

"LOOK here, Crazy." Cardona arose as he spoke. "I've had enough of this stall! If you think you're getting anywhere by trying to hold back on what you know, you're making a bum guess! I've been looking for you a long while. Now I've found you, you're coming clean!"

"Honest, Joe—"

"You're talking like a phony. You've got the inside on a lot of stuff that you're going to spill. Maybe you know more about Crofton than is healthy for you. Well, you'll squawk just the same."

"Don't worry about Crofton. He's forgotten you for the time. If you thought he was coming after you, you'd have been on your way long before this. Here's my proposition. Take it or leave it. Spill what you know, right here, or come along to headquarters."

"Don't pinch me, Joe!" blurted Crazy. "I ain't safe nowhere but here. I ain't safe when you're here. Gee, Joe, if dey—"

He caught himself. But Cardona had noted the slip. He nodded wisely. Crazy edged back upon the cot.

"So there's somebody else in it, eh?" quizzed Cardona. "Well, we're getting somewhere. Other mugs in the racket with the Unseen Killer? Just the birds I'm looking for. Who are they?"

"It isn't dem, Joe. It's de Unseen Killer I gotta watch out for. I ain't kiddin'. He's liable to be snoopin' in here right now—"

"Who are these other birds?"

Crazy hesitated. He looked toward the closed door. He licked his lips; then stared at Cardona. Leaning forward on the cot, he began to talk.

"Say, Joe," he pleaded. "I wanta get out of it. I pulled a boner. No foolin'. Listen: I'll give you de name of de guy you want; but get me away clear before you do anythin'. See? It'd be curtains—"

"From him?"

"Maybe from him, if he thought I was pullin' de double cross. Maybe from de Unseen Killer. Dat's what de guy tells me—de guy you want to know about. He says, 'Watch out for Crofton' an' it sounds like he means it—"

"Who's the guy?"

Crazy paused before mentioning the name. He was intent. So was Cardona. Neither noted the door from the hallway, slowly opening. Nor did they see the muzzle of a shining revolver as it edged through the space. It was not until the gun had stopped its motion that Crazy happened to glance nervously in that direction. The stoolie came up from the cot.

"Stop him, Joe! De Unseen Killer is comin'—"

AS Crazy voiced the second phrase, the revolver spurted flame. The boom of the weapon sounded through the room. Smoke curled from the muzzle. Crazy Lagran's lips spread silently. The stoolie sprawled forward from the cot. He plopped hard upon the floor.

Yanking his police gun from his pocket, Cardona sprang for the door. The revolver muzzle went quickly out of sight. Joe yanked the door open and thrust himself into the darkness, boldly seeking the unknown slayer. A flashlight came out in the detective's left hand. Joe pressed the button.

The gleam spread along the hall, toward the stairway. Joe stood startled. No one was in view. Then he heard a sound almost behind him. He wheeled. Before he could bring the flashlight into play, an arm come swinging through the darkness. Joe tried to ward off the blow.

It was a glancing stroke on the side of the head. Cardona staggered. He lost his flashlight. A foot kicked it into the room where Crazy's body lay. Cardona, staggering like a drunken man, still held his gun. It was of no service. Dizzy, Joe sprawled at the head of the stairs. An evil laugh came from the darkness.

Joe's assailant moved over and crouched above the detective's form. Half groggy, Cardona was trying to rouse himself. He gripped for the man in the darkness. He tried to raise his gun. Then the fellow had passed him. Blindly, Joe turned.

Crazy's killer jabbed a gun muzzle against Cardona's ribs. He was about to fire. Weakly, Joe thrust out an arm and encountered a living form. Then came a sound from the hall at the head of the stairs. Cardona's enemy looked up.

A window was moving upward. Someone was moving in from outer darkness. The window showed in dim outline; beyond it, only a strange blot of blackness. Dropping, the man on the stairs forgot Cardona. He aimed for the window and fired twice.

In response came the bursts of an automatic. High shots that whistled over the head of Crazy's killer. They were enough. Wildly, the man on the stairs dived downward. At the bottom, he yanked open the door and leaped out into the street.

A flashlight blinked a tiny circle at the head of the stairs. Keen eyes saw Joe Cardona. The detective was coming to his senses. A soft laugh—token of The Shadow. Keenly, The Shadow saw into the room where Crazy Lagran lay dead.

The stoolie killed; Cardona coming to life. No reason for The Shadow to remain. Too late to prevent Crazy's death, he had arrived in time to save Joe Cardona. Sweeping past the detective, he reached the street. There was no one in view, but The Shadow heard the shrill of a police whistle.

Evidently the last shots had been heard. Swiftly, The Shadow took to the night.

ONE block away, Hawkeye was on the move. Again the hunch-shouldered agent was taking up a trail. For Hawkeye had come to Mosey's hockshop. While The Shadow had entered by the rear wall, Hawkeye had been out front.

Hawkeye had seen a man come lurching from the doorway by the hockshop. He had taken up that trail. Right now he was less than half a block behind a thickset man who was heading through the darkness.

Hawkeye's quarry reached the nearest avenue. He started to walk along at a rapid pace. He—like Hawkeye—could hear whistles; the whine of a siren. They were too close for comfort. The fellow kept moving.

Hawkeye looked about in anxious fashion. His eye spied a taxi parked near an "el" station. Hawkeye grinned. No cab would be here as a rule, especially when the dragnet had this district on the go. Hawkeye hurried to the cab.

Leaning in by the driver's seat, he blurted quick words. A nod came from the shrewd-faced man behind the wheel.

The cab shot forward as Hawkeye dropped clear. Ducking into a doorway, Hawkeye watched the vehicle head up the street.

The man at the wheel of that cab was Moe Shrevnitz, another of The Shadow's emergency aides. Cruising about the badlands, Moe had been helping in the search for Miles Crofton's hideout. Moe had happened to be at the spot where Hawkeye needed him.

The cab rolled along easily. It passed the thickset man who was pacing up the avenue. Moe jammed the brakes and swung over by the curb.

"Taxi?"

Moe saw the man nod. He caught a glimpse of a hard face. He opened the door. His fare clambered aboard. He growled a destination:

"Hotel Revano."

"Where is it?" questioned Moe, leaning close by the window.

The man gave the address. Moe nodded. All the while, his right hand, on the seat beside him, was scrawling the name "Hotel Revano" upon the top sheet of a handy pad. Moe straightened up. He released the emergency brake. His hand yanked the paper loose and crumpled it.

The cab swung out from the curb. The ball of paper went spinning clear, unnoticed by the growling passenger. One minute later, the cab had turned a corner. But Hawkeye was coming up. He had seen that wad of paper fall.

It took Hawkeye just four minutes to get to a telephone. He put in a prompt report of Moe's cooperation. Then he strolled out from the little store where he had found the phone booth. Wisely, Hawkeye headed away from the badlands.

MEANWHILE, Moe was driving for the Hotel Revano. He made good speed at the start, getting clear of the district that he knew his fare wanted to forget. But after that, Moe picked his streets badly. Traffic crossing avenues; thoroughfares half barricaded with repair work—these increased his running time.

The passenger was peeved by the time they reached the hotel. He paid Moe the fare and walked into the lobby, growling as he went. Moe leaned from his cab and waved to the doorman. The uniformed attendant approached.

"Say, buddy," volunteered Moe, "I'm sorry for you. If all the guys that come here are like that cheapskate, your job must be tough."

"How much did he tip you?" asked the doorman.

"Not a jit," returned Moe.

"What did you do?" questioned the hotel attendant. "Take him five miles out of his way?"

"No. Why?"

"That guy usually hands out a tip. Maybe he was sore about the way you drove him. Maybe he was just in a hurry."

"Him? That cheap guy? Say—I guess I'm lucky to have got my fare out of him. He don't look like a bird with dough."

"Guess again," laughed the doorman. "That's Chuck Galla. Friend of Trip Burgan, fellow that lives here."

"Trip Burgan?"

"Yeah—used to be a big-time gambler. Got money and hands it out pretty free, too."

"That don't sound bad. I guess maybe this guy just forgot the tip. Well, that's the way it goes. Say, buddy, there's two taxis here at your stand already. Think I'll get a break if I fall in line?"

"Sure. There ought to be some cab calls anytime now. Better roll in while you can."

Moe backed his cab. As soon as he was in line, he scrawled out the information that he had received. He tore the paper loose and folded it with one hand. Then he settled behind the wheel and waited.

Not long. Alert though he was, Moe failed to hear the rear door open. His first inkling that anyone had entered the cab came when a soft hiss was voiced through the window by Moe's ear.

The taxi man lifted the folded paper. A gloved hand plucked it from his grasp. The door on the street side of the cab opened softly. Blackness emerged; the door closed. Moe's job was done.

The Shadow had called Burbank. He had learned Hawkeye's news. Moe's dallying had enabled The

Shadow to reach the Hotel Revano a few minutes after Chuck Galla.

Joe Cardona had found a trail to Crazy Lagran. That trail had ended with Crazy's death. But there, The Shadow had entered. Through his agents, he had gained where Cardona had lost.

Already The Shadow knew the name of Crazy's murderer. He had learned the identity of Chuck Galla; he had located Trip Burgan, the big shot whom Chuck was serving. The manhunt in the underworld had brought results at last.

CHAPTER XVI
TRIP'S ORDERS

TRIP BURGAN was standing by the window of his inner room. Cigarette between his lips, the ex-gambler was staring out toward city lights.

Chuck Galla, seated in a chair, was watching him. The underling had broken the news of Crazy Lagran's death.

"So Cardona never lamped you, eh?" inquired Trip. "Well, that's one good point. But you should have bagged Crazy before Cardona got there."

"How'd I know Cardona was coming in?" queried Chuck.

"I told you to watch the dragnet," retorted Trip. "If you'd had your eyes wide open, you'd have done better."

"It wasn't the dragnet, Trip. There wasn't nobody else near there. Say—if the bulls had been around the hideout, I'd never have made no getaway."

Trip considered this statement. He stared from the window, thinking. Chuck began to feel uneasy as he watched his chief. Seated with his back almost to the door, Chuck kept waiting for Trip to turn in from the window.

Motion from the doorway. The door itself was moving. Slowly, almost imperceptibly, it opened inward until its edge provided a space a fraction of an inch in width. Trip did not see it. He was looking from the window. Nor did Chuck, who was watching Trip.

Blackness seemed to creep in from the opening. Long, splotchy blackness that stretched across the floor. A flattened blot took on the sinister aspect of a hawk-nosed silhouette—a perfect profile that became motionless upon the floor.

"I was lucky, Trip," admitted Chuck, suddenly. "But I used my noodle being lucky. That's what counts. For all Cardona knew, it might have been the Unseen Killer that bumped Crazy."

Trip chuckled. The thought pleased him. He swung in from the window. Facing his lieutenant, Trip failed to notice the profiled blackness on the floor.

"Then out in the hall," resumed Chuck. "That's where I headed. Across the hall. All Cardona could have seen was the barrel of my gat. Well, when he piled out, I had him. He went right past me toward the stairs, like I figured.

"When he turned, I slugged him. Knocked him cold there, in the dark. Then I"—Chuck paused momentarily—"well, I beat it, leaving him on the stairs. He'll have something to talk about."

"You mean he'll figure it was the Unseen Killer?"

"Right he will."

"Good!"

A pause. Then Chuck, emboldened by Trip's approval, put a question that had evidently been perplexing him.

"Say, Trip," he said, "this racket's got me beat. The way it's switched around, I mean. Why don't you give me the whole lay?"

"You've got it, haven't you?"

"Sort of halfway. That's all. First you fix up a ritzy hideout for this bird Crofton. He ducks in there and he ain't any too soon. That Unseen Killer stuff sure started quick enough. Of course it don't matter with Crofton, since that professor fixed him so nobody can see him. But just the same, it was a good bet for him to have his headquarters."

"That's plain enough. You've got that much through your noodle. Go on; let's hear what's biting you."

"Well, then you tell me to get hold of Crazy Lagran. To tip him off he'd better hide out. Up over Mosey's. I'm Crazy's pal."

"And then?"

"Well, it goes on. Crofton does his stuff. Boy, how he does it! They're kind of woozy over at the hideout, never seeing no sign of him. Just sticking food and messages in that little living room of his. Not knowing when he's in or when he's out."

"We've discussed that. Get to your point."

"I'm thinking about Crazy. He's in that dump hideout of his. Then the dragnet hits. You tell me to go down there and bump him off if they close in. And you tell me to do it right. So it'll look like the Unseen Killer got him. Why was that?"

"Because Crazy tipped off Joe Cardona about Crofton. That's why."

"Then what was the idea helping Crazy to hide out?"

"So we would know where he was."

"All right. And then I bump him for the finish. That's what I don't get."

"Why not?"

"Why didn't you have Crofton bump him? Crazy was scared of the Unseen Killer. Crofton could have—"

"Crofton can't bother with small stuff," put in Trip. "It looked like a cinch for you. It was an emergency, anyway. I see what's got you mixed up. Listen: let me explain."

Trip strolled halfway across the room. Facing Chuck at close range, he spoke as follows:

"CROFTON pulls his stunt. He gets his hideout. He stays there and goes when he wants. He's got his jobs to do. He had to get the old professor. He had to bag those two other guys: Hildon and Amboy. He's after dough. When he gets it, the cut comes to me.

"In the meantime, right after he slides out from the prof's, Crofton knows that somebody squealed on him. About him being with Rouser Tukin. That's plain, ain't it?"

Chuck nodded.

"All right," resumed Trip. "Crofton knows it's Crazy Lagran. Says so in one of those notes he sent me. He don't want to bother with Crazy. So I'm to get the guy. But it don't look so hot, killing Crazy. I see a better way.

"The old hokum. Crazy don't know I'm working with Crofton. So I tell Crazy—through you—that I've got a hideout for him. Get him worried when he calls me up. Worried about the Unseen Killer. Crazy ducks into the hideout over Mosey's. He's there to stay.

"Then comes the hitch. Crofton bumps Hildon; then Amboy. He don't want to bump Norgan if the guy will cough over the dough. See? But he decides to give him an extra day to worry. Instead of Norgan getting a note this morning, he gets one tomorrow morning. See that?"

"Sure."

"Well, it was foxy. But Cardona, like a sap, decides to run the dragnet. Why? Because he's dumb. Thinks he can catch a guy he can't see. Well, that puts us in a jam on account of Crazy. He had to be bumped before the bulls located him.

"So I put you on the job. You did it. And the only fault I had to find at first was that you didn't bump Cardona. But maybe it's just as well you didn't, because Cardona will think it was Crofton and it will have him buffaloed. There's the whole story, Chuck."

Chuck nodded. Then he began to scratch his head. Finally he delivered a wise, knowing grin.

"All right," he said. "If Crofton won't bother with small guys, why was he down there at Mosey's? What was he doing—checking up on me?"

"Crofton—at Mosey's?"

"Sure. When I bumped Crazy."

"You saw Crofton?"

"How could I have seen Crofton?" queried Chuck. "Nobody can see him the way he is now, can they?"

"I don't mean did you see him," growled Trip, in a tone of annoyance. "I mean, did you see anything odd happen—anything that must have meant Crofton was around?"

"Yes. I was going to rub out Cardona, while he was lying groggy on the stairs. Then I hear something—I look up—there's a window opening."

" Where?"

"Top of the stairs."

"What did you do?"

"Without thinking, I used my gat. Then a couple of slugs come my way in a hurry. That's when I ducked."

"But you saw no one?"

"Not a person."

Trip scowled. He paced over by the window. He turned and eyed Chuck narrowly. He knew that his lieutenant had told facts. Trip spoke steadily.

"That wasn't Crofton," he said. "He wasn't out of his hideout. Listen, Chuck, and keep it under your hat. I'll tell you who was there at Crazy's hideout. The Shadow."

"The Shadow!" Chuck shifted half up from his chair.

"Sit down," ordered Trip. "Yes, The Shadow. That's another reason why Crofton should have pulled his last job tonight. Got the swag tonight, instead of waiting until tomorrow. That's the one trouble with this game. It's too good.

"You can't tell what's going to happen when The Shadow works in. Well—it means one thing. Crofton's hideout closes up. By tomorrow night."

"On account of The Shadow?"

"Yes. The dragnet is bad enough. Especially if it keeps on. But you can tell when it's getting hot or cold. You can't tell about The Shadow, though. Look here, Chuck, you're sure you weren't spotted down there at Mosey's?"

"Not a chance."

"Well, I'm not taking it for granted. You slide out of here pronto. Stay away tonight, and don't go close to Crofton's hideout. Understand?"

"Sure. Where'll I stay?"

"Up at the Lyceum Hotel. That's a quiet place. Then in the morning, grab a cab and go down to Crofton's hideout. Talk with the boys. Then leave. Come up here in the afternoon."

"What then?"

"You'll find out. I'll talk to you then."

TRIP nudged his thumb toward the door. Chuck arose. The door was closing, so slowly that the eye could scarcely notice it. It was tight shut when Chuck placed his hand on the knob. Chuck opened the door and entered the living room, Trip following.

"Stick out here for a few minutes, Chuck," suggested Trip. "I'll be back. Just want to make a telephone call."

He picked up the phone and carried it into the bedroom. He closed the door so the extension wire ran beneath. Chuck sat down to wait in the dim-lighted living room. He stared toward a bookcase in the corner.

There was a space between the far end of the bookcase and the wall. Staring in that direction, Chuck noted a peculiar blackened patch that reminded him of a head and shoulders. The black-ness did not move. Chuck forgot it when Trip returned a few minutes later.

The gambler set the telephone on a table. He nodded for Chuck to leave. The lieutenant arose and went out through the door of the apartment. Trip smiled and gave a light chuckle. Only in private did he relax his poker face.

Then the ex-gambler went back into the inner room, closing the door behind him. He did not take the telephone. He evidently did not intend to make another call. Silence followed. Then blackness moved.

The Shadow emerged from beyond the bookcase. Tall, spectral, he stood like a living apparition. Eyes beneath his hat brim glowed like coals as they stared toward the door through which Trip Burgan had passed.

Then came a strange laugh—one that was almost a voiceless shudder. It was confined within the walls of the little living room. The Shadow wheeled. He turned and left by the door that Chuck Galla had taken.

By his eavesdropping, The Shadow had gained the definite information that he had sought. He had learned who was aiding Miles Crofton, so far as the establishment of a hideout was concerned. He knew that Chuck Galla was going to the place tomorrow; he knew where Chuck could be watched in the meantime.

More than that, however, The Shadow had been able to fit Trip Burgan's statements into the picture that he had already formed concerning the Unseen Killer. Where Trip had talked to Chuck with limitations, The Shadow had understood all.

The telephone call that had followed the conver-sation. Trip's final O.K. to Chuck, just before the underling left. These were the final points. The Shadow's plans were made. By tomorrow night, he would be ready with an amazing counterthrust against the Unseen Killer's schemes.

CHAPTER XVII
FORCES CONVERGE

THE next morning, Wallace Norgan received a new threat from the Unseen Killer. It was a typewritten message that came in the first mail. Its terms called for a repetition of the scene at Warlock's. This time, Norgan would have an opportunity of his own to deliver the wealth that the Unseen Killer wanted.

The note specified an announcement to the newspapers after arrangements were made to use Warlock's safe the second time. It also stated that unless Warlock had changed the combination, a note would not be necessary on the front of the safe.

Joe Cardona was not at Norgan's when the new note arrived. But half a dozen dicks were there; they put in a prompt call to Commissioner Barth. He called Warlock; found the corporation president willing to go through with the new arrangement; and then sent Norgan's statement to the newspapers.

The Unseen Killer!

His name, mentioned by the press, had stirred the underworld. Throughout the district where the dragnet had been working, furtive, husky voices were speculating regarding the prowess of crime-dom's newest product.

"A guy you can't see—"

"De bulls ain't got a chanct to snag him—"

"A big shot—"

These were the expressions made by those who still roved free. Tonight, those same speakers would be dodging the law, for the dragnet would work again. Yet crooks had no antagonism toward the Unseen Killer, despite the trouble that his deeds had caused them. They were all for him.

Not only in the badlands. Elsewhere, men of criminal tendencies were speaking of the Unseen Killer in terms of praise. One spot where his name was whispered was a small cigar store on Ninth Avenue, an ordinary-looking place in a quiet district.

One man behind the counter. Two loungers in front. Beyond them, a door that led into a small poolroom, where men were playing at two tables. This was a place that The Shadow's agents had failed to uncover during their prolonged search; it was also one spot that the dragnet had not located.

The cigar store and the pool room were the "front" that covered Miles Crofton's hide-out. From the pool room, one could step into a little hallway that showed stairs leading to the second floor. Crofton had a complete apartment on that upper story.

One exit only. That was the path from the hallway through the cigar store. The shop and the poolroom remained open late each night. Men were constantly on duty. The fellow behind the counter; the loungers in and out; the habitues of the pool-room—all were under the command of Chuck Galla.

These were no ordinary gorillas whom the police could spot. They were crooks from out of town; men whom Trip Burgan had imported. He had chosen them well, carefully eliminating any who might have been known in and about Manhattan.

The police had failed to suspect these men. So had The Shadow's agents. Trip Burgan, himself, had no record other than his gambling past. Thus no one—not even Hawkeye—had gained the needed trail, until last night.

Then had come the relayed leads. Fox Cullis had opened the way to Crazy Lagran; from Crazy, the trail had continued to Chuck Galla. Finally it had reached Trip Burgan. After listening to Trip and Chuck, The Shadow had reversed the course. He had ordered men to watch Chuck Galla.

That was last night. This morning, Chuck had come to the combined cigar store and pool room. He had gone upstairs; come down again; then left. Chuck was coming back again, later. That much was known to The Shadow.

MORNING had passed. Afternoon was waning. Men in the cigar store were alert. One of the squad was standing by the door, looking out into the street. He saw a huckster pushing a dilapidated fruit cart along the avenue.

"That guy's never been in this block before," growled the watcher. "First time I've seen him around."

"What of it?" queried the man behind the counter, taking a look for himself. "He ain't the first push-cart peddler to try this territory."

"Business ain't so hot around here."

"Tell me anywhere that it's likely to be good for one of them guys."

The lounger shrugged his shoulders. He nodded. The man behind the counter was probably right. Furthermore, he was boss while Chuck Galla was not around.

"All right, Hobey," decided the lounger. "I guess the pushcart guy's all right. But what do you think of that bird across the way?"

Hobey leaned over the counter. He looked across the street. He saw an antiquated truck pulled up in front of a lot where workmen had torn down an old building. A huge African, attired in overalls, was picking out chunks of wood and heaving them aboard his truck.

"Him?" questioned Hobey. "Say—you have gone bugs! First it's a pushcart man that bothers you. Next it's a fellow clearing out junk from an old house. Can't nobody do any work in this block without you worrying?"

"You remember what Chuck said about—"

"He told us to watch out for snoopers. Them guys ain't snoopers, are they?"

"I guess not, Hobey."

"All right then."

The lounger decided that Hobey was right. He

turned away from the window and forgot the men in the street. But in his first suspicious impression, the fellow had been correct. Both of those men outside had come here for a purpose.

The pushcart man was known as Pietro. The big African bore the name of Jericho. Both were special agents of The Shadow. This morning, Hawkeye had spotted Chuck Galla taking a cab outside the Lyceum Hotel. Hawkeye had popped into Moe Shrevnitz's taxi. They had trailed Chuck.

Pietro and Jericho had taken up guard duty, Pietro first, off and on during the day. With waning afternoon, Pietro was soon to go off duty. Jericho, coming up with his old truck, was taking on the job.

Dusk was settling. A telephone rang behind the counter in the poolroom. Hobey answered it. He spoke in short sentences. When he hung up, he looked toward the loungers and gave a low-voiced order.

"Chuck's coming down," he informed. "Maybe Trip will be with him. Guess they want to talk with that guy upstairs. You birds are to ease out. Tell the boys in the back room."

"All right, Hobey."

Jericho's truck had pulled away by the time men were sauntering from the cigar store. Pietro, passing for the last time, spied them but gave no indication. The huckster kept along to the end of the block. But he had counted the slouchers as they began to take their places in doorways and other secluded spots along the line.

When Jericho's truck came rattling back for another load of rubbish, it passed the pushcart man. Pietro made a sign; Jericho grinned and nodded. He kept on until he reached the old building across the avenue from the cigar store.

While he loaded more junk, Jericho was conscious of lurkers in the dark. He kept at his work, knowing that they would not bother him. This load would go to an old garage, two blocks away, where Jericho was dumping the stuff. The African knew that Pietro had already headed for that old garage. A message was on its way to The Shadow.

MEANWHILE, other of The Shadow's watchers were on the alert. Hawkeye was standing across the street from the Hotel Revano, awaiting the appearance of Chuck Galla and Trip Burgan. For Hawkeye had seen Chuck enter, half an hour before.

The two men came out. Hawkeye spotted them and flicked a cigarette into the gutter. Moe Shrevnitz, stationed in the hack-stand space, was prompt with his cab. He shot up in front of the door.

Neither Trip nor Chuck had asked the doorman for a cab. Apparently they had intended to set forth on foot for a few blocks. But Moe's timely appearance made them change their minds. They stepped into the cab. Trip growled an address on the East Side.

Moe repeated it aloud. His voice was clear from the front seat, for he had opened the window beside him. Trip and Chuck heard Moe's repetition of the destination. So did Hawkeye, slouching across the dusky street. Moe pulled away.

Hawkeye headed for a telephone. He put in a call. Like Pietro, he was relaying information to The Shadow. Through Burbank, these messages would reach their goal—The Shadow's sanctum.

After phoning, Hawkeye headed out, grabbed a cab and made for the same destination that Trip had given Moe.

SOME twenty minutes after leaving the Hotel Revano, Moe Shrevnitz's cab stopped beneath the overhanging structure of an elevated line. Trip and Chuck alighted. Trip paid Moe. The two headed into an old clothing store.

Moe swung his cab around the el pillars and parked on the opposite side of the street.

Soon a slouching figure came up beside the taxi. It was Hawkeye. The little fellow asked a quick question. Moe pointed out the clothing store. Hawkeye shambled across the street and went by the lighted front of the emporium. Seeing no sign of the men he wanted, Hawkeye found a courtyard at the side of the store and went through.

A blind alleyway was at the rear. There, Moe heard voices. He made out the shape of a rakish touring car. As he crept forward, he discovered that there were four men in the machine. Two gorillas in front; Trip and Chuck in the back.

A growled order from Trip. Hawkeye heard reference to the cigar store on Ninth Avenue. He edged back to the passage just as the touring car began to move. Lights blinked on. The car was on its way. Hawkeye headed back to find Moe.

IN the meantime, Moe had gained another passenger. Some one had entered his car from the darkness beneath the elevated. Moe had heard a hissed order to cruise about the block. He knew who was in his cab. The Shadow.

Hawkeye, scurrying through the space beside the clothing store, saw Moe's cab shoot away. The little man grunted angrily; then decided upon a course of his own. A report call; after that a quick trip to Ninth Avenue.

He waited for a few moments, though, to see if Moe would return. The taxi did not show up.

There was a reason. As Moe's cab had turned the corner, keen eyes had spied a touring car swinging from an alley. The Shadow had spotted it as a mobster-manned machine. He had hissed a new order to Moe. The taxi driver had taken up the trail.

Thus were forces converging. Trip and his minions; The Shadow and his agents; both groups were heading toward the spot where men of both sides were already on watch. Events were due in the vicinity of Miles Crofton's hideout!

CHAPTER XVIII
THE SHADOW'S STROKE

THE rakish touring car had reached its destination. It was evening by this time. The machine was parked almost unnoticed in front of the little cigar store, where only Hobey remained on duty. Chuck Galla alighted alone.

Chuck looked along the street. He saw a taxi stopping more than a block away. The driver got out and went into a hash house. Chuck was not suspicious.

A rattling truck came jouncing along the avenue and pulled up across from the cigar store. An electric street light revealed the figure of a huge African. Chuck watched the man go to a pile of debris and began to pick up chunks of lumber.

That meant nothing to Chuck. The whole district seemed clear. Chuck entered the cigar store. While he pretended to make a purchase, he spoke in a low tone to the man behind the counter.

"I'm going in the back room, Hobey," he informed. "You turn out the lights, like you was closing the joint, see?"

Hobey nodded.

"Trip's coming in," resumed Chuck. "He don't want nobody to see him. So you slide out as soon as you douse the glims. We're going up to talk with Crofton."

Again a nod.

"Crofton's going out with us," added Chuck. "So you move around with the mob and keep them posted. If anybody starts anything, hand it back. We don't want to be bothered when we travel."

Chuck walked into the deserted poolroom. He turned out the light that he found there. Groping in the darkness, he made sure that rear windows were locked. These opened on an alley. Chuck moved back into the cigar store.

Hobey had turned out the lights. He had gone outside. Staring from the front window, Chuck could barely discern the shape of the touring car. The sidewalk between the automobile and the storefront was completely dark. Chuck did not see Trip alight.

It was the opening of the door that told him his chief had arrived. Chuck spoke in the darkness. Trip answered with a low growl that formed a question.

"You told Hobey?" he asked.

"That Crofton was leaving?" questioned Chuck. "Sure. I told him that."

"What did he say?"

"Nothing."

"Didn't wonder why the guy was going with us?"

"No."

"All right. Let's go up."

They made their way into the hall; then up the stairs. They reached the top. Trip tried the latch on a window that opened above the alley. It was locked.

"Come on."

Trip groped to a door. He rapped. A nervous voice answered from the other side. It was Miles Crofton.

"Open up," whispered Trip. "It's me, Trip—with Chuck."

"All right."

THE door opened. The two men entered a pitch-dark room. They left the door ajar behind them. It was then that something occurred near the end of the hall. The window latch began to move. Under the impulse of a prying wedge of metal shoved between the portions of the sash, it was being unlocked from the outer side.

The Shadow had left Moe's cab. He had come along the alleyway. He had chosen this mode of entry to reach the second floor above the cigar store. The window opened. The Shadow's shape obscured the slight light that came from that direction.

Then The Shadow edged to the wall. Men were coming from Crofton's apartment. The Shadow could hear their whispered conference. He made out the identity of each speaker, although the three were completely in darkness.

"It's the best way, Crofton," Trip was saying. "Chuck's told the gang that you're going out with us. You do go out with us. They'll remember it."

"But without the hideout?" questioned Crofton. "It's going to be tough for me—"

"We've got a better place," interposed Trip. "With two new guys to keep watch."

"These other mugs were getting stale," put in Chuck. "Squawking about their job. Said it gave them the willies, looking out for a guy they never saw."

"This is the first chance we've had to talk together," reminded Trip, again speaking to Crofton. "I know you've been doing some worrying, even though you're sitting pretty."

"Not so pretty as you think," retorted Crofton's voice. "Try it yourself if you don't believe me. Listen, Trip, there's plenty to talk about right here, before we start."

"The car's out front," explained Trip. "The sooner it moves away the better. We can talk while we're riding. Listen, Crofton: I wised Chuck to the real lay, over at the apartment. The two guys that we picked to go to the new hideout are no dummies.

"We've got to talk about a lot of things in a mighty short space of time. So let's get going and chin about it while we're on the way. Come on— you head downstairs first and go right out to the car. Chuck and I will follow."

Crofton grunted an agreement. Footsteps creaked and bodies jostled as they reached the head of the stairs. The Shadow was close against the wall as he heard the trio pass. Then came Trip's voice from the head of the stairs.

"Blink a light, Chuck," ordered Trip. "Just to make sure it's all clear up here. Shoot it when—"

Before Trip could complete his sentence, instructing Chuck to wait for a few moments, the lieutenant obeyed the order. He clicked the button of a flashlight and shot the rays toward the edge of the window, intending to sweep it along the wall until it revealed the door that they had just left.

A chance action; but one that produced a startling result. A gasp came from Chuck Galla's lips. His flashlight stopped short, revealing a form against the wall.

Trip, staring into the gleam, put words to his henchman's cry.

"The Shadow!"

THE response was a shuddering laugh. A second flashlight clicked in The Shadow's hand. Trip and Chuck were carrying revolvers ready. They swung their weapons upward. The muzzle of an automatic loomed from The Shadow's fist.

Glare to glare; gun to gun; The Shadow was dealing with murderous fighters. It was a battle to death—two to one in favor of the foe. The Shadow's automatic thundered. Quick shots stabbed toward the crooks as the tall black form whirled sideways.

Revolvers answered. Bullets zimmed amid the crackles. Fast, at close range, the battle was a grim one. Trip and Chuck were dropping toward the steps as they fired; but their action was less timely than The Shadow's swift twist.

By split-second precision, The Shadow had outdone his foemen. Chuck Galla gave a venomous cough and went sprawling to the floor. A cry came from Trip Burgan as the gambler staggered on the stairway.

A fierce laugh burst from The Shadow.

While revolver shots had whistled wide, slugs from the automatic had taken toll. The Shadow had dropped Chuck Galla with a death bullet. He had clipped Trip Burgan. Yet Trip was still a fighter.

Staggering crazily down the stairs, clutching at the rail with a wounded left arm, Trip kept on firing toward the top. Chuck's light had fallen.

The Shadow's had clicked out. It was a battle in the darkness. Stabs from the revolver; flashes from the automatic.

Glare to glare; gun to gun; The Shadow was dealing with murderous fighters. It was a battle to death ...

Half sprawling at the bottom of the stairs, Trip managed to dive into the cigar store. He staggered toward the front, bearing up despite new wounds, determined to give the alarm.

From above, The Shadow was sweeping downward, hot on Trip's trail.

OUTSIDE, men had heard the shots. The two gorillas in the front of the touring car had swung toward the cigar store. They were trying to make out what was happening. Then, before their eyes could distinguish objects in the thick darkness, they heard someone scramble into the car beside them.

"Get going!"

It was Miles Crofton's voice. The order was given with fervor. A mobster turned; then his fellow crook grabbed his arm. Someone else was coming from the cigar store. They could barely see a man who faltered toward the car.

"Get him!" It was Trip. "Get him—The Shadow! Get going before he comes—"

Trip sprawled. The driver of the touring car shot the car into gear. It started from the curb. It did not go far. At that instant, a big man came bounding from across the street. It was Jericho. Wrenching open the front door of the touring car, the huge African yanked the driver from behind the wheel.

The fellow swung a gun, viciously. It whizzed an inch past Jericho's ear as the big man hoisted the gorilla over his shoulder. Then, with a powerful lurch, Jericho sent the gangster headfirst to the paving. The gorilla rolled over and lay still.

The second man was at the wheel, aiming for Jericho. The African was an open target. He was springing forward to deal with this new enemy. Jericho might have been too late to stop the shot; but someone else was in time.

A gun barked from the old truck across the street. The gorilla slumped by the wheel. Jericho yanked him clear as two men came bounding from the truck. The first was Cliff Marsland; the other Harry Vincent.

The two had come up in Jericho's truck. They had been waiting, hidden, for this moment. Cliff had dropped the second gorilla with a well-aimed shot. Two mobsters eliminated, he piled into the darkened rear of the touring car.

Instantly, Cliff was locked in a terrific struggle. Someone had risen to meet him. Harry could see Cliff's shoulders lunging against a foe beyond. To aid Cliff, Harry piled in through the door.

All this in brief seconds. Astounded watchers, lurking in doorways, had been nonplused by the rapidity of action. Coming to life, they opened fire toward the touring car; toward Jericho.

The African dived for his truck. It was the best move. As he reached cover, he drew the fire. Then, before the marksmen could spot their quarry, they

learned of a new enemy. A fierce laugh sounded from a spot just outside the cigar store. Flashes appeared with the booms of automatics.

The Shadow!

CROOKS accepted the challenge of the hidden foe. They fired for those stabbing targets. The Shadow, on the move, was drawing their fire. Close by darkened building fronts, he was eluding the evil sharpshooters.

He was doing more. He was picking living targets. He was pulling shots away from the touring car where Harry and Cliff were still wrestling with a foe that grappled as fiercely as a fiend.

Then, whirling rapidly up the avenue, came Moe Shrevnitz's cab. Speeding in zigzag fashion, Moe lay half crouched behind the wheel. With a terrific skid, the taxi whirled about in the middle of the street, while crooks began to aim toward it. Moe leaped from the cab and gained the front seat of the touring car.

Crooks leaped from their hiding places. Maddened, they wanted to get The Shadow. They wanted to stop the departure of the touring car.

They were too late. The rakish machine shot forward. Moe looked quickly over his shoulder, to see Cliff and Harry struggling with an enemy who was obscured beneath them. He kept on, while bullets whistled through the top of the car.

The Shadow was again drawing the shots of crooks. Men were sprawling from his bullets.

Hobey, still in a doorway, shouted a wild command. He wanted to concentrate the fire; for The Shadow had dropped back to a doorway of his own.

Crooks wheeled. As they met the challenge of the automatics, a new fire came to The Shadow's aid. A wizened face thrust itself from the interior of Moe's abandoned cab. Hawkeye had joined the jehu before Moe's mad arrival. A sharpshooter in his own right, Hawkeye was gunning for crooks.

Caught flatfooted by shots from two directions, the last of the imported mobsters took to flight. All save Hobey. He thought that he had found The Shadow's range. He fired across the street. His bullet flattened against a brick wall. An answering report from an automatic. Hobey rolled from his doorway.

Hawkeye was out of the cab, firing at two mobsters, the last of the tribe. One sprawled. The other turned to aim past Hawkeye. An automatic roared. The last crook fell. Turning, Hawkeye saw The Shadow.

A hissed command. Hawkeye leaped into the front seat of the cab. Whistles—sirens—cops were coming up from the block below. With a mocking laugh, The Shadow entered the cab.

Hawkeye, an improvised taxi driver, stepped on the gas. The cab shot away. When officers arrived, they found only dead and wounded crooks. Those who were still alive could do no more than utter incoherent gasps. Then, from the back of the rickety truck came Jericho.

Feigning fright, the big African talked with chattering teeth. Fighting mobs. Crooks against crooks. That was his story. The police believed it. Some had come and gone in the taxi, Jericho said. Others had started trouble in the cigar store across the way.

But Jericho told no more than that. He gave no mention of the touring car that had sped away before the departure of the cab. His story told, Jericho went back to his truck. The cops told him to wait around a while.

As he waited, Jericho pondered. He shook his head doubtfully. He knew that The Shadow was all right; but he was thinking of the men in the touring car. Harry Vincent and Cliff Marsland; the assailant whom Jericho had not seen.

Two against one; Moe at the wheel. The odds had been with The Shadow's men. Yet Jericho feared that they were not enough. He was sorry that he had not gone along, for he had witnessed the power of the enemy.

Mentally, Jericho could picture the tables turned. Cliff and Harry staggered by swift blows. Moe going down beneath a grasping clutch. The touring car stalled in darkness. An enemy escaping while agents of The Shadow lay helpless.

Jericho could only hope that his fears were false. Impatiently, he waited for the police to send him on his way.

CHAPTER XIX
DEATH RESUMES

THE new note from the Unseen Killer had specified a repetition of the procedure that he had previously prescribed. Wallace Norgan was to place all the required funds in Findlay Warlock's safe or suffer the penalty of death.

Worried, Norgan had decided to go through with it. Commissioner Barth had agreed not to interfere with the Unseen Killer's action. Shortly before eight thirty, the commissioner had arrived at Warlock's accompanied by Joe Cardona.

Findlay Warlock and Marryat Darring were already there. Norgan arrived very soon, under the guard of six detectives, headed by Markham. With him, Norgan had a box that was larger than the one which he and Amboy had brought.

Norgan opened the box to display actual securities. He removed them from the box in bundles and carefully arranged the stacks inside the open safe. Others stood away, watching him. The task completed, Norgan himself closed the safe and turned the knob.

The group went downstairs, leaving Joe Cardona in charge under the same conditions as before. No message had been required in an envelope. Warlock had not changed the combination. Doors to the study were left open. At nine o'clock they were closed. At nine fifteen, they were reopened.

It was almost nine thirty. That was the time specified for a return to the study. While waiting for the dead line, Commissioner Barth began to pace about. He stopped in the middle of the living room to eye the others.

Warlock was seated placidly before the fire. Darring was leaning against the wall. Norgan was nervously resting in a corner. Barth made an anxious comment.

"I left word for Cranston," he declared. "At the Cobalt Club. I wanted him to be here. I wonder what is keeping him?"

Barth would have been amazed had he known. Tonight, Lamont Cranston had been temporarily nonexistent. But The Shadow had been in action. He had found it more important to visit Ninth Avenue than to come to Findlay Warlock's.

The Shadow knew that Norgan would be safe, so long as he actually delivered the funds. Moreover, The Shadow knew that Norgan would not welch tonight. The Unseen Killer was too potent an enemy to bait for a third time.

Nine thirty. Time for the doors to open above. Wallace Norgan, suddenly restless, arose and walked from the living room. Barth had not posted a detective in the hall tonight. Norgan started upstairs.

"Call him back," ordered Barth, suddenly, as he glanced toward the clock. "It's not after nine thirty. We must not clip the time too close."

Marryat Darring responded. He strode from the room and ascended the stairs in Norgan's wake. When he reached the open door of the study, he found Norgan comparing watches with Cardona.

"Nine thirty," announced Norgan. "I have followed the conditions. I am going in."

Before Cardona could stop him, Norgan pressed past and hurried into the study. He crossed the room and reached the wall safe. He began to unlock it. Warlock had openly mentioned the combination at the time the funds had been placed within.

Cardona had followed Norgan. Darring was close behind Joe. They saw the door come open. A snarl from Norgan. The wall safe was empty! As with the black box, the real wealth had been removed.

WILDLY, Norgan began to reach about inside the safe, pressing his hands against the walls, bottom, top, and sides. He seemed to be looking for something other than his purloined wealth.

Had the man gone mad? Cardona looked at Darring, who shook his head in a puzzled manner.

Norgan wheeled. Excitedly, he pushed his way past the other men. He started for the door; when he reached the hall, he began to shout for the commissioner. Never pausing, he dashed down the stairs, heading for the living room.

Darring turned and hurried in the same direction, anxious to know what had happened.

Cardona was about to follow; then he paused to bark instructions at the dicks who were stationed outside the doors. The Unseen Killer had grabbed a bundle of big dough. Joe did not intend to meet with new criticism for negligence. It was bad enough to have had Norgan in the study, opening the safe on his own. But, after all, the cash had been Norgan's.

Downstairs, Wallace Norgan had reached the living room. His square-jawed face was hideous with rage. There was no semblance of fear remaining. Wainwright Barth stood amazed. So did Findlay Warlock.

"The money is gone!" shouted Norgan. "All my wealth! The safe is empty, Commissioner. I have been tricked!"

"Tricked?" questioned Barth. "You knew what happened to the box you put there before. The Unseen Killer—"

"A double cross," sneered Norgan. "The Unseen Killer is not alone in this game. Someone is working with him. You can arrest his pal."

"His pal?"

"Yes." Norgan pointed to Warlock. "There's the culprit. He knows what happened to my millions."

"I?" parried Warlock.

"You!" accused Norgan.

"What do you mean, Norgan?" quizzed Barth. "Have you found some evidence?"

"No," jeered Norgan, "I've lost some. The case and securities weren't all that I put in that box. I put in something else—unnoticed—something that proves my—"

"Look out!" gasped Warlock, pointing.

Norgan swung about. Barth turned. The shining muzzle of a revolver had come between the edge of a curtain and the side of the doorway. Before Norgan could spring forward, the gun belched flame.

Wallace Norgan sagged. Like men stricken with paralysis, Barth and Warlock stood motionless, stunned by this new tragedy. The gun barrel was pulled from sight. The only evidence of its echoing shot was the form of Wallace Norgan, dead upon the floor.

THEN came a shout from beyond the curtains. From the foot of the stairway, out in the gloomy hall, someone was putting up a cry for aid. The voice was that of Marryat Darring. It carried triumph despite its tone of partial terror.

"Help me!" was Darring's call. "Help me! I've got him! The Unseen Killer!"

A gun thudded on the floor as Barth and Warlock sprang past Norgan's body. Outside the doorway, the two men stood astounded. So did another witness—Joe Cardona, coming down the stairs.

Marryat Darring was engaged in a desperate struggle with an invisible foe. With hands clutching at a throat that could not be seen. Darring was lurching back and forth. His body twisted, his legs sagged.

With a sudden choke, Darring dropped one hand to his own throat. He tugged to release invisible fingers. He succeeded. Throwing his arms about a form that no one could view, he shouted a warning to Joe Cardona, who was suddenly springing down the steps.

"His gun!" exclaimed Darring. "I can see it—where he dropped it—on the stairs—"

Joe stopped suddenly to reach for the weapon. At that instant, Darring went hurtling sidewise. His hands dropped; his arms spread out. He slumped and tottered under the force of an invisible blow. With a futile clutch for an escaping enemy, he sprawled on the floor.

Cardona was blocking the stairway. Barth and Warlock were in the hallway that led to the back of the house. The one opening was the front door; that stood wide. That was by order of the Unseen Killer, part of the conditions that he had proposed.

"Get him!" cried Darring, coming to hands and knees. "That's the way he went!"

Darring grabbed for the gun on the floor. Cardona yanked a revolver also. Darring fired through the front door. Joe did the same. They listened. There was no evidence of success. Detectives came dashing in from the street.

Darring came tipsily to his feet. He was weakened by his struggle. Still gasping, he spoke of the encounter that had been his lot.

"I—I heard the shot!" he exclaimed. "Just as I came down the stairs. I—I sprang for the curtain. He locked with me. I could feel his hands, his wrists, the gun. I wrenched at the revolver that I felt. It fell to the floor."

"I saw the gun," nodded Warlock, "when the Unseen Killer fired the shot."

"I saw the flash," added Barth. "I think—"

He paused as someone entered. It was Lamont Cranston. He had arrived just in time to hear this testimony. Barth greeted his friend and began to give the details of the crime that had occurred. Cranston nodded, solemn-faced.

"The mystery is deeper than ever!" concluded Barth. "Miles Crofton is a fiend. Unless we find him, the Unseen Killer, we shall have no end to murder in the city—"

The commissioner broke off as a detective entered to hand a note to Joe Cardona. The ace opened it; while Barth stood puzzled, he saw an expression of amazement come over Cardona's face. Excitedly, Joe turned and handed the note to the Commissioner.

"What is this, Cardona?" demanded Barth, before looking at the paper.

"A message, commissioner," returned Joe, grimly. "Read it. A message from The Shadow!"

CHAPTER XX
FROM THE SHADOW

"FROM The Shadow?"

Barth's tone was angered as well as skeptical. To the police commissioner, talk of The Shadow was absurd. Yet even as he gave indication of his wrath, Barth paused. He realized that The Shadow could be no more an incredibility than the Unseen Killer.

"Very well." Barth mollified his tone. "I shall read this message."

He adjusted his pince-nez. He looked at the paper. Then a scoffing smile appeared upon his lips. He handed the sheet back to Joe with a comment:

"You have a good imagination, Cardona."

The detective looked at the paper and blinked. It was blank. Joe gazed up to see Barth frowning. Angrily, the detective spoke.

"There was writing on this paper when I opened it," he said. "A message, signed by The Shadow— and I read it. Even if the writing is gone—well, that doesn't mean—"

"What was the message?" inquired Barth, testily.

"It said a box was coming," replied Joe. "To be delivered here. Its contents to aid us in solving crime. A box from The Shadow—"

Another detective entered. He spoke to Joe, meantime nudging his thumb over his shoulder toward the open front door.

"Two guys out there with a truck," informed the dick. "Got a box they want to deliver to Detective Cardona."

"Bring it in," ordered Barth. Then, noting Norgan's body, he added: "Take it upstairs to the study. Bring the men also. Markham"—he turned to the detective sergeant, who was standing by— "you take charge here while we go up."

The box went past the door. It was a large box, with a padlocked lid. It was more than four feet square and the delivery men staggered with their burden. Barth noted holes in the side of the box. His curiosity was aroused.

He ordered Cardona to bring Warlock and Darring upstairs. Motioning to Cranston, the commissioner invited his friend to join him. They reached the study, to find the delivery men standing beside their lowered burden, watched by two detectives.

"Where did you get this box?" demanded Barth.

"Found it on our truck," replied one of the delivery men. "Two fellows had put it there. They gave us ten bucks apiece to bring it around here. Said they were hiring another guy to go ahead with a note.

"Seeing as how it was going to a detective, we didn't see no reason not to bring the box. The guys looked all right. Talked like they were regulars. Couldn't see their faces close, though. It was dark where we had the truck."

"Hold these men," said Barth to the detectives. "Take them downstairs to the kitchen and wait there until we call for you."

"Say," protested the second truckman. "We haven't done nothing—"

"Don't worry," assured Barth. "We may need your testimony. That's all."

"O.K. Say—here's the key to the padlock. Them fellows gave it to us."

Dicks and delivery men departed. Barth eyed the box suspiciously; then ordered Cardona to stand ready with a revolver. Gingerly, the commissioner unlocked the box and raised the cover. He leaned forward; then stood staring.

Others approached. They, too, showed surprise. Inside the box, trussed and packed inside padded walls, was the huddled figure of a man. The fellow was gagged as well as bound.

Cardona put away his gun. He stooped beside the box. Lamont Cranston did the same on the other side. Together, they hoisted the huddled form out to the floor. As the man stared at them, Cardona pulled away the gag that half obscured his face.

"My word!" ejaculated Wainwright Barth, mopping his bald head. "It's Miles Crofton!"

"The Unseen Killer?" demanded Cardona.

"The same." Barth's surprised tone had changed to a note of accusation.

THE commissioner glared like a fierce eagle as he surveyed the captive. "Well, Crofton, we've got you. This means the chair for you."

"Cut these ropes," pleaded Crofton, anxiously. "I'll talk. I'll tell you everything. But—listen, Commissioner—I'm not a killer—"

"Keep him covered, Cardona," interrupted Barth. "Have your bracelets ready while we release him from these bonds."

Three minutes later, Miles Crofton was leaning wearily in a chair, his wrists handcuffed behind him. Commissioner Barth was eyeing him with a perplexed gaze. He could not understand how Crofton, supposedly invisible, had come back to view.

Crofton saw the commissioner's puzzlement. He understood. Weakly, he delivered a grin. Then, with a sigh of relief, he shook his head.

"I'll tell you the whole story," he agreed. "Straight from the beginning. That is, all I know of it. I was double-crossed; that's all. I've been in a crooked game, Commissioner, but murder wasn't my part."

"Proceed," ordered Barth.

"The whole thing started like a fake," declared Crofton. "It looked like a good game, though. I'd been a pal of Rouser Tukin's, but I wasn't in with his mob. That's something no one can ever hang on me. But I was pretty well worried when Rouser and his outfit ran into that mess. The time when Rouser was killed by the police.

"I went to see a fellow named Trip Burgan. Used to be a big-shot gambler. Trip seemed like a good guy. Loaned me some dough and advised me just to lay low. Said this Rouser business looked bad, but if I watched myself, I could keep out of trouble.

"I believed him. I know it was a stall, now, but I didn't think that then. Trip knew how he could use me. That was all. First thing I knew, he sent for me. Said he had a chance for me to keep out of sight and make some easy dough. Both at once."

Crofton paused to look about. Expectant eyes were watching him. His listeners seemed to be impressed with his story. Crofton leaned back in his chair and resumed.

"It looked like a good racket," he declared. "Working for Professor Melrose Lessep. Here was the story: Lessep had a cock-eyed invention that wouldn't work. Trip had found out about it somehow. He gave Lessep some dough and said that they could fake it and sell more stock in the idea.

"I was to work with Lessep. Trip had the idea; Lessep and I doped out the rest of it. A fake clear through. The trick lay partly in the cabinet and partly in that second motor. Then there was special wiring in the laboratory walls."

A thin smile had appeared upon the lips of Lamont Cranston. His keen eyes showed that he had learned all that Crofton was about to say.

"When the prof frosted up the walls," explained Crofton, "I revolved the back panel of the cabinet. I stepped through, to the back of the platform. That was a cinch. Nobody could see through the panels while I was doing it. They were all misty.

"When he used the second motor, the prof shoved in cords that had long, pointed plugs. One made a special contact with the cabinet; the other made a special contact in a dummy floor plug.

"The prof pressed one button on the motor. That made the door of the cabinet open, like I was responsible. Then he did a lot of hokum—all the while I was standing on the back ledge. Finally he shouted out to watch the door.

"That's when he pressed another gimmick. A special wire through the wall and into the door. It made the bolt move back automatically. Another push. The door opened. Then the prof touched the right button. It worked the light switch. Another pull made the front door shut."

"Amazing!" exclaimed Barth.

"WAIT a minute," objected Warlock. "You were still in back of the cabinet, Crofton."

"I'm coming to that," declared the prisoner. "In the dark, the prof pushed another one of his trick switches. It operated the bolt on the door into the back hall. That's how I made my getaway. When I closed the door, the prof swung the switch the other way. It shot the bolt again.

"Take me down to the lab. I'll prove all I've said. I worked plenty hard figuring out some of that trick stuff. The prof was stumped with a lot of it. But it worked fine the night we pulled it. The toughest part was finding enough time for the getaway."

"How did the professor know when you had made your escape?" questioned Barth.

"He could hear the door close," replied Crofton. "He was listening for it."

A pause. Barth was stroking his bald head, utterly confounded by Crofton's story. It sounded true, particularly the offer to make tests in Lessep's abandoned laboratory.

"Now comes the double cross," asserted Crofton, suddenly. "Trip Burgan had a hideout fixed for me over on Ninth Avenue. The idea was I'd have to keep out of sight or people might find out about the fake.

"Well, I hopped over there. A swell place—apartment with three rooms—guys to bring me everything I wanted. Only thing was, I couldn't let them see me. I was supposed to be invisible. Trip swore I'd have to play the game all the way.

"I look at the papers. They were brought up to my room. It kind of socked me when I found I was called the Unseen Killer. I sent a note to Trip. He sent back word to lay low. Somebody had squealed that I knew Rouser Tukin.

"Then I got a paper that told about Lessep being killed. Trip sent a note saying that he thought the prof had committed suicide. It looked worse than ever for me, and I knew murder was the game when I saw papers telling about Hildon and Amboy.

"But I couldn't make a move. Those gorillas—Trip had a crew of them under the place I was living—they would have bumped me if I tried to make a getaway. They were to rub out any guy that they found in the place. They'd never seen me. Since I was supposed to be invisible, they'd have plugged me for an intruder."

Crofton's voice showed strain. Thoughts of his recent ordeal were troubling him. It was with an effort that the man managed to conclude his story.

MILES CROFTON

"Tonight, Trip came to the joint," he said. "He and Chuck Galla. To take me away. I had to go. I was suspicious. I figured they were on the home stretch of their game and that they were going to rub me out, not needing me as a goat any longer.

"The dragnet was working. And they were scared of The Shadow. Well, just as we were going out, The Shadow showed up. Battled with Trip and Chuck. They had a car outside, with gorillas in it. I made for the car, figuring I'd rather bluff with the gorillas, even though they might be set to take me for a ride.

"Some fellows crowned those gorillas. Made off with the car, with me in it, two of them pinning me on the floor. One of them handed me a haymaker. I went out. When I woke up I was in that box and The Shadow was looking in on me."

"You're sure it was The Shadow?" challenged Barth.

"You bet it was," returned Crofton, in a positive tone. "Black cloak—slouch hat—all I could see was eyes. He talked to me and I listened. He knew everything, that guy. Said he was sending me to Joe Cardona. Told me if I talked, I'd come out all right. He'd do the rest in a pinch. Well, here I am."

Finished with his amazing tale, Miles Crofton

closed his eyes and settled back wearily upon the cushions of the chair.

CHAPTER XXI
NEW DEDUCTIONS

A BUZZ of comments broke loose when Crofton's story was completed.

Crofton did not open his eyes, even though some remarks were criticisms of his statement. He was tired. He was willing to rely upon The Shadow to substantiate the story that he had given.

"A hoax!" exclaimed Findlay Warlock. "Professor Lessep was no swindler! This wild tale is an insult to his memory!"

"I doubted the professor," put in Marryat Darring, "but not my own senses. I struggled with the Unseen Killer myself. If Crofton was not my assailant, who was?"

"Murder has been done," announced Barth. "Only an invisible criminal could have accomplished those killings."

Joe Cardona made no comment. He was puzzled. Barth looked at him; the detective merely shook his head. The commissioner reiterated his previous statement.

"Only an Unseen Killer could have done these crimes. Lessep—Hildon—Amboy—Norgan—"

"Odd deaths," came a quiet interruption. "Yet ones that do not belie Crofton's story."

Barth turned to Cranston. It was he who had spoken.

"Can you explain those killings?" challenged the commissioner.

"Possibly," rejoined Cranston, with a quiet smile.

"How?" demanded Barth.

"Lessep, to begin with," remarked Cranston. "No bomb was thrown at him. He died by a special device planted in his little office. One so clever that it passed unsuspected."

"How do you know that?"

"I found a used lamp bulb in his desk. I happened to try it. The bulb was not burned out."

"This is no time for a hoax!" cried Barth. "What did such a bulb have to do with Lessep's death?"

"It proved," returned Cranston, "that there must have been some purpose in its removal. For instance, a special bulb, screwed into the lamp above Lessep's filing cabinet. One that was left loose—"

"For what purpose?"

Cranston stepped across the room. He unscrewed a light bulb in its socket, leaving it loose. The others watched the demonstration, particularly Joe Cardona.

"Picture Lessep coming into his laboratory," remarked Cranston. "To get those photographs.

The last act he was to perform. He tries the light switch"—the speaker demonstrated—"and no light results. He decides to remove the bulb, thinking it burned out."

Cranston's long fingers began to turn the bulb. They stopped, apparently noting its looseness.

"A loosened bulb," he remarked quietly. "Lessep decides to screw it tight before removing it. He does so. Contact forms and—"

"He gets light," put in Barth, as the lamp came on.

"No," returned Cranston. "Not with the bulb that was placed there. That bulb was a bomb, its mechanism hidden by the frosted glass."

"Ready to blow when the current hit it!" cried Cardona. "That's the story, Commissioner! I see it!"

"DID you suspect this at the time?" demanded Barth, speaking to Cranston.

"Yes," was the reply.

"Why, then," asked the commissioner, "did you fail to mention it?"

"Because I suspected all that Crofton has told us. I knew there could be no Unseen Killer. Deducting from that basis, I knew that Professor Lessep had himself taken the lever from his machine; that he had typed the threatening note found on his desk. Lessep was a fanatic. I could well believe—"

"That he planted the bomb himself? As a means of suicide?"

"Yes. At the same time it was possible that an enemy had placed the bomb. I suspected one of two men. Lessep was dead. It was best to wait."

"Why?"

"In case the real killer would show his hand. So that he could be trapped in actual murder."

"You should have advanced your theory, Cranston. Hildon—Amboy—Norgan—"

"All died through their own errors."

"How so?"

"The killer did reveal himself," explained Cranston, "by his first notes. To Hildon, Amboy, and Norgan. Had they acted sanely, and informed you of the threats, I would have told you what I had learned. But they were avaricious. They had gained wealth by legalized crime. They kept their secret. Hildon died."

"Can you explain his death?" demanded Barth.

"I have a theory," said Cranston, quietly. "A sound one."

"Of how a visible killer could have left Hildon's room?"

"Yes."

"How?"

"By the side window."

"Impossible! It was locked on the inside. The panes were intact."

"Exactly. But suppose"—Cranston paused and adopted a tone that was almost speculative—"suppose some one had climbed to the porch roof outside the window. While Hildon was at dinner, the intruder could easily have chiseled away the painted putty that held one pane in place.

"Entering, leaving the glass on the roof, that man could have strangled a weakling such as Hildon. Then out through the window. The pane back in position. New putty, of the type that hardens rapidly. Quick-drying paint which—"

"That's the story, Commissioner!" exclaimed Joe Cardona. "It's no theory. Mr. Cranston is telling you facts. That's why the telephone bell was wadded."

"The telephone bell?" queried Barth.

"Yes," replied Cranston, with a smile. "So Hildon's body would not be found until morning. It was found sooner; but not too soon."

"You're right," agreed Cardona. "I was too dumb to think of the windowpane. That stuff had time to dry anyway. Say—maybe there's a lot of cracked putty on that roof—"

"There should be some," inserted Cranston, dryly. "Probably the murderer spread a cloth to catch most of it. But I advise you to go down there, Cardona. You will probably find traces now that you know where to look."

"CRANSTON," declared Barth, seriously, "this is something else you should have mentioned. Lives were at stake when—"

"Whose lives?"

"Amboy's and Norgan's."

"Not at all. Their wealth was at stake. They promised to deliver it to the Unseen Killer. That was why I waited. Had they delivered it two nights ago, the murderer might easily have been traced."

"You mean they tried to trick him then—"

"Exactly! That was fair, perhaps. But they played false with you as well."

"So they did. That's right. That's why Amboy died. But how—"

"I was interested at Amboy's," interrupted Cranston, quietly. "Detective Sergeant Markham gave us an excellent demonstration of how Peters Amboy might have died. But Markham was deluded by his belief in an invisible murderer.

"He mentioned—perhaps you remember it—that Amboy could have been killed while facing the wall. But he could not follow that theory because there was not sufficient space between Amboy and the wall.

"Yet Amboy did die while in that very position. The shot, Commissioner, came through the wall itself."

"Through the wall?"

"Yes. By way of the plug socket underneath the light switch. You remember it? The plug with the little hinged lid that dropped so easily into place?"

"I remember it," put in Cardona.

"Good," remarked Cranston. "Suppose, Cardona, that there is a similar switch and plug in the next apartment. Both on the same wiring. Picture a murderer stationed in the next apartment. A tricked murderer—one who has found a box containing blank paper—one who had planned this death beforehand.

"He comes to the empty apartment. He removes the light switch. He takes out the plug from Amboy's switch on the opposite side of the wall. He pushes a gun muzzle right through, into the darkened room on the other side."

"With the metal cap going up!" cried Cardona.

"Yes," agreed Cranston. "Then Amboy enters. He turns on the light. The murderer sees the glimmer. He fires at a man perfectly located. Back comes the gun. Down drops the metal plug cover—"

"And the killer fixes the whole works while Markham is looking at Amboy's body!" Cardona was excited. "All it took was nerve. Then a getaway from the empty apartment on the other side of the building!"

"Most amazing!" declared Commissioner Barth, sternly. "Yet it does you no credit, Cranston. A man has died tonight—Wallace Norgan—and you could have saved his life."

"Yes," admitted Cranston, in a solemn tone. "Unfortunately, I was too late in my arrival. I intended to be here, but"—a slight smile—"other matters detained me."

"Something more important than the saving of a human life?"

"Hardly"—keen eyes turned to note Crofton, half asleep in his chair. To The Shadow, Crofton, honest but duped, was more valuable a man than Norgan. "It was a matter of choice, Commissioner. However, I saw no danger for Norgan. If he had gone through with what he started, giving up funds that did not rightfully belong to him, he would not have died.

"But, apparently, he tried some trick. He blurted out the fact. That error cost him his life. Of course, had I been here, had I already revealed my theories—"

"Cranston," stormed Barth, "I extend you no thanks for what you have told us. We do not need your aid. Since you did not choose to speak before this, you can end your theorizing. I shall conduct the rest of this investigation."

"Very well." Cranston bowed slightly. "Suit yourself, commissioner. I believe that I have supplied enough information to enable Detective Cardona to furnish the rest. He is a capable man, Cardona. Given a clue, he seldom fails."

With that compliment, Lamont Cranston turned

and strolled from the room. His footsteps faded in the direction of the stairs.

WAINWRIGHT BARTH fumed. Then he turned to Joe Cardona.

"Bring Crofton with us," ordered Barth. "We are going downstairs into the living room."

Cardona roused Crofton. The others followed. In the living room, they found Markham, a police surgeon, and two detectives.

"Markham," said Barth, with sudden impulse, "hurry out and stop Mr. Cranston before he gets away. I want him to come back."

"Very well, sir."

Markham departed. Barth talked with the police surgeon; then ordered the prompt removal of Norgan's body. The corpse was taken out. Markham returned while it was on the way.

"Too late to catch him, Commissioner," he said. "The limousine had gone before I got there."

"Too bad," said Barth, sourly. "All right, Markham. Go down to the morgue with the body. Send the other men back to headquarters. Something else, also. Call the Cobalt Club and leave word for Mr. Cranston to communicate with me here."

Markham departed. Barth turned to Warlock and Darring. He made a comment.

"I was hasty," he admitted. "We owe much to Cranston. I see now that he was right. He wanted to wait until the Unseen Killer gained the spoils. That he might see him trapped with the goods.

"This man"—he indicated Crofton, half asleep in a chair—"is obviously innocent. There is no Unseen Killer—as such—but there is an unknown killer. He is the man we want. Cranston has proven that fact for us. A man smart enough to simply stay out of sight, without actually being invisible. He is the man we want—"

"And the man we can get," put in Cardona.

"If Cranston can furnish us with further clues," decided Barth.

"We have enough," returned Cardona. "He knew that when he left. He didn't have to tell us any more. He told us that there was no Unseen Killer. Well, if there wasn't, how did—"

Cardona paused as a sharp voice spoke from a few feet away. The detective turned; so did two others: Barth and Warlock. They were facing Marryat Darring. The black-haired man had drawn a pair of revolvers. He held the trio covered.

"How did I fight the Unseen Killer in the hall?" demanded Darring, with a laugh. "That was your question, eh? I'll answer it. I didn't fight him. I faked it. I'm the man you want!"

Darring's face had taken on a leer. His game of crime revealed, the master crook was gloating with the evil that he no longer could conceal.

CHAPTER XXII
WEALTH REGAINED

"SO it finally drilled through your head, eh?" questioned Darring, addressing Joe Cardona. "Filtered through the skull of the dumbest dick in the business."

"How long did you practice that act of yours?" retorted Joe. "Wrestling yourself, like you did in the hall?"

"A long time," acknowledged Darring. "That was part of the game—like the murders that I prepared. Trip Burgan was working for me. But I handled the killings myself.

"You're dumb, Cardona. But not so dumb as your boss, Barth. He pulled the prize muff, right here tonight, when he chased Cranston out. I wondered how long I could stall off while Cranston was here. But when he went, I felt easy.

"It will be curtains for the three of you, thanks to you again, Commissioner. Sending Markham away with the corpse. Well, when he comes back again, he'll find four more."

Darring paused. He held the others helpless. They were bunched together, three of them, under the muzzles of his guns. The fourth, Crofton, was still handcuffed. He could make no move, though he was wide awake by this time.

"Those three swindlers had plenty of easy money," remarked Darring, referring to Hildon, Amboy, and Norgan. "I saw that as soon as I took up the executive job with Centralized Power. I knew that they were too smart to have left a loophole for the law.

"You, Warlock, were a fool. I knew that when I looked into Professor Lessep's turbine inventions. When you told me about his scheme for devisualization, I knew the man was crazy. But it gave me an idea.

"Through Trip Burgan, I framed things with the professor. Trip did the talking. Lessep did not suspect that I was in it. He went through with the fake demonstration. Crofton vanished, as he told you.

"I wanted an Unseen Killer. One that I could use as a blind. That's why I had Trip Burgan tell a man named Crazy Lagran to turn stool. So Crazy could get Joe Cardona on Crofton's trail. It worked."

Joe Cardona glared angrily. He saw the rest. Crazy had been paid to give the tip-off. It worked two ways. It made Crofton a hunted man, marked as a killer. It also kept Crofton silent in the hideout that Trip had provided.

"The professor began to weaken," chuckled Darring. "I expected that. He kept calling up Trip. Something had to be done. Trip told him to ditch some of the apparatus. He did. I was with the rest of you. While we were looking for the missing lever, I put the bomb bulb in place.

"The professor did write himself that note—at Trip's suggestion. Well, his death added another boost to the stock of the Unseen Killer. It also put Crofton in a worse light than ever.

"Then, I began. I knew all about Hildon's house and Amboy's apartment. I had been both places, talking over matters that pertained to Centralized Power. I mailed them death notes—Norgan, too—and they failed to answer. So I killed Hildon. As Cranston elucidated."

Another chuckle. Darring was relishing this talk. He feared no interruption. In sneering fashion, he resumed:

"Amboy and Norgan double-crossed me. I found the black box. Loaded with blank paper. So I headed for the empty apartment and finished Amboy. I had no plan for killing Norgan. I knew he wouldn't dare to welch.

"But I gave him an extra day to think it over. Cardona pulled something in the interim. The dragnet. That meant bumping Crazy Lagran. Chuck Galla did the job. Neat enough to make Cardona think he had bumped into the Unseen Killer."

Darring paused a moment; then he glared venomously at Commissioner Barth who was blinking through his spectacles.

"You fool!" gloated Darring. "Cranston was right. Norgan should have been safe here tonight. But he tried some funny idea of his own—thinking that Warlock was behind the Unseen Killer's game.

"This house, that Warlock bought so cheaply, I fixed it and arranged its sale to Warlock. That's how he got the bargain. Why? So I could make it fit the Unseen Killer's game. Warlock was a good goat. I knew that if anyone began to wise up—like Norgan—he would blame Warlock because this was Warlock's house. Look, you fools!"

BACKING to the wall, Darring pressed the back of his hand against a spot near the rear doorway. A panel opened with a click.

Three men stared. They were looking into the interior of Warlock's wall safe. There, before their gaze, were the securities that Norgan had placed in the wall of Warlock's study.

"A dumbwaiter once," laughed Darring. "It made a perfect elevator. The upstairs safe has a solid front. But in back, the interior slides up and down.

When this box is on the ground floor, another container is on the second.

"When this goes up, the other rides clear to the third floor. When they put the black box in here, I came downstairs and pressed the molding. One safe lining slid down; the other lowered into its place.

"The same thing happened tonight. But Norgan must have suspected something. That's why he raised the fuss. Come here, Warlock"—Darring motioned with a gun—"and take a look inside. Don't touch those securities. Just tell me if you see anything else."

Warlock obeyed. Advancing, he peered into the opening. He nodded, falteringly, then spoke in a strained, quavering voice.

"I see a gummed label," he informed. "It is attached to the side of this interior—"

"So *that* was Norgan's trick!" snorted Darring. "Thought he ought to mark the inside of the safe. He didn't find the sticker after the swag was gone. He came hustling down to tell the police commissioner."

With a wag of one gun, Darring forced Warlock back to where Barth and Cardona were standing.

"I came here after the black box," he chuckled, "that night they left it in the wall safe. Started for my hotel with it, in a cab. I opened the box on the way and found it empty. That's why I went to kill Amboy. But tonight, the swag is here. I knew it would be; that's why I finished Norgan, when he began to talk smart. Well, you know now that there's no Unseen Killer. That's why I'm going to kill the lot of you, before you—"

He stopped. His eye had caught motion by the door. Turning his head, Marryat Darring stared squarely into a pair of burning eyes. There, in the doorway, stood the figure of The Shadow.

THE black-cloaked intruder had given no warning laugh. Only Darring had detected his arrival. Barth, Warlock, and Cardona were staring at Darring. Covered by the killer's guns, they did not dare to move.

From his chair, Miles Crofton spied the figure at the door. He smiled weakly. The Shadow had made good his promise.

Crofton, alone, was a witness of the deeds that followed. He saw the sweeping move that Marryat Darring made. He observed The Shadow's response.

Darring wheeled. Instinctively, he sidestepped, as he swung both guns toward the door. At the same instant, The Shadow shifted across the doorway. Crofton caught a glimpse of automatic muzzles.

A terrific roar filled the room as revolvers barked and automatics thundered. Tongued flame quivered from metal muzzles; pungent smoke wreathed upward from the weapons. Four shots seemed to come as one. Crofton stared.

No other shots were fired. Marryat Darring, his face venomous, stood like a statue. The Shadow, like a frozen silhouette, was rigid in the hallway. Then came the aftermath. Darring sagged.

The crook's arms fell. Revolvers clattered to the floor. The self-confessed killer sprawled forward. His rugged frame spread out upon the floor. Marryat Darring fell dead on the very spot where Wallace Norgan's corpse had lain but a little while before.

A strange laugh throbbed through the room. Like a whisper from a tomb, it brought a chilling awe with its terrible mockery. Paneled walls flung back sibilant echoes. Miles Crofton saw The Shadow swing away. He caught the flash of crimson—the lining of The Shadow's black-surfaced cloak.

Commissioner Barth sprang forward. He turned toward the hall. He saw no one. The Shadow had gone. Only the last vestige of a hissing echo seemed present in the room. Barth hastened toward the hall. Again, he was too late.

Joe Cardona was bending over Darring's body. He saw that the master crook was dead. Triumphant until the very last, he had met the death that he deserved. The man who had perpetrated the hoax of the Unseen Killer had gone, had paid the price of crime.

WHEN Lamont Cranston arrived at Warlock's house, a half hour later, he was greeted with a warm handshake by Commissioner Wainwright Barth. The official did not suspect the dual role that his friend had played. He knew only that Cranston had paved the way to the exposure of Darring's crimes.

Barth knew that someone—Crofton said The Shadow—had fired those shots from the hall. Whoever the deliverer, whatever his purpose, Barth was satisfied. Like Cranston, he held no grief for the three who had died: Hildon, Amboy, and Norgan.

Findlay Warlock had spread out the securities found in the lowered section of the safe. Wallace Norgan, fearing the Unseen Killer, had included all the spoils gained by himself and his associates.

Letters, agreements, options, together with cash and securities furnished proof of the game that the three had played. Shares of stock in companies that held riparian rights in Centralized Power territory were proof that the swindlers had planned their game long ahead.

Warlock's company could gain prompt settlement through this evidence. With funds returned; with stocks of other companies obtainable, the Centralized Power Corporation could reorganize to the benefit of the men who had honestly invested in its future.

Miles Crofton stood exonerated from all charges. Darring's statements, heard by Barth and Cardona, cleared him even of complicity in Melrose Lessep's hoax; for Crofton had been forced into the deal against his will.

To a man, those who had died had been engaged in illegal undertakings. But the greatest crook of the lot was the one who had led others to their destruction. Marryat Darring, truly the Unseen Killer, even though he had gained no fabled invisibility.

Challenger of the law, vulture who preyed on others of his kind, fiend who had even plotted the destruction of those who had done his bidding, Marryat Darring had met one master whose power he could not break. The Unseen Killer had failed before the might of The Shadow.

THE END

INTERLUDE by Will Murray

It was probably inevitable that the Master of Darkness would one day encounter an invisible man. Leave it to the ingenious Walter B. Gibson to turn the idea on its head in 1934's *The Unseen Killer.*

Of course, the true Shadow was not capable of actual invisibility. He was a master of stealth, able to blend into his shadowy surroundings thanks to his all-concealing black cloak and slouch hat. In fact, Walter Gibson often invoked the black-garbed Japanese Ninja warriors to explain some of The Shadow's stealthy tricks. But a lot of it was owed to the Black Art Illusion, whereby an illusionist dressed in ebony stepping before a black velvet backdrop would become functionally invisible.

With the increasing popularity of The Shadow radio program in the 1940s, Gibson felt obliged to include some of its mystical Shadow lore. He rein-terpreted it freely, ascribing to the Master Avenger a kind of practical psychological invisibility:

> Using the system of remaining absolutely immobile, with even his thoughts fixed, The Shadow was practicing the ways of the Tibetan mystics.
>
> It was their belief that such concentration could produce the equivalent of invisibility. Through experience, The Shadow had demonstrated that complete immobility did reduce an observer's chances to almost nil.
>
> It produced the semblance of a power through which he could cloud minds…

The device Gibson delineates in this story did not emerge strictly from his imagination. We know its true source. Early in 1934, news reports surfaced of a young British researcher who conducted public demonstrations of invisibility. These were published in various newspapers and in the May 1934 issue of *Popular Mechanics.*

In these demonstrations, a subject would step into an open cabinet wearing what was described as an "Electro-helmet" and "spectral man-tle": Attired in a futuristic diver's suit-style rig, he would appear to turn slowly invisible from the feet up, dematerializ-ing before the eyes of observers. Only a cone of light remained—the ray that supposedly accomplished the seeming miracle.

The operation was described by a *Popular Mechanics* writer this way:

> With both hands he touches contact gloves above his head and an electric current is switched on. As the current becomes stronger, it is claimed that the man seems to become transparent, then gradually vanishes, the feet disappearing first, followed by the rest of the body, and finally the head. The subject then is said to be tangible but not visible. Spectators are invited to verify the man's presence in the cabinet by a touch of the hand, and maintain they can feel he is still there but are unable to see him. Even the eye of the camera does not reveal the secret. Photographs taken during successive stages of the vanishing act, show only what the human eye perceives.

The unnamed inventor exhibited his device throughout London, photographs were published showing the stages of dematerialization, but nothing more seems to have been seen or heard of it since.

Whether or not this was a hoax, with his extensive background in illusion and stage magic, Walter Gibson probably suspected that it was and saw the obvious plot possibilities in these published accounts, and produced *The Unseen Killer,* which was written early in 1934, around the time the first reports were surfacing.

Two years later, two Hungarian researchers began demonstrating eerily similar devices, as reported in the October 1936 issue of *Modern Mechanix.*

The first, Adam Gosztonyi, demonstrated a phenomenon identical to the London researcher's, except no such apparatus as an Electro-helmet or spectral mantle was necessary. Using what he described as alternating "rays of invisible light" and shadow, Gosztonyi made individuals and even dancing chorus girls disappear, but from the head down, often leaving the feet visible for some reason.

  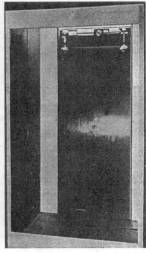

As with the man in the spectral mantle, the process was a gradual dematerialization.

Fellow Hungarian Stephen Pribil's device worked differently. Playing what were described as "invisible rays" on a small black-curtained tabletop cabinet, he showed that he could make objects like a colorful cigarette carton disappear. A hand thrust into the cabinet also turned invisible, and the sound of the unseeable fingers tapping an invisible object was audible. Pribil did the other experimenters one better: he also made radio cabinets transparent, then invisible, revealing the working tubes and innards within.

Like their counterpart in London, nothing more was ever heard of Gosztonyi and Pribil, and their "discoveries"—although Doc Savage appropriated Pribil's process in the 1938 novel *The Living-Fire Menace.*

We thought long and hard about whether or not to reprint *The Unseen Killer,* for it introduces a character who in the next novel becomes a full-fledged agent of The Shadow. Since the character has appeared in previous Nostalgia Ventures' reprints, there was a concern the story might be spoiled. Ultimately, we realized he had appeared in such a minor role, and *The Unseen Killer* is such a spectacular Shadow novel, that it would be a disservice not to bring this tale back into print.

Little is known of the inspiration for *The Golden Masks,* an exceptionally riveting Shadow novel that first appeared in the September 1, 1936 issue. Perhaps it was nothing more unusual than a desire to pit the Dark Avenger against a secret society similar to the Silent Seven, the Crime Cult and others of that ilk he had vanquished before.

Gibson had a strong interest in the occult, and wrote several books on the subject. In *The Mystic and Occult Arts: A Guide to Their Use in Daily Living,* co-authored with his wife Litzka, he told a fascinating anecdote about researching *The Golden Masks:*

> When I was writing the adventures of "The Shadow" and turning out two novels a month under the name of Maxwell Grant, I had to think up tricky devices whereby master criminals could accomplish their wicked designs. Sitting at my desk in my book-lined study in Maine, I decided that a clever device would be for crooks to raid a museum filled with odd, exotic masks, and then to wear them to hide their identities.
>
> But where would I obtain the data on such masks? From among my books, perhaps, but which book? Thus thinking, I looked through the bookshelves, passed by several, paused on two

volumes titled *Our Wonderful World,* which dealt with such subjects as great waterfalls, new ocean liners and huge skyscrapers, which I eliminated, and looked along to much more suitable books, including an encyclopedia.

> From sheer habit, I drew out the first volume of *Our Wonderful World,* which was wrong, as Volume II was the one that had the index. From further habit, I opened Volume I. Then, as I knew I didn't need it anyway, I started to put it back, but I first gave a passing glance to the opened page. It happened to be page 225, and the title, *Masks and Ceremonies of Magic,* which was the very subject that I wanted!

Gibson attempted to explain this phenomenon thusly:

> Closely analyzed, this example might be classed as an extension of ordinary senses, but with some surprising factors.
>
> Assuming that the article on Masks had been noted before—though the author had no recollection of such—it would require a strong photographic memory to bring it to the fore. Even more remarkable was the motor memory involved in opening the book to the exact page. You may have noted, in TV quiz programs, that persons gifted with photographic memory always make a conscious effort to stir it. Also, if you have ever tried to cut a pack of cards exactly in half, or want to try it now, you will realize they you must first make an estimate by the sense of sight; then confirm it by the sense of touch.
>
> But here, neither of those outer senses was in control. It was a case of looking elsewhere in opening the book and random. *Only the inner senses could have guided the action.* To charge it to mere coincidence would be no answer; out of dozens of books and hundreds of pages, the odds would have been too great. Hence, this sample is definitely acceptable as clairvoyance of the spontaneous type, especially since dozens of other cases could be cited that proved to be equally significant.

Street & Smith was a peculiar publishing house. It was so conservative that women were often absent from its pages. Yet it was surprisingly liberal in other respects. It was highly unusual to have any black characters in its pages beyond stereotypical waiters, railroad porters and the like.

But in *The Shadow,* Walter Gibson introduced Jericho Druke, the "giant African" in *The Chinese Disks.* In *The Golden Masks,* Jericho plays the largest role he ever played in a Shadow novel. By today's standards, of course, he's not a very well-developed personality. But by the lights of 1936, Druke was a radical departure from the prevailing view of black Americans.

Together these two novels display Walter Gibson's skills as a magician of the mysterioso as few other Shadow novels do. •

The Golden Masks

hid the faces of the most evil crew of killers The Shadow has ever opposed! But concealed under cover of black cloak and hat, the Master of Darkness unmasked the menace behind the gilded faces!

From the Private Annals of The Shadow, as told to

Maxwell Grant

CHAPTER I
FACES OF DOOM

THE outer office of the Oceanic Steamship Co. was deserted. The lights were out, but a big clock on the wall was visible. It showed the time as half past seven. The glow that revealed the clock dial came from the frosted panel of an inner office that bore the lettered statement:

JAMES LENGERTON
President

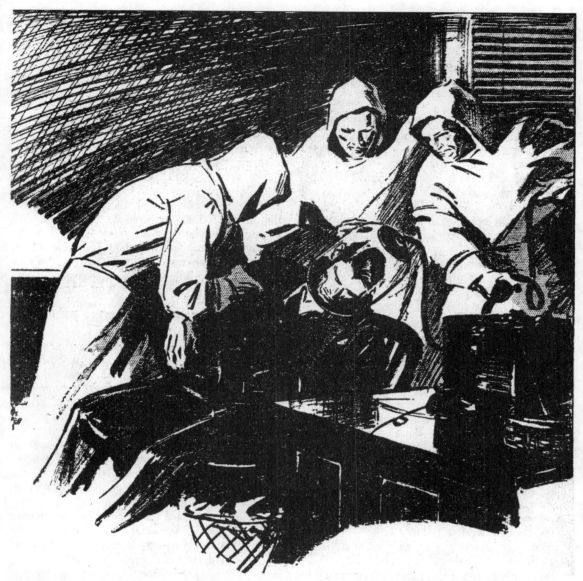

Within that private office, a tall, stoop-shouldered man was pacing the room in front of a large desk. This man was James Lengerton; his face, though firm, was haggard. At times, the steamship company president paused to thrust long, nervous fingers through his hair.

There was a *click* at the glass-paneled door. The barrier opened inward. Lengerton swung hastily; his face showed mingled expressions of suspicion and relief as his eyes recognized the man who had entered. The newcomer was a middle-aged man; square-built and of medium height. His face though passive, was as strained as Lengerton's.

"What brings you here, Froy?" questioned Lengerton.

"I received another letter," announced Froy, in a worried tone. "It came a short while ago. There was time to bring it here before eight o'clock."

"Let me see it." Froy handed an envelope to Lengerton. The latter noted that it was addressed to Burris Froy, 582 Exton Avenue, New York City. With shaking hands, Lengerton pulled the letter from the envelope; he scanned typewritten lines. Mechanically, he returned the letter to Froy.

"It specifies no new terms," declared Lengerton. "It is simply a reminder that I must have the cash ready by eight o'clock tonight."

"That is all," nodded Froy. "However, there is only half an hour remaining until eight o'clock."

"I know that, Froy. The cash is here. I shall leave the office before eight."

"Your decision is a wise one, Lengerton. I am sorry, though, that circumstances forced you to make it."

With this statement, Froy pocketed the letter. He turned about and went out through the door. He closed it behind him; Lengerton heard the footsteps fade away, then the muffled closing of the outer door.

MINUTES ticked by, while Lengerton continued his incessant pacing. Seven such minutes had passed when the glass-paneled door again opened. A droopy-faced man entered, stared in surprise at the sight of Lengerton.

The arrival was Lengerton's secretary, Sampler. It was plain that he had not expected to find his employer in the office. Stammering, Sampler stated that he had come for a file of shipping reports that he had intended to take home with him. The man's confusion was obviously honest. Lengerton cut Sampler short with a sudden remark.

"Sampler," declared Lengerton, "I am going to take you into my confidence, regarding a most serious matter."

Sampler nodded solemnly.

"Yesterday," reminded Lengerton, "a man named Burris Froy came here to see me. You remember him, Sampler. You ushered him into this office. He is a serious-looking chap. Very wealthy. A director in several banks."

Sampler repeated his nod.

"Recently," declared Lengerton, "Froy received an anonymous letter which he saw fit to show to me. It referred to certain securities that I purchased by proxy. Shares in Intercontinental Air Lines."

"You own such shares?" gasped Sampler, amazed. "Why, they have doubled in value, Mr. Lengerton! But—but Intercontinental Air Lines are expanding so rapidly that they threaten the shipping business—"

"Exactly," interposed Lengerton, tersely. "That is why I chose to control Intercontinental Air Lines. My shares cost me five hundred thousand dollars. Today, they are worth a million!"

"But—but if it were known that you owned those shares—"

"My standing in the shipping business would be ruined. That is why the letter was sent to Froy. It is blackmail, Sampler, with Burris Froy as the unwilling go-between. The letter threatened him with death if he did not communicate with me."

Turning about, Lengerton went to a safe behind his desk. He swung the metal door open; it was unlocked. Sampler gaped at sight of stacked currency, bundles of bank notes, all of thousand-dollar denomination.

"The terms were these," declared Lengerton, sourly. "I was told to unload all my holdings in Intercontinental Air Lines, which I did today, through my proxies. I was permitted to retain half a million, the amount of my original investment. That sum has been placed in the bank.

"The rest—an equal sum, all profits—you see before you. At eight o'clock tonight, the unknown blackmailer is to enter this office and pick up the money unmolested. That gives us"—Lengerton glanced at his watch—"less than twenty minutes to be out of here."

SAMPLER gaped helplessly. Lengerton seated himself behind the desk, drummed for a few moments, then yanked open a drawer. From it, he produced a stack of newspaper clippings, which he tossed on the desk with the comment:

"Look at these, Sampler."

The secretary did as directed. The clippings were ominous. They were of various dates; they were from newspapers in different cities. Each clipping carried its own strange tale. A few told of wealthy men, who had died suddenly.

Others mentioned important persons whose present whereabouts were unknown, but whose absence carried no suspicion of foul play. There were a few clippings that mentioned absent men who had returned; but who had refused to state where they had been. Sampler remembered several of these cases from the current news.

"Those came with the letter that Froy received," remarked Lengerton. "He believes that the people mentioned were victims of the blackmail ring. Some are dead; others are missing. Only the ones who will not talk have been allowed to return. Since their lips are sealed, it indicates that they must have experienced some terrible ordeal."

Lengerton gathered the clippings, thrust them into the desk drawer and angrily threw a sheaf of loose papers upon them. He glanced toward the open safe and grimaced. Lengerton did not relish the loss of a cool half a million.

"A double-barreled threat," mused the shipping president. "First, because I could not risk the exposure of my ownings in Intercontinental Air Lines. Second, the veiled warning of death or injury if I did not comply. Oddly, Sampler, it was the first threat that worried me. I would be willing to face the second."

"The first threat is ended, Mr. Lengerton," said Sampler. "Since you have already disposed of your airline holdings, there can be no exposure. At present, it is simply money that you must protect."

JAMES LENGERTON —president of the Oceanic Steamship Co.

A sharp gleam came to Lengerton's eyes. The gray-haired man pounded the desk with his fist. Hurriedly, Lengerton glanced at his watch. It showed twelve minutes before eight. Without further hesitation, Lengerton snatched up the telephone. Sampler listened while his employer called police headquarters.

Lengerton's statement was brief. He said simply that he was threatened by grave danger, that he must have protection before eight o'clock. After giving his name and office address, he promised that he would explain matters when the police arrived.

With a satisfied smile, Lengerton hung up the receiver. He glanced at his watch again and spoke to Sampler.

"I talked to an inspector named Cardona," declared Lengerton. "The fellow wasted no time over details. He says that he will be here with a squad of detectives in less than ten minutes. We have tricked our enemies, Sampler.

"Since eight o'clock is the deadline, they will wait until after that hour before they enter. If they are watching the office, they will probably think that I accidentally stayed too long. While they continue their vigil, the law will arrive."

Lengerton chuckled. His lips opened for another statement; suddenly, they froze. From his desk, Lengerton stared straight past Sampler, toward the door of the office. A horrified expression came upon Sampler's face, like a reflection of the terror that Lengerton had registered. Mechanically, Sampler turned about. He saw the sight that Lengerton had spied.

THE door of the office was open. Two men had silently stepped in from the darkened outer office. As they moved forward, side by side, three others followed, like slaves attendant upon their masters. The foremost pair had guns; the rear trio carried a cubical wooden box that measured more than a foot in each direction. The box was black, of ebony.

It was not the sight of leveled revolvers or the ominous black box that caused both Lengerton and Sampler to quail. The sight that horrified the trapped shipping president and his secretary was the appearance of the invaders themselves. They looked like monsters, those intruders; creatures who had shed their human features.

Each was clad in a robe of dull gold, with cowl-like headpiece that encircled cheeks and forehead. Each wore thin gauntlets of the same material. Their faces, amazingly lifelike, were also of gold. For a moment, Lengerton and Sampler thought that these were real countenances, gilded.

The trapped men then realized that such was not the case. The answer lay in the fact that every one of the five faces was identical. The leaders, with their glimmering revolvers; the followers, with their ebony box—any one of the group could have passed for another.

Each golden face carried an insidious expression. Each visage was perfect in formation; that fact simply added to the demonish touch. Golden lips were curved in half smiles that boded no mercy.

The only difference—and it was scarcely detectable—lay in the eyes that stared from golden sockets. There was variance in the colors of the five pairs of eyes.

The golden faces were masks, beaten from metal that was almost pure. Their thinness gave them realism, despite the fact that the golden features were immobile. Each mask hid the real face behind it; but the golden smiles seemed to tell the feeling that was held by every evil heart.

These Golden Masks were fiends to the core. They had come to claim wealth that they had demanded. Finding that their terms had not been obeyed, they were prepared to deal punishment upon the pair of helpless victims who cowered by the desk.

CHAPTER II
BEFORE THE LAW

AS he shrank before the threat of the Golden Masks, James Lengerton realized the error that he had made. He wished that he had closed and locked the safe; to leave with Sampler and meet the police outside the building. Such a move might have tricked these golden-garbed invaders.

Another thought flashed through Lengerton's brain. The Golden Masks must have guessed that he intended to offset their game. The fact that he had remained within his office almost until eight o'clock had been their cue for entry.

One of the two leaders snarled a command that produced no motion of the metal lips. Immediately, the three followers stepped to the desk. They placed the ebony box there and opened it. Another snarl made Lengerton stare at the enemy in front of him; hence the shipping president did not see what the box contained. Sampler observed it, however. The secretary gasped.

One of the golden-faced servitors was removing a large glass cylinder from the box. The cylinder was inverted; its mouth was covered with a sheet of rubber, that had a central slit. Sampler saw a rubber hose stretch snakily from the box as the Golden Mask lifted the cylinder high above his head. The hose formed a tubular connection between cylinder and box.

The cylinder came downward. From in back of Lengerton, the man who held the cylinder clamped it over the shipping president's head. Lengerton started a struggle; the other two servitors promptly gripped him, one on either side. Clamped between these captors, Lengerton could scarcely writhe.

The victim made a grotesque sight, his haggard face staring through the rounded wall of glass. The rubber cap beneath the cylinder had tightened about Lengerton's neck; his head was in an air-tight container.

The struggle that Lengerton made did not last long. The man who had capped his head within the cylinder reached a golden gauntlet into the black box. Fingers pressed a lever. A hissing sound followed.

Sampler saw a yellowish gas issue into the cylinder. The vapor coiled about Lengerton's head; increasing, the yellow cloud obscured the victim's face. Sampler caught one last glimpse of Lengerton's face; he could tell that his employer's breath had given out. Lengerton was forced to inhale the yellowish gas.

THE effect was completed in less than a minute. Lengerton's body sagged back into the chair behind the desk. His head tilted sidewise, carrying the glass cylinder to a precarious angle.

The men who held Lengerton let him slump; one of them caught the toppling cylinder and lifted it clear of the victim's head. Lengerton's neck wobbled; his head tilted backward and thumped against the back of the chair. One of the Golden Masks placed the cylinder back into the black box.

The other two raised Lengerton. The victim was staring, with goggly eyes, as though everything before his gaze was distorted. His muscles lacked action; but his body was loose, like that of a jointed puppet. He seemed to understand when one of the servitors snarled for him to walk; but he was unable to respond to the command.

Supporting their victim, the two Golden Masks moved Lengerton away from the desk. His legs acted mechanically, their footsteps draggy, as the two servitors walked him toward the door.

The last of the three masked underlings closed the black box and lugged it with him as he followed the others toward the door. Forgetful of his own plight, Sampler stared after them. He heard the draggy footsteps cross the outer office; he listened as the hallway door thumped shut.

Three of the Golden Masks had departed with their prisoner. Overwhelmed by the strange gas, Lengerton had reached a condition that made his removal easy. What Lengerton's fate would be, Sampler could not guess. Vaguely, the secretary realized that the Golden Masks had conquered Lengerton within a few minutes after their arrival. There would still be an interval before the police arrived.

During that period, Sampler knew that he would be at the mercy of the two Golden Masks who had remained. They were the leaders of the insidious throng. They stood with ready revolvers, holding Sampler prisoner. They did not intend to give him the gas treatment; for the ebony box and its glass cylinder were gone.

Had Sampler used reason, he would have seen that his own cause was not hopeless. Lengerton's money was still in the open safe. The leaders of the Golden Masks had further business here. It would serve them best to postpone murder until they were ready for departure. Given five minutes longer, the police would arrive.

Sampler's proper course was to stall, to plead with the Golden Masks; to promise them anything that would delay them. In his terror, the secretary did not grasp the possibilities that such a policy offered. He wanted a chance for flight; and he thought he saw such opportunity.

The leaders of the Golden Masks had turned toward the door. They were listening intently, even after footsteps had died. They wanted to be sure that their followers had made an unhampered get-away with James Lengerton.

The fixed stares on the golden faces made Sampler think that neither of the two men could see him. Shakily, Sampler edged along the desk. He gave a sudden spring toward the man who stood nearest to him.

THE golden-masked rogue spun away, with a fierce snarl. Sampler lunged wide. He was stopped by a sudden jab of the masked man's right hand. The Golden Mask thrust his revolver muzzle against Sampler's ribs; the gauntleted fist went deep beneath the secretary's coat. As Sampler tried to twist away, the Golden Mask fired.

The report was muffled by the folds of Sampler's coat. The secretary jolted; smoke coiled outward from his vest. With distorted lips that failed to give cry, Sampler sagged sidewise, flattened on the floor in front of the desk. The man with the gun looked down at his victim's sprawled body. The unchanged smile upon the Golden Mask seemed to denote the murderer's evil pleasure.

The other Golden Mask looked toward his comrade. His metal smile looked like an expression of approval. Calmly, both men put away their revolvers, pocketing them through slits at the sides of their robes.

One went to the safe, brought out the wads of currency and placed the money on the desk. The other found a cardboard box on a table in the corner. Together, they thumbed the cash, then packed their ill-gained wealth in the box.

Sampler's death had produced one result. Because the shot had been completely muffled, the

One of the members of the Golden Masks

Golden Masks showed no hurry. They were oblivious to the fact that the law was on its way here. They took four full minutes for work that they could have accomplished in less than two.

One of the evil pair tucked the pasteboard box beneath his arm. The other went to the door, turned the knob, just as his companion pressed the light switch. The inner office was plunged in darkness, just as the door came inward. Simultaneously, the man with the box remembered an important item. He snarled two words:

"The clippings—"

The other stopped him, with an evil hiss, pointed a gauntleted finger across the outer office, toward the door to the hall. Though both offices were almost completely dark, the rogue with the box detected his companion's gesture and looked in the direction indicated.

The outer door had a glass panel, like the one between the offices. Beyond it was the light of the hallway, dimmed because of the frosted glass. Nevertheless, it formed a semitransparent frame. Against that glass, visible from where the Golden Masks stood, was a shadowed outline that made both villains reach instantly for their revolvers.

THE shadow against the glass was a silhouette that showed a hawklike profile, topped by the brim of a slouch hat. Motionless, it formed an uncanny symbol—a shape that might have stood alone, without human form to produce it. Despite their evil prowess and the darkness that covered them, the Golden Masks were halted by the sight.

The Golden Masks were men of crime. They recognized the silhouette that blocked the hallway light. The hawkish profile told them that their trail had been crossed, that their path was covered by a master foeman whose presence meant destruction for workers of evil.

That superfoe had arrived just after the servitors had taken James Lengerton away. Though too late to deal with minions, he was in time to meet the perpetrators of crime, to halt the escape of the two leaders who had seen to the murder of Sampler.

That sinister profile against the door belonged to The Shadow. It symbolized a master of crime detection, whose ways were many, whose moves were hidden. Other crooks had seen that silhouette that marked the advent of The Shadow. They had learned—through their own doom—that it was futile to attempt open battle with an enemy whose actual form they could not see.

Evil though they were, the two Golden Masks feared to move. They crouched by their inner doorway, hoping to evade the search of eyes that they felt might penetrate the frosted outer pane.

Their revolvers were drawn; but the fingers within the golden gauntlets were numbed by fear. Neither rogue dared fire. A shot might prove useless; if so, it would be answered by a peal of mocking mirth. The Shadow would know the location of his huddled enemies.

Great was the terror that had gripped Lengerton and Sampler at the sight of the Golden Masks. Much of that same horror now held the Golden Masks themselves. Their golden garb was a mere masquerade that hid their actual identities. The blackness that enveloped The Shadow was a shroud that rendered him vague and invisible.

As the clock in the outer office ticked off the passing seconds, the masked murderers waited, banking all upon the hope that The Shadow would depart. That seemed their only chance of safety against this famed invader who had arrived before the law.

CHAPTER III
THE LAW'S BLUNDER

TEN seconds passed. Staring, the Golden Masks saw a slow motion of the silhouette beyond the frosted door. With eerie glide, the profile faded to one side. It did not return. Complete silence persisted until a slight click sounded from the outer hall. The dim light was extinguished. Total blackness reigned.

Without knowing it, the Golden Masks had held a temporary advantage. The Shadow had come to the office of the Oceanic Steamship Co.; just outside the outer door, he had discerned the light from the inner office. About to investigate, The Shadow had halted when the Golden Masks extinguished the inner light and opened the connecting door.

With no chance to fade away unseen, The Shadow had held his ground. He knew that men within the office would see his blackened silhouette; therefore, he had remained motionless, to make them think that his outlined profile was a ruse. The Shadow timed his stay to perfection; when he did withdraw, his deliberate move still bluffed the Golden Masks.

It was not until The Shadow pressed the hall switch that the rogues realized how close he had been to the outer door. Their knowledge came too late. The Shadow had gained the element that he wanted: darkness. The Golden Masks could risk no light. They were bottled in the office; there, The Shadow intended to keep them until their nerves reached a breaking point.

The Golden Masks were in a tight spot. If this situation had continued for a few minutes longer, they would have been due for a startling surprise. The Shadow had outguessed them; luck was all upon which the Golden Masks could depend. Chance favored them beyond all hope.

ONE minute after the hall light had gone out, the Golden Masks heard a distant sound, like the thud of approaching footsteps. It lasted for a few short seconds; The Shadow must have heard it also, for it came from beyond the hallway door.

The noise ended; without warning, a glare of light flooded the outer hall. Someone had approached to find the hall lights extinguished. The new arrival had supplied the brilliance of a bull's-eye lantern.

The flooding light showed a sight that the Golden Masks had not anticipated. The door from the hall was halfway open. Across the threshold was an unmistakable figure, cloaked in black. It was The Shadow, his gloved left hand upon the doorknob, his right gripping a mammoth automatic.

The light had come at a most inopportune instant. Had The Shadow been less advanced into the office, he could have dived away along the hall before the big light was flashed.

Had he been given a few seconds more, he could have sprung past the door which he had so stealthily opened. By finding darkness in the office, he could have shot it out with the surprised Golden Masks.

As it was, The Shadow stood trapped. His tall form was completely visible to the Golden Masks. Shouts from the hall told that he had been spied by the new invaders. The Shadow needed split-second speed in this emergency. He showed it.

Counting the men within the office as the most dangerous, because of their preparedness, The Shadow took his chances with those in the hall. Spinning outward, he wheeled and dashed along the corridor, away from the revealing light.

The Golden Masks came to life as The Shadow whirled. They fired rapidly with their revolvers; but The Shadow was gone too rapidly. Useless bullets bashed the far wall of the hallway, beyond the opened outer door.

The shouts in the hall were louder. Guns began to bark; at the end of the corridor, The Shadow heard bullets whiz past him. He swung into a side passage; heavy-footed pursuers dashed after him. The Shadow knew the false situation that he had encountered.

The men with the lantern were headquarters detectives. Sent to cover Lengerton's office, they had gone after the first intruder whom they saw there. The shots fired by the Golden Masks had simply spurred on the excited dicks. Without stopping to reason, they supposed that Lengerton and others who needed help had opened fire on the black-clad intruder at the office door.

As The Shadow raced along the side passage, the light reached the turn behind him. From a stairway ahead, two more detectives sprang up to block The Shadow's flight. The Shadow met the first man head-on, sprawled him to the stairs with a swift uppercut. As the second detective fired hastily, The Shadow grappled with him and swung the man between himself and the light.

The detectives at the turn could not fire; for their comrade was toward them. Hanging onto the fellow, The Shadow was prepared to haul him down the stairs, away from gun range. Just then, a chance incident started a new commotion.

One detective flashed a light back along the main corridor, to sight two figures hurrying from Lengerton's office. One glimpse told him that they were enemies. The Golden Masks were staging a getaway; they stopped the instant that the light flashed upon them.

Both crooks fired. The detective with the light dropped, wounded. Brief sight of the Golden Masks was lost; amid the gunfire, another detective doused the bull's-eye lantern. Blindly, the detectives fired along the darkened hall. The Golden Masks had dashed in the direction from which the headquarters men had originally come. The crook who carried the swag clung to it.

NEW shouts arose as the Golden Masks reached the beginning of the corridor. A loud, gruff voice was that of Inspector Joe Cardona. He had ordered his men ahead; he was moving up with others when the Golden Masks encountered them on a wide stairway by the elevators.

Arms slashed; guns blasted wildly; flashlights glimmered, to be knocked from the hands that held them. Fleeing men clattered down the stairway. The Golden Masks had broken through, unscathed.

Far distant, The Shadow heard the commotion. The detectives at the turn of the passage were dashing to join Cardona in pursuit of the Golden Masks.

The Shadow flung off the man with whom he grappled, left him at the top of the little stairway and dashed downward. It was The Shadow's only chance to head off the Golden Masks when they reached the street.

There were three flights to the bottom. The Shadow came out through a doorway that opened on a passage beside the building.

Shots were booming when The Shadow reached

the front sidewalk. A big sedan careened from the curb; revolvers spat from its windows as the automobile fled. Cardona and three detectives fired wasted shots. The Golden Masks were off to a getaway. No police cars were on hand to chase them, for Cardona had made his approach to the building a secret one.

There was a taxi near the curb, a little below the building. Before the police spied it, The Shadow sprang toward the cab. As he neared the taxi, he came into view. A detective shouted as he saw The Shadow, raised his arm to fire. Before the dick could fire, Cardona grabbed his arm and knocked the man's gun upward.

Joe Cardona had also spied The Shadow. An ace sleuth, the inspector recognized the cloaked combatant. Quicker in thought than the detective was with the trigger, Cardona not only saved The Shadow from a chance bullet; he also realized how great a mistake had been made.

If Cardona had guessed beforehand that The Shadow intended to visit Lengerton's, the inspector would have ordered his squad to stay in the background. Unfortunately, the law had bungled.

The Shadow snapped an order as he boarded the cab. The driver, a chance hackie who had parked near Lengerton's building, was quick in response. He heard a fierce whisper that commanded him to follow the car that had fled.

THE SHADOW'S commandeered cab sped past gaping detectives, who still could not guess why Cardona had ordered them to stand by. The taxi took the corner; the driver spied the car that carried the Golden Masks. The fleeing sedan was turning a corner two blocks ahead. It had gained too good a start.

When the taxi reached that corner, the sedan was out of sight. Though he did his best, the cab driver failed to pick up its trail as he threaded from street to street.

The Shadow ordered him to halt the cab. The driver obeyed. A five-dollar bill wavered past the hackie's shoulder and flipped to his lap. Clutching the unexpected fare, the cab driver looked into the back of the car, hoping to see his passenger. The cab was empty. The Shadow had dropped off into the night, closing the door silently behind him.

The Shadow, always in touch with important financial matters, had learned earlier that large sales had been made in Intercontinental Air Lines. Through confidential channels, he had gained sufficient data to link James Lengerton with the stock sales. Scenting mystery, The Shadow had paid that surprise visit to Lengerton's office. Ghostlike, he had arrived to trap the leaders of the Golden Masks. But the law's blunder had allowed a pair of master crooks to escape.

Though he had not even seen his superfoes, The Shadow had observed previous evidence of their depredations. Tonight, he had come closer to the Golden Masks than before. The Shadow was confident that his next endeavor would bring him face to face with these master criminals. All that The Shadow needed was one more clue.

Strangely, that clue would soon be in the making. New twists of circumstances were destined to bring The Shadow adventures of a sort that even he had never before experienced.

CHAPTER IV
MASKED MEN MEET

IT was midnight. Four hours had passed since the events at Lengerton's office. The early editions of the morning newspapers had reached the streets of Manhattan; newsboys were already selling them at Times Square. These "bulldog" extras carried sensational news concerning what had taken place at Lengerton's office. It had been inserted as a stop-press item.

"Big skyscraper moider—"

As a newsboy shouted the statement, a peak-faced man stopped to purchase an extra. The man was carrying a suitcase in his left hand; to it was attached a tag that bore the printed name of Clifford Sulgate. The initials on the suitcase corroborated the tag; for the letters were C. S.

With his free hand, Sulgate fumbled for change, found a quarter and gave it to the newsie. He did not wait for the twenty-three cents that the newsboy started to return to him. Instead, Sulgate walked hastily away and did not stop until he had reached the nearest corner.

There, by the light from a pineapple juice stand, Sulgate scanned the headlines.

Clifford Sulgate was the type of man whom one would expect to see near Times Square at midnight. He was dressed in a tuxedo; over that attire he wore a lightweight overcoat. His head was topped by an expensive Derby hat. Apparently, he had been to the theater, for a program was sticking out from his overcoat pocket. However, there was nothing in Sulgate's manner to indicate that he had enjoyed the show.

Sulgate's face was not only pale and dryish, but was almost the color of the gray hair that showed below his Derby. His lips twitched; his eyes kept blinking. As he studied the newspaper, he set down his suitcase in order to adjust his rimless spectacles. He fidgeted with the glasses until he had them as he wanted them; even then, his blinking and twitching were as frequent as before.

Sulgate's lips ceased their twitching when the nervous man chewed them tightly. Folding the newspaper, Sulgate thrust it into his pocket with the program. He picked up his suitcase and hurried along Broadway, noting the street numbers at each crossing. Several blocks above Times Square, Sulgate turned westward.

On the dimmer street, he paused to look at parked taxicabs. Enterprising drivers leaned out and called to the prospective passenger. Sulgate ignored the hackies until he came to one who was at the wheel of a green cab. The driver had his flag down, to indicate that the cab was hired. Spying Sulgate, the cab, driver gave a nod of recognition. Sulgate entered the taxi.

THE cab started eastward; it turned right on Broadway, then right again, on a westbound street. Away from the glare of Times Square, the driver calmly pressed a special lever located at his left. The effect was unusual.

Thick, tight-fitting blinds dropped at every window in the cab. Clifford Sulgate was confined in complete darkness. Moreover, sharp *clicks* denoted that the pressure of the lever had locked the rear doors.

The driver chose a twisting course; he drove the cab steadily, but without great speed.

Fifteen minutes later, the taxi pulled into a narrow alleyway between two bare-walled buildings. Continuing through the close-walled channel, it came to an inner courtyard. There, the cab wheeled about. The driver pulled the lever; blinds came up and doors unlocked. Clifford Sulgate stepped out, carrying his suitcase.

There was a dim door at one side of the court. Sulgate entered it, found the door of an elevator. He pressed a button; an elevator thrummed downward, on a long, slow trip.

When the car arrived, Sulgate opened the door and entered. The elevator was dark. Sulgate closed the door behind him. That done, he pressed a light switch. The elevator was illuminated; its glow showed Sulgate's twitching lips and blinking eyes.

Hastily, Sulgate took off his spectacles and put them into a case which he placed in an overcoat pocket. He doffed his overcoat and dropped it to the floor, with his Derby. He pressed an elevator button that bore the word "Up"; as the car ascended, Sulgate hurriedly opened the suitcase.

Gold cloth glimmered as the nervous man drew a long robe from the bag. Sulgate slipped the golden garb over his shoulders. From the bag, he brought another article—a mask of thin, beaten gold. He placed the mask on his face; kept it in place by adjusting the robe's hood about it. The edges of the hood completely covered every trace of Sulgate's gray hair.

From a man of ordinary, almost shrinking appearance, Sulgate had become a robed creature of insidious ilk. His metal face looked lifelike; its mold, its smile were identical with those of the Golden Masks who had invaded Lengerton's office.

The elevator reached the top of the shaft. The trip had been a long one; the floor at which it finally stopped was certainly a considerable distance above the ground. There was no way of determining the exact height, however, for the walls of the elevator were entirely closed and gave no glimpse of the floors that were passed.

Sulgate opened the door. He stepped into a gloomy, square-walled room, that had a golden door on the opposite side. A huge African was standing there as guard.

He was attired in a native costume, a leathery shirt crossed by a leopard pelt. The native's arms and legs were bare; they glistened like ebony beneath the light. The guard's muscles tightened; he raised a stocky war spear as Sulgate approached.

The guard was a full six feet six in height; he towered menacingly above the masked arrival. Sulgate stopped and spoke a password:

"Ashanti."

The guard lowered his spear. Sulgate approached the door and gave another countersign:

"Kumasi."

The African guard gripped a knotty handle in the center of the golden doorway. He pulled the barrier outward; let it close as Sulgate passed. That done, the guard brought Sulgate's bag, coat and hat from the elevator and stacked them with others that were in a corner by the elevator. The guard closed the elevator door, went back to his post, to await newcomers.

SULGATE, meanwhile, had entered a room where a strange scene was in progress. The room was well lighted; all about its walls were golden hangings, costly draperies that reflected their dull, yellow hue. Within the room was a throng of motionless men; more than a dozen, all attired in the same garb as Sulgate.

Metal faces looked toward the new arrival; all bore the same half smile that Sulgate's golden features carried. The only variance lay in the eyes that stared through the masks. Clifford Sulgate had arrived at a meeting of the Golden Masks; his own attire, his knowledge of the passwords, marked him as a member of that evil band. It was necessary, however, that he identify himself within the meeting room.

At the far wall stood a raised platform; it was set back in the wall like a small stage. Two of the Golden Masks were seated upon that dais, each on a golden throne. They were the leaders of the Golden Masks. Sulgate approached them. He spoke to the Golden Mask who sat upon the left.

CLIFFORD SULGATE— Wall Street business promoter

"I am Mu," declared Sulgate. His tone echoed, for the ceiling above the platform was a low one. "I speak to Alpha."

"Alpha replies to Mu," returned the seated man, solemnly. "Mu will give the first countersign."

"Ashanti."

Sulgate waited a few moments, then turned to the figure on the right. He spoke again:

"I am Mu. I speak to Omega."

"Omega replies to Mu," answered the second leader. "Mu will give the second countersign."

"Kumasi."

The procedure finished, Sulgate joined the crowd of Golden Masks who were standing about the room. Like them, he faced the platform, where Alpha and Omega sat with folded arms.

To Sulgate, the scene was not a new one; for he had long been a member of the Golden Masks. Nevertheless, the setting chilled him. Faces of gold were ominous; though he wore one that was identical, Sulgate felt a secret fear amid this masked throng. Even to a member of the organization, the Golden Masks were a mystery; for those like Sulgate had never gained complete initiation.

ONLY two of the group knew the real identities of all. Those two were Alpha and Omega, silent upon their thrones. All others were forced to go through the same routine as Sulgate; they were brought here by taxicabs, behind shaded windows and locked doors. The taxi drivers knew the faces of the men whom they were delegated to meet; but they did not know their names.

Those taximen were mere underlings, who knew the power of the Golden Masks and feared it; they maintained secrecy also because they were promised membership in the Golden Masks after their terms of apprenticeship were served.

Every member, like Sulgate, had a Greek letter name by which he identified himself. While the group remained motionless, another Golden Mask entered. He identified himself as Omicron, speaking to Alpha and Omega, as Sulgate had.

Sulgate often wondered who those leaders could be. All were capable of treachery; all were obedient to orders. All felt security in evil dealings, because of the protective power that the crooked society gave them. The Golden Masks formed a chain of graspers who used crime for profit.

Sulgate was a member of that chain; but tonight, he felt that he might be its weakest link. Sulgate had played a definite part in the move that the Golden Masks had made against James Lengerton.

Sudden regrets had seized Clifford Sulgate. Remorse was not the only emotion that gripped him. Sulgate was qualmish, fearful for his own safety. He was satisfied with the wealth that was already his; he had gained all that he wanted through association with the Golden Masks. Until this Lengerton affair, Sulgate had not been used as an instrument in crime. His present fear was that he would be employed again, more openly than before. That was more than he wanted.

Thanks to his golden mask, none could see the twitching lips and blinking eyes of Clifford Sulgate.

CHAPTER V
THE DESERTER

THE meeting of the Golden Masks had opened. A venomous voice was snarling gloating words. Alpha was the speaker; his statements referred to tonight's crime. The leader spoke facts that concerned Clifford Sulgate.

"Thanks to Member Mu," announced Alpha, "we learned that James Lengerton held a controlling interest in Intercontinental Air Lines. Lengerton's position in the shipping industry was such that he could not afford to let the fact be known."

A pause. Sulgate saw eyes turn in his direction. He repressed the nervous shudders that came over him. The tremor of his robed shoulders was scarcely visible.

"We required contact with Lengerton," resumed Alpha. "We chose a man whose complicity would not be suspected. He carried our message to Lengerton—and handled it capably. Allow me to congratulate you, Member Delta."

With a golden gauntlet, Alpha indicated a robed man who stood close to Sulgate. Member Delta gave a slight bow in acknowledgment, drew his shoulders proudly upward. His mask formed an impressive screen in front of his actual face. Had it been lifted, the features of Burris Froy would have been revealed.

Member Delta was the banker who had visited Lengerton with the anonymous communications. Those had been faked for Lengerton's benefit. It was true that no suspicion had been placed upon Member Delta.

Lengerton, in his talk with Sampler, had taken it for granted that Froy had acted in good faith. In calling the police, Lengerton had not mentioned Froy's name.

"We had trouble with Lengerton, however," concluded Alpha, dryly. "Those difficulties were overcome through the power of the Golden Masks. Member Omega will tell you how capably we handled the situation."

Omega bowed to Alpha, then addressed the throng in an insidious tone that was the counterpart of Alpha's.

"Lengerton placed half a million dollars in his safe," stated Omega, "to be there for our collection. Alpha and I went to the office in person, accompanied by three of our members. We awaited Lengerton's departure. He delayed.

"That delay was a sign that we did not like. It showed that Lengerton lacked proper respect for our threats. We entered before the stated hour. We found Lengerton in conference with his secretary. They had called the police—a fact which we learned later.

"Alpha and I lost no time. We ordered our followers to give Lengerton the proper treatment. They applied it and carried him away. We had been liberal with Lengerton, allowing him to keep half of the proceeds from his stocks. Since we hold him prisoner, we shall force him to disgorge the funds that he preserved."

Gloated chuckles of approval came from the Golden Masks who stood about Sulgate. The nervous man joined; his chortle was hollow, for his lips were dry, were twitching inside their mask. Sulgate's fellow members did not note his forced tone.

"As for the secretary," added Omega, "his death was necessary, for Lengerton had confided in him. The secretary's name, so Member Delta tells us, was Sampler. My companion, Alpha, disposed of Sampler with a single bullet."

There was a new buzz of commendation. Omega waited until all was quiet, then added a triumphant sequel to his account.

"The police arrived to trap us," he announced. "They learned the futility of combat with two members of the Golden Masks. We departed through their very midst. With us, we carried Lengerton's half a million dollars as a contribution to our cause."

THE proud statement brought restrained applause from the thronged members. Alpha and Omega exchanged dark-eyed glances. They had agreed to create the impression that they had handled a simple task. Wisely, they had refrained from mention of the actual circumstances that had aided them: the presence of The Shadow.

It was Alpha who broke the pause. He came to new business; a sort that pleased the members with its promise of further gain.

"Through one of our members," announced Alpha, "we have learned of a man who possesses great wealth that he can afford to lose. I shall not state the name of the member who brought this information; nor shall I disclose the identity of our future victim. I shall, however, appoint a member to contact the person whose wealth we intend to gain."

While Alpha was speaking, Omega reached in the slitted pocket of his robe and brought out a parchment scroll. He unrolled it; brought it to Alpha. Together, the leaders studied the scroll and nodded. It was Omega who spoke.

Gazing at the throng he announced:

"As a reward to Member Mu for his past cooperation, we shall appoint him to the duty of new contact. Member Mu, you will find your instructions on this scroll."

Both leaders were looking straight toward Sulgate. The nervous man was rooted where he stood by fear.

The evil leaders waited. Sulgate's legs came back to life. Swaying slightly as he approached the platform, Sulgate steadied as he reached the leaders. Summoning all his grit, he stared up toward the pair, reached out his right hand and took the scroll with his golden gauntlet, then returned to his place.

The rest of the meeting was chaos to Sulgate. The leaders spoke of other matters. Various members made reports. Sulgate scarcely heard a word that passed. He managed only to thrust the scroll within his robe and maintain a firm position on the floor.

When the meeting ended, Alpha and Omega resumed their thrones. The other members started toward the door, leaving Sulgate resting alone and conspicuous in the center of the floor. Suddenly realizing his position, Sulgate got up and followed the departing members.

Sulgate was the last man to take the elevator. He sagged when he stood alone; the car was halfway to the ground before he could summon strength enough to divest himself of his mask and his robe.

THE outside darkness nerved Sulgate somewhat; for there was only one taxi in the courtyard. It was the one that had brought him to the meeting. Sulgate entered the cab; when the curtains clicked shut, he sank back upon the cushions.

During the trip, his breath sounded in long, deep gasps. Though he was away from the meeting of the Golden Masks, Sulgate did not feel safe while still within this vehicle that the organization owned.

The cab dropped Sulgate near Times Square. City lights gave him courage; the glare also served as an excuse for the blinking of his eyelids, which he could not control. Sulgate had put on his spectacles; they improved his vision and gave him more confidence. Knowing that the taxi driver might be watching him, Sulgate did his best to appear steady as he walked away with his suitcase.

Sulgate went directly to the taproom of a large hotel. The place was only half filled; he chose a table near a side door and parked his hat and coat with the suitcase, on a chair at the right of the table. The gray-haired man then ordered a stiff drink; when he had finished it, he followed with another. Then he got up and headed toward a phone booth.

His fingers shook badly as he dialed a number. He had to begin the process over again. At last, Sulgate managed the connection. He seemed reassured by the drawly voice that answered.

"Hello, Bronden..." Sulgate gulped as he spoke the name. "Yes, this is Mr. Sulgate... Bronden, I—I can stand it no longer!... Tonight is the time for the break. I shall join you within the next hour...

"No, no!" Sulgate's tone was excited. "Not at home! I would not dare come there, Bronden... Yes, you must leave at once. Be sure that no one knows that you have left; that no one follows you... Yes, meet me at the apartment... You say that everything is ready there? Good!..."

COMING from the telephone booth, Sulgate mopped his forehead with a handkerchief. He returned to his table; a waiter approached and Sulgate ordered another drink. Nervously, he polished his glasses, put them back on his nose and looked about as if testing them. It was an excuse to see if any newcomers had entered. Sulgate saw none.

When the waiter returned, Sulgate asked for the check and paid it. He gulped part of his drink, but did not finish it. Just as some people walked in from the front door, Sulgate picked up his overcoat and suitcase. He planked his Derby hat on his head and made a rapid departure by the side door.

A taxi was pulling up to the curb, to discharge passengers at the hotel. It was just the sort of vehicle that Sulgate wanted; for he knew that it could not have been posted here by the Golden Masks.

Sulgate boarded the cab, gave the driver a fictitious address. His plan was to change his destination later, then transfer to another cab in order to reach the apartment that he had mentioned in his conversation with Bronden.

Clifford Sulgate was in flight from the Golden Masks. Depending upon Bronden, a servant long in his confidence, he was bound for a hideout where he felt sure no one could locate him.

Like other lesser members of the Golden Masks, Sulgate had not heard the full tale of the episodes that had involved the leaders. Therefore, the deserter knew nothing of The Shadow's entry into the game. Had he heard of how The Shadow had arrived to trap the leaders of the Golden Masks, Sulgate might have lost much of his confidence.

The Shadow had located James Lengerton, whom the Golden Masks had threatened. Similarly, The Shadow, wide in knowledge and versed in deduction, might uncover Clifford Sulgate in the hideout that the deserter had chosen.

CHAPTER VI
WHERE THE LAW HALTED

EVENTS of the next two days brought startling developments in the case of James Lengerton. The Golden Masks, through their use of violence, had forced a police investigation. Lengerton had disappeared; it seemed a certainty that he had been carried away a prisoner. Sampler's murder strongly supported that opinion.

There was a natural consequence. The proxies who had unloaded Lengerton's holdings in Intercontinental Air Lines began to talk.

One rumor had it that Lengerton's associates in the shipping business had learned that he was planning to jump to the field of air transportation, that to block him, they had hired strong-arm men to make him change his mind. Foreseeing trouble, Lengerton had unloaded his air holdings; but he had been too late.

The other rumor was that big promoters in the field of aviation had resented Lengerton's effort to snatch a large plum from their basket; and that they—not the shipping men—were responsible for the trouble that had occurred.

There was one man, however, who stoutly insisted that these rumors were the bunk. That man was Inspector Joe Cardona. He was playing a hunch; and he based it on certain evidence which he had discovered in Lengerton's desk. This evidence consisted of the clippings that concerned other cases similar to Lengerton's. Cardona believed that those clippings had been sent to Lengerton as a warning. Government men and private investigators did not share Cardona's opinion.

They considered the clippings as evidence of doubtful value. All related to cases wherein there was no proof of crime; some had even been investigated and cleared of any crooked connection. All investigators, except Cardona, fluctuated between two opinions: first, that Lengerton had gathered the clippings himself, because of some mental quirk; second, that the clippings had been planted deliberately by the masked men who had seized Lengerton, as a device to throw the law from the true trail.

Joe Cardona would have been pleased had he known that there was one investigator who shared his opinion that the clippings were important; particularly if he had been told that the investigator was The Shadow. Where Cardona followed a hunch, The Shadow used a process of deduction.

The Shadow recognized that if Lengerton had been fearful, he would have called the police sooner. He saw also that if the Golden Masks had chosen to plant a false trail, they would have gone to greater measures. By this process, The Shadow eliminated the other theories and accepted the one that Cardona held.

Although he had gained no details of such an organization as the Golden Masks, The Shadow could picture such a society. Accepting the newspaper clippings as evidence of their past activities, The Shadow knew immediately that the members of the evil band were surely headed by supercriminals, powerful and methodical. They had covered past crimes to perfection. Lengerton had been their first slip.

There was a new bit of news that interested both Joe Cardona and The Shadow. That concerned Clifford Sulgate, whose quiet disappearance caused some comment, the day after James Lengerton was carried away by the Golden Masks. Sulgate was a business promoter who had Wall Street connections. He also owned a considerable amount of real estate.

When he suddenly slipped from sight, Sulgate left a few business matters unattended. Those caused his disappearance to be reported. Joe Cardona was assigned to the case; the inspector held a long conference with the police commissioner. The result of that huddle was divulged by Cardona himself.

IT was eight o'clock in the evening, precisely forty-eight hours after the fray at Lengerton's, when Joe Cardona stalked into his office at headquarters. Stocky of build and brisk in action, Cardona nearly cracked his swivel chair when he sat down heavily in back of his old desk.

A satisfied smile showed on Cardona's swarthy face. It was noted by a stolid man who had awaited his arrival. Joe's present companion was Detective Sergeant Markham, the inspector's one confidant.

"How'd you make out, Joe?" questioned Markham. "Did the commissioner take to your theory on Sulgate?"

Joe nodded.

"The commissioner agrees with me," announced the inspector, gruffly. "He thinks I've found a link."

A streak of black slid across Cardona's desk. Joe looked up to see a dull-faced man clad in overalls. The fellow had entered the office with mop and bucket. He was Fritz, the janitor; he had overheard Cardona's statement and was staring stupidly, moving his pasty lips, as if trying to make sense out of Cardona's words.

Cardona and Markham paid no further attention to the fellow; Fritz was dumb and harmless to them.

"A dozen guys have told us that they unloaded stock for Lengerton," declared Cardona, to Markham. "As near as we can figure it, Lengerton took in a million dollars in cash, through those proxy sales. He only banked half of it."

"What became of the rest?" queried Markham. "Was it grabbed along with him?"

"We don't know," returned Cardona. "There's two things we've got to find out. First, why did Lengerton unload in such a hurry? Second, what did he do with one half of his dough?"

"Somebody ought to be able to answer one question or the other."

"Sure." Cardona nodded emphatically. "But maybe that somebody wouldn't want to be asked. That's where Sulgate comes into the picture."

CARDONA opened a briefcase that he had brought with him. From it, he produced report sheets and some heavier, folded papers. It was plain that he had used every source to gain data that concerned Clifford Sulgate.

"Sulgate knew Lengerton," declared Cardona. "They weren't much more than acquaintances; but they had a lot of friends in common. In the Wall Street bunch, particularly. There's a chance that one of Lengerton's proxies let something slip about that airline stock. It may have reached Sulgate."

Markham nodded steadily as he heard Cardona's comment. Continuing with his assumption, Cardona took up various theories.

"When I talked with the commissioner," said the inspector, "we agreed that maybe Sulgate was the bird who threatened Lengerton. That seemed like a long guess, though; too much like the stuff that the newshawks are shouting. A better hunch, maybe, is that Sulgate was close to Lengerton. Maybe Lengerton slipped him that missing dough, to try and buy back some of the stock. It might have taken a nosedive on the market, with so much of it being unloaded.

"Or maybe Sulgate has some cute business of his own; he may be in a jam like Lengerton was. Whatever the answer, he's ducked out of sight. He lived out on Long Island; we've made a thorough check-up there. We haven't landed a trace of him."

Once again, Cardona had taken up the trail that The Shadow had also followed. In some details, The Shadow had worked more thoroughly than the law, in this search for Clifford Sulgate. But Cardona was coming to a point that had as yet escaped The Shadow. It was something that Cardona had chanced upon by luck, through one of the many men whom he had sent out to gain information.

"Look at this," announced Cardona, opening one of the folded papers, to display a huge chart that was printed in several colors. "This is what made the commissioner sit up and take notice."

"Looks like a map," interjected Markham. "A big one, too; but it only shows a couple of city blocks."

"It's a fire insurance map," explained Cardona. "A new one, too. It shows who owns the buildings. Look at this block, Markham; it's made up of old apartment houses. Look who owns them."

"Clifford Sulgate!"

"That's right. He bought up every apartment house in that block, except one. He did it through a little realty company that he owns. The commissioner got a phone call from a cousin of Sulgate's who was going out of town; he said he had some of Sulgate's papers in the house. We sent a man up there; he came across the deeds to these properties."

"Then that shows that Sulgate was doing some buying on the side like Lengerton. Only he was grabbing properties instead of stock."

Cardona shook his head.

"These old apartment houses aren't important enough to count," declared Joe. "Sulgate didn't exactly cover the fact that he owned them. He just sort of tucked the business into a pigeonhole. It gave me a swell hunch, though; but it didn't work out."

Tapping each of Sulgate's properties that were indicated on the map, Cardona added:

"I figured that maybe Sulgate had picked one of his own apartments for a hideout. The commissioner liked the idea; he sent a whole squad up there to check on every apartment. The hunch was a fliv. They accounted for everybody in every apartment. Sulgate wasn't living there."

Fritz had approached the desk to stare at the colored printing. Cardona grinned as he saw the janitor study the map in puzzled fashion. With a gesture to Markham, Cardona arose; both headed toward the door.

IT was after their footsteps had faded from the corridor that Fritz showed an amazing change of expression.

The janitor's dull eyes lighted; his pasty lips pursed, to form a slight smile. From those lips came the whisper of a strange, knowing laugh; a dim echo of a strident tone that told the janitor's actual identity.

Fritz was The Shadow.

Stalled in his search of Clifford Sulgate, The Shadow had adopted this disguise in order to visit headquarters. He had wanted to learn, at first hand, if Joe Cardona had gained any important information on the subject of Sulgate. The law had acquired such data; but it had halted at the point indicated by Cardona.

Since a search of the apartment houses owned by Clifford Sulgate had failed to reveal traces of the missing man, Cardona had decided to press this clue no further. But The Shadow, as he viewed the large map on the desk, began new deductions from the place where the law had halted.

In analyzing Sulgate's circumstance, The Shadow had picked the actual part that the man played. The only way that the Golden Masks could have handled such big blackmail jobs as the plucking of James Lengerton was through the cooperative efforts of men whose own status held them above suspicion.

Clifford Sulgate could have known enough to be the betrayer of James Lengerton. Since the deal had gone through, there was little reason to suppose that crooks had turned upon the man who had aided their game.

Sulgate's disappearance indicated that he had become faint-hearted. His nerve gone, Sulgate had decided to dodge the Golden Masks. But his hideout would have to be a clever one in order to escape both the police and the Golden Masks.

On the very map that Joe Cardona had studied in vain, The Shadow saw the one spot that a wise schemer could well have chosen. It lay in the block with Sulgate's apartment houses. The Shadow rested his finger upon the one apartment house that Sulgate did not own.

Where else could be a better place?

Cardona's searchers had ignored it. After combing the apartment houses all about it, they had given up the hunt. Sulgate, in all probability, had counted upon the Golden Masks to do the same as the law.

Moving quickly, The Shadow stepped outside. Reaching an obscure locker, he donned his garments of black and let the overalls of Fritz slip to the floor. The Shadow was now on his way to the old apartment house that Clifford Sulgate could have chosen for a hideout.

CHAPTER VII
THE FUGITIVE'S STORY

THE block indicated on Cardona's map lay east of Fifth Avenue. The apartment buildings in that area formed an assorted lot. They varied from four to six stories in height; all had been built during the days when automatic elevators first came into vogue.

The one building that was listed under another ownership stood half a story higher than the apartment houses on either side of it. Its floors were a trifle squattier; hence the extra height included six stories instead of five. That fact was scarcely noticeable from the street. Persons entering the building weren't perplexed when they found that the automatic elevator went up five floors only.

The apartments in this building were good ones;

yet prospective tenants never were shown the best that the place had to offer. The largest and most ample apartment in the building was located on the unsuspected sixth floor. It was reached in a most peculiar manner; by ladder through the top of the elevator, when the car was halted at the fifth floor.

THE secret apartment was at present occupied. Two men were seated in a plain, well-furnished living room, where blinds were drawn. One was Clifford Sulgate; the bespectacled man was less nervous than usual. That was partly due to the calmness of the man with him; a stocky, square-faced fellow who was patient of expression. Sulgate's companion was his faithful servant, Bronden.

"I feel safe here, Bronden," announced Sulgate, in a confident tone. "We have provisions enough to last us for two months. In case of an emergency, we have the telephone"—he gestured toward the instrument, which stood on a handy table—"and its number is unlisted."

Bronden nodded methodically. He stroked a squatty hand through his short-clipped hair and settled back in his chair.

"Today brought me an enjoyable experience," clucked Sulgate. "Watching the police from this front window, while they searched every house but this one. Even if they had come here, they would not have discovered this apartment."

Another matter-of-fact nod from Bronden. The servant was used to hearing his master discuss this subject. Bronden seemed indifferent to any thoughts of danger. Sulgate noted the servant's attitude and became emphatic.

"The Golden Masks are shrewder than the police," he insisted. "We must never discount that fact, Bronden. I have told you enough about the organization for you to recognize its power. You will recall how I insisted upon the utmost secrecy in the preparation of this apartment. There must be no slips."

"I followed every instruction, Mr. Sulgate," responded Bronden, blandly. "There will be no slips, sir. You can depend upon me. But I advise you, Mr. Sulgate, to make no error of your own."

Nervously, Sulgate began to wring his hands. Thought of the future made him jittery. He turned to Bronden with a look of appeal.

"I've got to steady myself," asserted Sulgate. "It's this waiting that makes me shaky. I shall feel more settled after the deadline has passed. Tomorrow night is the limit."

Steadying, Sulgate motioned toward the rear door of the room. "Make me some coffee, Bronden," he ordered. "Black coffee, good and hot. It will steady my nerves."

BRONDEN arose and went through the doorway, closing the door behind him. Sulgate sat clutching the arms of his chair; restless, he came to his feet and began to pace the room. He paused suddenly, conscious of a slight draught. He eyed the window shades suspiciously, then resumed his pacing.

There was one thing that Sulgate had not noticed. One side of a window shade had inched toward the center; its space no more than an eye's width. In fact, as Sulgate turned away, an eye gleamed from that very gap. Like a detached creature, a gloved hand crept through the space and grasped the window sill. It moved along the bottom of the shade, waited there while Sulgate turned about.

The nervous man did not observe the halted hand. He turned away again; the black fingers slowly lifted the shade. There was no crinkle as the blind came up; nor was anything visible beyond, except blackness. From that inkiness, however, came a motion; as if a huge fragment of the night were taking living shape. Blackness swung inward, over the sill; as the shade eased down behind it, a tall form was revealed. Burning eyes bored straight toward Sulgate.

Turning about as he reached the door, Sulgate looked straight toward the window. Horror froze the nervous twitching of his lips, caused his eyelids to stop their blinking as if riveted in their open position. The gasp that Sulgate delivered was spontaneous. His hands, as they clamped to his breast, acted of their own, then stilled. For long, tense seconds, Sulgate stared. Slowly, recognition dawned.

Clifford Sulgate had heard of The Shadow, even though the Golden Masks had not mentioned the part that the black-clad avenger had played in the fracas at Lengerton's. Sulgate knew that The Shadow was a crime hunter. The fact that The Shadow was here stood as proof that he had delved into the ways of the Golden Masks.

Sulgate was sure that The Shadow knew all. Desperately, the hunted man sought for some way to avoid The Shadow's wrath. His jittery brain grasped the only answer. He must tell The Shadow the full truth. As Sulgate tried to find words, The Shadow spoke in a sinister whisper. His words added impetus to Sulgate's decision.

"Speak," ordained The Shadow. "State all facts concerning the organization which you no longer serve."

Sulgate replied, in quavering tone.

"I served the Golden Masks," he told The Shadow. "There are—I mean there were—at least twenty of us. All sworn to secrecy. Only Alpha and Omega, the leaders, knew the identity of the others. We all had similar names; I was known as Mu."

The Shadow's silence signified that Sulgate should continue.

"All members were gained by secret approach," resumed Sulgate, his lips twitching as he spoke. "I received letters; telephone calls—from whom I do not know—and though they were vague, they promised wealth. After I was initiated to the Golden Masks, I learned that different members gave information that led to helpless victims. I supplied the facts concerning James Lengerton. I do not know who approached him."

Sulgate's tone was quavering, but sincere. As the deserter paused again, The Shadow prompted him, with a statement that came as a command rather than a question:

"Your meeting place—"

"I do not know its location," gasped Sulgate. "We were taken there secretly. There were two countersigns: Ashanti and Kumasi. The masks that we wore were brought from the Gold Coast in Africa."

This information told much to The Shadow. He was acquainted with the African Gold Coast, a district peopled by a tribe called the Ashanti. Their capital was Kumasi; gold was plentiful in that land. In fact, the Ashanti were famous for their handicraft with the precious metal. The Shadow had seen thin masks of beaten gold, fashioned by those natives.

"I feared the Golden Masks," gulped Sulgate. "I remained a member only through dread. Knowing that matters would reach a crisis, I secretly prepared this apartment as a hiding place. One man aided me—one whom I could fully trust. He was my servant, Bronden, who is here with me."

His statement ended, Sulgate felt a surge of new fear. He had admitted his complicity in the case of James Lengerton. He sought to make amends.

"I couldn't get out soon enough," pleaded the nervous man. "I had to supply some information to avoid suspicion. I don't know what happened to Lengerton. But I did desert the Golden Masks in time to avoid an ugly duty."

REACHING to a table, Sulgate managed to wrench open the drawer. He pulled out the rolled scroll that the Golden Masks had given him; he uncoiled it and thrust it before The Shadow's eyes.

"Look!" begged Sulgate. "Before tomorrow night, I am supposed to visit a man named Roger Barfield, at the Hotel Romera. I am to advise him to buy certain stocks for half a million dollars, securities that have already been offered to him. Those stocks are worthless; if Barfield buys, the whole half a million will be acquired by the Golden Masks."

"Should Barfield refuse—"

Again, The Shadow's words came like a command for Sulgate to proceed. The deserter supplied the answer, by pointing to a paragraph on the scroll. The Shadow had not deigned to read it; he had kept his eyes full upon Sulgate.

"The instructions are here," faltered Sulgate. "I am to prepare threatening letters; anonymous ones mentioning a plantation in Dutch Guiana. Barfield, I suppose, will understand; just as Lengerton did about the aviation stock."

Sulgate's hands were shaking. The Shadow took the scroll; rolled, it and placed it beneath his cloak. He had found a new and important mission—one that could lead him directly to the Golden Masks. The sooner his move the better.

The pressure upon Roger Barfield was different than that which had been applied to James Lengerton. In this new case, Barfield was to be swindled through a forced purchase. Since stocks had already been offered him, they must have been handled by some other member of the Golden Masks. Through conference with Barfield, The Shadow could gain the name of another member of the band—one who was not a deserter, like Sulgate.

By moving quickly on this trail, The Shadow might be able to push operations against the Golden Masks before tomorrow night. He could stir up trouble for them—enough to make the organization worry about matters more serious than the punishment of Clifford Sulgate for his desertion.

In fact, by quick moves, The Shadow would have a chance to render Sulgate's position quite secure. The leaders of the Golden Masks might believe that The Shadow had captured Sulgate; hence they would consider Sulgate a prisoner rather than a deserter. It was obvious that no search had yet begun for Sulgate; furthermore, the man had assured The Shadow of Bronden's fidelity. Keen to visualize the trail ahead, The Shadow chose departure as the immediate course.

Without a word to Sulgate, The Shadow turned about and glided toward the window. He swung outward into darkness; his shape was blotted as Sulgate stared. The blind came downward, followed by the *click* of the clamp as the window was closed.

Sulgate stared after The Shadow in amazement, then looked toward the table drawer for proof that his senses had not tricked him. He froze in his tracks; he still seemed to hear that eerie whisper that no imagination could have produced.

Sulgate realized fully that his experience had been a real one. The closing of the window was proof that The Shadow wanted the whole episode kept silent. Sulgate resolved that he would not even speak to Bronden regarding the strange occurrence.

CLOSING the table drawer, Sulgate went back to his chair and sat down, his nervousness apparently ended after The Shadow's strange visit.

The rear door of the room opened. Expecting Bronden with the coffee, Sulgate turned around. He faked a twitching movement of his lips as he swung about to face the servant. The twitching became real. Gasping wildly, Sulgate came up from his chair.

Bronden had entered; but the servant was not bringing coffee. Instead, he carried a leveled revolver; his usually sober face was wearing an ugly leer. His head craned forward, Bronden came closer and closer. Sulgate raised his quivering hands, tried to back away. He staggered against the chair, shifted forward, to regain his balance, just as Bronden arrived.

The servant jabbed the revolver muzzle against Sulgate's heart and pressed the trigger before his master could twist away. The report was muffled; Sulgate's gargled cry was but a trifle louder. As Bronden stepped back, Sulgate staggered sidewise, twisted about and spread-eagled on the floor. He gave a long, convulsive quiver; then stretched dead.

Bronden pocketed his smoking gun. With a contemptuous snarl, he stepped to the wall, plucked away a large picture and pulled down a microphone with its wires. That done, the square-jawed man went to the telephone and dialed a number. He recognized an easy voice at the other end of the line.

Bronden spoke a single word:

"Ashanti."

Across the wire came the answer:

"Kumasi."

"This is Gamma," announced Bronden. "I have important news, Omega. The Shadow was here."

A sharp question followed; Bronden replied:

"Yes. He talked to Mu. I heard it over the dictaphone. I eliminated Mu after The Shadow left. The Shadow is on his way to the Hotel Romera."

There was a pleased chuckle from the telephone receiver. It brought an evil leer to Bronden's countenance. Bronden hung up, stared gloatingly at Sulgate's body, as he planned for its removal.

Bronden, previously a member of the Golden Masks, had tipped the leaders off to Sulgate's plans. They had let the deserter proceed under Bronden's watchful eye, giving him the full time limit. The Shadow's visit had meant death for Sulgate. Lone-handed, Bronden had not dared to act until after The Shadow's departure.

The Shadow had set forth to deal with the Golden Masks. Posted by Bronden, the members of that insidious band would be prepared for him. The Shadow was due for danger that he had not yet divined.

CHAPTER VIII
THE SHADOW'S ROUTE

SWIFTNESS was The Shadow's forte. Tonight, it had begun to serve him ill. He had reached the roof, gone to another building and descended so promptly, that he was out of hearing range when Bronden fired the bullet that ended the career of Clifford Sulgate.

Near the apartment house where Sulgate had died, The Shadow boarded a waiting cab. Its driver was one of The Shadow's own agents, Moe Shrevnitz, the speediest hackie in New York. The cab headed for the Hotel Romera, stopped only once, while The Shadow entered a drugstore to make a telephone call.

On this brief mission, The Shadow presented an appearance quite different from the guise in which Sulgate had seen him.

That visage was the one best suited for The Shadow's coming quest. It was the countenance of a man named Lamont Cranston, a globe-trotting millionaire, for whom The Shadow frequently doubled. The role of Cranston was the proper one to impress Roger Barfield, whom Sulgate had mentioned as a traveler and man of wealth.

Riding in the cab again, The Shadow reached the Hotel Romera, which was a secluded but fashionable establishment. Peering from the window of the cab, The Shadow saw a hunch-shouldered man slide way into a gloomy spot. That sight did not disturb him. The man was his own watcher, a clever spotter named "Hawkeye." Through the telephone call to his contact man, Burbank, The Shadow had arranged for Hawkeye to be on the job. The Shadow wanted news of any events outside the hotel while he interviewed Roger Barfield.

When he gave his name at the desk, The Shadow had only a short wait. The news of a visitor was telephoned up to Barfield, who must have recognized the name of Lamont Cranston. Soon, The Shadow rode up to the tenth floor in an elevator. He eyed the operator, decided that the man was an ordinary employee.

Similarly, The Shadow looked over the tenth-floor corridor, en route to Barfield's suite. He saw no signs of watchers.

KNOCKING at Barfield's door, The Shadow was promptly admitted, by the man whom he had come to see. Roger Barfield was an eager-faced man of middle age, thin-nosed and wide-mouthed, with eyes that carried a friendly sparkle. He was partly bald; what hair he had was rumpled. That, and the hunch of his smoking jacket, indicated that he had been drowsing when he received the call from the desk.

"Glad to see you, Mr. Cranston," welcomed Barfield, in a booming tone. He shook hands, closed the door and conducted The Shadow into the small living room of the suite. "I have heard of you often, as a globe-trotter like myself. I am pleased that our paths have crossed."

As The Shadow took a chair, Barfield tendered a box of expensive cigars, and raised thin eyebrows, as if inquiring why he had been honored with a visit. The Shadow's thin lips formed a smile.

"I have called to ask you a rather important question," stated The Shadow, in a leisurely tone that was Cranston's. "Recently, I was offered some securities of doubtful value by a man who talked across the telephone. He did not give his name; but he stated that he was conducting a transaction with you."

Barfield pursed his lips and nodded. He inquired, dryly:

"What stock did the chap offer?"

"He spoke of several," replied The Shadow. "Metropolis Oil and Century Motors were two of them. I find that both are bad."

"What kind of a voice did the fellow have?"

The Shadow shook his head.

"That is hard to tell," he replied. "I merely talked with him across the telephone."

"Was it rather sharp?" queried Barfield. "Like this? Abrupt? Short-clipped?"

He gave a good representation of an odd, thin voice. The Shadow nodded, slowly.

"That's the bounder," chuckled Barfield, in his own, deep tone. "He wanted me to buy shares in some Mexican mines that I happened to know about. They've been forgotten for the past thirty years; so has the fact that they were salted the last time that they were sold."

"Did the chap state his name?"

"Not at first. He sent me a letter, afterward. Oddly, he seems to be a man of some importance; not a stock promoter at all. Wait until I show you the letter, Mr. Cranston."

BARFIELD rummaged about the room, finally found the letter and gave it to The Shadow. The letterhead bore the name of Sidney Tallam, with the address 685 Marview Place. There was little to learn from the letter itself; it simply reminded Barfield that the offer was still open.

"That's his home address," announced Barfield, opening a telephone book. "There is also a Tallam Manufacturing Co. listed in the directory. I have learned that Sidney Tallam controls that business; its product is automobile accessories. Apparently, Tallam is a wealthy man."

Closing the telephone book, Barfield puffed at his cigar, then shook his baldish head.

"All I can guess," he announced, "is that Sidney Tallam has been stuck with an oversupply of bad securities and wants to pass them along. After all, that is his privilege, if any dupe is foolish enough to buy."

"Perhaps," agreed The Shadow, "but certain forms of persuasion should be taboo."

"What do you mean?"

"I had another telephone call," replied The Shadow. "It was also anonymous. I was advised to purchase the stocks mentioned. I was told that refusing such an action might give me worry about certain events that had occurred in the past."

The Shadow's statements had been a probe; they were becoming more direct as he learned facts from Barfield. The words took immediate effect. Barfield glanced sharply toward his visitor, then chewed hard on the end of his cigar.

"I was afraid of something like this," he said, slowly. "Do I understand you correctly, Mr. Cranston, when I think that you mean this game is blackmail?"

"You do," replied The Shadow. "I have had previous experience of this sort. I felt that when your name was mentioned to me, the purpose was double. I have been to Dutch Guiana, Mr. Barfield."

Barfield stared steadily for a moment; then his face registered consternation. He tried to restrain himself; at last, nervous eagerness overwhelmed him.

"I see," he nodded. "You would know that I might be blackmailed on account of my experience in Dutch Guiana. That would make you think that you would be due for the same dose, because of some similar episode in your own past."

The Shadow chanced a new remark; he phrased it in a subtle fashion, his tone leisurely but filled with reassurance.

"Of course," remarked The Shadow, "I never owned a plantation in Dutch Guiana, but—"

He stopped. Barfield's face had taken on alarm. The baldish man was shaky. He sank to a chair, dropped his cigar to the floor. Leaning forward, Barfield gripped his baldish head with both hands. "That would be it!" he groaned. "Yes, you have struck it, Mr. Cranston!" He looked up suddenly, his eyes wild. "I've done my best to keep that matter hushed! Tell me"—Barfield strained forward— "what do you know about it?"

"Not a great deal. Enough to feel sympathetic toward you."

BARFIELD looked relieved. He sagged back in his chair, thought for a moment, then spoke in frank tone.

"I bought that plantation in good faith," he affirmed. "It was the treacherous overseer who misruled the men. He instituted what was practically slave labor; he left the country when I found it out. I wrote some letters, asking for advice. Later, I learned that I and members of my family could be held culpable. The offense would be a penal one.

"My brother, my nephew are still at the plantation. If my old letters were turned over to the Dutch authorities, both of them would be sentenced to prison. My property would be seized; I would be ruined. I own lands in Sumatra, Java, other Dutch colonies as well as Guiana. Yes, it would be worth a half a million dollars to hush. That is the amount that Tallam wants for the Mexican stock."

Barfield again buried his head in his hands. The Shadow watched him quietly, then asked:

"Had you thought of blackmail until I mentioned it?"

"No." Barfield looked up as he spoke. Trembling, he reached for a fresh cigar. "But your opinion, Mr. Cranston, is sufficient to warn me. I am in a bad mess. I hope that you are not so unfortunate?"

"My position is secure," announced The Shadow. "Therefore, I should be able to help you, Mr. Barfield. Suppose I induce Tallam to concentrate upon me? I may be able to learn more of the game."

"That might save me," agreed Barfield, eagerly. "Yes, your exposure of the swindle would certainly end the operations of these rogues, if they are such. But wouldn't Tallam be surprised, if you came to see him? You say that he did not mention his name over the telephone."

"He named you. I can tell him that I dropped in to see you. That you gave me his name. In fact, I think that I shall call upon Mr. Tallam this evening."

Noting the address on the letter, The Shadow returned it to Barfield. The baldish man came to his feet, stammering his thanks. The Shadow halted him with a quiet smile, clapped Barfield on the shoulder. They walked to the door together; there, Barfield shook hands warmly.

DESCENDING in the elevator, The Shadow showed a slight smile. Everything that Barfield had said fitted with the instructions given to Clifford Sulgate. In his talk with Barfield, The Shadow had drawn the man out; everything fitted perfectly to show this game as another crime attempt by the Golden Masks.

One point, however, impressed The Shadow. The Golden Masks, in all their past activities, had been careful not to leave a trail. It was not likely that they would appoint one of their number to the actual task of unloading bad securities. Though The Shadow did not know the identity of Burns Froy, he was positive that whoever had visited James Lengerton had done so in a friendly fashion, claiming to be under threat; in as bad a boat as the victim.

This looked like a cunning reversal of the system. The Shadow pictured Sidney Tallam as a dupe. His assumption was that the Golden Masks had forced Tallam to buy bad stocks under threat; succeeding in that, they had told him to unload his worthless holdings on Barfield and turn the new proceeds back to them.

Perhaps they would do the same with Barfield later, using him as a means to shove the same stock on another hopeless victim.

The Shadow had completed these quick deductions when he stepped aboard his cab. He left Hawkeye on duty, to watch Roger Barfield; for The Shadow expected that soon someone might visit Barfield from the Golden Masks. The leaders would have to appoint a substitute in place of Clifford Sulgate.

Seeing new possibilities in Sidney Tallam, The Shadow believed that the retired manufacturer would merely be a link back along a chain of dupes. Therefore, he regarded his coming visit as one that might not bring great results. Keenly intent upon his new conclusions, uninformed of the fact that Clifford Sulgate had been overheard and murdered by Bronden, The Shadow had carried his previous deductions farther and farther from the proper course.

THE proof of this was demonstrated by Roger Barfield, soon after The Shadow left him. Seated in the living room of his hotel suite, the baldish man was listening intently for any sounds outside his door. Satisfied that there were none, Barfield displayed a wide smile on his thin-nosed face.

He placed his finger on the opened page of the telephone book, noted Sidney Tallam's number. He picked up the telephone, called the number. A crisp voice gave an abrupt hello. Close to the telephone's mouthpiece, Barfield uttered the word:

"Ashanti."

Tallam's voice responded:

"Kumasi."

"This is Omega," undertoned Barfield. "I have good news, Alpha. The Shadow arrived here sooner than I expected; so I have sent him along to you. He calls himself Lamont Cranston. Be prepared to receive him."

Cackled acknowledgment came from the receiver as Roger Barfield hung it on the hook. Confident that his fellow chieftain of the Golden Masks would overpower The Shadow, Roger Barfield leaned back in his chair and twisted his wide lips into an insidious leer of triumph.

CHAPTER IX
WHERE BULLETS FAILED

THOUGH The Shadow's deductions had caused him to overlook an existing menace, he did not neglect precautions in his coming mission. The Shadow regarded Roger Barfield as a future victim of the Golden Masks; he was inclined to class Sidney Tallam as a past dupe. The fact that there had been no spies watching Barfield at the Hotel Romera did not lull The Shadow into the belief that there would be none at Tallam's residence.

Just as he had put Hawkeye on watch at the Hotel Romera, so did The Shadow decide to cover Tallam's home. He made another stop, put in a call to Burbank. The Shadow ordered Harry Vincent on duty, to cover Tallam's. In choosing Vincent, The Shadow had picked the most experienced agent who served him.

There was one important point, however, that The Shadow did not overlook. Harry Vincent, though competent, did not possess Hawkeye's ability at slipping out of sight. To watch Tallam's house, Harry would need a suitable hiding place. Therefore, The Shadow gave instructions for Harry to contact Moe Shrevnitz and use the latter's cab as a lookout post.

The cab reached Marview Place. Swinging a corner, it passed the front of a tall, pretentious apartment house, where several taxicabs were lined up at a hack stand. The Shadow whispered an order to Moe; the driver nodded. He was to park in back of the other cabs, to await Harry Vincent. Moe might be able to remain in that line for an hour or more without attracting attention.

Number 685 was farther on than the apartment house; and across the street from it. Sidney Tallam's home was a huge, old-fashioned house with brownstone front, that had once been the most impressive building in this neighborhood. It fronted on the swanky street known as Marview Place.

Moe stopped his cab just past the entrance of the apartment house. The Shadow stepped to the sidewalk; he was still attired as Cranston, but his move was not conspicuous. With him, The Shadow was carrying the bag in which he had placed his cloak and hat. His automatics were in special pockets under the coat of his business suit. The Shadow waited until Moe had turned the next corner. Then he strode across the street, slackened his gait and strolled past a lighted patch in front of Tallam's.

The Shadow's stroll enabled him to note the house more closely. He saw that it stretched deep back from the street. He noticed that there were passages between it and the houses on each side. One of these, at least, must lead to a side door in Tallam's house.

THE SHADOW ascended the brownstone steps and rang the doorbell. He waited half a minute; when the door opened, The Shadow was faced by a huge African servant, who was more than six feet tall. Though the servant was garbed in American attire, The Shadow recognized immediately that the fellow must be a native-born African. His appearance tallied with statements made by Clifford Sulgate. The Shadow identified this servant as a member of the Ashanti tribe.

As The Shadow stepped through the doorway, the servant spoke in slow English; he inquired the visitor's name. The Shadow produced a card that bore the name of Lamont Cranston; on it, he wrote that he represented Roger Barfield. He requested the servant to take the card to Mr. Tallam. The Ashanti ascended a broad stairway, leaving The Shadow in a sumptuous lower hall.

The presence of the Ashanti servant merely served to strengthen The Shadow's recent deductions. Considering Sidney Tallam to be a dupe of the Golden Masks, it seemed logical that the organization would have men posted in Tallam's own home, particularly if they had already swindled him and had to keep him silent. This African servant would be the best sort of watcher that the Golden Masks could use.

While he waited, The Shadow momentarily compared Tallam's situation with that of Sulgate; for he had not entirely rejected the possibility that Tallam might be a lesser member of the Golden Masks. The fact that Sulgate had a servant like Bronden; and had presumably had no Ashanti in his employ, was sufficient to curb The Shadow's temporary suspicion.

Sulgate had been so emphatic regarding Bronden's supposed loyalty, that The Shadow had taken the deserter at his word. Lacking suspicion of Bronden, The Shadow had not gained the inkling that he needed.

The big Ashanti returned to the ground floor. Stolidly, he ushered The Shadow upstairs, conducted him to a room at the side of the house. Entering, The Shadow found Sidney Tallam; he also viewed one of the most curious rooms that he had ever seen.

TALLAM was a stoop-shouldered man attired in a gray suit that exactly matched the color of his thin hair. His face was sharp and pointed, its skin smooth and dryish. Tallam's eyes were dark; they had a keen glint. His lips were thin; they held a pursed smile. The hand that Tallam extended was scrawny; but its grip was firm.

As for the room, it looked like a combination living room and library. Its center portion was square-shaped; but small. The reason was that the room possessed three deep alcoves, each a trifle higher than the regular floor.

One of these alcoves was at the far side of the room. In its center was a desk; at the back were windows. On each side, the alcove had shelves of books that towered to the high ceiling. There was a similar alcove at the front of the room; it had bookshelves and windows; but no desk.

The alcove at the rear of the room had no windows, for it backed against an inner wall of the house. The rear of the third alcove was composed of bookcases; in its center was a chair and a table that supported a large dictionary. This alcove also boasted a huge globe of the world. Almost a room in itself, the alcove was the library; the bookcases in the other niches simply held extra volumes.

Sidney Tallam waved The Shadow to a large armchair in the center of the room. Taking a chair close by, Tallam looked quickly at the briefcase that The Shadow had brought. Tallam's manner indicated that he expected his visitor to discuss some business, that the briefcase contained documents that would be produced during conference.

"I expected to hear from Mr. Barfield," announced Tallam, in a crisp tone. "I wanted to see him in person. I mentioned that fact by telephone. Why have you come instead, Mr. Cranston? Is Mr. Barfield ill?"

"He is somewhat indisposed," returned The Shadow, calmly. "Being interested in the Mexican mining stock that you offered him, he consulted with me. Like Barfield, I am a traveler; but I know more about Mexico than he does."

Naturally, The Shadow had taken a new tack with Tallam. He wanted the retired manufacturer to accept him as Barfield's representative; should Tallam call up Barfield by telephone, the latter would support The Shadow's claim. That, at least, was The Shadow's logical assumption, since he had not yet learned that he was dealing with the two leaders of the Golden Masks.

"I see." Tallam's words were abrupt; his nod a short one. "I presume that you have looked into the mining propositions. I trust that you have recognized its merits."

"On the contrary," informed The Shadow, quietly, "I have classed the stock as very doubtful."

An expression of well-feigned worry showed on Tallam's dryish face. The Shadow was not sure that it was an actual revealment of Tallam's feelings. Nevertheless, there was a chance that it was real. The Shadow decided to sound the man further.

"In fact," he declared, "I wondered how you happened to buy such stock, Mr. Tallam. You have a surprisingly large amount of it; for Mr. Barfield informs me that you want a half a million dollars for its transfer."

Tallam began to chew his lips. He was succeeding temporarily with his bluff. Tallam's game was to make The Shadow think that he had expected no difficulties in the deal with Barfield. That would fit with the idea that Tallam was wise enough to know

that The Shadow held: namely, the belief that Tallam was but a helpless instrument in the toils of the Golden Masks.

"I cannot say why I bought the stock," began Tallam; pretending confusion, he added: "That is, it would be difficult to recall the circumstances that forced—or rather induced me to make so large a purchase. I was assured—convinced, in fact—that the stock was good. Indeed, I am rather well conversant with mining matters in all parts of the world."

"That interests me," asserted The Shadow, with a show of enthusiasm. "Forgetting Mexico for the moment, Mr. Tallam, what is your opinion of the fabulous claims concerning gold deposits on the African Gold Coast?"

TALLAM looked startled; he started to come up from his chair. His hands twitched slightly; his eyes took on a faraway stare that indicated a fearful recollection. Calming himself, Tallam shook his head.

"I know the rumors that have come from Africa," he declared. "How great quantities of gold have been found in possession of the natives. There is some tribe there that once had large amounts of gold. I forget the name of the tribesmen—"

"The Ashanti?"

"That sounds like it. It seems to me that the British authorities once instituted a search for some golden thrones that those natives were supposed to own. Wait just a moment, Mr. Cranston; I can easily refresh my memory by reference to the encyclopedia."

Rising suddenly, Tallam moved with spry step toward the alcove at the rear of the room. In his haste, he let his face lose its forced expression. In a single instant, The Shadow knew the truth. Tallam was dropping his role of dupe; that indicated that he must be more than an ordinary member of the Golden Masks.

The Shadow's mind flashed back to Clifford Sulgate. The Shadow had classed the deserter as what he was: a rogue at heart, but a man who had feared for his own hide. Though The Shadow had found Sulgate shivering with fear, there was a chance that leniency had been a mistaken move on The Shadow's part.

Sulgate could have seen an opportunity to put himself back in the good grace of the Golden Masks by passing the word that The Shadow had taken up the trail.

Though The Shadow had not struck upon the actual truth, he had gained its equivalent. It did not matter who had given the tip-off: Sulgate or Bronden. The job had been done. Quick suspicion caused The Shadow to class Roger Barfield as one of the Golden Masks. Just as quickly, he dropped all thoughts of the man whom he had recently interviewed.

SIDNEY TALLAM was the man who mattered at this moment. The Shadow saw the rogue for what he was: one of the leaders of the Golden Masks. Tallam's start for the bookcase in the deepest alcove was proof that the crook intended action. Coming up from his chair, The Shadow made a move of his own.

Whisking his briefcase open, The Shadow shot a glance through the open door to the hallway as he pulled his black cloak into view and dropped it over his shoulders. No one was in the hall; if Tallam summoned aid, The Shadow would have time to meet him. Seizing his slouch hat, The Shadow clamped it to his head; he looked straight toward Tallam.

Tallam spun about. In his right claw he gripped a .38 revolver that he had snatched from the globe.

The gray-haired crook had reached the bookcase at the back of the alcove. He was drawing out a volume of the encyclopedia. Tallam's back was toward The Shadow; his whole attitude indicated that he thought his visitor was still duped by his bluff. Tallam drew one hand away from an upright post of the bookcase. He began to thumb the pages of the big book, still with his back toward The Shadow.

Calmly, The Shadow drew on black gloves. Edging backward, he watched both the hall and the alcove. Though the light of the living room was subdued, both the hall and alcove showed considerable glow. Tallam could not move; nor could men approach, without The Shadow's observation.

Tallam laid the encyclopedia volume on top of the big dictionary. He turned toward the globe; spun it and touched a spot with his finger, as though looking for the Gold Coast in Africa.

The Shadow caught a partial view of Tallam's profile; he saw the smug smile that the man's lips showed. Like a form of vengeance, The Shadow stood motionless; one .45 leveled toward Tallam, the other automatic covering the hall.

The Shadow was prepared to deal instant death if Tallam made a false move; for Tallam was a murderer. Either he or his companion of the other night had dealt the fatal shot that slew Lengerton's secretary, Sampler.

Tallam's move came. The gray-haired man shifted slightly, bringing his back toward The Shadow. Tallam slipped one clawlike hand to the top of the globe; suddenly, he lifted a portion of the big sphere, like the lid of a box. Tallam's body did not quite cover the action. The Shadow saw the lid come up.

Tallam spun about. In his right claw, he gripped a .38 revolver that he had snatched from the globe. Though he gave no utterance, though his motion was strangely silent, Tallam displayed the venom that he felt. His lips had taken on a leer, as if to deliver an elated snarl. His finger was on the trigger of his revolver, itching for a quick tug. The muzzle was speeding its aim toward The Shadow.

BEFORE Tallam could complete his aim, The Shadow fired. His right-hand automatic delivered three shots with quick precision. At considerable range, The Shadow was taking no chances with the murderer. He expected the arrival of enemies from the hall; he wanted to deal with them without interference from Tallam.

As his third shot echoed, The Shadow halted, staring straight toward the alcove. Sidney Tallam still maintained his pose, leering and unwithered by The Shadow's fire. Upon the floor at the step up to the alcove lay three small objects, silvery and flattened. They were The Shadow's bullets. They had been halted five paces short of Tallam, their flight stopped in midair!

Tallam, though he gloated, did not utter a sound; nor did he fire. Dark faces appeared at the doorway to the hall. There, The Shadow saw the Ashanti whom he had met below, accompanied by two others. One carried a revolver; the second a dagger; the third held a spear. They made no effort to enter, nor to use the weapons.

Their arrival had been soundless.

The amazing answer dawned upon The Shadow. Reaching the bookcase, Tallam had pressed a switch. Unheard, unseen, sheets of bulletproof glass had slid across to cover the front of the alcove and the doorway of the room as well.

Sidney Tallam, Member Alpha of the Golden Masks, stood protected and his trio of Ashanti servants had the same security. Vicious in pose, Tallam showed a hatred that was imitated by the savage faces of the tribesmen who served him.

The Shadow was trapped, in the power of the Golden Masks!

CHAPTER X
THE SLEEP OF SILENCE

CALMLY, The Shadow put away his automatics; he folded his arms as he let his keen eyes gaze about the room. Viewing the floor, he could discern the bottom edges of the glass barriers that had enclosed him. He saw that the front and side alcove were also fronted with plates of glass.

Thus there was no chance to reach the windows. The Shadow was confined to the comparatively small area that formed the central portion of the room. Once noting the glass, he could tell when any barrier started to slide back.

The Shadow hoped that his pose of indifference would coax Tallam to silently open either his own glass door or the one that blocked the Ashanti. This would allow an attack from either or both directions. By giving his enemies what looked like an advantage, The Shadow saw prospects of a battle. If it came, he could show his foemen that his quickness on the draw would block them.

Tallam, however, did not budge the glass barriers. Instead, the Golden Mask turned to the bookcase behind him. He reached into the space from which he had removed a volume; there, he pressed a hidden lever. The bookcase performed a slow revolution, showing a room beyond.

Tallam went briskly through the opening. Soon after the bookcase had assumed its original position, he appeared in the hallway with the Ashanti. The Shadow saw him give an order. The tribesmen marched away and Tallam followed.

The Shadow approached the doorway to the hall, pressed his gloved hand against the glass plate that blocked it. Men were gone from beyond; though the barrier was heavy, The Shadow had a way to attack it when unobserved. In the lining of his cloak, he carried two powders, which, when mixed, formed a powerful explosive.

With these substances, The Shadow had disposed of heavy barriers in the past. The glass wall, however, looked more formidable than most. It had no hinges; its upper and lower edges ran in grooves. It had moved deeply into the far side of the doorway. Thus there were no weak spots in the barrier; no crevices for explosive powders.

HENCE The Shadow was deliberate as he examined the barrier; it was a few minutes before he decided upon his attempt. All would depend upon that single stroke. The Shadow could not risk failure.

Stooping, he removed one glove, slid his fingers along the stretch where the glass filled a metal groove in the floor. This was the spot to attack. Should the glass crack, The Shadow could break through. He was confident that explosives could succeed where bullets had failed.

Stepping back toward the center of the room, The Shadow moved behind a large armchair. He wanted to make sure that no spying eyes saw him obtain the powders from the lining of his cloak. He raised one side of the cloak, began to tug at the hem. Curiously, his fingers slipped from the cloth.

The Shadow's hands were numb. As he moved his arms, he found them strangely slow in motion. He felt his body sway; his legs were failing him. Though mentally alert, The Shadow was becoming physically powerless. Steadying himself against the armchair, he sensed the cause.

A sweetish odor had begun to fill the room; looking upward, The Shadow saw thin coils of yellow vapor floating from the arms of a high chandelier, like incense from a burner. The chandelier was beyond The Shadow's reach; though he might have attacked it sooner, he could no longer do so.

The Shadow was experiencing the same ordeal that James Lengerton had undergone. Sidney Tallam had released a soporific vapor that carried a paralyzing effect. The Shadow felt a limpness throughout his entire body. He gazed toward the doorway; beyond the glass, he saw the ugly face of an Ashanti servant who had come to view the prisoner's plight.

Quickly, The Shadow considered the outcome. The fact that he still retained mental alertness made him decide that the gas was not deadly. It was probably an anesthetic; its effects would wear off within a given time. Flashing to thoughts of the past, The Shadow recalled cases of men who had disappeared, then returned to their homes, to maintain silence regarding their absence.

Undoubtedly, they had been subjected to this gaseous treatment; threats of its repetition had caused them to avoid all mention of what they had undergone. The Shadow reasoned also that the length of time during which a victim would remain powerless would be determined by the amount of gas he breathed.

To strive against the overwhelming vapor would be useless. A long fight would only increase the succeeding period before recovery. If the Golden Masks intended to slay him when he was powerless, The Shadow's doom was sealed. There were reasons, however, why they would prefer to keep him prisoner.

They had probably guessed that The Shadow had agents who would search for him; alive, he would be bait for the capture of such agents. Stronger, however, was the fact that The Shadow had posed as a man of wealth.

Persons with money were the sort the Golden Masks required as victims. Such men, when prisoners, could be forced to turn over their wealth. The Golden Masks, though they had murdered often, preferred to let their victims live. They applied death only to those who would not accept their terms; they had even spared James Lengerton, although he had partly blocked them. They had slain Sampler; but that was because they had considered the man as useless.

SAGGING as he watched the face of the Ashanti guard, The Shadow decided to make the best of his plight. Slowly, he yielded the little strength that he still retained. His hands lost their pressure against the chair; the weight of his body did the rest. The Shadow lost his balance, tumbled helplessly to the floor. Though he still was capable of slight motion, he did not show it.

The Ashanti loped away along the hallway. Staring upward, The Shadow could see the yellow gas still wreathing from the chandelier. He could detect a slight hiss that announced the escape of the vapor, which was immediately absorbed by the air of the room. Soon, the yellowish curls were gone. Simultaneously, the hissing ceased.

Sidney Tallam appeared at the doorway, then went away. Shortly after, the bookcase revolved in the rear alcove. Tallam again stepped to view. He pressed a lever; sheets of glass slid back. Tallam stepped forward to view The Shadow; the three Ashanti entered from the hallway.

At Tallam's rasped command, the Ashanti lifted The Shadow, inert from the floor. They tore away his black cloak, pulled away his gloves and gave these garments to Tallam, along with The Shadow's hat. It had rolled from The Shadow's head; one of the Ashanti picked it up for Tallam. The big natives found The Shadow's guns; took them from him. They also gathered all the contents of The Shadow's pockets.

Tallam spoke in the Ashanti tongue. He ordered the servitors to overlook such minor items as The Shadow's watch and some coins that were in his pocket. Tallam took the wallet that The Shadow carried as Cranston's; the crook decided that it might contain papers that held useful information.

Carrying their prisoner, the Ashanti marched from the room. Tallam followed them, bringing The Shadow's outer garments. The course led to the rear of an upstairs hall; there, the carriers descended by a back stairway. They reached a basement and stopped by a massive steel door, which marked the back wall of the house.

Tallam unlocked the barrier and slid it back. The Ashanti descended a short flight of steps; they came to a corridor that formed a long, dimly lighted passage deep underground.

THOUGH he lacked all power of motion, The Shadow was conscious of all that occurred during the trip. He saw doors on each side of the dim corridor. They were of glass, like the barriers that had trapped The Shadow; but these openings had steel doors, also. The spaces between the outer glass doors and the inner steel ones measured approximately three feet.

Tallam stopped at one door. He pressed a switch beside it. The Shadow saw the inside door slide back. The departure of the steel sheet revealed a lighted dungeon; small, stone-walled and windowless. Motionless in a chair by the far wall sat a haggard-faced man whose eyes stared bulgingly toward the door. The Shadow recognized the prisoner as James Lengerton.

Hands moved feebly; lips tried to utter words. The Shadow knew that Lengerton was recovering from a powerful dose of the yellow gas. Probably Lengerton had inhaled a heavy mixture, the strongest that could be given. That meant that the gas, applied to its fullest power, would render a victim helpless for forty-eight hours.

Tallam pressed the switch that closed the steel door. Lengerton was behind a double barrier. Stepping across the passage, Tallam reached another door; there he pressed two switches. Glass and steel slid back. The Shadow was carried into a lighted cell that resembled Lengerton's. He was dumped unceremoniously upon a cot. Lying by the far wall, he was able to watch the departure of his captors.

The Ashanti left the cell. The Shadow saw Tallam turn to speak to a square-jawed man who had arrived. Tallam addressed the newcomer as Bronden; he chuckled the name so that The Shadow could hear it. That information lifted the last doubt concerning the tip-off.

Contemptuously, Tallam flung The Shadow's cloak and hat upon the prisoner's cot, along with the black gloves. He and Bronden left the cell. The two barriers closed when the switches were pulled.

The Golden Masks had acted as The Shadow had hoped. They believed their prisoner helpless; they were confident that he could not escape the dungeon in which they had placed him. Therefore, they had chosen to keep him alive.

WHEN the doors had closed upon The Shadow, Tallam abruptly ordered Bronden to keep charge of the dungeon corridor. His duty of watching Sulgate ended, it was obvious that Tallam intended to use the man at this headquarters.

Tallam and Barfield, Alpha and Omega of the Golden Masks, had taken Gamma into their closest confidence. Bronden was the only one of the lesser Golden Masks who had gained that particular honor.

Followed by two Ashanti servants, Tallam headed upstairs. He ordered one to duty at the front door; the other, to go outside and make a short patrol of the neighborhood. Tallam continued up to his living room. He took his place behind the desk in the central alcove and began to prepare a letter. He stopped this work to put in a brief telephone call to Roger Barfield.

Twenty minutes later, the Ashanti doorkeeper arrived to announce that Barfield had entered. There was no need for Tallam to order that Barfield be conducted upstairs. Tallam's partner entered while the servant was still making his slow report. Motioning Barfield to a chair, Tallam ordered the Ashanti to return downstairs.

As soon as the pair were alone, Tallam chuckled the details of The Shadow's capture, which he had chosen not to discuss at length over the telephone.

Barfield listened with an air of evil pleasure; when Tallam had finished, he described points of The Shadow's visit at the Hotel Romera. That discussion ended, the heads of the Golden Masks turned to the sort of talk that The Shadow had anticipated.

"I sent Seeklat outside," declared Tallam. "I wanted him to make sure that no spies are close at hand."

"That is not likely," assured Barfield. "I saw no suspicious persons when I left my hotel."

"If The Shadow has agents," decided Tallam, abruptly, "they would probably be competent enough to keep out of sight. It would be best for you to stay here, Omega."

"As we originally planned," nodded Barfield. "Very well, Alpha. If The Shadow does have workers, we should be able to trap them as easily as we did their chief."

"More easily. We may find a way to lure them. We are wise to keep The Shadow alive. For more reasons than one. He played the part of a wealthy man tonight."

"Which may mean that he has money. If so, I think that we can manage to acquire it."

Wise leers passed between the two conspirators. These men of the Golden Masks had known success in the past, even when they had dealt with stubborn prisoners. They were ready to try for results with The Shadow. Tallam's next remark showed, however, that any such action would not be immediate.

"Here are the papers for tonight's meeting," declared Tallam, passing them across the desk. "I am following your suggestion, Omega. We shall use Member Epsilon, otherwise Jay Jaffley, as contact in our next endeavor."

"It will work well," assured Barfield. "Jaffley is a prominent insurance man, which classes him as something of a conservative. Since we are after a promoter like Freeland Ralbot, we need a contact man who will impress him."

"None could be better than Jaffley," agreed Tallam. "He poses as a man of the utmost integrity. When he produces anonymous letters that hint of fake promotions engineered by Ralbot, we can take it for granted that Ralbot will be bowled over."

"It's always a good setup," nodded Barfield, "having a contact who rates higher than the fellow who pays the coin. Froy was a good bet with Lengerton. Jaffley will be even better with Ralbot."

TALLAM swung the bottom of the bookcase at the right side of the desk. From behind dummy volumes, he produced two flat suitcases and gave one to Barfield. These bags contained the robes and golden masks that were worn by Alpha and Omega.

"We shall go out by the long passage," remarked Tallam. "I shall speak to Gamma, to tell him that he will not be needed at the meeting. While we are below, Omega, we shall take a look at our prisoners. There is one whom you will be greatly pleased to see. I doubt that he has yet become accustomed to his new quarters."

With this reference to The Shadow, Sidney Tallam led the way downstairs. Roger Barfield followed, his wide mouth spread in a grin that was as ugly as Tallam's leer.

To these companions in crime, the capture of The Shadow was but another link in a long chain of evil successes. Though they had been chilled by The Shadow's arrival—the night when he had taken them unawares—they had played their recent game well.

Forewarned, these evil geniuses had acted with perfect teamwork. They had bluffed The Shadow, trapped him; small wonder it was that they had lost their fear of the superfoe whom they had blocked. To their way of thinking, The Shadow was in a snare that no living being could untangle.

In that surmise, the leaders of the Golden Masks were wrong. No trap was *ever* hopeless to The Shadow.

CHAPTER XI
THE SHADOW'S RUSE

DURING the interval that he had spent in the underground cell, The Shadow had experienced a slow but steady recovery from the

effects of the gaseous treatment. Lying upon his cot, he found that he could lift his arms, that they were strong enough to half raise his body.

Relaxing, The Shadow indulged in a calm smile. He had acted wisely when he had pretended total collapse in Tallam's upstairs trap. Through that ruse, he had gained prompt removal from the gas-laden atmosphere. Tallam had thinned the paralyzing vapor the moment that he had opened the glass barriers.

Because the process had been halted in its early stage, The Shadow had escaped the usual result. Thus he possessed an advantage that the Golden Masks did not recognize. The Shadow was no longer totally helpless; during the next forty-eight hours he would be capable of action.

Tallam, himself, had given The Shadow a weapon. He had thrown The Shadow's cloak upon the cot. Though guns were gone, The Shadow still had the explosive powders that were hidden in the lining of his cloak. Unfortunately, those materials had become useless to The Shadow.

This cell had a double barrier; steel within, bulletproof glass without. There was a three-foot space between the heavy doors. Even if The Shadow blasted the steel barrier, he would be blocked by the glass beyond it. He could not hope to shatter both with one explosion.

Since the far door was glass, any guard who chanced to pass along the outside corridor would see the wreckage of the steel door. The Shadow's advantage would be lost before he could follow it through.

CONSIDERING his plight, The Shadow came to the conclusion that his best policy would be to keep up a pretense of helplessness. Should he find a chance for a break, he could use it. If the Golden Masks came to remove him, he would be able to give battle once the doors were opened.

The only flaw in this plan lay in the fact that the Golden Masks formed an active band. They would not be idle during the next two days. In all probability, they would proceed with further crime; the very sort that The Shadow had planned to prevent. The only way to thwart the Golden Masks would be through some outside contact, gained without the knowledge of The Shadow's captors.

There were other prisoners here. Tallam had let The Shadow see

James Lengerton. To The Shadow, it was obvious that other cells contained additional captives. Some, perhaps, were helpless like Lengerton; others might have already regained their power of locomotion, like The Shadow. Certainly, none of them had managed a means of communication with the outside world; nor had any thought out a plan of escape.

Those facts, however, did not deter The Shadow.

Looking about his cell, The Shadow noted its simple furnishings. In addition to the cot, the room had a chair and a table. Both were flimsy; but chair rungs or table legs might do for cudgels in a pinch. There was another item, however, that pleased The Shadow more.

This was a wall bracket, made of brass. It had a curved arm, twelve inches in length, that could be unscrewed from the plate that was fitted to the wall. The bracket could be of value later. Its present purpose was to hold the single incandescent bulb that provided the room with light. There was a small switch attached to the bracket. Evidently, prisoners were allowed to choose either light or darkness after they had recovered from the yellow gas.

Rising slowly, The Shadow walked shakily to the wall and examined the bracket. He steadied himself; for a moment, his fingers touched the lighted bulb. The Shadow was considering a plan; he decided to postpone it, until he felt stronger. It was well that he made that decision.

As The Shadow moved back toward his cot, there was a *click* at the steel door. It indicated that the barrier was about to open. With all the effort he could summon, The Shadow threw himself upon the cot and rolled into the position that he had formerly held. His eyes were toward the door. He saw the steel sheet slide back.

Beyond the glass barrier was Bronden. The square-jawed man was beckoning to others. As The Shadow stared, keeping his eyes in a fixed position, he saw Sidney Tallam and Roger Barfield arrive beside Bronden. The appearance of Barfield removed the last question concerning the set-up of the Golden Masks. The Shadow knew positively that Tallam and Barfield must be Alpha and Omega.

Barfield smiled uglily as he viewed The Shadow. To him, the prisoner's bulging gaze meant that the paralyzing gas had taken full effect. While Barfield gazed gloatingly, Tallam spoke to Bronden.

Though The Shadow could not hear the crisp words that Tallam uttered, he could observe the precise motion of the crook's pursed lips. Tallam's words were plain.

"We are going to the meeting," Tallam told Bronden. "You will remain here, in charge. Keep Lothkal on duty; tomorrow, Seeklat will obtain more men."

The names Lothkal and Seeklat would have been difficult to note, if they had come from the lips of an ordinary speaker. Tallam's clippy pronunciation made the names clear. The Shadow knew that Lothkal and Seeklat must be Ashanti servants. Probably, Tallam and Barfield had decided to keep closer guard, since The Shadow was among their prisoners.

It would be Seeklat's job to find more men of Ashanti origin, if any were in New York. This indicated that the Golden Masks were not oversupplied with tribal henchmen.

Tallam ordered Bronden to close the steel door. As Bronden went to obey, Tallam motioned to Barfield. Together, the two walked away, taking the direction opposite the one by which they had arrived. A few moments later, the steel barrier slid shut.

THE brief interlude had brought important facts to The Shadow. The Golden Masks were meeting tonight; that meant that his conjecture regarding new crime was probably correct. The fact that Tallam and Barfield had continued along the passage proved that there must be a secret exit that would bring them above ground some distance from the brownstone house. Therefore, The Shadow's agents would not observe the crooks when they departed.

Offsetting these two factors were others that The Shadow regarded as advantages. With Tallam and Barfield absent, only Bronden would be in charge. He was not as keen as either of his chiefs; a clever ruse might easily deceive Bronden. Furthermore, the fact that Seeklat was to obtain new African henchmen was something of great consequence to The Shadow.

In fact, it gave him the very thing he wanted. The Shadow had already thought out a mode of communication to persons outside the house. The trouble had been the choice of a message. That difficulty was ended.

The Shadow lay idle for a full ten minutes; the closing of the steel door had made him safe from observation. He gazed toward the light that projected from the wall; his lips, still those of Cranston, formed a slight but confident smile.

When he was sure that Tallam and Barfield were well on their way, The Shadow arose. His legs were stronger; his steps were unwavering as he went to the wall.

There, The Shadow reached into the pockets of his vest. He found the few ordinary items that Tallam had left him—a handful of small change and a gold watch. Among the coins, The Shadow found a copper cent. He turned off the wall light, unscrewed the bulb and inserted the coin. He screwed the bulb tight, turned on the switch.

Instantly, a fuse was blown somewhere in the house. The Shadow had knocked out an entire circuit. He unscrewed the bulb and let the coin drop into his hand. He replaced the bulb, but kept the coin in readiness.

SEVERAL minutes passed. Suddenly, the light came on again. Its glow showed The Shadow, standing with his watch in his left hand, studying the dial. His right hand held the penny; quickly, that same hand unscrewed the bulb. Bringing his hands together, The Shadow balanced the cent on the metal end of the bulb, pushed both up to the light socket.

He accomplished this with amazing rapidity; in less than five seconds, the bulb was back in position. The Shadow did not screw it fully into place; he withheld the final action while he eyed the second hand of the watch. At the proper instant, he gave the bulb a quick, short turn to the right.

Again, the lights went out.

Unscrewing the bulb, The Shadow caught the coin, he inserted the bulb alone, so that it would bring the light the moment that another fuse was used. The Shadow knew, from the light's behavior, that Bronden must have gone to the fuse box when the lights blew for the first time. The new short circuit would be followed by another replacement.

While The Shadow waited in darkness, his lips phrased a whispered laugh that was confined to the stone walls of his cell. His present game would necessarily be brief; probably too short to complete all that he wanted.

Bronden would not replace fuses indefinitely; sooner or later, the fellow would look for the real cause of the extinguished lights.

That, however, would not matter. Confident that Harry Vincent was on outside watch, The Shadow was sure that the present ruse would bring the result that he required.

CHAPTER XII
THE AGENTS MOVE

THE SHADOW was correct in his assumption that Harry Vincent was on duty. Harry had contacted Moe's cab soon after it had parked at the hack stand near the big apartment house. Seated in the rear, Harry had joined Moe in keeping watch on Tallam's house.

Both had expected The Shadow to reappear from the front door. A long while had passed; then, instead of The Shadow, another person had approached the cab. It was Hawkeye. The little spotter had trailed Roger Barfield from the Hotel Romera. He had spied Moe's cab and come to contact.

Harry saw Barfield enter Tallam's. A brief chat with Hawkeye left Harry undecided whether Barfield's arrival boded good or ill. Harry had decided at last that The Shadow had sent for Barfield, in order to have a showdown with Tallam. Nevertheless, Harry had suggested that Hawkeye prowl about the outside of the brownstone house.

Hawkeye had returned to the cab just prior to The Shadow's action with the lights. Joining Harry, the spotter whispered news.

"There was a big gazebo came out of the house," informed Hawkeye. "He took a gander all around the place, like he figured somebody was casing the joint. He nearly spotted me; I didn't lamp him at first, there in the dark. He looked as husky as some of them Ethiopian soldiers they've been showing in the newsreels. Maybe he *was* one of them; but why's he here in New York?"

Before Harry could reply, Moe piped quick news from the front seat.

"See that?" queried the cab driver. "A bunch of lights just went out downstairs. Take a look at the house."

Harry did. He noted the sudden absence of lower lights. Trained to study any unusual occurrence, a prompt thought came to Harry's mind. Perhaps The Shadow would want a later report concerning those very lights. It would be well to know how long they remained extinguished.

HUNCHING low in the cab, Harry produced his watch and a fountain-pen flashlight. He threw a glimmer on the watch dial. He estimated roughly that eight seconds had passed since Moe had seen the light go off. He told Hawkeye to write down figures when he gave them; he ordered Moe to report when the lights reappeared.

A few minutes later, Moe snapped:

"They're on."

"Three minutes, twenty seconds," said Harry. "Put that down, Hawkeye. Then wait while I check it exactly. I had to make a guess at the start—"

"Off again!" called out Moe, from the front seat. "They went out just like before."

Moe's quick tone caught Harry's instant attention. His eyes already on the dial, Harry noted the exact second with camera-eye accuracy. His voice showed certainty as he spoke to Hawkeye.

"Leave it at three-twenty," said Harry, "as the time that the lights were off. Put down ten seconds as the period that they were on again. I caught that to the dot."

To Moe, Harry added:

"Watch for the lights to come on again."

Two minutes and forty-three seconds passed.

Moe snapped the news that lights had come on. As Harry announced the new time to Hawkeye, Moe ejaculated that the lights were off. Again, Harry had it to the dot. He told Hawkeye:

"Five seconds." Two minutes marked the next absence of the lower lights. Once more the glow reappeared. This time, the lights stayed on for exactly eighteen seconds. Harry gave the figures to Hawkeye. Again, the agent waited. The interval was longer than before.

There was a reason for the new situation—one that The Shadow recognized within his cell. Standing in darkness, The Shadow heard the *click* that announced the opening slide of the steel door. He knew at once that Bronden suspected that the new prisoner was tampering with the lights.

Instantly, The Shadow made a sweeping dive for the cot. He did not have to worry about the light bulb; that was in place, ready to tell when the new fuse was inserted. His actions with the coin were to come afterward.

Just as the door slid completely open, the lights appeared, both in the cell and the corridor. Holding his fixed stare, The Shadow saw Lothkal, the Ashanti guard, staring through the outside glass. Half a minute later, Bronden appeared, to question Lothkal.

Though he eyed The Shadow suspiciously for a short while, Bronden finally decided that the prisoner could not have been responsible for the blown fuses.

He pressed the switch that controlled the steel door; The Shadow was again confined from sight. He did not move, however, for he expected that Bronden might again try to catch him off guard. Furthermore, The Shadow's progression had been broken.

WATCHING from the taxi, Harry Vincent soon realized that such must be the case. The lights had come on again, to stay. Studying the figures that Hawkeye had transcribed, Harry could not fathom them, at first; suddenly a solution struck him. He confided to Hawkeye and Moe.

"The chief is in trouble," informed Harry, bluntly. "I think he is a prisoner. He knows that we are watching; the only way he could reach us was by blowing the lights. If I'm right, that gives me an idea."

Holding his flashlight to Hawkeye's paper, Harry picked out the figures that told how long the lights had been on.

"He couldn't have controlled the time that the lights were off," mused Harry. "That's when someone inside was putting in new fuses. All that The Shadow could do would be to extinguish the lights *after* they came on again."

"Ten—five—eighteen"—Harry named the numbers that Hawkeye had written for those intervals—"those are all that count. Let's take them as letters, according to the alphabet. Ten is J; five is E; eighteen is R."

"J, E, R," spoke Moe. "Guess there aren't many words that begin with those letters. But what good will one word be, even if we do guess it?"

"Jer," remarked Harry slowly. "Jera—Jera—Jeri—I've got it! The word is Jericho! The chief wants Jericho Druke!"

Moe and Hawkeye knew instantly that Harry had scored a hit. Both knew Jericho Druke, a husky African who ran an employment agency in Harlem. On several occasions, The Shadow had called Jericho into service, and had found him capable and reliable.

It was up to Harry Vincent to guess why and how Jericho would be needed. Fortunately, the answer was easy. Harry had been informed of recent events, through Burbank. The Shadow had foreseen that facts might be useful to his agent.

"The Shadow has been trapped," declared Harry, grimly. "Tallam must belong to the Golden Masks; maybe Barfield does, too, since he came here in such a hurry. That big fellow you spotted, Hawkeye, is one of the Ashanti.

"We can't try to crash that house, particularly if The Shadow is a prisoner. There's no use telling the police; they would bungle matters worse than we would. There's only one man who can get in there; and The Shadow has named him. That's Jericho."

"I get it," put in Hawkeye. "If Jericho can meet up with one of this Ashanti bunch—make them think he belongs to the same tribe—"

"They may able to use him," finished Harry. "The sooner we can stage the stunt, the better. Slide out, Hawkeye, and keep watching the house. If you spot any Ashanti leaving it, trail the fellow. Learn where he goes."

As Hawkeye edged from the cab, Harry leaned forward and spoke to Moe.

"We'll get away from here," declared Harry. "The less watchers, the better; so the job belongs to Hawkeye. I'll call Burbank. He can get in touch with Jericho and have him meet us."

Moe nodded. He waited a few minutes, for the cab ahead of him was about to move farther toward the front of the hack stand space. As soon as the head cab started, Moe wheeled his own machine out into the street and drove for the next corner.

GAZING from the window, Harry took a last look at the brownstone house. The old mansion looked grim and ominous; its windows were too deep for the lights within them to give any view of the interior.

Harry was more convinced than ever That The

Shadow was a prisoner. How desperate his chief's plight, Harry could not guess. He knew, however, that The Shadow's call for Jericho was the surest way to get results. With one worker inside to aid him, The Shadow might accomplish huge results. If Jericho could pass as an Ashanti, fine.

Particularly since Harry and the other agents would stay close by, with Hawkeye watching the house. If he contacted The Shadow inside, Jericho could pass word to Hawkeye, outside. The arrangement would be perfect, if it could only be accomplished. That was the part that worried Harry Vincent.

If, at that moment, Harry Vincent could have gained a momentary glimpse within The Shadow's cell, the agent's troubled mind would have been relieved. The Shadow was stretched upon his cot, his eyes still gazing toward the light that glowed from the wall bracket.

Motionless lips delivered a whispered laugh that chilled the confines of the cell. The Shadow was confident that his trick-signaling had been noted and understood by the outside watchers. He seemed confident that Jericho would manage entrance to Sidney Tallam's stronghold.

Though he remained a prisoner of the Golden Masks, The Shadow was already planning future moves to quell the activities of that insidious band.

CHAPTER XIII
THE NEXT MORNING

AT ten o'clock the next morning, Seeklat stepped from the side door of Sidney Tallam's mansion. The big Ashanti was attired in American clothes; there was nothing conspicuous about his departure from the house.

Part of Tallam's clever method was to let Seeklat come and go. The Ashanti spoke English well enough to excite no suspicion. It was easy for him to pass as an ordinary servant, employed in Tallam's household.

Moreover, Tallam was running no risk. Seeklat, like the other imported tribesmen, was sworn to primitive loyalty. No amount of persuasion or torture could induce any Ashanti to betray a chief.

If trouble should strike at Seeklat, it would simply give Tallam and Barfield a warning of enemies. Though they pretended otherwise, the leaders of the Golden Masks cared nothing about the fate of their Ashanti followers.

Tallam had told Bronden that Seeklat was to look for new recruits to serve with the Ashanti servants. That was true; but Tallam had another purpose, also. He believed that if The Shadow's agents were on watch, Seeklat might spot them; or they might attack the Ashanti. In either case, Tallam would gain a lead toward The Shadow's aides.

That was one of two reasons why Tallam sent Seeklat out by the side door of the house, and not by the distant secret exit which Tallam had used last night with Barfield. The other reason was that the Golden Masks wanted to preserve the secret of the distant exit. They knew that if Seeklat used it and was spied far from the brownstone house, observers might guess that the secret way existed.

When he reached the front street, Seeklat walked southward. Though the big Ashanti strode along with eyes straight forward, there was little that escaped his observation. Seeklat had spent his boyhood with an Ashanti tribe; his stride was the jungle stalk. While his gaze was ever prepared for sight of prey, Seeklat also possessed the sense that told when he was watched.

Experience in civilized surroundings had not dulled this sense of Seeklat's. It sometimes tricked him, however, for passers occasionally kept looking at the huge Ashanti through curiosity. Seeklat's unusual height was the cause of such stares. Today, Seeklat felt that he was being watched. As he turned a corner, he managed a glance over his shoulder that swept the street that he had just left.

A HUNCHY, wan-faced man slid out of sight as Seeklat turned. It was Hawkeye; the little spotter found refuge behind a pair of close-placed ash cans. He was quick enough to escape Seeklat's gaze; but the Ashanti had not finished.

At the end of the next block, he made another striding turn. This time, Hawkeye outguessed him. The spotter was deep in a doorway when Seeklat looked back.

Hawkeye was still on the trail when Seeklat reached an avenue that was topped by an "el" railway. The Ashanti ascended the stairs on the southbound side. Hawkeye scurried into a cigar store and made a quick telephone call. At night, he would have risked following Seeklat aboard an "el" train; by daylight, the chance of observation was too great. However, Hawkeye was playing a good bet with his telephone call.

No "el" train had arrived by the time Hawkeye came from the cigar store. It was several minutes before one arrived; soon after it had pulled away from Seeklat's station, Moe Shrevnitz arrived with his cab. Hawkeye boarded it; they sped along beneath the "el" line. The cab caught up to the "el" train at the third station.

From then on, they kept at an even speed with the train. After a few more stations, Hawkeye sighted Seeklat coming from an "el" station. The spotter dropped from the cab, threaded a new trail. As before, he kept from Seeklat's view. The Ashanti seemed less suspicious of followers at this distance from Tallam's house.

The course led to the waterfront. Near a line of dingy, battered piers, Seeklat entered the side door of a tawdry restaurant that was frequented by seamen. Hawkeye congratulated himself on having kept clear of the Ashanti's notice; for the spotter was now able to come from cover.

Hawkeye's own attire and appearance marked him as the sort found near the waterfront. Boldly, the hunched spotter entered the eating place.

Rough-clad men were lounging at a long bar; others were seated at battered tables. Hawkeye chose a corner near the back; he ordered a bowl of Chili. Keenly, the spotter noted a door that led to a back room; also a telephone booth in a corner beyond it.

A SQUATTY Portuguese was standing near the bar. He looked like the mate of some tramp steamer. The fellow was chatting amiably, in good English. Everytime he threw his head back for a laugh, gold coins shook from the lobes of his ears. As the Portuguese ended one guffaw, a barkeeper leaned forward and cupped his hand above the Portuguese's earring. When the barkeeper whispered, the Portuguese nodded. Hawkeye saw him head for the back.

Almost beside Hawkeye, the Portuguese opened the door toward himself; he went through and pulled the door behind him. As the door was swinging freely shut, Hawkeye shoved his foot forward to deflect it. The door stopped short, not quite closed. Hawkeye hunched himself over his bowl of Chili; squinted through the narrow opening.

The Portuguese had entered the back room to talk with Seeklat. Hawkeye could see both men; he caught the words that passed between them.

"You bring men?" queried Seeklat, in a low but deep tone. "Three men?"

"I bring one man," replied the Portuguese. "But maybe I get two."

"I want three." In emphasis, Seeklat held up one hand. He used his thumb to crook his forefinger inward, thus displaying his three last fingers. It was the peculiar style used by native Africans to denote the number three. The Portuguese shook his head until his earrings jangled.

"Bring one," he declared, emphatically. "One more, maybe. Best I can do."

With that, the mate of the tramp ship came out from the rear room. Hawkeye let him swing the door entirely shut; he watched the Portuguese go out by the front. Hawkeye saw instant opportunity. He hopped across to the telephone booth; made a quick call to Burbank. If Jericho should come here prompt-ly, chances would be good for him to contact Seeklat.

IN about half an hour, a rough-clad African solemnly entered the eating place and walked through to the rear room. Hawkeye was positive that the arrival was an Ashanti. Probably the Portuguese ship had brought one such native to America. There was no sign of the Portuguese mate. He had simply sent the Ashanti to Seeklat. That was just the way Hawkeye had wanted it.

The spotter paid for his Chili, left by the front door and stopped to shove a cigarette between his pasty lips. Eyeing a near corner, Hawkeye saw a stalwart African waiting there. It was Jericho; the man from Harlem was as husky as any Ashanti, although he did not resemble the members of that tribe. Hawkeye gave a signal, then moved on his way. The rest was up to Jericho.

Approaching the restaurant, Jericho stopped a moment, then entered. He saw the rear door, went through it. He came upon Seeklat and the other Ashanti; Seeklat had just signed up the new recruit. Seeklat eyed Jericho with a suspicious glare, then queried:

"You from ship?"

"Je ne comprends pas," grunted Jericho. "Mon pay est Abidjean, Cote d'Ivoire. Je parle que Francais."

Seeklat recognized the names that Jericho uttered. The prospective recruit was claiming that he talked French only; that he came from the town of Abidjean, on the Ivory Coast; the latter being a French colony that adjoined the British Gold Coast.

Seeklat was familiar with that portion of Africa. It seemed likely that a Portuguese ship that had brought an Ashanti would have picked up a hand from the Ivory Coast. In a native babble, Seeklat questioned the Ashanti whom he had just recruited. The native looked at Jericho, gave a noncommittal reply. He was not sure whether or not Jericho had been aboard the Portuguese vessel.

ORDINARILY, Seeklat would have rejected Jericho, since he was not an Ashanti. Two reasons made him decide to hire the new man. Seeklat needed Jericho; furthermore, he was impressed by the latter's size. Jericho looked as powerful as any of the Ashanti who served the Golden Masks.

Seeklat beckoned. Jericho followed him, along with the Ashanti. Seeklat took the pair to the "el" station; they rode back to the original station and walked to Tallam's. There, Seeklat took the two indoors, left them downstairs while he went up to report to Tallam.

DURING this interval, Jericho remained as solemn as the Ashanti who stood with him. There was a good reason for his soberness. Jericho had a ticklish game to play. He knew nothing of the Ashanti language; in fact, little of any native jargon used in Africa.

But in discussing that dilemma with Harry Vincent, Jericho had happened to mention that he could speak some French. He had once been employed as doorman at a French restaurant; through contact with waiters and chefs, he had picked up phrases of the language.

That statement had given Harry an idea. He had instructed Jericho to pose as a native of the Ivory Coast, to use his French to the best of his ability. Thereby, Jericho could avoid questions put to him either in English or in the Ashanti tongue.

When Seeklat returned, Jericho sensed that a test was to come. He and the new Ashanti followed Seeklat upstairs; they were conducted to the living room. There, they saw Sidney Tallam, seated at his desk. There was another man in the room; Roger Barfield was looking through the books in the rear alcove that served as a library.

Tallam studied the new Ashanti, spoke to him in the native tongue, choosing words carefully and slowly. The Ashanti made a reply. Tallam was satisfied. He turned to Jericho, put a slow question in French. Jericho understood and answered. Tallam smiled.

He did not realize that if he had been able to snap the question more rapidly, it would have slipped past Jericho's comprehension. Nor did the poorness of Jericho's accent perturb him. Tallam's own French was none too good; and he did not expect the glibness of a Parisian speaker from a native of the Ivory Coast.

Telling Seeklat that both men would do, Tallam drew a revolver from his desk drawer. He carried the weapon forward, let Jericho and the Ashanti examine it to see that the cartridges contained solid bullets. By this time, Barfield had turned about and was facing the living room. Tallam aimed toward his partner in crime, deliberately fired the revolver.

LAST night's phenomenon was duplicated. The bullet never reached the man in the alcove. It seemed to *zing* back in mid-air; as it fell gleaming to the floor, Tallam fired again. Jericho and the Ashanti stared bewildered at sight of bullets lying on the floor. They did not guess that a glass plate covered the entrance to the alcove. Tallam had modulated the lights of the room.

Tallam spoke to the recruits. In Ashanti, then in French, he explained that both he and Barfield were invulnerable, that they were potent witch doctors, who could deliver death as easily as they could prevent it. Though Jericho knew that the

stunt must be a trick, he pretended the same awe as the Ashanti, who thought the power real.

Barfield, meanwhile, had pressed a switch in the bookcase. Once the glass barrier had glided back in invisible fashion, he came from the alcove. Tallam ordered Seeklat to go downstairs and take the new Ashanti with him; in French, he told Jericho to remain. As soon as the others had gone, Tallam made a remark to his partner.

"We'll keep this fellow up here," said Tallam, indicating Jericho. "Since he knows no English, he's a good man to have around. We can talk while he is here."

"Maybe you'll need him as an extra guard," remarked Barfield. "Unless you bring back one of the Ashanti at the meeting place."

"We'll use this fellow if necessary," decided Tallam. "But there's no use pushing him. He can't talk Ashanti anymore than he can English; so there's no way for him to understand orders in either language. I'll keep him with me, since I talk French."

With that, Tallam briskly ordered Jericho to patrol the hall outside the living room. Jericho obeyed the command; as he paced the hall, he could catch snatches of conversation between Tallam and Barfield. As time passed, Jericho decided that he was doing the best that he could, for the present.

Talk of guards had convinced Jericho that there were prisoners, with The Shadow among them. If the cells lay below, an attempt to reach them without proper orders would be a foolish, perhaps suicidal, effort. It was better to stay here, close to Tallam and Barfield.

These men, so Jericho had been told, were the leaders of the Golden Masks. If harm was to befall The Shadow, it would be through their order. Thinking that Jericho could not understand English, they would think nothing of discussing their plans with him close by.

Until he learned that The Shadow's life was threatened, Jericho Druke intended to play his part as a new and supposedly ignorant recruit in the service of the Golden Masks.

CHAPTER XIV
CHANCE SERVES THE SHADOW

THE day passed slowly to Jericho, after his arrival at Tallam's. But the passage of time upstairs in Tallam's house was rapid compared to the slow monotony of life in a cell below. To The Shadow, the lingering hours spoke of futility.

Though The Shadow had no way to learn whether or not his agents had received his message, he believed that they had actually gained it. He was sure that steps had been taken to put Jericho into

Tallam's household; but there was a chance that some hitch had delayed that game.

The Shadow realized also that Jericho might already be inside; but in no position to reach the cell rooms below. Though The Shadow was confident that he could eventually escape through Jericho's aid, he hoped for an earlier opportunity.

For a while, no plan occurred to The Shadow. Retaining his fixed position on the couch, he watched the occasional opening of the steel door. At those times, spaced a few hours apart, either Bronden or Lothkal looked in to make sure that The Shadow was still powerless.

It was when Lothkal made another such inspection that The Shadow learned a new fact. As he held his fixed gaze, he saw through the glass outer door; there he observed an Ashanti servant standing outside of Lengerton's cell. While The Shadow watched, the native pressed a switch. The glass door of Lengerton's cell slid open; but the inner steel one did not. The Ashanti stooped and picked up a tray of dishes.

The Shadow's view was suddenly ended as Lothkal pressed the switch that closed the inner door of The Shadow's cell. In that glimpse, however, The Shadow had viewed enough to gain a plan.

Since Lengerton had recovered from his gas treatment, he was receiving food. The system appeared simple. An Ashanti opened the glass door and placed a tray there, then closed the glass door and slid back the steel so that the prisoner could pick up the tray. Later, the steel door was opened, to let the prisoner put the tray outside it. That done, the steel door would be closed.

The Shadow saw possibilities through this. He had two hours to wait; for he could not try his plan until after the next inspection. Looking at his watch, The Shadow saw that it was six o'clock.

That fact spurred him to his purpose. He was sure that the Golden Masks plotted new moves. Night was the time when they would act. It would be wise for The Shadow to move by eight o'clock.

TWO hours moved slowly. Promptly at eight, The Shadow saw the steel door slide back. For the first time, he let Lothkal see that he was no longer under the influence of the gas. Slowly, with pretended weakness, The Shadow came up from his cot. Lothkal flattened his nose against the glass and watched.

The Shadow staggered toward the door, stopped suddenly and clapped his hands to his eyes, as though the dazzle of the cell light troubled him. Shifting toward the wall, he found the light switch, turned off the incandescent. He continued toward the glass door, blundered against it and fell back in the cell, within the line of the steel door.

Lothkal's large features showed a grin. Apparently, The Shadow had not remembered the glass barrier. The big Ashanti slid the steel door shut. The glow from the outer passage was ended. The Shadow lay in total darkness.

A few seconds later, The Shadow arose. He acted with great rapidity. He sprang to the darkened wall, found the bracket and wrenched it with his fists. He unscrewed the rod; ripped the wiring loose.

Reaching his cot, he seized his black cloak; he tore away a strip of the sable-hued cloth. Working with all possible speed in the darkness, The Shadow wrapped the brass rod in the strip of cloth. He donned his cloak and hat, put the cloth-covered rod out of sight.

The Shadow completed his preparation in good time. The steel door slid back again; this time, it was Bronden who peered through the glass. Lothkal had reported The Shadow's recovery. Bronden wanted to see proof of it.

For a few moments, Bronden saw nothing, for the cell was dark. Bronden thought nothing of that fact, for Lothkal had told him that The Shadow's first act had been to turn off the light. As Bronden stared, he saw The Shadow.

Shakily, groggily, the cloaked prisoner again blundered up against the glass door and sagged back, this time in the path of the steel door.

Bronden leered. This interested him. He laughed at The Shadow's weak effort. Wearing cloak and hat, the prisoner was trying to offer feeble challenge, as Bronden saw it. Yet The Shadow was totally helpless, in the power of the Golden Masks.

Bronden scowled a warning through the glass barrier. He intended to slide the steel door shut. He motioned for The Shadow to move back. Weakly, The Shadow obeyed, rolling into the cell. Bronden pressed the switch; the steel door slid into place.

IN watching The Shadow, Bronden failed to notice something else. In his fake sprawl close to the glass door, The Shadow had planted the brass rod on the floor. Cleverly, he had shoved it against the side of the doorway that the edge of the steel door was to meet.

Bronden did not see the cloth-covered rod, for it was black. Nor did he hear the crunch that came when the steel door closed into its place. The outer glass prevented the sound from reaching Bronden's ears; but The Shadow heard it.

On hands and knees, he probed the edge of the steel barrier, to discover a slight crevice. The brass bar had stopped the steel door from coming fully shut. Donning his gloves, The Shadow forced his fingertips into the tiny space.

At first, he could not budge the steel door. He shoved his knee sidewise, against the inner end of the brass rod. The leverage helped; the steel door gave a fraction of an inch. The Shadow squeezed his fingers through, gave every ounce of his strength. The door slid farther open. The Shadow jammed his knee into the space.

Once he managed to work himself to his feet, his task was ended. The Shadow pushed his body between the door and the frame; he leaned against the door edge with a powerful shoulder. The door opened farther.

The Shadow kicked the brass rod back into the cell. Squeezing completely through, he pressed against the glass door and released the steel one. Massive, hidden springs drove it shut with a muffled clang.

The Shadow was confined in closer quarters than before. He had left the cell in order to occupy a three-foot air space between the steel door and the outer glass one. Cloaked and hatted, The Shadow was invisible; for the surface of the steel door was blackened. Moreover, The Shadow shifted to the side of the space that was shaded from the nearest corridor light.

To keep himself unseen, The Shadow needed to remain absolutely motionless. He did so; but for another reason, also. The air supply was limited between these sealed doors. The Shadow was in the same situation as the Hindu fakirs who allow themselves to be buried alive for hours.

The Shadow knew the secret of the fakirs, how they could endure such tests without obtaining their fresh air. Complete immobility was the first requirement; for motion would create friction and thereby use up precious oxygen.

Slow breathing was also necessary. Steadily, easily, The Shadow drew in his breath, held it, then exhaled with the same slow process. He waited several seconds, then drew another retarded breath. He was conserving his air supply to the limit.

An Ashanti paced into view. It was Lothkal, back on guard duty. The huge watcher stopped at The Shadow's door, glanced at the glass and the steel within it. Backed by a darkened barrier, the glass reflected the passage lights. Lothkal did not see The Shadow. He paced onward.

SOON Bronden arrived. He spoke to Lothkal, gestured toward The Shadow's door and shook his head. The two walked from The Shadow's view. Apparently, Bronden had reported upstairs; he had been told to do nothing more about The Shadow for the present.

It might be that Tallam and Barfield had decided to deny food to The Shadow. If so, the glass door might not be opened until morning. That would mean a twelve-hour stretch for The Shadow; a long period to remain rigid, clamped between two barriers.

A long time, too, to go without fresh air. Nevertheless, The Shadow was prepared for the ordeal.

He had more space than in an ordinary coffin, wherein a living burial can last for a few hours. Every additional square inch of space meant more oxygen. As he calculated, The Shadow decided that under ordinary conditions, he would have enough air to last from seven to eight hours.

He was determined to make that supply stretch to twelve if so required. His breathing became slower than before, so slight that it was almost imperceptible. Body rigid, eyes fixed, The Shadow had assumed an almost hypnotic condition, with his face turned toward the inner steel door. He had reduced his breathing to the absolute minimum. It would stay at that timing.

Minutes passed. The Shadow showed none of the strained impatience that comes with close confinement. He counted upon time to bring its break; though he was prepared for a twelve-hour wait, he believed that the break would come sooner.

Perhaps Tallam and Barfield had merely postponed the matter of a food supply. If they intended to fare forth tonight, they would probably make plans concerning The Shadow before they left; for the matter of his early recovery was something that they could not ignore.

By this time, Jericho might be in the house, almost prepared to make some move that would bring aid to The Shadow. These were the possibilities upon which The Shadow counted as he waited. The likelihood of one chance or another had been the chief reason why The Shadow had undertaken this bold move.

Long hours of contemplation had not dulled The Shadow's keen perception of the future. His senses were at their fullest sharpness. A break would come. The Shadow could foresee it. When the time arrived, inaction would be ended.

Blotted from the view of men who stood five feet away, The Shadow was prepared to use opportunity when it came.

CHAPTER XV
WORD FROM WITHIN

ASIDE from gaining an advantage place between the barriers of his cell, The Shadow had hoped that word of his imprisonment would reach Jericho. It did; and by a very direct route. Bronden had come upstairs to report immediately after his inspection of The Shadow's cell.

Tallam gave the order that The Shadow was to receive no food for the present. After Bronden had gone, Tallam began to discuss his decision with

Barfield. Standing as close to the living room door as he could, Jericho overheard their conversation.

"His early recovery is not surprising," asserted Tallam. "This room has a large cubic area. The vapor did not completely saturate it. I calculated that the effects might pass in about twenty-four hours."

"Logical enough," agreed Barfield, "but since he has recovered, why not feed him? You know how it has worked with the others. The better we treat them for a while, the more they fear another gas treatment."

Tallam shook his head.

"This prisoner is a different case," he declared. "Soft treatment will not lessen The Shadow's resistance. He needs another stretch of inactivity. We shall give it to him."

Tallam opened a small cabinet beside his desk. Inside were knobs, each marked with a number. They corresponded to the cells that held the prisoners. Tallam chose the one that represented The Shadow's cell. He turned the knob.

"Five minutes will suffice," declared Tallam, tersely. "The cell is filling with gas, enough to render him powerless for twelve hours longer."

"Unless," warned Barfield, "he manages to somehow plug the pipes."

"Impossible," explained Tallam. "The openings are high on the walls and in the ceiling. They can scarcely be detected, and they are out of reach. Furthermore"—he chuckled as he pointed to a dial above the buttons—"this indicator marks the flow of gas. Any obstruction would produce a zero registration on the dial."

Confident in his tone, Tallam sat back and watched the indicator; he timed the period by a small clock on his desk. When five minutes had passed, Tallam announced:

"That settles The Shadow for the next twelve hours. There is no possible way in which he could have escaped the charge of gas. Remember, Roger, the vapor will persist until the doors are opened. If our prisoner attempted to hold his breath, he merely postponed the outcome."

Tallam turned off the knob. The dial dropped to zero. Barfield looked pleased; he liked Tallam's precise methods. The keeping of the prisoners and their treatment was Tallam's task. Barfield served as field general of the Golden Masks.

"Cell five." Tallam spoke musingly, then turned another knob. "That is where we have Gilden Cleatland, the Texas millionaire. He is supposed to be on a yacht cruise; instead, he is enjoying our hospitality."

"You are giving him another dose of gas?" inquired Barfield. "I thought we intended to talk to him tomorrow?"

"We shall," promised Tallam, "but he has experienced too long a recovery. Twelve hours more of helplessness will convince him that it would be wise to forget those oil options."

"And let us bag the million dollars that they will bring."

"Precisely. Keep your eye on the clock, Roger, while I watch the dial. Tell me exactly when the five minutes are up."

JERICHO heard much of this conversation; but he did not grasp its importance during the first two minutes. When the truth dawned upon him, Jericho almost forgot himself. He was on the point of driving into the room; battling it out with Tallam and Barfield. However, he managed to curb himself.

From what Tallam and Barfield had said, Jericho understood that The Shadow was merely being reduced to helplessness, not receiving permanent injury. Since Jericho thought that he would eventually have to manage a rescue entirely on his own, he decided it best to let the present deed be done. Tallam and Barfield would be less wary when The Shadow was helpless. That would give Jericho a better opportunity for action.

Moreover, Jericho saw the futility of an attack. Barfield had been immune from Tallam's bullets, while standing in the rear alcove. Chances were that the leaders of the Golden Masks would be safe in the side alcove, where they were at present. Jericho realized that if he attacked, he might be trapped; and his service for The Shadow ended.

When Barfield announced the end of the five minutes, Tallam turned off the knob that controlled the gas jets of Cleatland's cell. His chuckle told that he thought two prisoners were immobile. Barfield thought the same. So, for that matter, did Jericho.

It never occurred to Tallam and Barfield that The Shadow could have chosen a new prison between the doors of his cell. In that airtight space, he was completely immune to the yellow gas that had filled his larger prison.

Tallam glanced at the desk clock and noted the hour.

"We must leave for the meeting," he told Barfield. "Bronden can remain here as before. Member Gamma will not be missed. We shall have a while to wait at the meeting place."

"Matters will go all right at Jaffley's," assured Barfield. "Ralbot is due there within the next hour."

"Every detail is covered," added Tallam. "Member Epsilon is competent. He will see to it that our new prisoner is shipped to the meeting place."

"The truck is ready," reminded Barfield. "It is stowed in back of the garage by this time. It wasn't wise to let it be seen around Jaffley's house until after dark."

"You put the usual driver on the job?"

"Yes. The fellow who used to handle the cab that brought Member Mu to the meetings. It was best to arrange for him to take the truck to the meeting place, rather than let him know about our head-quarters here."

"Quite right. We can bring the prisoner here afterward. Well, Roger, let us start. By this time Freeland Ralbot is on his way to visit Jay Jaffley. Good luck to him."

THE two arose and walked from the living room. Jericho had resumed a slow patrol by the time they arrived in the hall. Tallam spoke a few words in French, ordering the new guard to remain on his present duty. Stolidly, Jericho watched the two men depart toward the rear of the floor.

Jericho quickly guessed that he would not have a long time here alone. Someone would have to take the place of Tallam and Barfield, in this vital center spot. The only man who could act in that capacity was Bronden. He would probably be upstairs within the next five minutes.

Believing that The Shadow was powerless, Jericho saw no chance for immediate gain through a rescue of his chief. He wanted Tallam and Barfield to be well away before he took up that task. But Jericho did see a present opportunity. Stepping into the living room, he went to Tallam's desk, picked up paper and pencil, to scrawl a note.

Jericho remembered what he had heard Tallam and Barfield say. A man named Freeland Ralbot was on his way to visit another named Jay Jaffley. There was a truck hidden behind Jaffley's garage, ready to receive a new victim, who would be carried to the meeting place, then here. Jericho put down those facts.

The huge African stepped to the window in back of Tallam's desk. He pressed against the pane, gazed downward into the area beside the house. Close to the window, Jericho knew that he could be seen if anyone happened to be watching from below. Tallam had left the desk light burning; it gave sufficient illumination to outline Jericho's form.

Three minutes passed. They were all that Jericho could allow. He hoped that Hawkeye had sneaked along below, that the little spotter had spied him. Taking a chance on it, Jericho tried to open the window. He found that the heavy wooden sashes were bolted into place. The thickness of the glass indicated that it was bulletproof.

Using his full strength, Jericho pressed upward against the lower sash. The bulging of his huge muscles told that they possessed gigantic power. The bolts were too solid, even for Jericho; the wood-work could not stand the strain. It gave a trifle as the bolts resisted. The lower sash moved up a fraction of an inch, the bolts loosening within it.

Jericho did not want to break the sash beyond repair; for it would attract Bronden's attention when the lieutenant arrived. As the sash gave a tri-fle more, it reached the condition that Jericho required. Though the bolts were still in place, the wood about them had yielded.

Jericho forced the lower sash just far enough upward to produce a slight crack between the sash and the sill. Jericho shoved the note through the space, let it flutter down into the darkness.

Jericho gesticulated at the window; a signal to Hawkeye, should the spotter be below. That done, Jericho eased the sash into its original position. He eyed it, saw that it appeared to be in its solid con-dition. That meant that Jericho would not have to fight it out with Bronden as soon as the lieutenant arrived. Bronden would think that all was well; he would never guess that the new guard had managed outside contact.

JERICHO returned to the hall; he had spent six minutes in his efforts. Bronden had not arrived. Resuming his stolid pacing, Jericho made ready for the man's appearance. Everytime he passed the doorway of the living room Jericho eyed a telephone that rested on Tallam's desk.

He would have liked to make an outside call, to Burbank; but he was not sure that it would be safe. Tallam had so many mechanical arrangements in the house that it was possible he had provided against any unauthorized calls.

Jericho could picture a glimmering light some-where below, that would tell Bronden if the tele-phone were in use. Therefore, he decided to depend upon Hawkeye. Jericho had been assured that any signal he made from within the house would be promptly noted.

Unfortunately, Jericho had not fully understood the import of the message that he had sent. He was not to be blamed, for Tallam and Barfield had not been too specific in their conversation. Their men-tion of Member Epsilon had made their speech somewhat ambiguous. Odd consequences would be due as a result of Jericho's message.

Offsetting that was the fact that other results were due within this very house. They, too, were something that Jericho did not foresee. They con-cerned The Shadow, whose present plight was far different from the sort that Jericho had pictured.

The Shadow, like Jericho, had counted upon a break. He had forced it, by letting his recovery be noted. Sidney Tallam, contemptuous of his prisoner, had shot through another blast of paralyzing gas. His partner, Roger Barfield, had witnessed the deed.

The Golden Masks had no suspicion of Jericho; they were totally untroubled about The Shadow. Therefore, they felt full security. Their mental attitude had reached the very state that The Shadow had hoped it would.

CHAPTER XVI
FROM THE DARK

STANDING encased between glass and steel, The Shadow was at that moment watching men who stood in the passage outside his cell. Sidney Tallam and Roger Barfield had reached the underground corridor. They stood in conference with Bronden.

The Shadow's hat brim was pressed in front of his eyes; only the slight up-tilt of his head enabled him to observe the men beyond the glass. At one moment, Barfield glanced in The Shadow's direction; he saw nothing but the blackness beyond the glass.

That was not surprising; for there were men present far keener of sight than any of the Golden Masks. They were two of the Ashanti: Lothkal and the new recruit who had come with Jericho. The Shadow saw Lothkal speak to the new tribesman, as if instructing him. The Shadow knew that the man was a newcomer.

That meant that Jericho was quite likely to be within the house, since Seeklat had obtained at least one new guard.

Tallam, as he spoke to Bronden, gestured toward two cells. One was The Shadow's. Bronden nodded his understanding. Carrying suitcases, Tallam and Barfield made their departure along the underground passage.

Bronden gave an order to Lothkal. The Ashanti went to the cell that Tallam had first indicated. It was the one that held Cleatland, the wealthy Texan. Bronden pulled one switch; the glass door slid back. He pulled the second switch to open the steel barrier. Darkness showed beyond the gap; Bronden entered and found the light. When he turned it on, The Shadow could see a sprawled figure on a cot.

Cleatland had evidently been asleep, with the light out, when the new shock of gas had overpowered him. Bronden ordered Lothkal to remain at the open doors while the cell cleared of gas. He showed Lothkal his watch; tapped it, to indicate the time that the doors were to remain open.

About to walk away, Bronden pointed to The Shadow's cell and made another remark to Lothkal. Bronden headed in the direction of the house; The Shadow promptly guessed the reason for the remark. He knew that Tallam had poured gas into the cell that he had left.

Soon, The Shadow's cell would be opened; if the same process took place, the glass door would slide first. That would leave The Shadow free. Time lingered, however; it was fully fifteen minutes before Lothkal closed the doors.

The Ashanti could apparently tell time quite well without a watch. Moreover, he seemed to expect Bronden's return. If Bronden came back before The Shadow's cell was opened, it would mean a battle with three fighters: Bronden and the two Ashanti. Eyeing the huge Africans, The Shadow saw heavy odds ahead. He hoped that Jericho might manage to come along with Bronden.

WHILE The Shadow considered these possibilities, a different one took place. Lothkal stopped by The Shadow's door, waited there impatiently. Finally, he spoke to the new Ashanti, told the recruit to go upstairs and find Bronden. Lothkal held up five fingers and the Ashanti nodded. Lothkal had signified a number of minutes.

The recruit went from the passage. Lothkal stood stolid and immobile, staring toward the closed doors of Cleatland's cell. The Shadow timed the minutes with his slow drawn breaths. At the end of five, Lothkal stirred. The Ashanti had counted the time interval almost exactly with The Shadow.

Lothkal scowled, seeing no sign of the recruit's return. He swung toward The Shadow's cell, placed a huge hand upon the switch that controlled the glass door. Lothkal waited, allowing almost a minute more. His hand seemed reluctant to pull the switch; but finally his hesitation ended. Lothkal started the glass door on its opening slide.

The Ashanti was looking straight toward the barriers as the glass one opened. The removal of the reflecting surface gave him a chance to observe The Shadow, for the darkness was less intense when the glass was gone. In fact, Lothkal did see The Shadow; but his first glimpse came an instant late.

Just as the glass edge cleared him, The Shadow swung outward. His period of immobility was ended. He snapped to action with the power of a long-held spring. Whipping forward, he shot his cloaked arms toward Lothkal. Viselike fingers gripped the Ashanti's throat before the fellow knew what was upon him.

That first advantage was vital to The Shadow. The fight that followed proved it. Weaponless, The Shadow had attacked a formidable battler, who towered a full head above him. Lothkal had more than sixty pounds of additional weight. Moreover, he was schooled to bare-handed combat. Ignoring the grip upon his throat, Lothkal seized The Shadow's shoulders, swept his cloaked adversary in the air. He tried to fling The Shadow across the passage. He would have succeeded, but for a quick move of The Shadow's left foot. Flying wide, The Shadow hooked Lothkal's right knee.

**The Shadow … had all but choked Lothkal to death, for the big fighter
had resisted to almost the final moment.**

THAT changed the combat. The Shadow had literally climbed up to the Ashanti's height; and Lothkal could no longer shake him off. Desperately, Lothkal performed a sidewise roll, flung himself to the floor of the passage, in hope of crushing The Shadow beneath him. He was doubly foiled.

Not only did The Shadow maintain his hold; he kicked his foot free as they fell. As Lothkal crashed face forward to the stone, The Shadow escaped his weight with a sidewise twist. The only hold that he retained was that merciless clutch upon Lothkal's windpipe.

Lothkal lashed about like a huge crocodile. The Shadow clung, twisting his opponent's head at will. Lothkal's eyes bulged; big veins formed streaks upon his forehead. He grabbed The Shadow with both his hamlike hands, hoisted him straight upward in the air. The Shadow scaled feet first; but Lothkal could not fling him away.

The Shadow's burning eyes met the Ashanti's bulging gaze. Gloved fingers jabbed harder, deeper. Lothkal rolled, relaxed suddenly. It was his last trick and it partially succeeded. The Shadow's sideslipping weight caused him to loosen his hold for the first time. It was Lothkal's opportunity; had he made the most of it, the odds would have been his. But Lothkal tried to gain the edge too quickly.

As he twisted his head sidewise, he hoisted up on one shoulder, shot a big hand in to grip The Shadow's fingers. Instead of trying to regain his grip, The Shadow let Lothkal's hand intervene, then jabbed both his own hands forward with all his weight behind them.

Lothkal's head bobbed backward; his skull cracked against the stone wall of the passage. Even that jolt could not stun the giant Ashanti; but it shook him. His hand slipped away; The Shadow's fingers instantly regained their former hold, to begin another grind.

HALF a minute later, Lothkal subsided. The Shadow arose and viewed his prone enemy. He had all but choked Lothkal to death, for the big fighter had resisted to almost the final moment. The Shadow observed that Lothkal was still alive; he had reason to suppose that the Ashanti would soon recuperate.

The Shadow pulled the switch that controlled the steel door of his cell. Grabbing Lothkal's body, The Shadow hauled the unconscious fighter through the doorway. Holding his breath, The Shadow hunched Lothkal face downward; yanking off his cloak, he threw it over the Ashanti's body and tossed the slouch hat to the floor beside him.

Taking a breath as he reached the passage, The Shadow sniffed the strong, sweetish gas that was coming from the cell. He closed the doors quickly, so that the remaining fumes would be sufficient to

overpower Lothkal. That accomplished, The Shadow eased against the wall, to recover from the effects of his battle. The struggle against Lothkal had stiffened him, for he had exerted all the strength that he possessed in holding that neck clamp.

It was a few minutes before The Shadow could decide upon his next move. There was no sign of Bronden or the Ashanti recruit. Though neither would prove as formidable as Lothkal, The Shadow could see no wisdom in waiting for a double struggle so soon after his tiring fray with Lothkal. If Jericho came with them, it would put the situation in The Shadow's favor; but The Shadow was not sure that he could count on Jericho's arrival.

The Shadow looked at the doors of other cells. Beyond them were prisoners who needed release, but some were at present paralyzed by gas. If The Shadow opened those doors, he would have to call upon the men who were fit to carry out those who were not.

All this would mean immediate hazard. Any moment, some arriving Ashanti might give an alarm. Meanwhile, Tallam and Barfield were on their way to plot new evil with the other Golden Masks. As he considered the situation, The Shadow saw where he held a marked advantage.

His victory over Lothkal; his planting of the victim in the cell might keep Bronden lulled, until the return of Tallam and Barfield. Nothing would happen to the men in the cells. The best plan was to take up the trail of the men who headed the Golden Masks.

If Jericho were here in the house, The Shadow could learn that fact better by making outside contact than by attempting to find Jericho himself. Present moments were precious; for they gave The Shadow a last opportunity to depart before Bronden or others arrived.

CLOAKLESS, hatless, wearing the garb of Cranston, The Shadow hurried along the passage, following the direction that Tallam and Barfield had followed. He came to a closed door, found the switch that controlled it. Opening the barrier, The Shadow descended to a narrower, lower passage; and closed the door behind him.

The new passage ran for more than a hundred yards, with several short turns, and occasional flights of steps. Its width varied, as did its height; the lights that illuminated it were very few in number. At times, the walls changed from brick to stone; their condition was not always the same. These clues explained its construction.

The passage had been hewn between the foundations of old buildings in the backstreets. Tallam had probably picked the course, through a study of the neighborhood, and had put Ashanti servitors to work. How long the job had required, The Shadow could not tell; but it must have taken several months and the feat was a remarkable one.

Nothing had been neglected. Certain walls had been patched, so that they would not fall through into the cellars of houses. Where the passage crossed streets, it dipped, to avoid water mains and gas pipes. The Ashanti must have been patient as well as capable in order to complete this long burrow.

However, The Shadow had long since decided that Tallam held them in a state of awe. Under the direction of a man whose power they dreaded, it was not surprising that they had finished their assigned task.

The Shadow reached a final turn; the passage widened to form a small square room. Despite his cautious tread, The Shadow clicked a loose stone; before he could halt, a huge man stepped into view from beyond a corner of the room.

The fellow was an Ashanti guard, dressed in leather shirt and leopard skin. He held a sturdy war spear, with a sharp point; he had the weapon at shoulder level, the instant that he appeared. Long fingers gripped the spear; an arm was ready to drive the pike straight for The Shadow's body.

Attack would have been useless. A feint was almost hopeless. One move; one step forward, The Shadow would have been an instant victim. Stopping where he was, The Shadow still stood in danger. The Ashanti was giving him brief moments only. That time space was sufficient. It made The Shadow know that the guard's action was a challenge.

In the calm tone of Cranston, The Shadow spoke the first word that Sulgate had mentioned as a countersign:

"Ashanti."

The jungle-garbed guard half lowered his spear. Meeting the Ashanti's gaze, The Shadow added:

"Kumasi."

The Ashanti turned to a metal door. Above it, The Shadow saw a wired object that looked like a loudspeaker. The guard drew a large bolt, pulled the handle of the door and slid the barrier aside. The Shadow strolled through, came into a small stone room. He heard the door slide shut behind him.

Outside of a few battered chairs, the room had no other furniture. There was a slope in the corner that denoted a flight of stairs; and The Shadow saw a small closet beneath the slant. He opened the door; probing deep in darkness, he found wires and touched a tiny round microphone that was set in the baseboard.

Anyone coming into this room from outside could gain admission through to the passage quite easily. He had only to open the door of the closet and speak the word: Ashanti; followed by Kumasi. The guard would hear and open the metal barrier.

Because of visits from Barfield and Bronden, with other persons in prospect, Tallam had instructed the distant guard to pass any one who gave the countersign. That had served The Shadow well; by avoiding battle with the outside guard, he had again managed to keep his escape unknown.

THERE was a door in the far wall of the room that The Shadow had reached. Passing through it, he found himself in the rear of an old garage, which was only about half filled with cars.

A partition cut off this empty section of the garage; and there was a back door that could be reached without going past the cars. The Shadow chose that secluded exit; reaching a street, he took survey of his whereabouts. He knew the neighborhood well enough to recognize that he was almost two blocks from Tallam's house.

With swift strides, The Shadow made in the direction of the brownstone house. There was no need for stealth, for this neighborhood was unwatched. It was not until he turned the corner of Marview Place that The Shadow slackened his stride.

He saw Moe's cab at the hack stand across the street; he was about to head for it when he noted a hunched figure edging out from beside Tallam's mansion. Close to the wall of another building, The Shadow made a half a dozen quick strides. A wizened face turned suddenly toward The Shadow; a quick hand jabbed to a jacket pocket.

The Shadow caught the moving arm; in hissed tone, he gave the command:

"Report."

Eyes blinked both wonderment and delight. The Shadow had encountered Hawkeye; the spotter was completely flabbergasted to find his chief at large. For a moment, he could not speak; then, flattened against the wall, he whispered hoarsely.

"I got a tip from Jericho," the spotter told The Shadow. "Shot it to Burbank; he sent Vincent on the job. Here it is."

Hawkeye pushed Jericho's message into The Shadow's hand. Pocketing the paper, The Shadow ordered the spotter to join him in the cab. Both took a separate course; they arrived almost without notice. Moe heard the opening of a door, however; he turned around, then gave an audible gasp as he heard The Shadow's hissed whisper.

The Shadow ordered Moe to drive to the garage two blocks away. As they rode past the lighted corner, he held Jericho's message to the window; read it by the light of the street corner. The cab reached the garage and stopped there. The Shadow ordered Hawkeye to leave the cab and keep watch near the rear door of the garage.

As soon as Hawkeye had left, the cab rolled

away. Upon the seat, he discovered a bag which he knew contained hat, cloak and guns. Burbank had ordered Moe to carry this new outfit in readiness. No matter what plight The Shadow might find, Burbank always anticipated his return.

The cab reached a corner drugstore. The Shadow alighted, entered the store and went to a telephone booth. He dialed Burbank's number. A methodical voice responded:

"Burbank speaking."

"Report."

THE SHADOW'S whispered word did not astonish Burbank. Stationed for long intervals in a hidden contact post, handling the threads that linked The Shadow with his active agents, Burbank was too methodical to be astonished. It was his task to move the active agents during intervals when The Shadow was unable to give instructions.

"Vincent has gone to Jaffley's," stated Burbank, taking it for granted that The Shadow had already learned of Jericho's message. "Address 810 Shore Road, Silverbrook, Long Island. Telephone temporarily disconnected. Impossible to communicate with Jay Jaffley, except by personal call."

The Shadow questioned Burbank as to the time of Vincent's departure. He learned that the agent had left fifteen minutes before, in his own car. Briefly, The Shadow new instructions to Burbank; told him to have agents in readiness for new action. That done, The Shadow came from the drugstore.

His leisurely manner ceased the moment that he boarded the cab. His call was for speed, and Moe gave it. The cab wheeled eastward, headed for the nearest East River bridge. It was bound for Silverbrook, a Long Island suburb within the New York City limits. Moe could reach Jaffley's within the next half an hour.

Temporarily, The Shadow had dropped Sidney Tallam and Roger Barfield, the insidious chieftains who ruled the Golden Masks. They could come later; for the present, The Shadow was faring forth to block a scheme of crime. Alone, Harry Vincent might fail. He had gone to carry a warning to a victim threatened by the Golden Masks. That was not enough.

Knowing the insidious measures of which the Golden Masks were capable, The Shadow saw the need of action. Moreover, in his brief reading of Jericho's note, he had found its details meager. Much might be beneath the surface of the scheduled episode at Jay Jaffley's Long Island residence.

The Shadow knew. He had been at grips with the leaders of the Golden Masks. He knew their subtle methods. The Shadow alone could offset the strategy of the Golden Masks. From the dark, he had struck to gain escape. From the dark, The Shadow would strike again.

CHAPTER XVII
THE COMING VICTIM

AT the very time when The Shadow was starting his swift trip to Long Island, a coupé pulled up in front of Jay Jaffley's home at Silverbrook. The young man who alighted from the car was Harry Vincent. The Shadow's agent had made an unusually rapid trip to his destination.

Harry had started from the Hotel Metrolite, in New York; he had been there, temporarily off duty, when he had received Burbank's call. Harry's coupé had been outside the hotel; he had taken a direct street to an East River bridge. On the Long Island side, he had caught traffic at an ebb. As a result, Harry had not lost a single minute in his trip.

As he viewed Jaffley's house, Harry recalled certain facts that Burbank had given him over the telephone. At his contact post, Burbank kept stacks of reference books from which he could obtain needed information. The contact man had gained data concerning Jay Jaffley and Freeland Ralbot, for both were men of some prominence.

Jaffley rated high. He was an insurance man of considerable standing. Ralbot, on the contrary, was a promoter of questionable record. Several of his enterprises had been investigated; and although Ralbot had been cleared in every case, he was not the sort to be accepted with full confidence.

Therefore, Harry had formed a definite idea of the setup. Jay Jaffley, a wealthy man of a conservative type, was to receive a visit from Freeland Ralbot, a man of doubtful character. Secret steps had been taken to post a truck in back of Jaffley's garage; in readiness to receive a captured victim. Unquestionably, underlings who served the Golden Masks would be on hand to make the seizure.

Noting the secluded situation of Jaffley's house, Harry saw how easy it would be for a man like Ralbot to take Jaffley unaware. Aided by a strong-arm crew, Ralbot would have no trouble carrying Jaffley from the house. Harry pictured Jaffley as another Lengerton, due for serious trouble if he failed to accept the terms offered by the Golden Masks.

There were no cars in front of the house. Harry took it for granted that Ralbot had not arrived. Knowing that time was short, Harry went directly to the front door and rang the bell. He was admitted by a butler, who nodded when Harry asked if Mr. Jaffley was at home. Harry gave his name; the butler went away and returned to announce that Jaffley would see him.

HARRY found the insurance man in an enclosed sun parlor near the rear of the house. Jaffley was short of stature, keen-eyed and dark-haired. He received Harry with an affable handshake; but it was apparent that he wondered why this stranger had come here. Harry waited until the butler was gone, then opened conversation.

"Mr. Jaffley," he said, "I understand that you expect a visit from a man named Freeland Ralbot."

Jaffley nodded. His face looked puzzled. He seemed to wonder how this visitor had learned of tonight's appointment.

"I suppose that Ralbot will be here shortly," resumed Harry. "Therefore, I should like to give you a warning before his arrival. The man is not to be trusted."

Jaffley smiled indulgently. He seemed to be impressed by Harry's clean-cut appearance and obvious sincerity. Otherwise, he might have displayed anger at Harry's blunt statements.

"I know all about Ralbot," remarked Jaffley. "The fellow has a doubtful past. Men like myself have invested in his enterprises, and have lost money doing so. I do not intend to make a similar error. I thank you for your warning, Mr. Vincent; but unless you have new and startling information regarding Ralbot, we will simply waste time in discussing him."

Harry took the opening that Jaffley's statement offered.

"I have new facts," declared The Shadow's agent, slowly. "Startling ones, too. Freeland Ralbot is more than an ordinary swindler. He is linked with a criminal band that has managed to evade the law in all its operations."

The insurance man registered intense interest.

"Let me mention the most recent case," declared Harry, making his tone more brisk. "A shipping man named James Lengerton was forced, under threat, to dispose of a million dollars' worth of air-line stocks. Lengerton has disappeared; his secretary was murdered."

"I know!" exclaimed Jaffley. Then, in a startled tone: "You believe that Ralbot was responsible?"

"Not necessarily," returned Harry. "But I believe that he is linked with the organization that threatened Lengerton. Tell me, Mr. Jaffley; have you received any veiled threats from an unknown source?"

"None at all."

"Then Ralbot is probably the missionary of the group in question. He will make the threats."

"If he does, I shall turn him over to the law."

Jaffley spoke with assurance. His smile showed a contempt for any threat that Ralbot might make. Harry saw need to play a stronger hand.

"The threats will come," he promised, "but Ralbot will probably be cagey enough to insist that he is acting against his will. He will deliver an ultimatum from the criminal band. If you refuse it, you will suffer."

Jaffley laughed; his tone showed disbelief and annoyance. He acted as though he took Harry for a crank.

"Tell me then, Mr. Vincent," suggested the insurance man. "If such an organization exists, what is the name of it? And how could such a band manage to harm me? Why do you think that they would strike immediately? Answer those questions, and perhaps I may believe you."

HARRY hesitated a moment; then, realizing that Ralbot might arrive at any minute, he staked everything on a complete reply.

"The organization is called the Golden Masks," he declared solemnly. "It is composed of criminals who have harmed others, and can, therefore, molest you. As proof that the Golden Masks intend to strike tonight, you will find a truck hidden in back of your garage, ready to carry you away if necessary."

Harry's words hit home. Jaffley came to his feet in alarm. He started to call a servant. Harry halted him.

"I would not advise sending men to the garage," warned Harry. "A dangerous squad may be posted there. Your best step, Mr. Jaffley, is to leave here at once. Tell your servants that you will return shortly, that you want Ralbot to wait for you. You can go with me, in my car. We can call the police, have them capture Ralbot and his crew."

Jaffley nodded, then paused. He eyed Harry sharply, then questioned:

"Just how do you think Ralbot would work his game?"

Harry decided that a prompt answer would be the best method to convince Jaffley that departure was necessary.

"He will blackmail you," Harry told the insurance man. "That is the method that was used with Lengerton and others. Ralbot may know something that you would prefer to have forgotten."

Jaffley shook his head emphatically.

"My past is entirely clear," he declared. "That could not be Ralbot's method, Mr. Vincent."

"Then he will simply demand a sum of money—"

"Wrong again, Mr. Vincent. Your answers do not fit the circumstances. I suppose you think that Ralbot approached me regarding his visit here tonight?"

"Of course."

"The case is quite the opposite." Jaffley's smile became hard. "Ralbot's visit is of my arrangement. He is coming here with cash and stacks of securities, which he intends to show me as proof that he is worthy to be my partner in a huge enterprise.

"When Ralbot arrives"—Jaffley reached to a table and picked up a small folio, from which papers protruded—"I shall show him these. Ralbot will read confidential reports and affidavits concerning some of his past promotions. These papers are faked; but Ralbot may not suspect it."

Laying the folio aside, Jaffley indulged in a harsh laugh.

"Freeland Ralbot will either turn over to me the quarter of a million that he has with him," declared Jaffley, "or he will become a victim. You are right, Mr. Vincent, when you say that the Golden Masks are dangerous, that they have made arrangements to carry away a victim. But I shall not become the prisoner. The man who will be taken is—"

"Freeland Ralbot!"

EJACULATING the name, Harry came to his feet. In an instant he had seen through the game. It was Jaffley, not Ralbot, who worked with the Golden Masks! The whole situation was the reverse of the one that Harry had pictured!

With Jaffley at their service, the Golden Masks had the edge on Ralbot. Jaffley was a man with a high reputation, falsely built. Ralbot was one upon whom doubt had been cast. No one would ever suspect that Jaffley, a man of supposed integrity, had been instrumental in an attack upon a person of Ralbot's poor repute.

Just as The Shadow had walked into trouble with Barfield and Tallam, so had Harry entered a mesh by this visit to Jaffley. With his quick realization, Harry saw need for fast action. He jabbed his hand to his coat pocket, gripped an automatic with his fingers. His only chance was to whip out a gun and cover Jaffley before the crook could move.

Harry never pulled the weapon. As Jaffley leaned back to deliver a disdainful laugh, two husky servants pounced through from the house door. Jaffley had witnessed their sneaky arrival, while Harry had not. The brawny pair was upon The Shadow's agent before Harry could bring his hand from his pocket.

Though his arms were clipped from in back, Harry put up a fierce struggle. He twisted half free, dragged his foemen in Jaffley's direction. Then Jaffley himself came into the fray. He jabbed stout hands for Harry's throat, choked the prisoner into submission while the others stopped Harry's flailing arms.

As he sank back in the grip of his captors, Harry saw Jaffley step to a cabinet at the side of the porch. From it, the crook brought a huge glass jar inverted, and with a rubber-sheeted bottom. A coiled hose unwound as Jaffley came toward Harry.

While the servants gripped their victim, Jaffley clamped the jar over Harry's head. Rubber edges rubbed against Harry's face, then formed a collar about his neck. Another servant arrived to steady the glass jar while Harry tried to struggle. Jaffley sprang back to the cabinet, pulled a lever there.

Gas hissed about Harry's ears. His nostrils scented a strong, sweetish odor. The scene faded in a cloud of yellowish vapor which swirled before Harry's eyes. Through it, he caught glimpses of Jaffley's leering countenance; he could see the grinning faces of the servants who held him.

WEAKNESS followed. Harry's whole body seemed paralyzed. His eyes bulged; they could stare, but he could not move them. His neck loosened; Harry's head thumped the inside of the glass jar. He could not feel the thud.

Yellow blurred his eyes; he was lost in a swirling chaos. Harry's sense of time was gone; the period that followed seemed interminable, for Harry had no way of measuring the minutes that passed.

Actually, the time of Harry's ordeal was short; for Jay Jaffley was in a hurry to dispose of this victim. The dark-haired man choked off the gas within four minutes after the flow had begun. Jaffley gauged his action by watching for the sag of Harry's body.

Once the gas was off, Jaffley wasted no additional time. He ordered the man who held the cylinder to lift it. Away it came; the servants cleared it by spreading the rubber bottom. The gas that drifted out was quickly absorbed by the air of the enclosed porch.

Hurriedly, Jaffley replaced the cylinder in its cabinet, along with the coils of hose. Harry, his eyes fixed in a rigid stare, could see the events that followed. Though his body seemed nonexistent, his mind was clear. He heard the order that Jaffley gave.

"Take him out to the truck," rasped the self-admitted crook. "Tell the driver to take him to the appointed place, then return at once. There will be another man for him to carry."

The servants lugged Harry through the door to the house, choosing that route to gain a back door that led outside. Propped between two huskies, Harry was no burden. His legs dragged, walking almost of their own accord, as Lengerton's had done that night when he had been removed from his office. Like Tallam and Barfield on that other night, Jaffley watched the victim's departure.

Standing with one servant still beside him, Jaffley listened. Soon, he heard the throb of the truck's motor. In less than fifteen minutes after his arrival at this house, Harry Vincent was being carried away, a prisoner of the Golden Masks.

The truck's motor faded into the distance. As the sound ended, a new noise came. It was the tingle of the front door bell. With a hard grin, Jaffley turned to the servant beside him.

"It is Freeland Ralbot," remarked Jaffley. "Admit him and bring him here at once."

As the servant left to obey, Jaffley's hard manner altered. Once again, he was smugly pleasant, as he awaited his next victim. Jay Jaffley felt sure that the leaders of the Golden Masks would express their full approval of Member Epsilon's smooth work tonight.

CHAPTER XVIII
THE ASHANTI MASK

HARDLY had Jay Jaffley seated himself beside the sun-porch table when the servant reappeared, bringing a portly, gray-haired man. Jaffley looked up to see a pudgy, wide-smiling countenance. He recognized Freeland Ralbot. Jaffley arose to shake hands with the visitor.

Ralbot looked the part of a glib promoter. He was jolly, affable, warm with his handshake. He placed a briefcase beside his chair, sat down and began to put an unnecessary apology for being late.

"I just left a big conference," confided Ralbot. "Whatever your proposition is, Mr. Jaffley, I can line up half a dozen investors who will be waving money in their fists. Stock promotion is my specialty."

"So I understand," remarked Jaffley, in a dry tone. "I have heard a great deal regarding your former enterprises."

Ralbot showed a flicker of worry, then shook his head and smiled.

"They didn't all pan out," he admitted. "When a big deal falls through, there are always squawks. I didn't make it a practice to be too particular in choosing investors. Some of them talked big, then didn't put up money when it was needed. Whenever a proposition flopped, they blamed it on me."

"I understand."

"I know you do, Mr. Jaffley." Ralbot spoke in a tone of real sincerity. "That's why I agreed to put up a quarter of a million of my own money, to match the amount you've promised. With half a million as a starter, we can get plenty more investors interested in this new mutual insurance company. Insurance is your business. You stand high in that line."

Ralbot paused to motion toward the briefcase.

"The funds are there," he told Jaffley. "The total profits from all of my promotions that turned out successfully. I'm putting it all in your hands. Just give me full receipt; and sign our business agreement. If—"

Jaffley waved an interruption. A servant had stopped by the door; he could hear the others coming into the house.

"You have the key to my coupé?" queried Jaffley, speaking to the servant. Then, as the man nodded: "Very well. Drive it into the garage. Return here afterward."

As the servant went away, Jaffley turned to Ralbot, to ask:

"Did you drive here?"

"I came by train," replied Ralbot. "A cab brought me up from the station. Say—it's great out here in the country. Fresh air everywhere."

He paused to sniff; his fatty forehead furrowed.

"You must have some fine flower beds, Mr. Jaffley," remarked Ralbot. "There seems to be a perfume in this sun porch."

"Yes," agreed Jaffley, with a slight smile. "You must come here in the daytime, Mr. Ralbot. The flower gardens are magnificent. But let us get back to business, Mr. Ralbot. Before we proceed further, I want you to look over these."

JAFFLEY handed Ralbot the folio that was on the table. The promoter drew out papers with his pudgy hands, began to study the documents. His gaze narrowed; his lips stiffened as they lost their smile.

"These are lies!" exclaimed Ralbot. "I never swindled the investors who put money into those Pacific Coast companies! I can disprove every statement!"

"Some of those are signed affidavits," remarked Jaffley, indicating certain papers. "Look them over more carefully."

"The men who signed them have committed perjury!" stormed Ralbot. "These are lies, I tell you!"

"What if they were made public?" queried Jaffley, in a speculative tone. "Do you think they would help us in the promotion of a new insurance company?"

"Of course not," retorted Ralbot. "But there is no need to make them public. They would cause me annoyance, of course."

"I see. Then they would just about ruin any new promotion that you might undertake."

Ralbot chewed his fattish lips. He saw Jaffley's point. Spiking these charges would be a difficult task; one that might not work out to Ralbot's benefit. Jaffley emphasized it.

"If the signers of these affidavits appeared in court," he told Ralbot, "and stood by their sworn statements, the burden would be thrown on you. Perhaps those men believe that they were swindled. I think that a jury would be inclined to stand by them. Of course, if we could manage to get new affidavits from the same persons, repudiating those, matters would be better. Similarly, I think that the confidential reports could be forgotten."

"Maybe you're right," admitted Ralbot. "You want me to settle these matters before we go ahead with our new promotion. Very well. Twenty or thirty thousand dollars would do it. I can scrape that together, without touching the quarter million that I am turning over to you."

"You misunderstand me," returned Jaffley. "The terms are these, Mr. Ralbot. You can keep these affidavits and reports. I shall obtain retractions and forward them to you. Everything will be perfectly smoothed, out of the money that you leave with me tonight."

"About twenty thousand dollars of it?"

"No, no. All of the quarter million. It is quite simple, Mr. Ralbot. I keep your funds, but give you no receipt. You leave here, a bit wiser than before you came. Wise enough, in fact, to say nothing about the matter—"

Ralbot bellowed an interruption as he came to his feet. He shook a fat fist in Jaffley's face.

"This is a holdup!" roared Ralbot. "You're a crook, Jaffley, but you can't get away with it! I'm too wise for you! There are securities here that need my signature for proper transfer—"

"So I supposed," interposed Jaffley. "Of course, you will sign them?"

"Never! No threat can make me do so!"

Jaffley snapped his fingers. His three servants appeared with precision. Ralbot turned clumsily about, gaped as he saw the strong-arm crew in the wide doorway.

"Will you sign over your securities, Mr. Ralbot?"

"No." Ralbot scowled the retort, in reply to Jaffley's question. "You can't thug me into it, Jaffley. If this mob of yours murders me, the law will know that something is wrong. You'll never cash that stuff, Jaffley. It will be too hot for you."

"You will be persuaded later," remarked Jaffley. "Fortunately, I know that you have wisely refrained from telling anyone that you had business with me. I know a form of treatment that makes men glad to do as they are told, and keep quiet into the bargain."

ANOTHER snap of Jaffley's fingers. As one, the three servants sprang upon the pudgy man. They buckled Ralbot's arms behind him, stifled the cries that he tried to give. Two were enough to hold Ralbot. The third servant produced the gas cylinder. Jaffley nodded for them to proceed. Calmly, he walked into the house.

Purple of face Ralbot collapsed before the cylinder was clamped over his beefy head. He was no match for the men who grappled with him; the two who held him were actually propping his shaky body when the third applied the big glass jar. Substituting for Jaffley, that third servant turned on the gas. A new supply of the yellowish anesthetic enveloped Ralbot's head. The servants gave good measure. Five minutes were gone before the cylinder was lifted. Two men still supported Ralbot; the third drew away the big glass. Ugly-faced, Jaffley's servitors surveyed their handiwork, jesting as they looked at Ralbot's bulgy eyes,

which formed a ludicrous sight as they stared from above the victim's fatty cheeks.

The man with the cylinder turned away, just as the others swung Ralbot about. He chanced to observe the inner door before the others. The gulp that he gave was so sudden that it halted the others in alarm. They saw their comrade staring with a glassy gaze that was as fixed as Ralbot's. For a moment, they thought that he had received a dose of the paralyzing gas.

Then their own eyes bulged.

This trio had expected Jaffley to return. Instead, an intruder had stepped from the house door. He had come like a ghost, this invader, and his garb made him appear as a being from another plane. He was cloaked in black from head to foot.

Jaffley's minions were faced by The Shadow. Eyes burned upon them. Looming automatics displayed their yawning muzzles.

A hissed command told crooks to stand as they were. The two who held Ralbot trembled; the bulky man slipped slowly from their clutch, to flop in huddled fashion on the floor. The third man was shaky; the glass cylinder nearly clattered from his hands. The Shadow stepped forward, to back him to the table.

The Shadow gestured with a gun; trembling, the servant turned to set down the cylinder. The jar gave a *clang* as it thumped upon the table. The glass delivered a sharp echo; it was that resonant sound that changed the situation.

The peculiar *clang* drowned another noise; that of approaching footsteps. The Shadow did not hear them for the moment. He was an instant late when he sensed the approach of danger. The Shadow wheeled about, in the very midst of his three foemen, to see another enemy coming from the house door.

It was Jay Jaffley. He had arrived, carrying a suitcase with him. At sight of The Shadow, Jaffley had leaped forward. The bag bounded from his hand and fell to the floor; with his other fist, Jaffley whipped forth a revolver from his pocket.

JAFFLEY'S attack was instinctive. Another fighter might have depended on his gun alone, or made a bare-handed forward spring. The Shadow could have frustrated either form of attack. But Jaffley's double mode of action put The Shadow at a disadvantage.

For the instant, he could risk neither a quick shot nor a grapple. The Shadow faded; in so doing, he sidestepped almost into the arms of the men who had dropped Ralbot. He twisted, expecting to be away before they saw their opportunity to fall upon him. A hoarse shout from Jaffley inspired them to action.

One from each side, the bruisers grabbed for The

Shadow's arms. Each was lucky enough to gain a hold. As they wrested The Shadow back, his gun hands swung up; the weapons pointed above Jaffley's head. With a snarl, Jaffley aimed; his men bent at The Shadow's arms, to poise their prisoner in front of Jaffley's gun.

The Shadow doubled as the grip tightened. He lunged forward; his feet swung up from the floor. Jaffley, jabbing his gun close to The Shadow's chest, was at the very spot The Shadow wanted him to be.

As the weight of his body lurched him from the clutching servants, The Shadow hit Jaffley's shoulder, feet foremost. His body had the drive of a battering ram. Jaffley spun about, hit the floor. His revolver clattered away.

Coming to hands and knees, Jaffley saw his gun lying six feet distant. Twisting into a sprawl, The Shadow was throwing his body upon the weapon, hauling the men who grasped him. They were stumbling with their temporary prisoner. Neither one dared to loosen his grip.

The third servant had dived for the corner where the cabinet stood. He was reaching in his pocket for a revolver. Jaffley saw the futility of shots while The Shadow was twisted in a struggle with two men who were too valuable to lose. He roared a command to the man at the cabinet, telling him to start the gas.

The servant obeyed. Jaffley seized the glass cylinder; he pounced toward The Shadow, coming low, to avoid the gun muzzles that still pointed upward. Gripped tightly, The Shadow was motion-less for the moment. Jaffley saw his chance to jam the hissing cylinder over the head that wore the slouch hat. With a long sweep of his arms, Jaffley brought the big jar forward.

With a hand that was tight against his body, The Shadow pressed the trigger of an automatic. His aim was not for Jaffley; he fired at a closer target. Tilted at the upward angle of a howitzer, The Shadow's .45 was set for a mark it could not miss.

Flame tongued straight for the glass-filled cylinder. A bullet crashed the rounded object, shattered it in Jaffley's very grasp. Glass clattered everywhere; chunks pummeled The Shadow's hat as he ducked his head. Large slivers rattled about Jaffley as the dark-haired crook sprang back with a loud cry. Unlike the barriers that were in Sidney Tallam's house, the glass jar was not shatterproof. The Golden Masks had not foreseen a catastrophe such as this. In one well-chosen shot, The Shadow had changed the entire fray.

Like Jaffley, the men who grappled with The Shadow tried to avoid the chunks of flying glass. It was an instinctive move on their part—one that The Shadow himself might have performed, had he not known that the smash was to come. In that brief falter, the servants lost their hold upon The Shadow; for his lurch was a forward one.

The only man who could have stopped The Shadow was the servant by the cabinet. He not only saw the cloaked fighter snap upward, free and ready for battle; he spied the end of the hose that had been attached to the gas cylinder. From it, a sweep of yellow vapor was pouring into the confines of the enclosed porch.

THE fellow tried to perform two actions at once. He aimed for The Shadow with his gun; with his other hand, he grabbed for the valve that controlled the gas. Hastily, he snapped the revolver trigger; a bullet sizzled six inches wide of The Shadow's cloaked shoulder. That one shot was the servant's last chance.

The Shadow stabbed a reply. His bullet clipped the man's gun arm; sent the rogue spinning to the floor, howling as he fell. The wounded man forgot the lever on the cabinet. The flow of gas maintained its hiss.

The two men who had grappled with The Shadow were coming to their feet, while Jaffley dived to regain his lost revolver. The Shadow drove directly toward his foemen. As the first tried to grab him, bare-fisted, The Shadow sprawled him with a sledgelike blow from an automatic. The other servant stopped halfway to his feet, yanking a revolver, to aim. The Shadow beat him to the shot, winged his shoulder with a scalding bullet.

Only Jaffley remained. He had taken his revolver on a pickup; he had the gun leveled as he swung about in the doorway. Jaffley hoped to drop The Shadow, then take to flight. He saw The Shadow spinning toward the wall, almost beside him. They were separated only by the width of a door that was opened outward, flat against the wall of the sun porch.

Gripping an automatic, The Shadow's left hand had reached the wall to stop his spin. His right was still aiming its gun toward the man whom he had wounded. Instead of pausing to aim, The Shadow hooked the loose door with his left handgun, swung it shut with a terrific slam. Jaffley ducked sidewise from the doorway, stabbing vicious shots. Like the man at the cabinet, he made the mistake of trying two moves at once.

Jaffley had not only lost his aim; by leaping back to a corner of the porch, he had increased the range. His shots zimmed wide. Right-handed, The Shadow fired for Jaffley's body. The single bullet found the crook's heart. Jaffley's leap ended in a long dive to the floor. A member of the Golden Masks, Jaffley was a murderer. His doom was earned.

The Shadow viewed the three servants. One was stunned; the wounded men were groaning as they crawled along the floor. Those two had no fight left. Their gasps were coughed; for yellow gas was forming a rising layer on the low level of the floor. Thrusting his automatics beneath his cloak, The Shadow hoisted Freeland Ralbot.

The Shadow breathed the full strength of the sweetish gas as he stooped to the floor; but his stay was only a matter of seconds. Shoving Ralbot's loosened form through the doorway, The Shadow stepped inside the house. He closed the porch doors; through the glass, he saw Jaffley's servants succumbing to the creeping gas. Soon they would forget the pain of their wounds. None of them would talk or act for many hours to come.

Leaning Ralbot's body against his shoulder, The Shadow steadied the gassed man in balanced position. With a free hand, The Shadow picked up Jaffley's suitcase, then walked Ralbot along in mechanical fashion. Halfway to the front door, The Shadow was met by Moe Shrevnitz, who had dashed in from the cab after hearing the shots. Together, they took Ralbot out to the taxi.

COMMOTION had begun in a neighboring house. Shots had been heard; probably a call had gone to the police. The Shadow ordered Moe to drive for Manhattan, to place Freeland Ralbot in some safe spot. With that, The Shadow moved away in darkness, taking Jaffley's bag with him. The cab sped off.

Soon afterward, sirens sounded. The Shadow heard them, from a lurking spot behind a hedge, where he had a distant view of Jaffley's house. Far enough away to elude any searchers, The Shadow shielded a flashlight and focused its rays upon Jaffley's suitcase. He opened the bag. Gold glimmered from within.

There, set upon a crinkly robe, was an Ashanti mask; the one that Jaffley wore as Member Epsilon. Golden lips wore their half smile. That fixed face seemed to express the insidious spirit that guided the Golden Masks in their reign of crime.

Jericho had written the title of "Member Epsilon" in his note to Hawkeye. The Shadow knew that it was the name that Jay Jaffley bore. As Member Epsilon, Jaffley had intended to attend tonight's meeting of the Golden Masks.

That was a fact that would be useful to The Shadow; but there were other facts that he also recognized. The Shadow knew that Harry Vincent must have been captured and carried away, a prisoner in the truck. Since Freeland Ralbot was to be a later victim, the truck would soon return.

Posted on the route by which the truck was due to come, The Shadow intended to await later developments. He needed a trail to the hidden meeting place of the Golden Masks; and he had chosen the best way to gain it.

The flashlight's glimmer ended. The lid of the suitcase closed. The Shadow waited silently. His vigil was intent as the minutes passed. Opportunity had come The Shadow's way, and it was a golden one. Golden in the shape of an Ashanti mask that was to become The Shadow's passport to a throne room of crime.

The Shadow's .45 was set for a mark

CHAPTER XIX
THE DOUBLE TRAIL

ONE factor had aided The Shadow immensely in his escape from the dungeon of the Golden Masks. The Ashanti whom Lothkal had sent upstairs to Bronden had not returned within the specific time. That was why Lothkal had decided to open the doors of The Shadow's cell, for no word had come to restrain him from that task.

There was a simple reason why the new Ashanti had not returned. He had met Jericho in the hallway on the second floor.

Jericho had let Bronden pass through to the

it could not miss. Flame tongued straight for the glass-filled cylinder.

living room, for he knew that the lieutenant was too important a person to be dealt with early in the game. With Tallam and Barfield gone, Jericho had formed a simple and primitive plan. That was to dispose of persons who would not soon be missed, taking them one at a time. While still debating on the merits of such policy, the arrival of the recruit had caused Jericho to proceed.

Meeting Jericho in the middle of the hall, the Ashanti had stopped to talk in sign language. He pointed toward the doorway of the living room, to indicate that he had a message for Bronden. Jericho had answered with a headshake, and a pointed finger toward a side door that led into a darkened bedroom.

Wondering, the Ashanti had entered; and Jericho had followed, to close the door after him. When the door had opened a few minutes later, only Jericho had returned, to resume his patrol in the hallway.

During the next hour, Jericho stopped often at the living room, to see Bronden seated at Tallam's desk, deeply engrossed with stacks of papers. At intervals, Jericho had been tempted to creep in upon him; but he had remembered the peculiar immunity that the alcoves offered. Therefore, Jericho waited.

It was Bronden who ended the idle spell. He appeared suddenly at the doorway; looked at Jericho and demanded:

"Where's Lothkal? Didn't he come up here?"

Jericho looked blank. "Did he send that fellow who was with him?" queried Bronden. "I told him to let me know before he opened the other cell."

Jericho stared soberly. Bronden suddenly recalled that this new servitor did not speak English. With an impatient gesture, he ordered Jericho to follow him. Wisely, Jericho obeyed. He guessed that Bronden was going down to the cells. This would be a good opportunity to see what could be done to aid The Shadow.

WHEN they reached the cell passage, Bronden stared in puzzlement. He had expected to see Lothkal. Motioning to Jericho to remain on guard, Bronden went to the front of the passage, opened the big door and raised a shout for Seeklat. Soon, the fellow appeared from somewhere. Bronden questioned him in English.

"Where is Lothkal?" demanded the lieutenant. "He was supposed to be in charge here, with the new man."

"Not see Lothkal," replied Seeklat, solemnly. "Me sleep."

Bronden looked toward The Shadow's cell. Angrily, he thrust his hand into his pocket and brought out a large revolver. Ordering Seeklat to back him, motioning Jericho to do the same, Bronden pulled the switches that controlled the

doors of The Shadow's cell. Ready with his revolver, he produced a flashlight as soon as the door came open. Flicking the light, Bronden threw the glow upon the floor.

The lieutenant chuckled harshly when he saw the prone, cloaked figure. He waited for the gas to thin. All the while, Jericho was tightening in preparation for a double struggle. If harm threatened The Shadow, he intended to take out Bronden first.

About to enter the cell, Bronden stopped. He turned to Seeklat.

"This doesn't tell us where Lothkal is," snarled Bronden. "He knows enough to stay on duty. Where could he have gone to, Seeklat?"

Bronden had brought away the flashlight; but the glow from the passage stretched across the threshold of the cell, once the doors were opened. In answer to Bronden's query, Seeklat stared. Trained to sharp observation, Seeklat had noticed a bulkiness about the cloaked figure on the floor. He pointed; then announced:

"Look there."

"Where?" demanded Bronden. He turned the flashlight toward the walls of the cell. "Lothkal isn't in here. Wait, though—there's something—"

Bronden had spotted the broken wall bracket. He went over to examine it. Sensing that something was wrong, he turned about to see Seeklat stolidly stepping into the cell. Framed against the light from the passage, Seeklat pointed to the cloaked shape and again stated:

"Look there."

With a sudden understanding, Bronden came over with his flashlight. He stopped and pulled away The Shadow's hat and cloak. He fumed as he saw the figure beneath. There was the face of Lothkal, staring upward with huge, bulging eyes.

Bronden stood dumbfounded. The odor of gas still persisted in the room; Lothkal was plainly paralyzed by the fumes. Yet The Shadow had managed to withstand the dosage, to overpower Lothkal and leave the Ashanti in his place.

Jericho viewed all this from the door. He repressed the elated grin that crept to his lips. To Jericho, also, the escape was a mystery; but he was used to such exploits on the part of The Shadow.

Events had taken an amazing turn. If any one should be blamed for cooperating in The Shadow's escape, it would be the new Ashanti, whom Jericho had left in an upstairs closet. Bronden himself knew that Jericho had been guarding the second floor. Bronden, however, was too excited to think of anything but the fact that The Shadow was at large.

"You stay here, Seeklat," snapped the lieutenant. "Keep this big fellow with you. Better wake the other men who are asleep. Have everyone ready when I get back."

Bronden hurried to the rear of the corridor; there, he stopped to open the door of an unoccupied cell. He brought out a suitcase of his own, then headed toward the distant exit. He was off for the meeting of the Golden Masks, to inform the leaders that The Shadow had escaped.

Seeklat motioned to Jericho. His gestures signified that the latter was to stay on patrol duty in the passage. Seeklat intended to rouse the remaining Ashanti tribesmen, to have them ready when Bronden returned. That would mean a search of the house, for traces of The Shadow.

Jericho regretted that he had been lenient with the recruit whom he had bound and gagged upstairs. If the fellow could be found unconscious, his plight might be attributed to The Shadow. But Jericho felt sure that the recruit had recovered; he knew that the man would tell who had attacked him. Foreseeing trouble, Jericho took the best way out.

He sprang for Seeklat, as the huge Ashanti was turning toward the front of the passage. Seeklat sensed the attack, swung quickly to meet his antagonist.

JERICHO was powerful; he had proven that in his quick disposal of the man upstairs. There, Jericho had dealt with an opponent just about his equal in size. Seeklat was more formidable. The huge Ashanti was almost the twin of Lothkal, whom The Shadow had overcome only by a super-human fight.

Inches taller and pounds heavier than Jericho, Seeklat had an advantage as the battle began. He did not have the edge that Lothkal had held over The Shadow; for Jericho was heavy enough to hold his footing when Seeklat tried to sling him. Nevertheless, the fray looked hopeless for Jericho.

It was a strange match, this one. Seeklat fought with the savage instinct of a jungle battler. Jericho used methods that he had employed against thugs. In the back of Jericho's head were recollections of surprising methods that he had seen The Shadow introduce in conflict.

The fighters were eye to eye; Seeklat glaring like a savage war dancer, Jericho grinning as though he enjoyed the fray. They staggered back and forth across the passage, each trying to hurl the other against a wall. Each stopped himself by a brace whenever his back neared the wall. Both were able to absorb the jolts.

Though the fight was equal for the first few minutes, it was obvious that Seeklat would wear down Jericho. The latter knew it. He watched for a break. One came, just as Seeklat jammed Jericho against the wall beside Lengerton's door.

As he took the jolt and rallied, Jericho saw beyond Seeklat's shoulder. Across the passage was

the doorway of the cell that had once held The Shadow. Bronden had left the two doors open. The space became Jericho's objective.

Heaving against Seeklat, Jericho drove the Ashanti backward. Seeklat let himself be shoved, expecting a quick opportunity to rally. As they reached the far side of the passage, Seeklat braced. He prepared for a rebound when his shoulders struck the wall.

Jericho gave harder impetus. Seeklat let his shoulders go back. Instead of encountering solid wall, they went through the open doorway. The huge Ashanti toppled off balance; Jericho hurled him to the floor inside the cell, only three feet from Lothkal's prone body.

Seeklat was not through. His hands grabbed for Jericho's throat. Seeklat's head came up; Jericho drove a big fist to the Ashanti's jaw. The blow flattened Seeklat; but failed to stun him.

Jericho was smart enough not to try again. Instead, he sprang away from Seeklat's clutch and leaped from the cell before the Ashanti could regain his feet. Jericho yanked the lever that controlled the steel door.

Looking toward the cell, Jericho caught a last glimpse of Seeklat's glaring face beyond the closing barrier. The Ashanti was too late to make the exit. He pounded against the steel door from inside. Jericho pulled the second lever; closed the glass barrier. It deadened any noise that Seeklat made.

The gas had thinned within the cell. Seeklat would not succumb like Lothkal. Nevertheless, he was bottled up helplessly. He had lost his chance to rouse the other Ashanti servants. Jericho began to pace the passage. His idea was to be on duty when Bronden returned, to dispose of the lieutenant when he inquired for Seeklat.

THERE was a reason, however, why Bronden did not return. The lieutenant had headed for the meeting of the Golden Masks, to appear there as Member Gamma. Bronden had passed the secret exit; he had gone through the side door of the garage. Carrying his bag, he was walking briskly, pausing at intervals to make sure that no one was on his trail.

Bronden soon satisfied himself that he was unfollowed. He was wrong. Hawkeye had spotted him and was artfully keeping him in sight. The course led along secluded streets; darkened flights of steps and doorways gave the trailer an easy task. Following Bronden was much simpler than trailing Seeklat.

After a circuitous route of nearly one mile, Bronden came to a large warehouse. He turned and entered an alleyway between the warehouse and another building. Listening, Hawkeye heard the echoes of Bronden's quick footsteps, then noted that the sound made a sudden fadeaway.

Hawkeye guessed that there was a larger area at the end of the alley. He was right. Bronden had gone to the same place where Sulgate and other members of the Golden Masks had traveled by cab. Holding the full confidence of Tallam and Barfield, Bronden had been given the location of the meeting place.

Hawkeye decided to enter the alleyway. He reversed his decision suddenly, as he saw headlights swing from a corner of the outer street. Diving away, Hawkeye made for the building across the alley from the warehouse. He found a doorway and hunched himself there.

The headlights were those of a truck. The vehicle slowed as it came to the alley; it turned in and rolled through to the courtyard. Hawkeye bobbed from his hiding place. He peered into the alley, saw the truck's tail-light, stopped some distance ahead. Hawkeye crept in the direction of the truck.

When he reached the side of the truck, Hawkeye heard mumbled voices from the front seat. Edging closer, he caught snatches of conversation between two men.

"Take the note up in the elevator," growled one speaker. "Give it to the big guy there. He'll recognize you."

"Maybe I'd better wait there—"

"Not a chance. The guard won't let you stay. We gotta scram and stow this truck somewhere."

"But we was supposed to bring in another mug from Long Island—"

"And we couldn't get near the house. The bulls was there. That's all in the note. If we're needed, they'll know where they can get us."

One man alighted, while the other remained at the wheel. Hawkeye edged back along the truck; he stopped abruptly as his ears caught a slight sound near the back of the vehicle. Hawkeye breathed tensely; his presence was suddenly detected. Not by the truck driver, but by an unseen being who stepped from behind the truck.

AN action that had occurred more than an hour ago was suddenly repeated. A gloved hand clamped Hawkeye's arm. Hard-pressing fingers were as sure a symbol of identity as was the subdued hiss that sounded in Hawkeye's ear.

The Shadow had come from the truck. He had boarded it on Long Island, near Jaffley's house. He had ridden into Manhattan, straight to the meeting place of the Golden Masks.

The Shadow drew Hawkeye out through the alleyway. They stopped in the doorway; there, Hawkeye heard a suitcase thump as The Shadow set it down. In brief tones, The Shadow gave

instructions. Hawkeye was to report to Burbank, with orders for the contact man. Hardly had The Shadow completed his instructions before a whine sounded from the alley. The truck was backing out to the street.

Both The Shadow and Hawkeye escaped observation as the truck pulled away. The Shadow gave a commanding hiss; it was the order for Hawkeye to start off and deliver his call to Burbank. Nodding, Hawkeye stepped from the doorway. He darted a look up and down the street, to see that the way was clear. He paused a moment, to blink; he turned toward the doorway and saw its dim outline in the darkness.

The Shadow was gone, taking along the bag that he had brought. Though The Shadow had stepped away, Hawkeye had not seen him in those sharp glances along the street. The answer dawned on Hawkeye as he started off upon his mission.

There was only one place where The Shadow could have gone so suddenly. That was into the alley that led to the courtyard. Realizing the fact, Hawkeye gained an inkling of The Shadow's own plans.

The Shadow had gained the end of a double trail; one that both he and Hawkeye had traced. Lone-handed, The Shadow was going to the meeting of the Golden Masks.

CHAPTER XX
THE MASKS REPORT

WITHIN their room of gilded draperies, the Golden Masks were in session. Upon their platform, with its crimson backdrop, stood Tallam and Barfield. Masked, their identities were unknown to their followers. Here, Tallam and Barfield were known only as Alpha and Omega.

Except to one man, who stood near the platform. He was a member who had but recently entered, to identify himself as Gamma. This man was Bronden; called to the dais, he had delivered a confidential report to the leaders.

Tallam was speaking, in the harsh voice of Alpha. His words came through the fixed smile of motionless metal lips.

"Member Gamma brings an unusual report," rasped Tallam. "He states that a prisoner has escaped us. Such an event has never occurred before. Nevertheless, it gives us no occasion for alarm. The prisoner was an enemy who sought to thwart us. While he was making his escape, we captured another who will serve as hostage in his place."

Tallam turned about; Barfield did the same. As token of their mutual authority, Alpha and Omega each gave a clap with their golden-gloved hands. Crimson curtains parted, to show a room beyond. From it stepped two Ashanti warriors.

Across their shoulders, they carried two spears, like the bars of a stretcher. Thongs formed a crude resting place between the spears. Upon the improvised stretcher lay the prisoner. The captive was Harry Vincent.

Advancing to the front of the platform, the two Ashanti set the stretcher near the edge. They lifted Harry from it, placed him at the feet of Alpha and Omega. Lifting the lashed spears, the warriors went back through the curtains. The draperies closed.

Tallam gestured a gauntlet toward Harry, while the Golden Masks thronged slowly forward to view their prisoner. In the tone that he used as Alpha, Tallam pronounced:

"This prisoner is a tribute from Member Epsilon. Soon we shall have another captive; the one whom Epsilon was assigned to bring. Our new prisoner will be Freeland Ralbot, whose capture will produce a quarter of a million dollars for our coffers."

There were subdued buzzes from the lesser Golden Masks. Some of them had heard of Ralbot. Tallam silenced the slight commotion, then looked toward the door as Barfield pointed in that direction.

THE Ashanti who guarded the outside barrier had entered. Spear in one hand, he was placing the fingers of his other hand to his forehead, as token of his servitude. Tallam noted a sheet of paper that the Ashanti clutched in the hand that held the spear. He sent Bronden to bring it. As soon as Bronden received the paper, the Ashanti retired to his post.

"Let me have the message, Member Gamma," ordered Tallam. Receiving the paper, he opened it, then said to Barfield: "Read it with me, Omega."

The two studied the paper. It was the message from the truck driver. Tallam crumpled the sheet, rasped a command for silence.

"Our plans have been hindered," he informed. "Men went to gain the prisoner we wanted; but they have not brought him. Possibly Member Epsilon has failed to capture Freeland Ralbot. Since Member Epsilon has not appeared, this meeting must be adjourned."

Deep silence gripped the Golden Masks. Lying on the floor, Harry Vincent could sense the stillness. His eyes, staring upward, saw the gold faces of Alpha, Omega and Gamma. Harry knew that all the other members must be wearing identical masks.

In his urge to count the remainder of the throng, Harry instinctively turned his neck. He had moved it but an inch when he found himself wondering at his own action. Ever since he had been paralyzed by the gas, Harry had realized the futility of attempting motion. At times, he had felt a slight bodily sensation, but had classed it as his imagination.

The response of his neck had told him the truth. Jay Jaffley had been too brief with the gas dosage. He had removed the cylinder the moment that Harry had become limp. Instead of being under for a forty-eight-hour spell, Harry had already recovered.

Elation seized Harry, then faded. Though he wanted to rise, he restrained himself. He kept his eyes straight upward, fighting against a growing desire to blink them. None of the Golden Masks had noted Harry's slight motion. It would be suicidal to let them know that he had recovered.

Harry's only hope was to pretend that he was helpless, on the chance that he would be able to make a break later on. He was too concerned with his own situation to wonder about what had happened at Jaffley's. Harry still thought that The Shadow was a prisoner. Harry had taken it for granted that his own mistake had made Ralbot's capture a certainty.

Barfield, as Omega, pronounced his agreement with Alpha's order for adjournment. The lesser members stepped back to the center of the room; Bronden joined them, for as Gamma, he was but one of the group. The leaders went through a brief ritual, turned about to take their places on their thrones, as final token that the meeting was ended.

AT that moment, the outer door opened. Tallam and Barfield halted, as a new member of the Golden Masks stepped into view. The only absentee was Member Epsilon. The leaders gazed with eyes that showed elation as the newcomer approached the platform. They were ready to receive Jay Jaffley's last-minute report.

Approaching Tallam, the final member paused; in low monotone, he pronounced:

"I am Epsilon. I speak to Alpha."

"Alpha replies to Epsilon," voiced Tallam, eagerly. "Epsilon will give the first countersign."

"Ashanti."

The newcomer turned to Barfield:

"I am Epsilon. I speak to Omega."

"Omega replies to Epsilon," answered Barfield. "Epsilon will give the second countersign."

"Kumasi."

Immediately, Tallam and Barfield hissed in low tones. Breathlessly, they called for Epsilon's confidential report. Bronden edged forward, to try and overhear it. To Harry Vincent, lying face upward at the very feet of the men on the platform, all the words were plain.

"Ralbot offered trouble." The words were calm as they came from the mask of Member Epsilon. "Others came to his aid. I was forced to carry Ralbot away myself."

"Your servants?" queried Tallam. "What happened to them?"

"I left them to explain matters to the police. There was a great commotion at the house. People reported it."

"Ralbot's money?" quizzed Barfield. "Did he bring it?"

"Yes. I acquired it. I have placed it in a safe spot. Ralbot received the gas treatment. I have put him where no one will find him."

WORDS of approval came from Tallam and Barfield. Their eyes glistened with evil delight. Harry Vincent, looking straight up, saw the eyes of Member Epsilon. He seemed to sense that they were looking downward toward him. By this time, Harry could no longer repress a blink. He winced as his eyelids closed. He thought his game was finished.

Instead, Harry heard another low tone from the metal lips of the arrival who called himself Member Epsilon.

"I brought certain of Ralbot's documents with me," announced the newcomer, "so that you would have proof of my success. Let me give them to you, Alpha. Then you and Omega can announce that all went well."

As he spoke, the masked arrival drew away his golden-hued gauntlets. He performed the action with his hands palms upward. Tallam and Barfield saw the gold circle of a ring within the third finger of his left hand; to them it meant nothing.

To Harry, staring upward, unnoticed by any save Member Epsilon, the ring revealed the truth. He could see a glimmering stone on the lowered back of the hand. The gem was a resplendent fire opal that showed depths of ever-changing hues. Harry recognized the jewel the instant that he saw it.

The gem was The Shadow's girasol!

Lone emblem of The Shadow, that stone was a mark of identity. It meant that Member Epsilon was The Shadow.

Alone, The Shadow had come here not only to effect Harry's rescue, but to deal with the Golden Masks within their own domain.

CHAPTER XXI
MASKED BATTLE

QUICK realization came to Harry Vincent. He knew that The Shadow must have escaped from imprisonment; also that his chief had reached Long Island in time to conquer Jay Jaffley and take the latter's place.

The flash of the girasol told all that; it specified more that Harry understood. The Shadow had seen Harry's motion; he knew that his agent was recovered and ready for action. Harry gave a response.

Tightening, he set his muscles, delivered a slight nod with his head against the floor. This signified

that his recovery was complete. The Shadow, however, had taken that for granted. He had experienced a prompt recovery of his own, after the gas treatment in Tallam's house.

Stepping down from the platform, The Shadow thrust his ungloved hands into the slitted pockets of his golden robe. His move was not too hasty, for he was still playing the part of Jaffley. The Shadow was actually reaching for automatics, not for documents. Before he could gain them, a sudden interruption came from Bronden.

The lieutenant saw Harry move. Bronden uttered a warning cry. Tallam and Barfield thought that the warning referred to a false move by Member Epsilon. They reached for their own guns, just as The Shadow whipped forth his weapons.

A laugh burst from the false lips of Jaffley's mask. Weird and shivering, it echoed from above the platform.

Half turning, The Shadow aimed one gun for Tallam and Barfield; he pointed the other .45 toward the lesser members, congregated in the center of the room.

TALLAM and Barfield sprang back, their guns unleveled. The Shadow stabbed his first shot toward the murderers. He wanted to drop those leaders, knowing that their fall would throw confusion into the ranks of the Golden Masks. He fired one shot at random; he had Barfield covered for the second. But as The Shadow pressed the trigger, a chance attack spoiled his aim.

Bronden was leaping for The Shadow. Though wild in his dive, he managed to clutch the robed fighter's arm. The bullet that The Shadow dispatched went wide of Barfield, who made a dive after Tallam, toward the curtains.

The Shadow flung Bronden aside. Harry, rolling from the platform, pounced upon the fellow, snatched away a gun that Bronden tried to draw. The Shadow aimed for the curtains; just then, a darkish face and ebony arm appeared between them. One of the Ashanti had arrived with a war spear. He flung the weapon for The Shadow.

Diving forward, The Shadow was beneath the spear as it slithered toward his robed form. The point barely grazed the cowl above The Shadow's golden mask. Almost to the platform, The Shadow aimed, ready to riddle the crimson curtain with a fusillade of shots.

From the edge of the dome, a glass curtain thudded to the platform. Either Tallam or Barfield had pulled a switch, to release one of their bulletproof barriers. The leaders of the Golden Masks were cut off from The Shadow's vengeance. They were ready for flight by another exit, trusting to their followers to dispose of The Shadow.

In this swift conflict, The Shadow had not forgotten the danger from the horde behind him. The rest of the Golden Masks had waited momentarily, dazed and startled by the kaleidoscopic shifts near the platform. The Shadow's shots; Bronden's leap; the dive by Tallam and Barfield; the fling of the Ashanti's spear—all had come within scant seconds.

Nevertheless, the horde of Golden Masks had moved by the time The Shadow wheeled. Most of the crooks were armed; more than a dozen of them were whipping revolvers from the pockets of their robes. Had The Shadow halted against such numbers, he would have been doubly doomed. First, from the crowd itself; again, from some return attack by Tallam and Barfield, who had delayed their flight to watch through the glass barrier.

Harry Vincent had rolled to a corner, dragging Bronden. Half shielded by the prone lieutenant, he was ready with the revolver to give The Shadow aid. For the moment, the odds seemed hopeless to Harry. Then came the move that changed the entire scene.

The Shadow flung himself squarely into the ranks of the aiming throng. Guns barked; they were too late. The Shadow had arrived. From then on, the crowd of Golden Masks began to break.

Grappling with the first foemen whom he met, The Shadow stabbed shots; slashed with his automatics; pitched men into sprawling groups. He was wheeling through the melee, first low, then high. Guns were aimed too late in his direction; slugging fists missed him as they descended downward.

For The Shadow had a perfect camouflage. Every face about him was the same as his own. All lips wore the leering smile that adorned The Shadow's mask.

It was like a battle in darkness, where one fighter, sought by a group, holds a marked advantage. To The Shadow, every leering face of gold represented a foeman. To the Golden Masks, only one was the enemy they sought; and there was no way to single him from the rest.

But, where darkness would have forced The Shadow to hit or miss tactics, light did not. Every shot he fired, every blow he sledged, was a perfect hit. From beyond their screen of glass, Tallam and Barfield saw that the outcome would be victory for The Shadow.

They could not intervene. If they raised the glass and tried to mow down The Shadow along with all their followers, they could expect sudden bullets in their own direction.

Tallam and Barfield dropped their curtains, took their path to flight. Harry saw them go; he turned to watch the battle on the floor. He could not fire to aid The Shadow; he was unable to pick out his chief.

Some of the Golden Masks ripped away their Ashanti faces, shouting as they did so. They thought that they could thus confine attention to The Shadow. Nearly a dozen of the fighters were down; of the eight who remained, only two retained their masks. One of the unmasked men shouted to get both.

Five unmasked men sprang upon the pair; riddled them with bullets. As they stepped back, sure that one of the victims was The Shadow, a fierce laugh made them turn. They saw one robed fighter standing alone, unmasked.

The Shadow had whipped off his mask with the others, knowing that they could not recognize one another. He had revealed the face that he had worn at the time of his capture: the visage of Lamont Cranston. Five members of the Golden Masks had taken him for a bona fide member of the band. They had slaughtered two of their own number.

Bewildered, the five survivors were covered by The Shadow's guns. Some of them had used all their bullets in that last slaughter. The others were too few to fight. Harry had sprung forward to join The Shadow, bringing a third gun into play. Sullenly, the five Golden Masks let their revolvers drop to the floor, amid the sprawled bodies of their comrades.

At this moment of The Shadow's triumph, there came a double attack that threatened disaster. Bronden, flattened upon the floor, came to hands and knees unnoticed. He recognized The Shadow. With a quick move, Bronden snatched up a revolver that a Golden Mask had dropped.

Simultaneously, the outer door swung wide. The Ashanti guard was there; he singled out The Shadow. Viciously, he raised his arm to fling his spear.

The Shadow spotted both moves from where he stood. He picked the Ashanti as the more formidable. An instant more, both spear and bullet would be on their way. There was a chance to stop the Ashanti's lunge; but it was impossible to prevent Bronden's snap of the trigger.

Fading, The Shadow fired. He clipped the Ashanti; the big warrior twisted to the floor. His lunging aim went sidewise; the spear skidded from his hand and pierced a curtain on the far side of the room. As the spear slithered wide, Bronden's gun barked. The Shadow's feint was sufficient. The bullet hardy grazed his golden robe.

THE SHADOW delivered an answering shot as Bronden tried to take new aim. So did Harry, for he had spotted Bronden's move. These bullets spelled the end of Member Gamma. Bronden's supporting arm gave way; his chin thudded the floor. Others of

Fading, The Shadow fired. He clipped the Ashanti; the big

the Golden Masks, about to leap for revolvers, stopped short.

With Harry following, The Shadow circled to the outer door. He and his agent passed through the opened doorway, covering the remnants of the Golden Masks. The Shadow gave a command; Harry clanged the big door shut and bolted it.

Five Golden Masks were trapped in their meeting room, between bolted door and locked glass barrier. With them were the dead and wounded who had lost out in the fight against The Shadow.

In the outer anteroom, The Shadow ripped away his golden robe. He yanked open a suitcase that was in the corner; from it, he drew garments of black. He and Harry entered the elevator; The Shadow donned his own garb and they descended.

warrior twisted to the floor. The spear skidded from his hand.

Outside the alley, The Shadow contacted Moe's cab. He and Harry boarded it. There was no need to inform the law of what had happened. Already, sirens were sounding close at hand. The heavy barrage of shots had been heard, despite the thickness of the warehouse walls. Soon, the meeting place of the Golden Masks would be uncovered.

Moe expected a command to start. Instead, The Shadow ordered him to wait. A whispered laugh sounded within the taxicab. The tone carried deep significance.

The Shadow had another quest; the pursuit of Sidney Tallam and Roger Barfield, leaders of the Golden Masks. He was willing that the law should share in the final victory.

That was why The Shadow ordered the cab to wait.

CHAPTER XXII
THE SWIFT TRAIL

THE wait that followed The Shadow's command was of less than one minute's duration. That interval ended, a police car wheeled suddenly into view from the nearest corner. It stopped near where Moe's cab was parked.

The lights of the taxi were out; but the headlamps of the police car showed that the vehicle was a cab. A burly policeman came from the patrol car, flashed a light into the front seat. Moe held his arm before his eyes to avoid the light.

"How long have you been here?" demanded the policeman. "Hear any shots?"

"Some were fired in the warehouse," came a calm reply from the back seat. "You will find an elevator entrance in the courtyard at the end of the alley."

The policeman flashed his light toward the rear seat, wondering about this speaker who seemed to know so much. As the glow fell upon The Shadow, the cloaked passenger gave a single word to the driver:

"Start."

Moe shot the car ahead, snapping on the lights as the gear whined forward. The policeman fell back from the running board, shouted madly for the patrol car to take up the pursuit. It did; but Moe had wheeled around the corner by the time the pursuit began.

More police arrived. The lone cop informed what had happened. Another police car went off in pursuit; a squad of bluecoats hastened through the alleyway to investigate the warehouse.

Matters had worked as The Shadow wanted them. Riding ahead, he knew that the law would find the trapped members of the Golden Masks. But although the cab had gained a long start on the first car, The Shadow did not call for full speed. Instead, he ordered Moe to slacken.

Within a few blocks, the police car gained close range, picking up the trail through Moe's obedience to The Shadow's order. Guns began to pop; Moe wheeled around a corner. The Shadow ordered him to increase speed to the limit. As the cab roared for the next corner, The Shadow added:

"To Tallam's."

NEW police cars joined the chase within the next three blocks. Moe stuck to his task, changing his course to avoid a blocking car. The direct route was closed; but Moe still had a chance to make a circuit that would bring him to Tallam's house.

The Shadow counted Moe to be the speediest taxi driver in Manhattan. Moe proved the claim on this night. He sped through red traffic lights; took corners on two wheels. He hit the straight stretches like a racer.

Shrieking sirens followed close behind, with gunshots punctuating their wails. Moe outdistanced the pursuers; when he cut back toward Tallam's, he was a full block ahead of the nearest police car.

The cab came into Marview Place from the wrong direction; but that was a small matter. Moe whizzed across the path of another car, skidded his cab to a stop on the left side of the street, squarely in front of Tallam's brownstone steps. The door on the sidewalk side swung open; The Shadow propelled Harry Vincent to the curb, then followed.

"Through by the near side of the house," ordered The Shadow. Harry made for the spot indicated. To Moe, The Shadow added: "Travel. Lose the trail."

The cab shot away. The Shadow sprang for the brownstone steps. He fired two shots, just as the first patrol car swung from the corner. Instantly, the officers saw that the cab had discharged its passenger. The headlights of the police car gave a momentary view of The Shadow, on the house steps.

As the police car halted, The Shadow sprang from the side of the steps. He swung away through darkness to join Harry. Officers piled out, focused their flashlights upon the spot that The Shadow had left. They saw no one. A bluecoat pointed to the house door.

"He must have gone in there—"

The suggestion was sufficient. The police hammered at the door. Others who arrived took to the spaces beside the house, searching for other means of entry. They were too late, however, to find The Shadow and Harry.

The Shadow had led the way through to a rear opening between two buildings. With Harry following, he threaded a swift course for a new objective: the garage that offered secret access to Tallam's home.

More police were coming; they were forming a cordon around the block; but The Shadow whisked Harry across a street and off through a darkened stretch between two old houses. The Shadow and his agent had a clear path.

ON the street in front of Tallam's, a car pulled up. It had come from headquarters; the man who stepped from the machine was Joe Cardona. The inspector received a prompt report, then turned to Markham, who was at the wheel of the headquarters car.

"Get this, Markham," stated Cardona. "I told you The Shadow was on the move, when we heard about that find on Long Island. Well, they saw The Shadow up by that warehouse that's been raided. They grabbed a bunch of phonies with gold faces when they broke in there.

"Now The Shadow's been seen here. They think he's gone into this house. If he has, he's got some more of the tribe to handle. We're going in there and give him a hand."

With that, Cardona issued an order for the police to smash down the front door without delay. Bluecoats set to work, while Cardona stood with ready revolver, to be the first man through.

MEANWHILE, The Shadow and Harry had reached the old garage. Stopping in darkness, they heard motion ahead. Hawkeye's whisper came to The Shadow's ears. The spotter had spied Harry, even though he had not seen The Shadow.

"They blew in here a couple of minutes ago," voiced Hawkeye. "Two of 'em, with a couple of those big guys that work for 'em. They left their car in the garage."

"Marsland and Tapper," returned The Shadow. "Where are they?"

"Due any minute."

"Wait for them."

Ordering Harry to follow, The Shadow entered the garage. As he had expected, Tallam and Barfield had experienced a delay in getting a car for themselves and the two Ashanti who had fled with them. The delay had been even longer than The Shadow had estimated. There was still a chance of overtaking the leaders of the Golden Masks.

The Shadow reached the room outside the secret entrance. Harry saw him go to the door of the closet, open it and speak one word:

"Ashanti."

A pause. There was no response. The Shadow added:

"Kumasi."

Nothing occurred. The Shadow knew then that Tallam and Barfield had ordered the inside guard to admit no others. A huge door blocked further progress; but The Shadow had provided for it.

He had provided for other things as well, such as a call by Burbank to the police, telling them where they could find Freeland Ralbot, the owner of money and securities that had been recovered at Jaffley's Long Island home. But most important for the present was a means of entry through this secret door that led to Tallam's dungeon room.

There were hasty footsteps from the rear of the garage. Hawkeye arrived, followed by two others. One was Cliff Marsland, square-shouldered and firm of jaw. Cliff was a good teammate for Harry in the attack that was to come. The other was "Tapper," a man whom The Shadow seldom used. The Shadow had ordered Tapper on duty tonight; and he had brought a useful service along with him.

AT The Shadow's order, Tapper opened an elongated box that he had gingerly placed on the floor. He produced a drill, approached the metal door and quickly cut three short holes. From the box, he brought a container that held a powerful charge of explosive far more potent than the powders that The Shadow ordinarily used.

The Shadow stooped forward. A fuse fizzed. As The Shadow gestured, his agents hurried out into the desolate garage. The Shadow followed them, closed the door of the little room. Quietly, he commanded Harry and Cliff to be ready with him; he ordered Hawkeye and Tapper to remain here on guard.

Only the burning time of a short length of fuse remained. When that period had ended, The Shadow would be ready for his final foray. He had coaxed the law to the task of battering in through the front of Tallam's house. While that attack was in the making, The Shadow had prepared this surprise.

Soon Tallam and Barfield, leaders of the Golden Masks, would find themselves harassed from two directions. Yet The Shadow did not count the conflict won. Even though he had vanquished the massed horde at the meeting place, he knew that there would be heavy strife ahead.

The final battle would come inside the portals of a stronghold where Tallam and Barfield were prepared to resist attack. The lives of helpless prisoners were at stake. Vast wealth, the swag reaped by the Golden Masks, would be on hand.

The Shadow knew that strategy, as well as force, would be the deciding element in the final fray.

CHAPTER XXIII
THE LAST TRAP

TALLAM and Barfield had stopped when they reached the passage between the dungeon cells. They had good reason for their halt. They wanted to talk with Seeklat, to learn if Lothkal had been located. They wanted to find out what else had happened since Bronden had brought news of The Shadow's escape.

With Tallam and Barfield were the two Ashanti warriors who had come with them from the meeting place. The four made a formidable group. Tallam and Barfield still wore their golden robes, though they had stripped the masks from their faces. They were carrying revolvers; the native-garbed Ashanti had their short spears.

Tallam and Barfield had not found Seeklat. The only man whom they discovered was Jericho. Standing on sentry duty, the big African looked like a loyal guard. In fact, Bronden had reported him as such.

In English Tallam queried for Seeklat. Jericho stared, expressionless. Tallam put the question in French. Jericho pointed to the door at the front of the passage. Tallam went through the door; beyond it, he raised a shout for Seeklat.

Soon, two Ashanti appeared. They were the men whom Bronden had ordered Seeklat to summon. They shook their heads as they returned with Tallam. They had not seen Seeklat. Nor had they seen Lothkal. They had been asleep.

"We know where The Shadow stowed Lothkal!" snarled Tallam to Barfield. "In his own cell, for that's where Bronden found him. But what's happened to Seeklat?"

"Maybe The Shadow came back here," suggested Barfield, "and managed to handle Seeklat like he did Lothkal."

Tallam nodded slowly, then looked toward The Shadow's cell. He reached for the levers that controlled the sliding doors. Jericho saw the action; his muscles tightened. Jericho pressed a revolver that was in the pocket of his coat.

He was in a bad spot. There were six enemies against whom he must contend. Once Seeklat should be questioned, Jericho's part would be known. Jericho saw hopeless battle due within the next few minutes. All that he could hope for was to thin the ranks of the enemy before he fell.

A LUCKY interruption halted Tallam. There was a clatter at the rear of the long passage. In came the Ashanti who guarded the rear exit. He was shaking his spear, babbling his native dialect.

One of the other Ashanti translated the words:

"Him say man speak through wire. Give words the same like you give."

"What else?" demanded Tallam. He spoke to the arriving guard. "Tell me the rest yourself."

The guard thought slowly to find the English words.

"Make noise, man do," he declared. "Noise on door. Noise like I make here."

To illustrate the sound, the big guard scratched the point of his spear upon the stone floor. Barfield interjected a statement to Tallam.

"They're going to blow the door!" he exclaimed. "We'd better get back there!"

"Wait," suggested Tallam. "We can handle them later."

He pulled the levers on which his hands rested. The door of the cell slid open. From within came Seeklat, blinking at the light. Seeklat's face showed viciousness and anger. Just as Tallam was about to question him, a distant rumble sounded. It came from the rear corridor, the long echo of a heavy blast. There was a quiver of stone underfoot.

"They've blown it!" shouted Barfield. "Quick, Tallam! We've got to stop them!"

"The prisoners!" bellowed Tallam. "Get them through to the front! We'll hold the door between here and the house!"

Tallam gestured to Seeklat, to help him open the cells. The order was useless at that moment. Seeklat, staring past the Ashanti warriors, saw Jericho. With a savage roar, Seeklat forgot all else. He drove between the warriors, his hands shooting straight for Jericho.

THIS time, Jericho had no need for silent action. His revolver was out; he was prepared to meet others after Seeklat. Jericho fired a shot straight for Seeklat. The bullet found the Ashanti's body, but did not stop his charge. Plunging on, Seeklat fell squarely upon the enemy who had crippled him.

As Jericho rolled to the floor, Seeklat's two Ashanti sprang for him. Jericho gave two shots; one Ashanti staggered. The other grabbed Jericho's throat with one hand, wrenched away his gun with the other. The Ashanti warriors leaped up with their spears.

Shots ripped from the rear of the passage. Tallam and Barfield leaped toward the front of the passage, shouting for the Ashanti to forget Jericho. It was too late.

Three invaders were closing the range, firing as they came. The Shadow was foremost, his automatics blasting. Cliff and Harry were close behind their chief. Their guns were booming past The Shadow's shoulders.

Ashanti warriors swung to hurl their war spears. One managed the deed; but his throw was short, thanks to the low ceiling of the passage. Then he sprawled wounded with the others, who were already crumpling beneath a hail of high-aimed bullets.

Shots were devastating along this corridor. At long range, the bullets ricocheted. Jericho lay safe beneath Seeklat's body; falling Ashanti sprawled about him. Only Tallam and Barfield were safe, for they were protected by the bodies of their servitors.

The golden-robed men dived through the door to the house. They had no chance to close it. The Shadow prevented that with his swift fire. The leaders of the Golden Masks were off to flight.

The Shadow paused, only to order his agents to remain below. Their task was to release the prisoners, to see that the wounded Ashanti offered no more fight. Jericho was on his feet, beside Harry and Cliff. Promptly, Harry and Cliff took charge of the passage, with Jericho standing by to follow orders.

AS The Shadow reached the first floor of the

house, he heard the front door shatter. A flood of police poured inward; shouting, they took to the stairs. The Shadow knew that they had spied Tallam and Barfield at the top. The crooks had reached the second floor. The Shadow headed for the rear steps.

Foremost in the law's charge was Joe Cardona. He had spotted the leaders of the Golden Masks, making for the front of the second floor. Joe took the step by twos, a whole squad behind him. He reached the hallway where Jericho had once stood guard. Cardona saw the light of the living room.

He reached that objective, paying no heed to closed doors on the way. As soon as he entered, Cardona saw Tallam and Barfield. They had reached the alcove at the rear of the room; they had donned their golden masks, to face the police.

Twin faces showed their half smiles. Hands that wore golden gauntlets were raising revolvers. Cardona and seven of his men aimed to fire at the Golden Masks, hoping to riddle them where they stood. Tallam gave a tug at the rear bookcase.

Police revolvers spoke. Bullets mashed flat, seemingly in midair. Glass barriers had dropped in time to save the Golden Masks. Cardona and his men gaped, amazed; then they sprang forward.

One member of the squad blundered against the glass sheet that protected Tallam and Barfield. He sank back. Another officer discovered the glass that barred the doorway to the hall.

There was a hiss from the chandelier. Greenish vapor poured forth; Cardona detected an odor that resembled chlorine. This was not the yellowish gas that paralyzed its victims for a temporary period. It was a deadly vapor that would kill within fifteen minutes.

The Golden Masks had pronounced doom upon the men whom they had trapped. To ridicule their victims, they hauled away books at the sides of the alcove. They brought forth bundles of crisp cash; huge stacks of gold; trayloads of resplendent gems.

Tallam tugged a cord. The floor of the alcove jolted; it quivered upward. The floor was an elevator that could carry the Golden Masks to a heavily barred third floor. By an exit through the roof, they could escape across the tops of adjoining houses, carrying their swag with them. These partners in crime intended to divide the shares that they had promised to the lesser members of their band.

Cardona fumed as he held his useless revolver. The Golden Masks stared through the glass, their eyes glowing with delight at the sight of men who were to die. Intent upon that view, they did not notice what occurred behind them. Only Cardona saw the next event.

Slowly, the center of the rear bookcase began a revolution. It was high enough from the rising floor

to do so; but as it turned, the floor reached it. The pressure of the heavy bookcase stopped the elevator's rise. Instantly, the Golden Masks wheeled.

ON the threshold of a dim room beyond the bookcase stood The Shadow. He had guessed the game that the Golden Masks would play. He had picked the right room; the one by which he himself had once seen Tallam make an exit. Entering that room, he had solved the secret of a hidden spring that operated the bookcase.

Tallam and Barfield did more than turn. They leveled their revolvers as they wheeled. Simultaneously, The Shadow raised his automatics; but not with long sweeps of his arms. He tilted them upward from his hips, tugged the triggers as he aimed at two angles. His short move enabled him to beat the gun thrusts that Tallam and Barfield offered.

Joe Cardona saw silent flames spout from the muzzles of The Shadow's guns. No flashes came from the weapons held by the Golden Masks. Instead, the robed men sagged. One dropped his revolver and huddled motionless upon the stopped floor. The other tried to hold his balance, also attempted to deliver a shot. He failed in both endeavors. His efforts ended with a headlong spill.

No crash or thud marked those falls. The heavy glass deadened the sound, just as it had blocked the roar of The Shadow's guns. Cardona saw The Shadow manipulate hidden levers, then step away, through to the rear room.

The hiss from the chandelier ended. The greenish gas faded. A click reached Cardona's ears; it marked the closing of the rear bookcase. The fact that he had heard the sound made Cardona guess something else that had occurred. Springing forward, Joe reached the alcove. No barrier stopped him. The Shadow had raised the sheets of glass.

Golden masks, hastily donned, had fallen from the faces that wore them. No longer were Sidney Tallam and Roger Barfield an insidious, smiling pair, whose countenances made them appear as a pair of demonish twins. Their own faces were on view; Tallam's vicious, with its pursed lips; Barfield's drawn into a contorted smile that showed fiendishness rather than mirth.

The faces of these supermen of crime were fixed in death, like the golden masks that they had worn in life. Their long career of evil had been ended by The Shadow. With the death of its founders, the organization of the Golden Masks was dissolved, never to be revived.

SOON afterward, Joe Cardona and a squad of men found the dungeon rooms in the passage that led underground from the house. There they were greeted by James Lengerton and half a dozen other prisoners who had been released. Men of prominence—some whose disappearance had not yet been guessed—began to pour their stories to the law.

All had the same tale. They had failed to listen to threats. All had been treated with the paralyzing gas and then imprisoned. During each respite, they had been subjected to new demands. Failure to agree had been followed by another period of forced immobility.

In three cells, Cardona found prisoners who were undergoing the treatment that the Golden Masks had devised. One was Gilden Cleatland, the last to be gassed. Cardona knew that these men would recover within the next two days. Then their stories could be recorded like the others.

The Shadow and his aids were gone. The ex-prisoners had been placed in charge of the wounded Ashanti servants, who had become peaceable when told that their masters were dead. Staring along the passage, Cardona saw the door at the rear. He knew that The Shadow had come from far beyond it, and had gone again by the same route.

As he listened, Cardona fancied that he heard a quivering tone that echoed from some distant underground corridor. Faint, fading, it formed an evanescent peal of mirth that spoke of final victory.

Though other listeners had not caught it, Cardona was sure that he had heard The Shadow's laugh of triumph.

THE END